NO FLESH

SHALL

BE SPARED

💀 💀 💀

carnell

ZED
P R E S E N T S

ZED Presents...
Publishing

First Edition
October 2010
Printed in the USA

ISBN 978-0-615-40393-9

carnell
www.zombiesexist.com

Cover art and interior illustrations by Aaron Acevedo
www.aaronace.com

"Burning Season" & "Visions" © Faith and the Muse & Elyrian Music 2003
Used with kind permission
For more information on Faith and the Muse go to
www.mercyground.com

ZOMBIFIED font by Chad Savage
www.sinisterfonts.com

ZED Presents... Publishing
424 W. Bakerview Road, Suite 105-272
Bellingham, WA 98226 USA

"Death closes all;
But something 'ere the end,
Some work of noble note, may yet be done,
Not unbecoming men that strove with Gods."
- Alfred, Lord Tennyson, *Ulysses*

💀 💀 💀

"When the dead walk, Senores...
We must stop the killing...
Or lose the war."
Dawn of The Dead

Motherhood

Before...

Cigarette smoke swirled in the bright beams of light pouring in through the windows of Kathy Mae Gilbert's trailer home. The smoke danced like willowy strands of ether within the pillars of luminosity that stabbed their way through her thin, Kmart curtains. Inside the trailer, the air was a dank, cough-inducing fog bank that never seemed to go away, satisfied just to hang in the air and whirl over the faded velveteen couch. Next to the sofa, a worn, faux-leather La-Z-Boy roosted, the sheen of its fake hide rubbed off in the spots where it came in repeated contact with human skin. The furniture sat like squatters in front of an old, wood-veneered Motorola television set. Against one wall, half a dozen boxes from a move made six months ago waited to be unpacked. The place was a shit-hole, but for Kathy Mae it was home, a squalid fortress of solitude to come to and rest her bones after working double shifts at the Hog & Dog diner and do exactly what she was doing now: sit and smoke and pretend for a moment that her life had gone a different way.

Kathy Mae had been a smoker since she was twelve and never once did she consider quitting. Her Daddy taught her to smoke when she was little. It had been one of his parlor tricks when guests came over to drink beer and work on cars. "Watch my li'l girl... she's so damn growed up... she even smokes!" But even before that, she'd always thought smoking was cool. People in the movies smoked and they looked cool. Daddy smoked and he was also cool. These days though, Daddy was also dead and buried. Throat and lung cancer claimed him several years ago. Kathy Mae could still remember seeing him sitting on the porch of his house, smoking through the tracheotomy tube in his neck.

Before she knew it, nicotine had its hooks into her and she was fully addicted by the time she hit high school. Her smoking was like a lethal legacy handed down, just one of many bad habits given to her by her parents. Hell, she'd even smoked, despite her doctor's warnings, through the entire length of her pregnancy. And why the hell not? She never wanted kids and would have been all too happy to have left her womb a barren landscape. Unfortunately, Billy Ray Beaumont saw to it that was not to be.

Billy Ray had sweet-talked Kathy Mae at the Leslie County Swap Meet and wined and dined her on a spectacular buffet of frozen pizza rolls and Mad Dog 22. Theirs was a union made in hillbilly heaven, but from the start it had been destined for failure.

One dark and stormy night, when he informed her that he'd forgotten to bring a condom (a "jimmy," he'd called it), she was just liquored up enough to say "What the fuck." Billy Ray didn't have it in him to drive straight, what were the odds that he could shoot straight?

Pretty good from the sound of the screaming brat in the other room.

"OK, you little shit dispenser!" she shouted. "I'm comin.'"

She stalked into the other room and lifted the screaming baby by one arm out of the laundry basket where he, more often than not, spent the day sleeping and crying and swimming in his own shit. The baby wailed loudly and kicked its legs in the air, to little effect. The child, Johnny Garth Beaumont by name, had been brought into the world with a criminally low birth weight a little over a year ago and he'd gained precious little in the way of body mass. The little shit had been colicky for the last week or so and Kathy Mae's nerves now bore the stretch marks of his foul mood.

"Jeezus H... Will you shut the fuck up!?!" Kathy Mae screeched into the baby's wailing face.

Johnny continued to blubber loudly and flail his spindly limbs.

Kathy Mae slapped him twice sharply across the back of his legs and tucked him into the crook of her left arm. She unbuttoned the front of her grease-stained waitress uniform and hauled one of her pale breasts out from the sweat-sodden depths. Roughly, she pushed the nipple into the baby's mouth, hoping he'd nurse or, at the very least, quiet down. Either one would have been just fine for her. She looked down, annoyed, and sighed in frustration when he didn't. Johnny didn't seem to want her nip, he just continued kicking and crying like a banshee. His lone tooth, sticking up from his gum-line like a headstone, glimmered dully in the dim light.

"Fucking kid..." she said. "I cain't give you what you want to make you stop cryin' if'n you don't tell me what it is you fuckin' want!" The last word sounded like the desperate cry of someone at the end of her rope.

Johnny spit the anemic areola from his mouth, threw his head back, and let out another ear-splitting wail. The baby's eyes were full of tears, the corners caked with a gummy sludge. A high fever raged like a fire within his little brain and nothing Kathy Mae did or could do would stop it. The baby had lain for far too long in the cold trailer; his body rife with a combination of the flu, colic, and rampant malnutrition. Kathy Mae's breast milk was pitifully inept at providing the nutrients he needed in order to fight off the host of viruses that now coursed through his system. All his mother's body was able to give to him was a lethal mixture of nicotine, alcohol, and cheap diner food with just a splash of methamphetamine.

"Gawd damn ya, ya ankle biter, eat will ya!?"

Kathy Mae propped up the child's head and pressed his face against her breast with all her might, thinking that she could make the baby eat with a combination of brute force and strong will.

The child managed to pull back from her far enough to catch a quick breath and let out another wail of pain and frustration. Kathy Mae took the sides of his head in her hand and pressed his face back to the meat of her breast.

Johnny's mouth and nose were smothered by the drawn flesh that surrounded the fatty tissue of Kathy Mae's breast. He tried in vain to move his head in order to pull some air through his turned-up nose, but Kathy Mae's grip was too strong and his underdeveloped muscles were far too weak. His little hands beat against her chest futilely. Saliva coated both the nipple in his mouth and his face, but still Kathy Mae pressed on.

"Eat will ya, goddamnit? Eat!"

Johnny's lungs screamed out for oxygen, but his mother, either in apathy or anger, ignored his plight. His tiny fists beat with less and less force against her bony chest, his strength draining from him like water through a colander. The smell of tobacco and speed sweat was the last thing to flit through his diminishing senses before Johnny Garth Beaumont died in his mother's indifferent arms.

After a few minutes, Kathy Mae drew the baby from her breast and roughly wiped his mouth of spent lactate with the back of her hand.

"You done?" she asked, not registering in the sparse light the child's slightly blue tinge. "You just lay here for a minute and I'll change ya just as soon as you shit that out."

She laid Johnny down on the tattered, yellow sofa and went off to fetch herself another cigarette.

An hour or so later, Kathy Mae had damn near forgotten about Little Johnny and his crying. He'd been so quiet since she'd fed him last that it was almost like he wasn't even on the planet. She figured that, by now, it had to be just about time to change him.

"A goddamn cow on a milking machine, that's all I am to you," she said as she walked over to the couch. She plopped herself down on the sofa, puffs of dust springing up into the air.

Johnny lay where she'd left him and, thank the lord, he seemed to be sleeping peacefully for once. She picked him up brusquely, his body limp in her hands. She slid him like a football into the crook of her arm and checked the back of his diaper. Finding it empty, she once again pulled her tit from her uniform. As she did so, she felt the child stir slightly in her arms.

"Now you take this with no more of your goddamn complainin'," she said, pressing her breast to his cobalt-tinged lips. She slid her nipple into the baby's slack mouth and sat back into the well-worn arms of the couch. The baby roused a little and his mouth began the gentle sucking sensation that told her he was feeding.

"You must be feeling better, ya brat. You're eatin' again."

Johnny awoke with little knowledge of his brief life or of his reprehensible death just a short time prior. All his brain knew was that the initial confusing whirlwind of sensations—the lights, the sounds, the tantalizing smells—had finally started to settle down. Slowly, they'd begun to focus in on just one: hunger. As he nursed, the hot fluid coursing over his tongue became distasteful; milky and acidic to his palate. It was a sour and nauseating excuse for a meal. And while Johnny had never gotten a chance to learn what life had in store for him, he had learned in his short stay on the planet that his mother's breast could yield something that *almost* resembled nourishment. Now, death showed him a new purpose for her breast. Instinctively, he clamped his mouth down harder, nipping at the soft flesh with his tooth, and sucked harder.

Kathy Mae sat dozing on the couch, her cigarette burned down to a cylinder of ash in her hand. Far off in her senses, she could still feel the baby nursing. He'd been at it for what seemed like an awfully long time. He would need to stop soon, she thought, since she was starting to feel a little woozy. She glanced up at the clock over the stove and realized that she'd been sitting there sleepy-eyed for almost half an hour. Her head felt light to her somehow and the floor seemed uneven beneath her feet. Her sight made the angles of the room seem... off. Her perception waffled like an image in a fun house mirror.

She tried to pull the baby away from her breast, but surprisingly, he wouldn't let go. From the way he was holding on, he must have been hungrier than she'd first thought. Pulling gently, she attempted to dislodge Johnny from her chest, but he had latched on too tightly. She tried again, harder this time, only his little hands kept pulling himself closer.

"Well, you've managed to mess up my only clean uniform, Johnny Boy. Good God, it feels all wet," she said. "I'm going ta have to go change now before my next shift at the diner!"

She reached up and forcibly dislodged Johnny's mouth from her nipple. Her hand came away wet and coated in a dark, viscous fluid. She looked down at the baby and saw his mouth straining to get back to his nursing. His eyes were closed. His mouth remained pursed and sucking at the air.

"Goddam, Boy! What the fuck? Did you bite me, ya little bastard?"

Johnny looked up to meet his mother's gaze. His eyes were unfocused and still gooey from his infection. His pupils were now clouded and opaque.

Kathy Mae's mouth dropped open as her child pushed toward her and latched back onto the place where her areola had once been. Blood flowed out of the side of his tiny mouth as he abruptly bit into her flesh in earnest. Pain screamed through Kathy Mae's drug-addled senses and instinct commanded her to push him away. She tried to get a decent grip on him, but his new-found vigor confounded her. He chewed and tore at her breast, insistently demanding the only sustenance his newly reawakened system could now tolerate.

Kathy Mae stood up and pulled the child forcibly away from her chest. In disgust, she held him at arm's length. With all of the wriggling and kicking, he jerked out of her grip and dropped like a stone to the ground. With an audible grunting sound, what little air that was held captive in Johnny's dead lungs came out in a rush. Kathy Mae tried to get to her feet, but her legs went all rubbery from the loss of blood. She stumbled and collapsed in a heap next to the couch. She tried to crawl away from her child, but her coordination was off and her limbs felt weak.

Pressing her back against the sofa, she looked across the floor and saw Little Johnny dragging himself rapidly toward her across the beer-stained rug. His mouth was still working busily and the pupils of his eyes shone creamy white. His expression seemed filled with a hunger that was like something she'd never seen before. As his cold, little hands grasped at her ankle and he began pulling himself up her leg, Kathy Mae drew a stuttering breath and started to scream.

☻ ☻ ☻

Exordium

The landing gear of the UH-60M Blackhawk helicopter touched down on the helipad, its hydraulics hissing like venomous snakes under the weight of the aircraft. The titanium and fiberglass composite four-blade rotor began to whine down as power was cut to the T700-GE-701D engine. Almost immediately after the three wheels touched the paved ground, a clacking sound came from one of the copter's side doors and it slid open on oiled rails. Two men jumped down heavily to the pavement— their boots making an empty and hollow sound— with their AR-15 rifles not drawn, but at the ready.

A quick survey of the landing space and one of the security men nodded back toward the darkness within the helicopter. From inside the cramped compartment, a man in an impeccably cut silk suit climbed out of the helicopter and out onto the tarmac. He surveyed the area, breathing deeply of the early morning's cool air.

The man, one James Masterson by name, wore the officious bearing and no-nonsense demeanor of someone who was born to lead and had spent a lifetime doing so. His manner was one that demanded respect and was, more often than not, granted it. Short dark hair crowned his head and gave him a distinct military look. His dark eyes gleamed from over an aquiline nose, intellect cataloging minutiae, silently gathering details that— in another place and at another time— could spell the difference between life and death.

"Sir," said one of the armed men, "the area is secure."

"Good job, Son," said Masterson as he absentmindedly brushed his seams straight. "Thank you."

His baritone voice splintered slightly from lack of use, many hours having passed since he'd last spoken to another human being. It had been a long flight from what still passed for San Francisco and, in spite of his best efforts to the contrary, Masterson felt tired and more than a little cranky. The search for this new man had been long and arduous, but after having seen some of the footage of him at work, both Masterson and The League felt it would all soon be worth it—well worth it.

At least that was the hope...

The man now sitting in the shadows of the copter's interior was as close to a natural fighter as Masterson had ever seen. His intuition was good, even if raw and untrained. His body was not large, but it was firmly put together: hard muscle mixed with a brain that could react, truth be told, even more effectively than Masterson's own. All of this was impressive, in spite of the fact that up until now the man had been working on instinct, a big set of balls, and pure dumb-fuck luck.

Thinking back to the tapes he'd seen on the guy, it was no wonder that The League had ordered Masterson to personally escort him back to this facility. It wasn't exactly irregular for them to send someone with Masterson's pedigree out into the field to do something as simple as a retrieval, especially when there was so much money potentially riding on this dude's ass. Better to protect their investment out of the gate with a trained and armed chaperone than lose it due to some bad planning.

Masterson turned at the hip and looked back into the inky black of the copter. "Cleese..." he said into the darkness, "Follow me."

From within the shadows of the copter, a figure pulled itself from the blackness and moved slowly toward the door. Anyone could see that this was a man whora-diated an innate sense of power with limbs that were both lithe and supple. His movements, although controlled, crackled with an energy that betrayed abilities learned in the blistering heat of battle. His build was forged in the Real World, not in some gym somewhere hefting weights. The man gave off the impression of a big, lethal cat that had been caught dozing. It was plain from his demeanor and body language that if something was to rile his ass up, there would surely be hell to pay.

Cleese's face came almost reluctantly into the light. His features were lined, hard-edged, and dominated by a pair of cold eyes that burned with an icy-blue fire. His mouth was little more than a cruel slash that tore angrily across the lower part of his face. His gaze was one that gave no bullshit and expected none in return. This was a face that had gotten him out of a lot of bad shit in the past, but then again, had gotten him into a lot of it as well.

He stepped out of the Blackhawk, his long black hair whipping about his face, strands riding the air being moved by the still-spinning rotors overhead. He looked around suspiciously—taking in the expanse of the compound spread out before him at a glance—and raised his eyebrows. The place he'd been brought to was an odd cluster of modern buildings set amidst large expanses of grass, all plunked down right here in the middle of no-fucking-where. The compound was made up of no more than a handful of what looked like semi-permanent structures and then noth-ing for miles. It was as if whatever it was that they were doing out here—when they did it—they didn't want much of an audience.

Masterson marched across the helipad, never looking back to see if Cleese was following. He simply walked, trusting that his every order, his every command, would be followed to the letter. His silhouette grew smaller until it finally turned and descended a flight of unseen stairs at the far end of the helipad.

Cleese looked at the soldier nearest him and cocked an eyebrow.

"Nice guy..." and he nodded in Masterson's direction.

"Your gear will be delivered to your quarters a-sap, Sir," said the soldier in a flat monotone. His gaze remained fixed and pointed straight ahead. He was a young kid of about twenty-five who looked as if he'd once called someplace like Kansas home. Cleese looked into the man's eyes, which were set back in deep, cavernous sockets. They were rimmed in redness and puffy from lack of sleep.

Cleese smiled to himself. He glanced over to the other soldier who could have been the first one's brother and saw the same weariness in his gaze. He looked back and forth between the two men. They both stared silently straight ahead and waited for him to comply with Masterson's orders.

As he always did when confronted by a new and potentially dangerous situation, Cleese assessed the myriad of possible outcomes should things turn ugly and he need to clock both of these bitches and head the fuck on out of here. He considered their guns, his inability to fly a helicopter and God only knew what else might lie beyond the walls of this place, and decided against it.

"Sir," reminded the first soldier as he almost imperceptibly jerked the gun barrel in the direction of the stairwell where Masterson had gone. "Mr. Masterson will be waiting. You'll need to follow the stairs down, head through the door. Mr. Masterson will be waiting for you in The Press Hall which is down the long corridor and to the right."

Cleese ran a hand through his hair and chuckled as he slowly crossed the helipad. A few scant hours ago, he was asleep and dreaming in his bed. Then, a knock on the door later and he was being escorted onto the Blackhawk only to now find himself here. It was turning into quite a night. He couldn't wait to hear what this Masterson fella had in store for him now that they'd arrived here in this Disneyland of the Damned.

Still chuckling softly, Cleese strode across the asphalt and toward the stairway.

Space Station #5

Back when the poop hit the prop, things had been rumbling along pretty well for most of the world's population despite the usual moguls and pitfalls that always had a way of cropping up. Life, as they say, could oftentimes get in the way of Living. Economies see-sawed, despots rose and fell, morality shifted along its slippery slope toward inevitable oblivion, but in the end it was pretty much status quo.

In the spirit of global unity, several of the more affluent nations of the world came together under NASA's banner, and after several years of development set up an orbiting research station. It floated serenely in space and real strides in medical and technological science were made. Brave new strains of substances were generated up there in the cold, vacuum of space that never could have been created here on Earth. We were all, as a planet, beginning to understand that the world was indeed a small place and, like it or not, we'd better all start getting along.

Sure, there were isolated instances back on terra firma in which dictators would venture outside their country's borders, but they were put down in short order like rabid dogs. A seemingly real and lasting peace was catching and spreading like a grass fire across the planet and, finally, everything seemed to be on track for ol' Mother Earth.

As so often happens, just when things seemed to be going their best, it all went to shit. A group of scientists in the U.K. discovered that the space station's orbit had begun to decay—microscopically at first—but within a week or two, it was a given that the whole shebang was going to come down out of the sky and fall onto all of our heads. The scientists and astronauts who'd inhabited the station only had enough time to grab their Buck Rogers suits and beat feet onto the shuttles hastily sent to retrieve them before it did just that.

When the station entered the atmosphere, its collapse and incineration was a light show like no other. Giant pieces came apart from the main hull like wings pulled from an overcooked chicken. Huge, multi-colored streaks ran like a street hooker's eye-makeup across the dark of the sky. Everyone came out to watch. It was like the Fourth of July, the Macy's Day Parade, and Christmas all rolled into one big burning ball of rapidly descending metal.

It wasn't until later, when the government asked what had gone wrong, that people questioned what exactly it was that was being done in that circling laboratory in the sky. Finally, CNN ran an interview with a rogue scientist (his face obscured for his protection by computer-generated pixelization) whose conscience outweighed his sense of national obligation, and he admitted that there were indeed some very nasty bugs being brewed up there. He went on further to insinuate that— maybe—a fiery combining of them probably wouldn't be in the planet's best interest.

But several days went by and nothing happened. After a week or two, we all thought that whatever danger there might have been had passed us by. It was that error in judgment that brought due a bill for which we would all be made to pay.

It was only when the first of the dead opened their eyes in, of all places, Harrisburg, Pennsylvania, that it was apparent how right that scrambled-pixel-faced scientist guy had been. Within hours, we had ourselves a nice little End-of-Times caliber catastrophe brewing. The contagion (if that was what it could be called) splashed across the face of the planet. Due to some of our antiquated views on death and dying, we'd gotten ourselves right fucked pretty quickly.

First, morgues and mortuaries started reporting cases of flat-line misdiagnoses. Then, hospitals were flooded with random biting and clawing attacks. The medical community was initially indignant, saying that these reports were unlikely especially considering the number and how spread out they were. The Center for Disease Control finally decided that the disaster could only be the result of either a series of chemical spills, bio-terrorism, or something heretofore unknown biologically.

And in a roundabout way, they were right on that last bit.

Soon enough, all protests and hypotheses were drowned out by the sheer number of police reports that came flooding in. There were just too many instances to be ignored, let alone enough time to try to explain them all away. When the dead finally got up from their beds and shuffled out from their tombs to roam the streets by the tens of thousands, the C.D.C. had fallen ominously silent.

So when it could do nothing else, the networks reluctantly began reporting the truth of what was happening and the news wasn't good. It was with sad and unbelieving faces that the anchors told us what we all already knew...

The Dead were returning to life and eating the Living.

☠ ☠ ☠

The Gunfire's Waiting

After entering through a pair of double doors at the bottom of the helipad's stairway, Cleese walked down the long corridor in front of him and followed it through a maze of very corporate-looking passageways. From what he could tell, the place was made up of offices and conference rooms mostly, but since the majority of the doors in the building were locked, it was hard to tell what else was housed there.

After a bit of searching and finally following the guard's instructions, he discovered a set of doors with a sign reading Press Hall above them. Inside, he found Masterson seated behind a long table in what looked like a lecture hall. The auditorium was laid out with long rows of theater seats each with desktops that could be folded up or down depending on the needs of whoever sat there. The desks were set in a large semi-circle, which surrounded on three sides the podium at the furthest part of the room. From the looks of things, this was where The League held their news conferences. Across both the walls and ceiling, squares of acoustic tile ran in a grid-like pattern; each tile dampening any sound within the room. As a result, even the door shutting behind him sounded muted and hollow.

Along the far wall was a set of blackboards, each on rails allowing them to slide back and forth, one behind the other. The lectern stood at the center of the stage; a microphone jutted up phallically from the middle of the podium. Masterson sat patiently at a table just to the right. His fingers were tented and his eyes closed as if he were trying to snatch up any bit of rest he could.

Cleese had heard of the technique before from men in the military. They called it "Alpha Napping" and it was a way to rest the mind (since brainwaves changed to restful Alpha Waves when the eyes were closed) when full blown sleep was a luxury the soldier couldn't afford. Cleese figured that the military must have been where Masterson had learned it. The guy had a look about him that said he'd spent some time in Uncle Sam's service. He noted the tidbit of information and catalogued it for later consideration.

Upon hearing Cleese enter, Masterson slowly raised his head and opened his eyes.

"Sit down," Masterson ordered and nodded toward a desk at the front of the room.

"Nice place..." he said looking around, but not moving.

"Sit down, Cleese. I won't say it again."

Behind him, Cleese noticed that the two security men from the helicopter had appeared at the exit. They dutifully closed the doors behind them and stood by at attention. Their rifles, cradled in their arms like sleeping children, spoke volumes as to the reason for their presence in the room.

Cleese smiled and shrugged, then walked down the center aisle a few rows. Choosing a seat midway down the gallery, he sat down heavily, just within earshot of Masterson. His choice of seating would, at the very least, mean that his disagreeable host would have to raise his voice in order to be heard.

Pity.

As he settled into his seat, Cleese gave Masterson the once-over now that they were in brighter light. There was no doubt that the guy was as hard as nails. His manner and the look in his eyes said that he'd seen some shit in his time, but given all of the events of the last few hours, he knew that Masterson was someone he simply wasn't going to like.

For the life of him, Cleese couldn't put his finger on exactly what it was that bugged him about the man, but it was there. God knew there were so many reasons to choose from. Maybe, it was that he was a "Suit" and Cleese hated Suits. Maybe it was the unceremonious way he'd barged into Cleese's room and had him yanked out of bed at gunpoint. The promise that the trip would be "worth his while" might have been enough to spark his interest in the beginning, but more and more, even that was failing to hold water.

And then there was that quiet-as-a-tomb airlift here. The chopper ride had been about as comfortable as a cavity search what with the guy just sitting there stone-faced the entire trip. He'd just sat there, staring straight ahead, not saying a syllable.

It was enough to almost creep a guy out.

Whatever the reason was, Cleese decided the least he could do was to put a little crimp in that anally-retentive timetable of his. The prospect of fucking with him was proving to be all too tempting.

It was only after some silent deliberation that he decided it was Masterson's sense of entitlement—that self-absorbed air of superiority—that rubbed him the wrong way.

All that other shit was just icing on an already unpalatable cake.

In the end, it came down to something as simple as chemistry...or a lack thereof.

The crux of it was that Cleese was certain that the guy was an asshole of the first order, and for that alone he deserved to be given at least some small ration of shit. And he'd learned from past experience to trust his gut whenever it grumbled. That oily feeling deep in the pit of his stomach had saved his ass more times than he could remember. So when it spoke up as it had now...he figured it best to pay it the strictest attention.

"I'm sure you're wondering why your presence here has been requested," said Masterson.

Requested?!? Is that what he called it? So then what were the firepower and military accoutrements for, setting a mood?

Cleese looked him dead in the eye and slowly—methodically—scratched his balls.

"It had crossed my mind," he said over the soft sound of his ball scratching.

"That was a rhetorical question, Smartass. From here on in, I talk...you listen," hissed Masterson, looking down at his clenched hands. "I ask questions and you answer them. Interrupt me again and I'll have you dropped back into that shit-hole where I found you."

Cleese grinned his best "I'd like to see you do just that" grin.

Masterson looked up at him for a heartbeat, silently considering whether he should make good on the threat. Finally deciding against it, he reached for the lone folder laying on the table near him. As he slid it across the table, it made a soft, whispering sound as if already betraying its secrets.

"Cleese, have you ever heard of the WGF?"

Cleese sat for a minute, quietly thinking. Of course he'd heard of them. Fuck, everyone had. The World Gladiatorial Federation and its subsidiary, The Undead Fight League, were huge—making the NFL, Major League Baseball, and NBA all look like sandlot pick-up games. The thing was...Cleese had never really given a shit for what many now called sport. He was, in his own way, a busy man and already had enough violence in his life. He didn't really feel the need to watch a televised slaughterhouse in Dolby Digital. He left that sort of thing for people who led less active lifestyles.

Cleese shook his head slightly. He'd wondered what cards this guy was holding up his sleeve and what the real reason was for his being brought here. Now, as the fine hairs on the back of his neck stood at attention, he was almost wishing he'd never agreed to get into that damn helicopter in the first place. Then again, with all the hardware his escort was sporting, it wasn't like he ever really had much choice in the matter.

Cleese took another moment and, looking around the room, thought back to a time before there was a need for such sport, back to when chaos first tore its way across the face of the planet, back to the day when The Dead first got up and started walking again. Hordes of Them had come spilling out into the streets, killing and eating anyone and anything unlucky enough to fall into their path. An unfathomable number of people died as a result of the initial Awakening and that only made the situation worse. Death led to more death. Soon, those who were murdered awoke and began killing. A basic understanding of exponential math should have told people just how fucked they all were.

It had been hell there for the first few days. Initially, the dead were able to move quickly and that was a major part of the problem. The Dead being as swift and as strong as they had been in life made them formidable foes, but as the days slipped by and rigor mortis and decomposition set in, they slowed right down. By that time however, there were so many of them. At one point, the tide almost turned in their favor as the days gradually turned to weeks.

It was closing in on months when the living finally got things back under control by giving the whole dog and pony show over to the good ol' U.S. Army. Those jag-offs sure as fuck fixed things up right quick. First, they'd assessed how badly contaminated specific areas were. It became clear early on that the really big cities such as New York, Chicago, Houston, and Los Angeles were fucked. Slightly smaller municipalities could be scoured in house-to-house search-and-destroy missions, but the major metropolitan areas were all chalked up as losses because just one of those things left upright and roaming would start the whole thing all over again. It was imperative that not one of Them be left "alive."

And so, with a suitably heavy heart, The President ordered the four cities leveled: from downtown to the suburbs and all points in between. After that, the deaths of all those innocent citizens—the ones holed up and awaiting rescue—were never a topic that was discussed openly. It was just a fact unquestioned, but kept like pocket change: a small, hard, terrible thing that people carried and never mentioned, but were never without.

Soon after the military had their way, people slowly found their way back to a place that resembled normalcy. The Dead were still a consideration, something everyone dealt with, but now, they were more of a reminder of what had been lost, both on a personal level and as a culture. There were still sporadic outbursts of undead activity, but the situation was nowhere near as dire as it had once been.

Once the authorities had gotten a solid handle on what was left and things finally started settling down about a year later, it was only natural for people to attempt to deal with everything they'd been through in their own way. It wasn't long after that that the network news picked up on a story of illegal Undead fight clubs that started cropping up in city after city. At these midnight, underground locations, one of the Living would climb into a ring or pen with a few of The Dead where they would fight, one-on-one, mano-a-mano. Weapons were added in an effort to level the playing field somewhat. After all, The Dead had their teeth and claw-like hands the least we could do was to give the Living a gun or two.

It was decided that too many combatants were being bitten, so some rudimentary hand and arm protection was introduced. After another year or two, things became more and more standardized and voilà! a new sport was born. It was pretty obvious that there were a lot of people left in the world who wanted to see Mankind dole out some righteous payback to the unholy sonsabitches.

And who could blame them after everything that had been lost? In some macabre way, people wanted a chance to fight that initial confrontation all over again...only this time they wanted more of a heads-up. This time, they all were longing for a change in venue and the hope of a different outcome.

A young producer at one of the networks had been taken to a match by a story source and pitched the idea to his bosses. He told them the matches were a television natural and with the proper marketing the phenomenon could be big; huge, in fact. Like *Survivor*, only this time getting kicked off the island was the least of your worries. This time, if you played the game wrong, it was your ass. What was extinguishing your torch and being sent home compared to getting your throat ripped open and having your intestines eaten live on national TV?

After all, with what the world had just been through—The Dead crawling out of their graves, family member murdering family member, corpses eating corpses—people had already become desensitized to the imagery of Death and of The Dead. Putting it all on TV was almost a fait accompli. Luckily for them, there was already a guy who was running the show and had a whole network of fighters, handlers, and support teams in place. The network's Standards and Practices thought it over and agreed that this was something they could turn a blind eye toward, if for no other reason than for the good of the Nation.

"Well...?" asked Masterson bringing Cleese back to the moment.

"Sure. Everyone has. Zombie fightin,' right? *Mad Max Beyond Thunderdome*-type shit."

Masterson looked at the seated man for a moment and, quite against his will, the corner of his mouth twitched.

"Yes, well...We prefer the term: 'UD Engagement,' but the sentiment is the same."

"Tomayto...Tomahto, Pal. Call it what you want. It's still kickin' a zombie in the ass to me."

Masterson picked up the folder before him, opened it, and looked at the contents once again. His eyes scanned the documents, and as if reciting a bedtime story to a child, he read what he saw aloud.

"Cleese, William Thomas. Born 1977... Idaho Falls, ID... to... Cleese, Elizabeth Margaret... Father... Unknown."

Masterson looked up over the rim of the folder and, just for a second, shot Cleese a wry glance.

"Is there a point to any of this?" Cleese said, casually flipping him off.

"You presently reside in what was once San Francisco, California where, at last report, you work as 'muscle' for a local loan shark and live in a rat-trap, walkup apartment." He raised his eyes once more and grinned. "Nice place, by the way."

"Fuck you."

"During The Outbreak, you achieved a bit of notoriety by fighting your way out of San Francisco armed only with a baseball bat. Since then, you've ridden that cred and managed to establish a bit of a reputation by supplementing your income with taking odd bar fight bets where you often cheat and seldom lose. You are not married and you have no children. All of your relatives have either disowned you or are dead. Sound about right, Tough Guy?"

"Yeah, so...? What the fuck is this... my *A&E Biography*?"

"Let's you and I be honest here, Cleese. You are a man with few options. You're a bottom dweller who lives a life based on thuggery and unlawful pugilism. You, quite frankly, have little in the way of anything remotely resembling marketable skills. You're a loser without a future and are, quite frankly, seemingly beyond redemption. However, The League sees something in you and has therefore asked me to bring you here to see if you have sense enough to try to change all of that."

Cleese leaned forward in his chair. Despite himself, his interest was piqued. He sensed that the other shoe was about to drop, that the real reason for his being brought all the way out here was about to be revealed.

Masterson leaned back in his chair and carefully closed the file. His eyes burned red and weary as he finally arrived at the point of all of this. He slowly rubbed his eyes and raised his gaze to meet Cleese's.

"Zombie fightin'..." He smiled slow and creepy, like a rattlesnake might if it had lips. "Ever do any of it?" Masterson asked, already knowing the answer.

Cleese smiled and scratched at the scruff on his chin. Now that he knew why he'd been brought here, he relaxed. He knew what he was being asked and it wasn't whether he'd ever fought the dead. Shit, everyone had done a little of that back in the day. When Masterson mentioned the bar fights and then the WGF, he was letting on that he wanted to know whether he ever opened a can of whup-ass on the undead... for money.

"A bit... but that was a long time ago," he said with an almost embarrassed grin.

Cleese looked deep into Masterson's eyes and let his smile grow a little bit wider. "How much?" he asked.

"Excuse me?"

"Let's cut the shit, shall we? How much are we talkin' about here?"

Now it was Masterson's turn to smile.

"A lot, Cleese. A helluva lot."

The two soldiers at the door grinned silently to one another as laughter rang out in the empty room.

Early Morning Constitutional

Cleese and Masterson stepped out of the Reception Building and into the early morning's soft light. Dew still sparkled on the sidewalks that separated the building from the helipad and another small structure which, from the multitude of cabling coming out of it, looked as if it held some kind of electrical power source.

As his eyes became accustomed to the growing sunlight, Cleese got his first real glimpse of the compound as a whole. He looked past the electrical shack and across a short stretch of lawn where he saw two large gymnasium-like buildings, one directly in front of him and another just to the right. Between the structures Cleese could see other smaller buildings and beyond that another larger expanse of grass—like some sort of immense soccer field. Off in the distance, he could make out the erratic pop of small arms fire, the shots' echoes snapping like whip cracks through the spaces between the walls. Other than that, there was really nothing but farmland for as far as the eye could see.

"We have four main buildings here at The Compound," explained Masterson as they walked. "The building we just left is accounting offices, lecture auditoriums, and corporate offices mostly. Over there, to the right, is the fighter's housing which we refer to here as 'cribs.' At the other end over there is the Mess Hall. We expect you to comply with a full training regimen while you're here, and so, we feed you well. You should prepare to gain some muscle weight while you train."

Cleese looked around and had to admit, the joint was impressive; sparse, but damned impressive. Someone had dropped a fair amount of coin on this bitch. He just couldn't figure why anyone would build it out here in the middle of nowhere.

"What's that?" Cleese pointed toward a large building which lay directly before them.

"That is where we're going now... The Main Training Hall. Inside, you'll find that it comes complete with a full gym, a mixed martial arts training space and, of course, a Training Octagon.

Masterson raised his right arm and pointed with his middle finger.

"Beyond that is The Chest which is what we call our equipment room and armory. Further on, is the Firing Range and Quarter Mile Track and, over on the far side of the compound, is the Holding Pen, which you can't really see from here, but is where we store the all of the training UDs."

"UDs?"

"Verbal shorthand, I apologize. Undeads or, as you and the rest of the world have been referring to them, 'Zombies.'"

Cleese looked at Masterson like the man just shit in his morning bowl of corn flakes.

"Are you telling me that you keep zombies here?

Masterson nodded. "It's what we do, Cleese. Get used to the idea that you will soon be dealing with Them on a very intimate basis."

"How many?"

"What?" Masterson asked, sounding annoyed.

"I asked how many of them do you keep here?"

"We store up to three hundred at any given time. The number ebbs and flows depending on the kind of training we're engaged in."

Cleese shook his head in disbelief and stumbled to a stop. His mind reeled at the thought of someone willfully keeping that many of those fuckers together in any one place, at any one time. The things could be a handful if encountered one on one—he'd seen that firsthand—but gather a half dozen or so together and you could end up having a very shitty afternoon. And to think, these fuckin' imbeciles were casually talking about "storing" them by the hundreds. He trotted to catch up with the still-walking Masterson.

"You ever have any of 'em break out?"

"Never."

"Never?" Cleese said with a slight chuckle.

Masterson stopped abruptly and Cleese had to skid to a stop to avoid running into him. He turned to look Cleese square in the eye for the first time since the two of them met in San Francisco. His gaze was direct and allowed no argument.

"Never." he said emphatically and turned.

An odd shadow, cast by a sun slung low over the horizon, danced across the man's back as he continued walking toward the training hall.

Monk

The two men entered the Main Training Hall and the heavy, metal door echoed loudly as it slammed shut behind them. The first thing Cleese noticed as he walked deeper into the building was the smell. It was a pungent mixture of leather, sweat and bitter antiseptic. The place reeked of hard work and exertion, of men pushing their bodies beyond their physical limitations and of painful learning.

It also smelled like death. A swirling odor of putrescence and decomposition hung over the room like a pall, tainting everything it touched. It was a smell that stuck to the back of your throat like paste and made gagging a very real possibility. It was, simply put, a smell that once experienced you never forgot.

Once, a long time ago, Cleese had broken into a local funeral home and made off with a couple of bottles of embalming fluid. Some freaks he knew in the neighborhood made a habit of dipping their cigarettes into the shit, letting them dry, and then smoking them. They'd called them "Sherms." Got real high on them, they did. The things also burnt their brains out like napalm. Cleese had to go into the mortuary's prep room to get the stuff. That place had the same smell to it then as this one did now.

As they walked deeper into the main part of the Hall, Cleese saw what looked like a locker room and showers off to the left. Directly in front of them was a large open space covered with interlocking mats on the floor . Up and further to the left was a weight training area where several workout machines glistened in the low overhead light. The mirrored wall at the far end reflected racks of free weights and a dozen or so treadmills. An open-beamed ceiling arched high above them, its supports fanning out like a ribcage. Hung sporadically from the rafters, large round lights threw pools of illumination over the interior.

"Here's the martial arts area, over there, the gym. You'll be expected to conform to our way of doing things here, our protocol," Masterson explained as they continued deeper into the building. "Here's the way it all breaks down... We hold fight and tactical classes every day at zero-eight-hundred and again at sixteen hundred. Your attendance there is mandatory. Later in the day, we offer gymnastics and Judo, which are elective. Some guys' fighting styles don't make use of it and so not everyone is required to come to class. You'll need to check the schedule for you and your trainer's spots in The Octagon."

"Is that when we fight the zombies?"

"No." Masterson sounded slightly annoyed. "It's where you train. Live combat is saved for the televised events. It was one of the first rules laid down by The League. When people tune in, they want to see a show. This isn't professional wrestling or any of that staged kinda bullshit. They don't want matches that appear planned or biased in any way..." and then under his breath, "not like you could plan, much less reason, with those damned things.

"It just keeps things honest and above board," he continued. "You will be required to train with the UDs as well as living opponents. The UDs will, of course, be wearing bite blocks and harnesses. It's to maximize your safety and minimize our liability."

As they walked together across the mat, Cleese saw an older man coming toward them from the opposite direction. He stood not quite as tall as Cleese, about fifty or so, with salt-and-pepper hair. His body was well-muscled and yet compact—solid, like a boxer's—only it looked as if capable of inflicting a lot more damage. Even though he was an older man, he still gave off a vibe that said he'd seen some shit in his time and, if troubled, he'd be only too happy to carve off a major chunk of your ass.

"Monk!" Masterson called out and waved a hand.

The other man returned the wave, but Cleese noticed that he didn't smile. He strode over and shook Masterson's hand. From their body language, Cleese immediately assumed that these men had known one another for some time. He also noted that although their acquaintance had been long, it was not particularly deep.

"Good to see you, Sir," Monk said. His voice was gruff and scratchy, like silverware drawn over broken glass. He immediately looked Cleese over, appraising him as if he were a racehorse. With a discerning eye, he circled Cleese and, every so often, poked or prodded at him.

"Monk, this is Cleese." said Masterson. "Cleese, the man before you is James Thelonius Montgomery. Although the last man to call him 'James' or 'Thelonius' is, I believe, still able to breathe as long as no one unplugs him. It's safest if you just call him 'Monk.'"

"How'z it goin'?" Cleese said with a jerk of his head and extended a hand and waited for it to be shaken.

Monk ignored him and looked accusingly at Masterson. A displeased look sat on his face like a fat man on a lawn chair and he shook his head in disgust.

"He's too skinny."

Masterson sighed. His shoulders slumped and he rubbed at his right eye with his fist.

"He's too skinny and he's too green," Monk continued. "He'll never be worth a shit."

"Monk, it's been decided" Masterson said calmly. "You've read the file."

"Hey, fuckin' ex-cuse me," said Cleese. "I am still standing here."

"And he's stupid." Monk ran his hand over his face, pulling his features into distortion. "Motherfucker doesn't even know when to keep his mouth shut tight."

"I recall someone once saying some similar things about you," Masterson smiled.

"I'm going on record right now as saying that I think he's the type to shit the bed, but ok. After all, you guys are the boss."

"Duly noted."

They both turned and looked toward Cleese, who scowled and held up his right hand, brandishing two fingers. His expression let it be known that it was not a gesture of peace he offered.

"Two things," he said with a tiger's slow smile. "Number one," he said as he dropped his index finger. His middle finger jutted from his fist in unabashed defiance. "Don't talk shit about me like I'm not here." He spun his fist around in a tight circle. "You have something to say, you say it to my face or not at all. And number two," the middle finger lowered slowly into a fist. "I get treated fairly here and I play nice, but if I think that anyone is trying to buttfuck me, I walk. No bullshit and no second chances."

He pumped his fist like a heartbeat.

"We work on a mentor system," continued Masterson, ignoring everything that Cleese had just said. "Every new recruit is paired with a veteran. Your mentor is Monk. The two of you will bunk together, train together, eat, sleep, and shit together. When in the pit, you are to know where your partner is at all times. Remember, the people who have forgotten that have been carried out of here in pieces."

Cleese looked at Monk and then back to Masterson.

"Is that understood?" Masterson asked.

Masterson looked quite pleased with himself, like a child who'd been given a job and been able to complete it to satisfaction. And why shouldn't he be? His package had been picked up and delivered in exactly the manner that The League requested. From here on, Cleese would be Monk's problem. Masterson was out of it unless, of course, the fighter fucked up. If and when that happened, he would personally pitch the son of a bitch out of a helicopter and throw him back into a world of shit.

For Monk's part, a look of dissatisfaction continued to squat across his features, like an old woman taking a dump. He'd been around this game for as long as it had been around and he'd seen more fighters come and more fighters go than even he was comfortable with. It was sad for him to think that this guy standing before him would no doubt be dead in a week, maybe less. From the look of him, Monk was starting to think that betting heavily on the "maybe less" would be a good idea.

"Ay-yup," Cleese said with a heavy sigh. "Let's do this..."

☠ ☠ ☠

Indoctrination

Over the course of the next few days, Monk showed Cleese how things worked around the compound. He learned there was a rigid five day schedule in place which started with a big breakfast, martial arts and weight training in the mornings, an enormous lunch, and then free sparring and what was referred to as "target specific training" in the afternoons. After that, it was more food, more training and more pain. It was a helluva lot of work, but despite some initial bitching Cleese found that he enjoyed it. It had been a long time since he'd worked his body this hard and in a short amount of time he regained some of the strength and vitality he'd lost years ago. Hell, he'd even gotten back some of that muscle definition he'd thought was buried forever beneath the avalanche of booze and bad bar food he'd once called a diet.

During the evenings, both mentor and student were encouraged to spend their time doing whatever activity they chose just as long as they remained together. Some of the teams played chess or played music; others drank and took in women. The more serious of them studied the day's lessons and pored over the compound's vast fight tape library. Whatever the two of them did, it was always in one another's company. The generally accepted theory was that if the two fighters were together at all times, constantly looking out for one another, a trust would develop. It was similar to an ethic that the Spartans once developed in their soldiers.

Besides, in this game, you could always use someone who was willing to watch your back.

Cleese was grateful when everything finally settled into a routine and he could get his first real look at some of the other fighters. There were a lot more of them here than he'd initially thought. They were an odd assortment of personalities that had been collected together for an equally odd assortment of reasons. Some of them had nothing left to lose, having lost their families and whatever passed for their lives back before The Dead first crawled from their dusky tombs. These folks started fighting back then and now continued doing it because that was all they remembered.

Others were nothing more than professional adrenaline junkies: guys who'd given up their snowboards, crotch-rockets and thrill-seeking base jumps for a pistol and a blade. They'd gotten hooked on the notoriety and developed a real jones for the high that only came from stepping within scrapping range of the ultimate, dangerous animal. Of course, the money was a pretty big incentive as well. Cleese noticed early on that a lot of these guys had wide-eyed, jittery looks about them and if local myth was to be believed, they usually ended up being torn to shreds in short order.

Another group, one who kept their members apart from the others, referred to themselves as The Budo Warriors. They'd attached a complex theology to the carnage that took place within the confines of The Pit. Each of them had given up his identity from Before and adopted a samurai-like outlook to their work here: "Live today to the fullest, for tomorrow, we die."

It was, in their minds, a perfect marriage of canon and confrontation.

Their leader, a good-looking bit of femininity named Chikara, was the stuff of legend around here: leader of the Budo Warriors, a woman without a sense of remorse, fighter beyond equal. She'd been in the League for almost as long as Monk and it was rumored that she'd come here after something she'd held dear was lost to the rampaging Dead. After she'd walked away from her life back in The World and joined The League, she'd not given a good goddamn whether she ever made it out of the pit alive. The League welcomed her mostly because she kicked ass and, as a woman, she was a rarity in this killing game.

At first, her technique was more balls than brains. Then she got wise and applied some intellect to her retribution. She periodically allowed the UDs to come in real close and almost get their grip on her—too close in many trainers' opinions— and then she'd lash out with everything but the kitchen sink. It was a fighting style that, although unorthodox, was completely practical and incredibly proficient.

Other fighters saw what she was up to and flocked to her and her cause. Hell, everyone loves a winner and if Chikara could offer these inexperienced men knowledge to help keep them alive a little bit longer than the initial five minutes of their first match, everyone had been up for it. Chikara had been smart about it, too. She wrapped whatever fighting technique she had to offer in a tattered veil of spirituality. If she could only free these men's minds, then their asses would soon follow. She'd doled out nourishing little spoonfuls of Nietzsche and Schopenhauer with a liberal dose of Zen Buddhism, Shintoism, and some cool lines from old Bruce Lee movies.

Soon enough, she had forged for herself a formidable team.

Monk explained to Cleese how all of the Budo Warriors believed that they were already one of The Dead and that the UDs were just another task set before them on their way to enlightenment... or God, whichever. Chikara made little differentiation between gods: hers, theirs or anyone's. Life was merely a test given to the faithful to prove their capacity to serve. God, Jehovah, Jesus, Buddha, Allah... none of these things made a bit of difference to Chikara. A person's relationship with his or her god was something that remained between them and their chosen deity. Chikara's only concern was whether or not you could pass the ordeal that was set before you.

On more than one lazy evening, Monk had shown Cleese a variety of the Warrior's fight tapes and they were an eerie thing to watch. To a man, the Warriors all had the same creepy, calm approach to their fighting: sometimes standing perfectly still until the very last second, then reacting with a lethality that took your breath away. They were, in many of the fighter's minds, combat personified.

All of the fighters—no matter how they saw their place in the world— did agree on one thing and it was that The League was all important. It was Life. It was Death. Fame... Prestige... Money... Horror... Pain... Fear... It was what defined many of them. For the fighters, there was only the Training ("The Way is in the Training") followed by the money and the glory of the live televised events. One always followed the other like clockwork; as regular as breathing—in—out—in—out. And soon, Cleese was told, he would catch on and come to understand.

After only a short while, Cleese discovered that he felt at home here and was growing to actually like this new routine. There'd never been anything even remotely resembling a regular schedule in Cleese's life up 'til now. He'd pretty much done as he pleased since he left home as a kid, but this new discipline just felt right to him. Sure, he'd not had to face a live (or rather dead) opponent, but he knew in time that he would, well aware of the fact that he'd be sparring with the harnessed UDs and all of this mundane shit of lifting weights and going over reaction drills was going to fly right out the fucking window.

Cleese was also pleased to find, despite the inhospitable temper displayed at their initial meeting, Monk was growing on him and vice versa. Sure, he was a foul-mouthed, hard drinking son of a bitch who'd come to the Leagues when they'd first been formed but he was also a man who knew a thing or two about fighting. In the short time they'd been paired together, Monk demonstrated to Cleese dozens of new ways to kill a man. Some were clean. Some were just plain nasty. The bottom line was that they were all effective and would, no doubt, prove useful once Cleese found himself down on the sand in the pit.

As the time dragged on, both Cleese and Monk came to consider themselves lucky to be paired with one another. Some of the pairings were not as good. Some had friction built into them from the get-go as a result of competing personalities. Others had one person exerting more control over the other and both of the fighter's styles suffered because of it. With Monk and Cleese, it was different. It became evident that they both loved the intellectual aspect of what some called the "sweet science;" that chess-like quality combat could sometimes possess. They also came to respect one another as fighters and it was that respect that made becoming friends all the more easy.

In Cleese's opinion, most of the other fighters were nothing more than cannon fodder, at best. Monk though... Monk was different. Monk was cut from a different kind of cloth all together. He knew something. He knew something special, but he was only willing to dole it out in tiny bits and pieces. He was like a gardener carefully watering and feeding a fragile young plant until it was able to support itself and bloom on its own.

He'd give Cleese ideas and concepts and then give him enough time and enough space to put them all together for himself. He would let it all sink in—from the scribblings he made in the sand to the lengthy discussions they'd had over fight tapes played at slow motion—and allow Cleese to internalize it, ponder it, and then turn it into something lethal, something that the crowd would suck up like mother's milk.

Yeah, training was good. Cleese felt better than he had in years, but he also knew that they'd be climbing down into The Pit with The Dead, putting both their lives and their asses on the line.

And when they did, it was going to be a wild ride.

The Squad

Cpl. Lance Johnson intently studied the field spread out before him. The air was still and birds could be heard singing hesitantly far off in the tree line. The weeds and brush carpeting the ground beneath his boots were only a couple of feet high, but he'd learned from past experience that death popped up where you least expected it. Since joining the squad, he'd seen more than a few men fall in fields exactly like this. They'd be walking along—running Point mostly—and then, suddenly, gone.

Dragged down into the brush.

Sometimes they'd go screaming, sometimes they'd go silently, but go they did. A subdued hiss would come up from the foliage and that sound would be the only thing to mark their passing. Well, that and their shrieking... By the time any of the squad could get there and shoot off the things that had swarmed all over the guy, he would be torn to shreds. Ripped to ribbons.

After awhile, when it happened the squad would just blast a hole wherever the man had been. With the stalks of green and brown moving and all of the commotion coming from the ground, it was usually safer to just put down whatever was there—friend or foe.

No one ever made it up intact after being swarmed over on the ground like that, anyway. The Dead were like sharks in that respect. Once they got their teeth in you, you were done.

Caught. Cleaned. Cooked.

The team had been on a House-to-House for the past few weeks, ever since their unit was called up and told that big shit was brewing over in Cress County. The Dead had come back to Life was the story they'd heard. None of them believed it, at first. After all, who would? Who'd ever heard of corpses getting up and eating the flesh of the Living outside of a goddamn horror movie?

Seriously... what the fuck was that all about?

The whole concept seemed fabricated by a combination of over-active imaginations, irrational fear and blatant stupidity. Any one of those things by itself was a dangerous thing. Add them all together and you had a catastrophe of biblical proportions.

Lance looked over toward Sgt. Masterson, the team's leader, and saw the big man rattle off a series of commands by way of a combination of intricate hand signals. His movements were practiced, concise and instantly understood by the men. One by one, they all dutifully complied.

Masterson was from the old school. He was a burly man in his mid-thirties with a dark flattop you could cut paper with and when it came to things like family and friends, it seemed that he'd made his choice a long time ago. The Corps had been his life and his love for as long as he could remember. There never seemed to be a good enough reason to change that. He readily admitted to being what was often referred to as a "lifer" and he was proud of that, however now that The Dead had come a "callin'", it looked more and more as if that life might just be the death of him.

Masterson motioned for the big black man known as "Ray Dog" and the guy they'd picked up on the road who called himself "Slider" to take Point. The Dog waved the M-60 in his hands in front of him like a divining rod and made his way past where Lance was crouched.

"'scuse me, Brutha..." Ray Dog said in his deep baritone.

Slider rose up and fanned the Mossberg shotgun back and forth as he came up on the right. Slider came to be a member of the squad when they'd run into him at one of the bivouacs popping up on the roads along the way. He'd been traveling west from Jersey when the shit hit the fan. The fact that he happened to have the Mossberg and a shit-load of ammo in the trunk of his car pretty much bought him a place on the team. His ability to clear a room with the weapon and keep his head while doing it kept him there. His nickname, he said, came about as a result of his love for White Castle burgers. If all the food in the world disappeared overnight, it would be those greasy little hockey pucks that he'd miss the most.

The two men crab-walked past the group and crouched near a split-rail fence for a second to get their bearings. Then they ducked under the strut and made their way carefully across the field in a fast moving crouch. The barrels of their weapons swayed back and forth, following each soldier's ever-wandering gaze. The rest of the squad dutifully followed along, each checking both the path in front of him and the one behind for even the slightest signs of movement.

Midway down the knoll, a dirt road cut across the field and angled down toward what looked like an old farmhouse. The building was still a good distance away, but its eaves could be made out over the tops of the trees. You could just see through the foliage that the structure was flanked by a small utility shed on the left and a large barn on the right, near the back. The barn looked to be set up for horses or cattle, maybe sheep. In another time, it would have been a place where folk could live out their entire lifetimes in peace. These days, it looked like a death trap.

Reaching the dirt road, the men stood up and let a little of their tension ease. Keeping their eyes moving and assessing their surroundings, they regrouped. Masterson made a few more quick hand signals and they turned as one and headed down the road in a two-by-three formation toward the house.

"Shit, Sarge, how many more of these Sweep and Clears are we going to do?" said the man they all called "A-Rab." He was one of those guys who was always complaining about how much work they all had to do, the conditions, the weather. It was always too hot or too cold or too wet or too dry for A-Rab. The Dog said once that A-Rab was the only guy he knew who could be getting laid and still find a way to complain about the pussy. All of it was whiny-assed bullshit, but carrying the M249 SAW as he was, he'd proven himself a valuable asset to the team. The gun could cut just about anything—living or dead—in half with a burst of its firepower. When you found yourself in shit as deep as this, that kind of weaponry made the difference between life or death; between being taken along or left behind.

"Can the chatter, Son. I have neither the time nor the inclination to listen to your bullshit today," Masterson hissed in clipped tones.

A-Rab looked down, dejected; his diaper having been suitably spanked.

The six men continued to walk silently down the dirt road, each one carefully checking every shadow and shade for even a hint of motion. Once they'd seen to it that the area was clear, they began to relax and talk amongst themselves, albeit in low, hushed tones.

"Hey, Bruce," Lance said to the small, Asian man whose real name was William Takahashi, "did you get a quick one from that broad you were sweet talkin' at that last compound?" Despite the fact that Takahashi was of Japanese heritage, the men had given him the nickname "Bruce" after Bruce Lee who, William theorized, was the only Asian guy they all knew.

Takahashi smiled broadly. "Let's just say that she was very grateful at our having rescued her from the top of that water tower."

"Yeah," laughed Lance, "but did she show you her appreciation."

Bruce winked and grabbed at his crotch.

"The only thing was..." Ray Dog whispered back over his shoulder, "she was horny again an hour later."

The group laughed and for a moment it almost felt as if things weren't so dire. For a second, they collectively forgot how bad things had gotten over the last few weeks, forgot about how most of the people they had known and loved were now dead. Dead or walking around with their faces torn off and trying to eat anything still left alive.

For a second, they were just a group of guys hangin' out and shootin' the shit.

Then, Masterson spoke and brought all of that to an end.

"Stow it, Ladies," he said in a whisper that to the men's ears seemed louder than any scream. "We've got movement."

As one, the men dropped into a crouch and immediately broke off into the brush on whatever side of the road was closest.

"By the shed... on the right," hissed Masterson.

Lance directed his attention toward the small shack that looked like it was a combination utility shed and place for a gas-powered generator. The squat building had the same look as the larger ones far off across the homestead: colonial and just a step out of time.

For a moment, things looked pretty normal. The birds chirped in the trees, the grass swayed in the soft breeze and none of the dumbfucks could be seen. Things looked clear. Then, just below the rise of the hill where the shack stood, a small blur of color could be made out.

Then, another.

"Sarge, you amaze me sometimes," Bruce said quietly. "You sure you don't have E.S.P? I mean, the way you track these fucks makes my head spin."

"Well," grumbled Ray Dog from the back of the pack, "I guess that makes you a dis-oriental."

The men all chuckled under their breath.

Suddenly, three of the reanimated dead staggered around the side of the shack. Two of them were men; white guys dressed like they'd worked as farmhands on this or a neighboring spread. The other was a woman who looked as if she'd almost been pretty once, in a plain sort of corn-fed way. But now something had gotten to her and gnawed off the lower half of her face, leaving her ravaged.

The two males circled the structure, trying and re-trying the door in a vain attempt to gain entry into the shed. The rusted lock that hung from the latch held firm despite their fevered efforts. Futilely, they both hammered their fists on the door's frame.

The woman stood by, momentarily distracted by the flies that circled over and around their heads. She seemed to be patiently waiting for her companion's labors to bear some blood-sodden fruit.

The team fanned out and cautiously approached as Ray Dog and Slider moved ahead. The soldier's approach was silent and skillful. The Dead never noticed a thing until they were almost right on top of them.

"Yo, Nigga," Ray Dog rumbled as he stood up and flipped the safety on his weapon to the fire position, "'Sup?"

Ray Dog pulled the trigger and cut the two men down with the M-60. The massive 7.62mm shells tore through the first guy's upper body, severing his right arm at the shoulder. The stream of bullets then back-tracked as the massive gun was swung back, effectively decapitating both of them.

The woman, who had been standing and swaying slowly and unsteadily on her feet, visibly jumped at the reports of the '60. She'd only begun to realize that her companions were down for good when Slider came up behind her and pushed the Mossberg's barrels up against the back of her head. He pulled the trigger and her expression of disbelief was blown apart by the back of her skull.

Masterson sidled up next to Bruce and whispered something in his ear. Without a word, the Asian took off at a run toward the farm's main house with his MP5 tucked under his arm. He stayed slightly crouched so as not to be seen, but his pace was just this side of "sprint."

The rest of the team secured the area and searched the shed, which they found empty.

"What d'ya think they were looking for?" Slider asked.

The Dog walked up behind him, pointing the barrel of his M-60 toward the ground.

"Your mom."

In a few minutes, Bruce returned and fought to catch his breath as he spoke directly into Masterson's ear.

"Ok, bitches, show time! Bruce here tells me that we have five—count 'em, five—more dumbfucks up around the house," Masterson explained. "I want The Dog and Slider to approach from the front. If any of these fuckers even thinks about trying to attack from there, you'll stop that train of thought before it ever gets on the track. A-Rab, you and Lance take the left flank. Bruce, you and me are on the right."

The team split up accordingly and each drew and checked his weapon, racking rounds and flipping off safeties. The change in their collective demeanor was abrupt but clear. What was before a group of guys jolly-timing it suddenly became a sharpened team of professional killers. This was not their first rodeo and, despite all the bullshitting and dickin' around, these were hardened soldiers. Some, like Masterson, spent a lifetime honing their skills while others had been dragged up a very steep learning curve. It was a field of study that to fail to learn meant death... or worse.

The farmhouse before them was an impressive two story structure with a large, wooden porch around its perimeter. On the right, a large willow tree snuggled up against the side of the house and blanketed it protectively in shadow. On the left, a storm cellar door led into the basement. The place seemed deserted, but they'd all seen that sort of scenario go sour a time or two before. It was how they'd lost Roehler and Fredrickson at the Home Depot and Dupont, Jackson and Miller at the gravel pit.

Having their instructions, A-Rab and Lance sprinted off, making their way around the left side of the house. Lance aimed his AR-10, sweeping the area for any unfriendlies and A-Rab came up behind with the SAW. Once they were set, the two men knelt down and waited for Masterson to give the "in position" signal.

On the right, Masterson and Bruce moved ahead and took up a spot next to the willow's trunk. The Asian moved slightly further to the right to cover the squad leader's flank.

Ray Dog and Slider stood calmly beneath the warm sun, feeling the weight of the artillery in their hands. It was turning out to be a nice day, weather-wise, and they were both grateful for the chance to drink some of it in.

"Hey, Dog," Slider said, "If we had us some Margaritas and some honeys, we'd be set, eh?"

"You know it, man."

The two men burst out laughing, but quickly cut their amusement short. They both knew the dangers of giving themselves away too early to these things. They'd been there to mop up when a squad of National Guard guys had their asses handed to them when they went wandering into a Starbucks making too much racket. Time and time again, being lackadaisical bred stupidity and stupidity bred carelessness and carelessness brought on a world of hurt.

Lance and A-Rab heard their friend's laughter and glanced over to see what was so funny.

The Dog saw the two men staring and flipped them off.

"Lance," Slider hissed, "on your nine."

Lance shot a glance over and saw a zombie coming around the back of the house. The guy looked like another farmhand, which made sense given the locale. It stumbled over something on the ground, but continued to gaze up toward the farmhouse's windows. It looked like it was searching for something, a way in maybe.

Who knew?

Who cared?

Lance raised the AR-10 and pressed it into his shoulder. As he zeroed in, A-Rab shot off a chirping whistle so that the rest of the team would know they'd found movement. Lance pulled the weapon tighter into his shoulder and prepared to fire.

From the same place behind the house, another one of the undead shuffled out behind the first. This one wore a business suit and his chest was caved in. The wound looked semi-circular in shape like it had been made by a car's steering wheel.

A-Rab saw the second zombie and bumped his elbow into Lance's side.

"Do it, Lance," he whispered. "I got ten bucks says you can't do that shit a second time."

"Ten bucks, eh?" Lance considered the proposition from behind the sights of his weapon. "You're on."

Lance pulled the rifle slightly tighter and did his best to keep it still. He took in a deep breath and held it, waiting. He slid his fingertips over the knurling on the thin, curling bit of metal and gently caressed the trigger.

His patience was soon rewarded as the second zombie stepped up just behind the first. Lance let out his breath in a soft sigh and gently squeezed.

The first of the .300 Remington Short Ultra Magnum rounds screamed out from the barrel of the AR-10. It was immediately followed by three more in a staccato burst. The bullets tore through the atmosphere, cutting a swath through humid air and shimmering sunlight. For a microsecond, all sound ceased: the wind halted, the trees went motionless, even the birds stopped their song. As the reports from the gun echoed off into the distance, a heavy and completed silence took its place.

It was in that quiet moment that Lance's initial bullet hit the first zombie just to the left of its nose. As the bone and muscle were torn away, the second and third bullets slapped into the hamburger that had, seconds earlier, been the thing's face and blew it out the back. Now, with a workable pathway made through the zombie's head, the fourth bullet flew through the carnage and struck the second zombie square in the forehead.

Both of the reanimated dead teetered and then fell like trees; one to the left, one to the right.

"Sonuvabitch!" A-Rab sighed.

"That'll be ten bucks, Caliph," Lance said with a wink.

At the sound of the gunshots, Masterson and Bruce stood up and headed 'round the back of the house at a quick clip. They figured that the sound would lure any remaining dead who were behind the house toward the left. It was their plan to come about from the right and flank them.

Ray Dog and Slider took the shots as a sign that it was Go Time and walked toward the front door with a deadly purpose. Slider took up a position to the side of the door and Ray Dog stopped once he got to the door mat.

"Should we knock?" The Dog said with an easy, wide grin.

Slider shook his head and laughed.

Ray Dog raised one of his size fifteen boots and kicked the door off of its hinges. "Knock, knock!"

Just inside, coming out of the family room and into the foyer, was a reanimated woman. She looked roughly forty or so, hair tied tight at the back of her head in a haphazard bun. The front of her dress was torn and bloody. A large gash extended from her throat and angled down into her dress. From beneath the hem of her dress, an oily loop of intestine dragged forgotten behind her, leaving a deep crimson snail trail in its wake.

Suddenly, from behind the house, another series of gunshots were heard. By the sound of it, it was Masterson's Bushmaster. The short staccato sound of pops was heard and then the echo trailed off across the valley. The dead woman turned, distracted by the sound.

The Dog gave a sharp whistle, dragging back the attention of the thing before him. For a second, they stood staring at one another and then the woman opened her mouth and bared her teeth. He fired a quick burst with the M-60 and obliterated both the dead woman and most of the hallway. Splinters of wood, stucco, and body parts were thrown violently into the air. When the smoke cleared, the place looked as if The Wild Bunch had been there.

"Clear!" Ray Dog shouted.

"Ya think?!?" Slider said still laughing.

From behind the house came the other's responses.

"Clear!" shouted Masterson.

"Clear!" yelled A-Rab.

Slider entered the front door and ran up the stairs, taking them two at a time. Ray Dog watched as he disappeared at the top of the staircase. Soon enough, a shotgun blast echoed through the building.

"Clear!" came Slider's shout from upstairs.

Minutes later, the squad regrouped on the porch outside the shattered front door.

"Ok," Masterson said, running his hand over his sweaty scalp. "no one get comfortable. We have one more structure to check."

They all looked further up the small hill, which angled up twenty or so yards to the right and back of the house. It was there that the barn stood waiting.

"We do this just like we always do, Gentlemen" he said. "Secure the perimeter, and then we compromise the front door. Anything Dead moves, if it even so much as wiggles, cap it."

The men nodded and shouldered their weapons. As a group, they headed up toward the barn at a trot. The road was more dirt driveway than real road with deep furrows from a tractor's tires cut into the hard ground. Years of repeated travel back and forth from the barn to the field had left some deep scars on the earth.

Several hundred yards away from the barn, Bruce detected more movement.

"I got a coupla more meatheads over here," he said. "One by the double doors at the front. One on the left."

Masterson raised a scarred pair of binoculars and aimed them toward the barn. In the lenses, he could see that the building was fairly large and painted in a stereotypical red with a set of double doors in the front. Above them was another set of doors with a winch suspended over it by a post. No doubt it was where they loaded hay and feed once upon a time. The building looked exactly like what it was: a barn. Even from this distance, the smell of straw was sweet and overpowering.

Standing in front of the doors were two more zombies: a man and a young girl. The guy was in his mid-fifties with gray hair and a severe beer belly. He was missing his left hand and forearm and there were huge, raking tears down his back. The girl was barely out of high school with short brown hair cut in a bob. She had no visible causes of death. Under the hot sun their skin appeared to be discolored with large blackened patches of flesh that looked bruised and rotting.

There was a slight family resemblance between the two. So much so that Lance thought maybe they'd once been Father and Daughter. Maybe not. It didn't matter. Now, they were hungry, disease-ridden predators and they were about to have their heads aggressively ventilated.

That's just the way things were.

The team headed up the roadway with eyes continuing to scour the landscape and their guns held up and at the ready. It wouldn't do anybody any good if they became too focused on what lay in front of them and forgot all about what might be hidden in the brush to their left or right.

Once they'd gotten to within a dozen or so yards from the barn, the two zombies caught the squad's scent on the wind. The man whirled around and snarled. He headed toward them at a speed that was faster than any of them thought possible. He had his weight and the fact that he was heading downhill on his side. No matter... one thing was clear.

The fat boy could run.

The girl stumbled along behind him like a retarded puppy. Her arms swayed back and forth like pendulums as she ran. From the look of things, she'd already followed him to the Gates of Hell and beyond. Following along behind him to go after a bit of food now was a given.

Bruce stepped forward and, without prompting, cut them down with the MP5. They both did a sort of herky-jerky dance as the spray of bullets tore through them and splintered the barn behind. Finally, several slugs slapped into the meat of their faces, blowing the tops and sides of their heads into the air like divots.

"Area clear, Sir!" Bruce said with a smirk as he dutifully stepped back in line.

"Good work, Son," Masterson said, patting the young man on the back. "We'll need to recon the interior and get our asses on to the next homestead down the road."

The group walked over to the double barn doors together, stepping over the now still bodies of the fat guy and the girl, and noticed the padlock that had been put in place on the door just as it had been on the shed. Slider picked up the lock and jerked on it.

"Fuck," Slider exclaimed, letting it fall back in place with a sharp banging sound. "The place is locked up tight. Somebody had enough time to secure the joint before they took off."

"Or got themselves ate up," The Dog said under his breath.

"Maybe that was them up at the house," Lance suggested.

They all looked back at the farmhouse they'd just secured. From this distance, they could make out the shattered front door hanging from its hinges. A sudden breeze whistled through the eaves.

"Ah, who gives a fuck?" A-Rab said, sounding disgusted. He stepped forward and unceremoniously shot the lock off.

"What?" he said wryly and shrugged his shoulders. "None of yaz ever hear of the Gordian Knot?"

The pair of doors was thrown open and the group stepped back to give themselves some fighting room should anything be waiting just inside. Oddly, no livestock came running out. It appeared as if the barn were empty; inside lay nothing but the inky darkness. On both sides, stalls that looked as if they'd once housed horses or sheep or some other kind of livestock were lined up. The place smelled like sweet hay mixed with the rich odor of manure.

The men fanned out and secured each of the stalls one by one.

"Looks empty, Sarge," Lance said.

"Well, those dumbfucks outside were after something," Masterson said. "Slider, why don't you take the Mossberg and check out the loft upstairs? The rest of you, check your magazines and reload."

"I'm on it," Slider said and he disappeared like a wraith into the shadows.

The squad pulled off their packs with a collective groan and set to swapping out their old magazines for fresh ones. No one had to tell them what it meant to be caught by The Dead with only a half-full weapon. Once the hardware was reloaded, they refilled their spent magazines from the ammo in their packs.

Soon, a shout from over their heads echoed through the empty barn.

"Nothing up here, Sarge. I did find somebody's stash of old *Playboys* though." There was a long pause and then, "Hellooooooo, Miss October."

"Ok, fine. Leave the stroke books and get back down here. We'll take fifteen to rest and finish reloading before we head off for the next farm."

Slider rejoined the men after a couple of minutes and the group soon fell into a congenial conversation.

"Look," Ray Dog said to Slider. "I ain't sayin' shit 'bout the effectiveness of your goddamn shotgun, you simple Jersey Fuck. I'm only sayin' you shouldn't be steppin' up and standin' in front of my '60."

"Will youse all listen to this fuckin' mulignane?"

"Careful with that mulignane shit, Cuz, or I'm gonna have to hang my size fifteens in your lily white ass."

The team laughed, having been longtime by-standers to this ongoing debate. Ray Dog was always complaining about having to check his fire because Slider would step into his firing line time and time again. He said Slider did it to take credit for his kills. Slider's position was that The Dog thought of his weapon in the same way that he thought of his dick—big, black and mighty deadly. He felt he needed to show a little of what a white boy could do to help him out.

The dispute had been going on for as long as they'd been on the patrol.

As the two men argued and the rest of the squad listened amusedly, a small almost invisible door moved slightly on its hinges in the shadows at the back of the barn. It wasn't anything anyone would have noticed unless they'd been looking right at it, but it did indeed move.

"Listen, White Bread, all I'm sayin' is that if you ain't careful, you're going to get the smoking end of this bitch straight in the ass."

Again, the door shifted. This time though, it came off the door frame and opened slightly. Over the din of the men's conversation, no one noticed or heard a thing.

Except Masterson.

The squad leader cleared his throat suddenly, and made a circular motion with his finger that told the men to continue talking. The men immediately raised their weapons and looked around in response. Masterson raised a finger and pointed into the shadows at the back of the barn.

"Shit, man, you know my ass is exit only," said Slider, continuing the ruse, as they all caught on to what was going down.

The small door continued to slowly swing open and deep in the shadows four dirty fingers slowly slid into view. As one, the team snapped their weapons to a firing position and waited for Masterson to give the go-ahead.

An older man slowly stepped out from behind the door. His face was smudged with dirt and sweat, his clothes matted with a dark oily substance. His expression was tired and his skin sallow. His cheekbones jutted out and gave him the appearance of someone who hadn't eaten in days, maybe weeks. He looked like something out of Auschwitz as he raised his eyes to meet Masterson's and slowly opened his mouth, yellow teeth flashing in the half-light.

Just as Masterson gave the signal to fire, Lance saw that the man's pupils were clear and unclouded by Death.

"Dumb fucks," shouted Masterson. "Smoke 'em!"

Before Lance could say anything, the other five men opened fire.

Bullets tore their way through the old guy and splintered the wood of the wall and door. Huge holes opened up in the wall, which only made the other rounds' passage to whatever lay beyond all that much easier. The Mossberg blew pizza pan-sized craters in the wall while the M-60, the SAW, and the smaller rifles threw up a hailstorm of metal. The sound inside the enclosed barn was deafening and as the MP-5 and the Bushmaster all fell on empty, the team heard Lance shouting.

"Wait! Wait! Wait!" he screamed, spittle flying from his lips. "Ohhh, you stupid motherfuckers! You stupid, stupid motherfuckers!"

The men all looked around, dumbfounded.

"He wasn't fucking dead, man!" Lance cried out. "He wasn't fucking dead!"

With the set of double doors in the front open and the Volkswagen-sized hole now blown in the rear, the wind soon blew the thick gunpowder smoke clear. The men all stood trying to sort out what the fuck Lance's trip was.

"Say wha...?" Ray Dog questioned now looking small and uncertain somehow.

Lance ran up to the bullet-decimated wall and bent to check the man's already rapidly cooling body. He waved his arm in an attempt to clear a bit more of the choking smoke.

"This guy wasn't one of Them, you fucking assholes!" He ran his hand over his face, pulling his features into distortion. His eyes quickly welled up with tears as he cried out, "Oh, fuck... oh, God!"

Masterson stepped over to the now dead man and bent to check to see if what Lance was saying was true. They all felt their hearts sink when they saw the look that passed over his face.

Lance stood up and continued rubbing his face with his hands.

"Oh, God..." he cried. "You stupid fuckin' fucks!"

He turned and kicked at the last remaining boards and stepped into the area beyond the shattered door. The place looked like the OK Corral. Bullet holes and splintered wood were everywhere.

Lance knelt down, trying to get beneath the last of the smoke. He coughed and continued to fan his hand back and forth in an effort to try and see more clearly. As the smoke finally dissipated, what he saw behind the obliterated wall was something that would haunt him until the day he died.

Lying on the floor were what was left of the dead man's family: a woman about the same age as he'd been, a girl who looked to be about seventeen, a boy who was twelve if he was a day, and a smaller kid who couldn't have been more than eight. The artillery had torn them into bits. Large, gaping wounds still bled and at even the most cursory of glances, it was evident that they were now just as dead as their patriarch.

Despite his best efforts to control his rising nausea, Lance vomited into the hay.

For a long time, no one spoke. Masterson walked away from the group and sat on some bales of hay, looking pale and flustered. He sat there for a long time and looked deep in thought as he regained control and considered all of the possible ramifications of this little fuck-up.

Finally, Masterson spoke up as he stood and began gathering his gear, "This place is clear, Gentlemen. We report it as such."

"Sarge," Lance shouted, "we just murdered these people!"

"Casualties of war, Son," Masterson said and the words sounded as if they tasted bitter in his mouth. "You ladies are to finish reloading. We move on to the next ranch in five."

The men all stood around and looked confused and a bit repulsed. Shooting zombies was one thing. This... This was something else entirely.

"Are we clear on this?" Masterson said and his gaze addressed them all sternly, especially Lance, and never wavered. "Gear up! You heard me, we leave in five."

"You can't be serious?" Lance said unbelieving.

Masterson turned on him. He took a menacing step forward and none of them—Lance in particular—failed to notice how his hand drifted toward the pistol he kept holstered at his side. His eyes narrowed and his jaw grew noticeably more taut and firm.

"Son, we have a job to do here and we're going to do it. Nothing is going to bring these people back, you hear me? This was a mistake," he said through clenched teeth. "A mistake that never happened."

Lance started to open his mouth to respond, but he felt A-Rab's hand on his arm as if to say, "Some fights aren't worth dying over, kid."

"Now... are we clear, soldier?"

Lance closed his mouth and reluctantly nodded.

"Good. Like I said, Ladies... Pack your shit. We leave in five."

As Masterson walked away, Lance felt a fleeting impulse to shoot the bastard in the back. God knew it would serve him right, but as the men slowly began to follow the Sarge's orders, he knew that he wouldn't do it. He knew that he'd do just as he was told and pray this whole thing would be over soon. With enough time and distance, it would all become just a vague memory of something that could only have happened in a dream. The squad would move on and someday The World would get a handle on all of this crazy shit. Life would go back to the way it had been before and all of it—The Dead, the killing, the bodies, and the blood—would fade from their memories.

But Lance knew today would be different, today would be with him forever. Deep down, he knew he'd remember the look in the old man's eyes and that moment, the one just before the bullets starting flying, would replay in his mind—in his nightmares—again and again, and every time he remembered it, he would get the same sick feeling in the pit of his gut as he had now.

Today though...

Today, the world was falling to shit and for better or for worse he was still alive. If he intended to stay that way, he knew he'd need to keep his mouth shut and just follow the orders that were given. So, with his face set and his eyes looking downward, Lance gathered his gear and tried to prepare himself for whatever might be lying in wait at the next farmhouse up the road.

0 0 0

The Monkey Dance

The light fixtures set in the ceiling of the weight room were turned off in an attempt to keep the room cool against the remaining heat of the day. Just below the lights, blades of circulating fans churned the warm air like dark and malignant butter. The hottest part of the day had almost passed, but in this place the heat never fully went away. It was always oppressively hot, day or night, and any cool breeze, no matter how slight, was appreciated.

The fighters working out were happy for the respite after a long day too full of sun and the bright lights of the Octagon. What each of them wanted now was to have some peace and quiet and to remain uninterrupted while toiling in the relative calm of the gym.

Cleese lay on his back across the bench press and looked up at his spotter. Monk's face floated there like a Macy's Thanksgiving Day Parade balloon. It drifted there and his stern, upside-down expression was almost comical. Cleese closed his eyes and tried to shut out all external stimuli. He ran his fingers through his long sweat-dampened hair and, being too tired and too hot to do much else, sighed. They'd been at this for a good couple of hours now and even though he felt exhilarated by the exercise his muscles burned from tendon to ligament. His flesh was hot to the touch and the flush of exertion burned warm and red across his skin.

They'd had a quick, but strenuous five mile run on the compound's quarter mile track to warm-up, then the two of them came to the gym to do some weight training and, more importantly, to try and calm their souls. Lately, Cleese felt like his nerves were on the short edge of frayed. Even Monk could tell how close he was to breaking. Damn, anyone with half a brain could see it. Too much had happened far too fast and he hadn't had the chance to just chill out, sort through his thoughts, and centralize his concentration on something he knew and knew well... his body.

It had been only a short time since he was brought out here to the middle of goddamn nowhere and asked to adapt to a new paradigm and an entirely new routine. He'd been dropped into a maelstrom that was about as foreign to him as a jump shot was to a circus midget. The whole thing was like nothing he could have ever imagined. Sure, he'd seen his share of weird before. Hell, he'd bartered in some pretty bizarre shit once upon a time, but this... this was just out there.

This made weird look like weird was on vacation.

If pressed, Cleese would have probably said that he'd been happy in San Francisco, back when his aggressive ignorance seemed like bliss. He'd had some money, plenty of broads, and access to pretty much everything he could have ever wanted or hoped for. Yes, he'd given up pieces of himself over the years in exchange for those things, but life had been good.

More or less.

However, deep down he knew that it was all just an empty replacement for the one thing he most craved: a place to truly fit in and call his own, without ties or caveats.

But as they say, that was then and this is now...

Now, he found himself sitting square in the eye of a shit tornado and from the look of things life was going to get a hell of a lot worse—or at least a heck of a lot weirder—before it ever got better.

That said... if this routine supplied him with anything, it was a place and a role. He was a fighter. And as a fighter, that meant he was a man who put his mettle to the test day after day in the most inhospitable—and most unimaginable—of places. He did what few others would do—what few others could do.

Or at least that was the plan... just as soon as he finished this training, completed this next set.

Cleese slowly opened his eyes and stared up at the ceiling and Monk's grinning Jack O'Lantern face. Jesus, he was a hideous motherfucker, hovering there and looking like Death and Ugly had a baby and it had been allowed to grow up. He closed his eyes once more and silently prepared himself for the next lift.

Raising his hands, he slid them across the straight bar that sat on two posts welded to the bench on each side of his head. He moved his hands roughly eighteen inches apart, stopping when he felt the knurling carved there under his fingertips. A quick check as to the position of the three forty-five pound metal plates on each side of the bar and he braced his hands against the steel. He took a deep breath, then another, and pushed against the weight. Once clear of the supports, he carefully moved the bar over him and held it there.

The plates rattled softly as he slowly lowered the weight to his chest. He felt the bar bounce gently off of his sternum and held it there. He contracted his pecs, forcing blood deep into the muscle. The flesh grew still warmer and, slowly uncurling like a serpent, pain raised its cobra-like head once more. With a grunt, he pushed at the bar, and the weight rose slowly and steadily to the fully extended position. Cleese methodically repeated the "lower–contract–lift" motion another six times and then, with a deep breath, set the barbell in its rack above him.

Once more, Monk's face came into focus wearing a grin which cut fiercely across the lower part of his face.

"You're a goddamn animal," he said, his voice brimming over with delight.

"That's what your momma said," Cleese puffed as he sat up.

"Like fuck..."

Cleese leaned over and picked up a small towel from the floor. He reached up and wiped at the side of his neck. As he caught his breath, he felt the serpent in his chest recede and the flush subside a bit.

"I gotta tell ya," he said as he slowly caught his breath, "this feels good. I haven't done this kind of shit in quite a while."

"Well, from what I hear, you weren't living the healthiest of lifestyles when they did your Retrieval."

"Yeah, well... We can't all walk the straight and narrow."

"Son, you ain't seen the straight and narrow since you were a dribble on your daddy's dick," Monk said as he reached down for an additional thirty-five pound plate. He slid it onto the left side of the bar and then went to do the same on the right.

"Hey, that additional weight isn't for me, is it?"

"Damn straight, Skippy. I wanna see you either beg for mercy or cry like a four year old school girl. Frankly, either one'll do."

Cleese laughed and wiped the other side of his neck. When he was done, he dropped the towel to the ground and lay back onto the bench for another set.

Monk slid the last plate on and pushed it against the others.

"You guys going to fuckin' gossip all day or give the rest of us a chance on that equipment?" a gravelly voice interrupted.

Cleese looked up and saw one of the other fighters standing there in sweat pants and a large red shirt. It was a guy he'd seen around who was known as Michaels. He was a big tub of shit who had somehow gotten it into his pint-sized head that his brawn automatically made him a proficient fighter. Michaels was one of the newer fighters, newer than even Cleese, and he'd already gotten himself a reputation as being an aggro asshole. From all accounts, he'd hit the ground running in that respect. As he stood there glaring at them, his hands were on his hips and his manner was severely impatient.

"Listen, Michaels," Monk said calmly, "there's another set of benches right there." Monk pointed toward three additional benches on the other side of the room. "Use one of those."

Monk turned his back on him as if dismissing him and walked over to spot Cleese on his next set.

"See, that's the thing, Old Timer," Michaels said, his voice dripping with caustic sarcasm and just a hint of menace. "I like this bench and I mean to use it."

Cleese slowly sat up and turned so that both of his feet were on the same side of the bench, just in case this fool decided to make good on his threat. He'd seen it happen too many times in the past where someone got rushed and his footing was compromised by stuff on the ground: a barstool, a drunken girlfriend or some other stupid shit. He didn't know this Michaels guy too well and what little he did know said that he was a prick. Not having his whole story made him decide to err on the side of caution.

"Step off, Cherry," Monk hissed. His voice was low and steady, but it was barbed with an implied warning. "You want none of this, I assure you."

Michaels took a step forward and squared his shoulders.

"Is that so?"

"It is at that," Monk said and looked him dead in the eye.

"Listen, Monk," Michaels growled, "some people here think you're some hot shit, but all I see is a washed up old man who's past his prime. Now, take your hippy pal here and get off my fuckin' bench."

"Not gonna happen," Monk replied, looking back toward the bench. "If you want to press it, we can talk to Masterson."

"Fuck Masterson," Michaels shouted and he took another step foward.

"Careful, now..." Monk replied, sounding casual and almost uninterested. "You know how the League feels about fighting amongst its staff. You wouldn't want to compromise your sit-chee-ation," he slowly returned his gaze to the big man's eyes and cocked an eyebrow, "now would ya?"

Michaels paused just for a second as if he was pondering how far he wanted to push it. Interestingly, Monk helped make the decision for him.

"Good thing, too... or I'd be handing you a big piece of your chubby ass right about now."

"Hey, fuck you, you old piece of shit."

Cleese stood up, having decided that he'd heard just about enough. If this little prick wanted his melon thumped, Cleese felt more than happy to oblige him. Besides, he'd dealt with assholes like this in bars for years. They were usually all bark and no bite and all you needed to do was whack them on the nose with a rolled-up newspaper and they quickly learned to behave. Moving rapidly, he took a step between the two men and smiled malevolently at Michaels.

"Hey, KoolAid..."

"You stay out of this," Monk warned. The last thing they needed was for Cleese to do something to get himself booted from the Roster.

Michaels glared at Cleese and leaned in.

"You should listen to your mommy, Frisco. You don't want me to hurt you, now do ya?"

Cleese smiled and motioned with his finger for Michaels to lean in even closer.

"Two things..."

"Cleese, no," Monk said again.

"First, don't ever call my home town 'Frisco.' We hate that shit."

Michaels' face broke out in a wry grin and sniffed in lieu of laughing.

"And second... the only thing you ever put a hurt on is a deli plate, you fat fuckin' pussy."

Michaels reacted as if he'd been slapped. His eyes went wide and his face flushed red. He quickly balled his hands at his sides into fists and slowly raised them.

Cleese smiled and knew he'd hit his desired mark.

"What did you say to me?" the fat man bellowed.

"I said..." Cleese leaned in even further and purposefully stuck his chin out, offering the man a target that was designed to be too good to pass up. "I said... that you, my rotund friend, are a poo..." specks of saliva flew from his lips as he enunciated the "p" and landed on Michaels' cheek "...say."

He stared deep into Michaels' eyes and smiled, watching as the man's blood came to a slow rolling boil. His patience was finally rewarded when he saw Fat Boy's right shoulder drop.

The punch was a wild haymaker coming from behind Michaels' back. Cleese had to give it to him, the boy was as stupid as a sack of hammers, but if he was anything, he was committed. With all of this strength directed into his arm and his vision obscured by his rabid anger, Michaels never saw Cleese's feet shift and his weight transfer to his push-off leg. As the haymaker came around, Michaels' left hand dropped and his jaw presented itself with everything except a colored bow.

Cleese ignored the offering and was already in motion even as he slapped at the incoming fist with his left hand. Coming around the other man's reach, he let Michaels' momentum spin him like a top. With a little hop, Cleese let loose a savage oblique kick to the nearest open target—the knee of Michaels' right leg. Predictably, the big lummox lost his footing as his knee collapsed. With a painful sounding grunt, he dropped down on all fours.

Cleese circled and, as the wounded man raised his head to scream out in pain from the leg strike, quickly boxed both of his ears. Michaels screeched anew and clutched at the sides of his head.

"Cleese," Monk shouted. He reached out and grabbed the bench's barbell. Once he saw that it was already too late, he leaned over and rested his head in resignation on the cold, metal bar. "God damn it!"

Michaels collapsed forward, clutching at his ears. Now in a full rage, he started to rise to a standing position despite the pain in his leg. When he'd gotten up on one knee, he noticed an empty dumbbell bar which was lying on the ground next to the bench. Boiling over with fury, he grabbed at it. As he rose to his feet, he swung it viciously at Cleese's head.

Having expected something of this sort, Cleese was ready. He caught his wrist as it came up and deftly wrestled the bar out of his grasp. He quickly twisted the arm and then maneuvered himself down and under the outstretched limb.

Now that all of the joints in Michaels' arm were twisted in on themselves, he had but two choices—return to the ground or allow his arm to be broken in several places.

As the fat man fell, Cleese silently thanked an old Steven Seagal movie he'd seen years ago for the move.

Monk raised his head and, seeing how things were progressing, grimaced.

Michaels' body hit the ground with another pig-like grunt and he immediately moved to cradle his wrenched arm. His face twisted up into a painful looking grimace and a small string of drool fell from his lips. As he rolled onto his back, he looked up and was horrified to see Cleese standing over him holding the dumbbell bar like a dagger. He gasped when he saw that Cleese was already in motion and bringing it down in a powerful strike aimed directly at his face. He cried out and raised his hands to protect himself.

Monk shouted out, "Nooo, shit!"

With a loud slap, the metal bar hit the rubber padding on the floor just to the left of Michaels' head.

"BAM, Motherfucker!" Cleese shouted into Michaels' twisted face. "It's just that fuckin' easy."

Michaels rolled up into a crouch and, wiping tears away from his eyes, shouted, "They were right! You are fucking crazy!"

Cleese casually tossed the bar aside. It hit the floor with a clatter and bounced under the bench.

"And that was me making you a fuckin' corpse! Now, get out of here before I fuck you up but good, you fat fuck!"

Michaels got to his feet and limped off like a spanked little boy, alternately cradling his arm and rubbing at his boxed ears. The men in the gym, who'd been watching the altercation with an expectant immediacy, all hooted and jeered. Most of them had been fucked with by Michaels and none had done anything about it, not wanting to run afoul of the League's restrictions on fighting. However they were only too happy to watch someone else risk their gig and dole out a little payback.

Monk came out from behind the bench and poked Cleese in the chest with his forefinger. "Well, that was just fuckin' stupid."

"Hey," Cleese said, raising his hands in mock contrition, "he attacked me. He threw the first punch."

"Still, you know the rules... 'No fighting!'"

"Hey, I'm new. 'Sides, I don't know no better."

Monk looked dumbfounded for a moment and then laughed.

"Yeah, well... you may just be right about that, but it could still cost you your spot."

"I somehow doubt it. I'll just plead ignorance."

Monk smiled and scratched at the back of his head. He had to admit it; it wasn't exactly something Corporate would toss an asset like Cleese out on his ear for. After all, Michaels had thrown the first punch. It could always be argued that Cleese was only defending himself. He'd sure as shit have enough corroboration for that story from the still-laughing men gathered around them.

It was a given that the Suits would be pissed as hell, but they'd also probably give him a pass on it. Michaels was a schmuck and everyone knew it. Most of the mentors had already discussed how much trouble the kid was getting to be. There'd been talk of officially punishing him by docking his earnings. From the decisive ass-whuppin' Cleese had just handed him, he was willing to bet that his days of being a tough guy and a pain in everybody's ass were pretty much over.

Monk looked over at Cleese with a newfound respect. Not only had he risked everything in order to respond to an insult, by goading Michaels into striking first he'd done so in a manner which offered minimal blow back.

This kid was definitely growing on him.

"Yeah, they'll totally buy that, you simple fuck. You truly don't know no better."

Cleese grinned and walked back over to the bench.

"Ok," Monk said as he walked back to the head of the bench, "see that something like that doesn't happen again."

"You got it," Cleese grinned and slid himself back under the bar. "We're still pals, right?"

"Fuck you..." Monk said and reached down to grab two more twenty pound plates. He slid a plate onto one end of the bar and then loaded the other one on the opposite end. He then nodded at the bar set across the bench's uprights, "and give me another set."

☠ ☠ ☠

Rules of the Game

"Listen up," Monk said one afternoon as the two of them sat, taking a break in the stands overlooking The Octagon, "'cause I'm only going to say this shit once."

The fighting space below them was a pit roughly thirty feet across with dull, brushed metal sides. The walls bore the marks of training sessions past, blood smears and bullet holes hung like macabre decorations across the vertical iron surface. At the spaces where the walls came together, there were metal X-frames which Cleese had previously seen spin on their central axes. The floor of the pit was mostly sand to aid the fighter's footing.

It also made cleanup a whole lot easier.

Cameras sat perched like paparazzi on the walls above and sent a steady stream of video to the media booth at the back of the Hall. It beamed an up-close-and-personal view of the action to the monitors there which recorded every fighter's training session. All of them were required to review the tapes and use whatever they learned to refine their techniques. Off to the side, a dimly illuminated scorekeeper's box sat high above the stands. Cleese noticed an ethereal, ghost-like shadow move behind the glass.

"Rules of the Game... Listen to 'em, learn 'em, and never fuckin' forget 'em." Monk said and leaned forward, his forearm resting on his knee. "Forget 'em and you will almost assuredly have your ass carried out of here with your toes pointing toward at the ceiling." His manner was secretive and almost conspiratory; as if great knowledge was about to be handed down in a lurid, oral tradition.

"You may think you already know this stuff, but as with all things, you don't know shit from shaving cream."

Cleese leaned back and closed his eyes. He gently prompted his mind to imprint the words he was hearing upon his memory; to sear them into the meat of his brain. They were just a few days away from Cleese's first training session with the UDs and he knew better than to blow this off.

This... this was important shit.

"One man goes inside," Monk explained. "He has his bare hands, a blade, and a side arm with one full clip. We use Beretta 92Fs with Teflon M882 hollow point rounds for side arms. We've opted for the meatier slide that's sixty grams heavier and one millimeter wider to improve control for when you're firing multiple shots in quick succession. The Beretta is used because it's a damn reliable weapon. The hollow points because they make for splashier bullet hits. These are televised events after all and we want to keep it exciting for the crowds. You'll have fifteen rounds in the first clip with one up the pipe."

Cleese nodded, taking it all in and mentally transforming principles into instinct.

"As the rounds progress, you'll come across a rash of shotguns out there:

Mossberg 500s, pump action Remington 870s, Winchester 1300s... even semi-auto Browning A-5s and Benelli M1s. There'll also be chainsaws, harpoon guns... a whole host of shit. We'll have a ton of weapons training available, so we'll make use of it all. You don't want to get caught out there with a locked and loaded weapon that you don't know how to use."

Monk dragged the back of his hand across his chin. His stubble produced a harsh, rasping sound. For a second, his mind seemed to slip away to a time when he'd first been given this speech. It seemed like a lifetime ago and the talk, quite literally, changed his life. After a moment, he returned to the here-and-now and continued with his explanation.

"Oh, and a word of advice: save your bullets for when you draw a crowd. The people in the stands came to see *Spartacus* not *High Plains Drifter* so be frugal, you get me? You go in shootin' up the place and you'll find that you're out of rounds when you need them the most. And then... Toes up."

Monk shrugged and broke away. He paced back and forth along the front of the benches. He'd found long ago that keeping himself moving helped him to think. At a time like this, it wouldn't do to forget something important.

"A match begins with three UDs released into The Octagon. Every two minutes, a buzzer will sound." He jerked to a halt, and pointed a finger at Cleese. "Listen for that sound, because that sound... is your ass."

Monk raised his right arm and made a tight circle in the air with his finger. The room echoed with the sound of a loud buzzer. Suddenly, the X-frames spun a quarter turn and locked into place with a hollow, metallic sound.

"Motherfu..." Cleese exclaimed. He'd heard the sound before, but for some reason, this time it made him damn near jump out of his skin.

Monk waved toward the scorekeeper's box as if in thanks. Inside the elevated room, the shadow Cleese had previously seen waved back before evaporating back into the gloom.

"At the sound of that buzzer, the eight corners of The Octagon will pivot like you just saw," Monk continued, returning his full attention to his enthusiastic student. "In your head you should assign each corner a number and remember what's what so you can keep 'em all straight in the heat of the moment. Once those spindles move, you're gonna find one of four things there."

He counted them off aloud, using his stubby fingers as a visual aid.

"One: a weapon. It could be a better pistol, a shotgun, a chainsaw. You'll never know, but whichever it is, you'll be damn glad to see it. Two: ammo. This ain't Halo or Quake out there, Buddy. There's no cheat codes, so sooner or later you're gonna need to reload. And that's as good as fuck a reason as any to conserve your ammo. Three: A very pissed-off UD. They'll be disoriented at first, but soon enough, they'll smell you and come a-runnin'. Four: Nothing... Nada... Bupkiss. There are eight spindles and we have to maintain some sense of drama. We don't want this to be a goddamn turkey shoot. Again, we gotta keep it interesting for the crowd. It is, after all, what they're paying for.

"Keep this in mind, by the time the next buzzer sounds you'll need to have thought about a lot of shit: your position in the Pit, the position, if any, of the remaining UDs around you, your weapon's status and what you need to replenish it, where the spindles are (which can be both a good thing and a bad thing depending on what is there when it next spins). Lotsa shit... You're a smart boy. You'll figure it all out.

"When that buzzer sounds, kill whatever's around—fast! You move on to get what you need, but only after those first UDs are down. Don't stand around fucking shopping. Kill—Grab—Move on. You with me so far, Champ?"

Cleese sat up and looked the ring over. His eyes narrowed and as he thought, he spoke his thoughts aloud.

"Ring. Spindles. Buzzer. Weapons. UDs. 'Kill—Grab—Move.'" He looked back at Monk and grinned malevolently. "Got it."

"Ok, genius, after six minutes and three rounds, the buzzer will sound each and every minute with the odds of a UD being 'spun' being higher. Think of it as a game and you're going on to harder and harder levels. At ten minutes, the buzzer will sound every thirty seconds. You reach fifteen minutes and you're done! Make it through and you're a hero, a media fuckin' god. Sound simple enough?"

Cleese sat thinking, going over the math in his head. No matter how he added it all up—it sucked. It also sounded crazy, but... as they say, "in for a penny, in for a pound."

"By my count, that's a fuckload of UDs, Monk."

"It's roughly fifty of the slimy bastards in those fifteen minutes. It's why you're being paid those big bucks, Pal. But none of that shit is gonna make a lick of difference 'cause, if you have to shoot, you're gonna aim for the head. Demolish the lumps of shit that pass for their brains as quickly as you can. Remember, it ain't considered a kill unless you destroy the brain or lop their heads from their shoulders.

"And don't get cocky and don't play to the fuckin' crowd. Not at first. You get the job done and you'll be back in your trailer gettin' your dick sucked by a big-titted blonde faster than you can say "wet and sloppy.""

Monk raised a hot dog of a finger.

"Fuck up..."

"I know... it's a vinyl body bag," said Cleese.

"Fuck the body bag, Bronco, that's for your momma to cry over. You get stupid out there and step in it, some UDs gonna be having your ass for an appetizer."

Cleese stared out over The Octagon, rubbing his hands over his eyes. This was some world of hurt he'd gotten himself into, but if he were to be honest a part of him was almost excited about trying this. He'd fought his way out of San Francisco back when the shit first hit the fan, but this... this was something else.

This was sticking your dick in a bear trap and callin' it pussy.

This was crazy and Cleese fucking well knew it.

"Come on, Cochise," said Monk slapping Cleese across the back. "We need to get you fitted for your gear."

He turned and walked away.

Cleese continued to stare down at the fighting ring, weighing his decision... and his options. The last place he'd called home had been a bit of a bust. He'd been out of work—honest work that is—since he bitch-slapped Stolie, the loan shark he had worked for. The man pushed Cleese one time too many and needed to be ghetto-cuffed if only on general principal. It was a mistake and Cleese knew it even as he was doing it. Then again, "job security" and "good sense" were never high on Cleese's list of watchwords.

When Masterson came calling, Cleese had already beaten down two guys with a broom handle earlier that night when they'd tried to muscle him over a boxing bet. Afterward, as he stood over their unconscious forms, he knew that he'd just stepped in yet another steaming shit-pile. Both of them were connected and that meant Mob. Whether he ended up getting into the Blackhawk or not, he'd probably not be living to see his next birthday. Making the choice between dying in his shitty apartment with a bullet in the back of his head or by whatever bullshit means Masterson might think up was pretty easy. The way he had it figured, either way, he was pretty far beyond fucked.

But then again...

It's not like any of it really fucking mattered. He knew that if he bought it, it wasn't like there was anyone there to really give a shit. With no wife and no kids (that he knew of) there was no one around who cared enough to mark his passing, much less mourn him. There really was nothing to lose here and, it would seem, a shitload to gain. All he needed to do was go ahead and slide his dick down deep into that bear trap.

From far off, he heard Monk's voice come drifting in.

"Yo, you comin'...?"

Cleese forcibly dragged himself back to the present moment. He took a long look at The Octagon and then another one back at Monk who stood waiting a dozen or so yards away.

"Fuuuuuck..." he hissed before getting to his feet and trotting off to catch up.

☠ ☠ ☠

Graveyard Shift

Before...

"Damn it!" hissed Jeffrey Adamson as he lost his grip on the long metal tro-car he held in his hands. The instrument fell, banging loudly as it bounced off of the bright aluminum embalming table and continued on, clattering against the linoleum floor.

Adamson, who stood just over six feet with a cap of short cropped hair and a dark-humored personality, was the living embodiment of his vocation of Fu-neral Director. While outwardly stoic and conservatively dressed, he was known by the people in his life as a bit of a contradiction; someone whose tastes ran from micro-brewed beer to the crudest of jokes. His music of choice was death metal. In more ways than one, he was not the person he seemed.

He stood next to the embalming table, dressed in black suit pants with, white shirt with cuffs rolled carefully up around his elbows, tie tucked discreetly between the buttons of his shirt, plastic apron and thick rubber embalming gloves. For almost an hour now, he'd been putting the finishing touches on the late Mrs. Abigail Harvey and fatigue was starting to gnaw at the fringes of his awareness.

The woman lying on the table before him had died (ahem, passed on) as a result of a life-long heart condition. One minute she was standing in her kitchen drinking a cup of coffee and watching "her stories" on TV and the next she was a mound of inert flesh wrapped in a faded housedress. A tremendous weight pressed and twisted deep in her chest and then it all—the dishes that needed to be done in the sink, the laundry waiting to be dried, the machinations of the cit-izenry of Port Charles—simply winked out. There was no choir of angels singing "Halleluiah" to mark her passing, just a spilled cup of General Foods Interna-tional Coffee Café Vienna and a soup of urine and feces congealing on the tile floor.

Luckily, the preparatory work for her upcoming service had gone well. The acrid embalming fluid that Jeffrey had pushed through her arterial system via the Sawyer machine had completed its chemical alchemy, preserving her tissues at least long enough to last through her wake and funeral. When she'd died, Mrs. Harvey had fallen face first onto the floor and remained there for as long as it had taken for her to be found and for the Medical Examiner to arrive and assess her cause of death. The dark purple discoloration from post-mortem lividity where her blood pooled had almost completely faded from the side of her puffy face.

After death, blood settled in whatever the lowest point was in the anatomy: the back, feet and hands. Gravity's laws demanded to be obeyed above all else.

Marilyn Monroe died lying flat on her photogenic face and it had been a certified mess by the time the embalmer was able to begin his ministrations. The timely removal of such settling was one of the trickiest parts of the job. If not caught early, the red blood cells would burst, forever staining the surrounding tissues. The condition was called "post-mortem stain" and it was best to clear the circulatory system out as soon as possible in order to achieve the most eye-pleasing results...

...for the family's sake.

With an exhausted sigh, Adamson squatted down and picked up the trocar. Standing up, he took a moment and checked it for damage or dirt. The instrument was an imposing length of rigid metal with a sharpened point at one end. Three small holes were visible just before the tip of the point. At the other end, a ribbon of rubber hose was attached to the handle. The pale rubber tubing snaked away, its far end plugged into to a delightful little apparatus called a hydro-aspirator which, in turn, was fastened discreetly under the table's drain. The metal instrument was used to remove any fluids trapped in the abdomino-thoracic cavity of the deceased by the use of the vacuum created as water ran through the aspirator.

The point of the shining steel shaft was designed to be inserted roughly two inches to the right of and two inches above the navel and pistoned back and forth allowing the vacuum to suck up all of the blood and other fluids from within the cavity.

Insertion point is two inches lateral and two inches superior to the umbilicus, perforating the rectus abdominis, he recalled from Embalming class.

Upon completion of this motion, Jeffrey would redirect the tube into the lower abdomen through the same hole in the skin and remove any blood, urine and watery wastes that remained in the lower gastrointestinal tract. Once all of that was done, he would use the same procedures to pour a highly concentrated formaldehyde solution called "cavity fluid" into the same areas in order to preserve the now perforated viscera. The procedure took a little getting used to since it was so similar to repeatedly stabbing someone in the belly, but with enough composure on the part of the embalmer, it soon became just another part of the job.

So much to do...

As he set about taking care of Mrs. Harvey's internal organs, he silently considered his busy night so far. He'd already embalmed Mr. Lodene and now that he was almost finished with Mrs. Harvey he only had one more case to complete before calling it a night. After that, there was minimal cleanup that needed to be done and then it was all quiet on the Western front until his shift ended.

Adamson enjoyed working the overnight shift at the Howard, Fine and Howard Funeral Home. The place was nice and had over the years developed a solid reputation. The late hours allowed him to work out from underneath the anally retentive eye of his boss, Mr. Marshall Howard, and let him care for the dead in the manner—and with the respect—he felt they deserved. In the past, he'd worked for too many firms that gave little to no care for the amount of consideration afforded to those who had passed on. For many people in this profession, the job was more about making money than any real sense of compassion; more about financial gain than offering any tangible psychological benefit to the bereaved. In some cases, the bodies themselves were tossed about like sides of beef in a slaughterhouse. In fact, many morgue workers often referred to the moving of bodies as "throwin' meat." This was the kind of sentiment that Jeffrey neither understood nor condoned. It was crucial to Jeffrey that the dead be given their due. Working the late shift allowed him to see that quality care was given to each and every case that came under his watchful eye.

"Jeez," he said aloud, his voice sounding alien in the silence of the room. He checked his watch and raised an eyebrow. "Four hours." He rubbed the back of his wrist across his forehead in an effort to relieve some of the tension there. "I've been at this shit for four hours."

He absentmindedly let go of the trocar still inserted deep into the belly of Mrs. Harvey and pulled the latex gloves from his hands with a loud snap. The lance stuck up phallically from her midsection and pointed toward the ceiling.

"Break time," he muttered, unstringing the stays at the back of his plastic apron. He stepped away from the table and pulled the cords from around his neck. The muscles in his back complained silently the moment his arms were raised over his head. As he took an appraising look at his handiwork, he draped the plastic apron across the foot of Mrs. Harvey's table.

Mrs. Harvey was a big woman with great rolls of flab cascading from her thick frame. Years of overeating with little or no thought ever being given to her health contributed to the stroke. A lifetime of Funyuns and root beer floats were not exactly conducive to longevity.

A doctor had once told Jeffrey as he'd signed off on yet another death certificate, "You never hear the expression big old man or big old lady... It's always little old man or little old lady." Most folks never seemed to get that.

On the table before him, the woman's hair laid slick with water against her skull, giving her face a "standing in a high wind" appearance. Her chubby cheeks hung like sacks of water from her face. All in all, it was a look that was not in the least bit flattering.

Adamson turned to the small sink behind him and picked up a bottle of green antibacterial soap. The stuff looked as if it might have smelled of mint, but instead gave off an aroma of old socks and fungus. He washed his hands, first one and then the other, repeating the procedure until he was good and sure they were disinfected. With the amount of bugs and disease he worked with, sanitization was an important aspect of his job. Any embalmer who didn't think that was so, usually ended up on a metal table himself. After shaking any excess water from his hands, he then dried them and unrolled his shirt's sleeves. He walked to the door of the room and turned to look back at his workspace, feeling a genuine sense of pride at how well the night's procedures had turned out.

One more to do.

He looked toward the last case which was a Mr. John J. Robinson, according to the toe-tag wrapped in one of the hospital's plastic shrouds. The man's arms crossed his chest, bound by a length of thin twine designed more to keep them in place than for any aesthetic purpose.

Jeffrey figured that after he completed the necessary work on this last guy, he would be free to spend the last few hours at the end of his shift either reading or doing homework for the Business Administration class he was taking at the local city college.

"I'll be bawk," he said in a put-on Austrian accent as he opened the door and stepped through. As usual, he made sure to close it until he heard the click of the bolt mechanism falling into place.

As he stepped into the dark hallway, Jeffrey heard the phone ringing in the main office. The radio he kept playing during his shift to remind him that there was still a world of activity going on somewhere out there droned on despite no one being there to hear it.

...due to the clear danger to countless people as a result of the situation that is occurring, this station as well as hundreds of others throughout this part of the country will remain on the air and pool their resources through the Emergency Broadcast System to keep you informed of all developments. At this hour, these are the facts as we know them...

Jeffrey rushed across the loading area, which was an open space that had once been a garage. At the far end was set a large roll-up door. The space was used so that employees could have enough room in which to "casket" the prepared bodies for upcoming services. A "ship-out container," which was nothing more than a flat piece of wood covered by a cardboard box designed to protect coffins while shipping them via airline or train, sat with an occupied casket sealed inside.

He quickly walked past and entered the office proper. He snatched up the handset of the phone just before the answering machine clicked on. As he lifted the receiver to his ear, he leaned over and twisted the volume button on the top of the radio to quiet it.

There have been rampant reports of the de—

As the radio fell silent, he subconsciously noted that the clock on the radio read 1:37 A.M.

"Howard, Fine and Howard Funeral Home. This is Mr. Adamson speaking. May I be of assistance?"

"Jeff!" said the voice from the other end. "This is Marshall..."

"Heya Boss, what's up?"

"I'm home, buried up to my ears in taxes since I got here. I managed to lock myself in my study with no distractions: no TV, no kids, no wife, no nothin'. Just me and Uncle Sam, all alone with his finger up my ass," and the tinny voice laughed in Jeffrey's ear. "I just wanted to call and make sure you were doing all right. How are the cases coming?"

"Marshall, you've called me every night since I started here a year ago, no matter if there were cases or not. Are we sure there isn't the word "micro" in front of your title of "manager," Buddy?"

Again the voice on the phone laughed. "Ok... you're right. I'm mothering you."

"The cases are going great. Mr. Lodene and Mrs. Harvey are pretty much done and I only have Mr. Robinson to do," Jeffrey said, reaching over to switch the coffee on to start a fresh pot. "Now, providing we don't get any new First Calls, you guys should be OK for the morning."

"Ok, that's just great. I have some death certificates to get filed in the morning and..."

A loud metallic clatter interrupted the man's next thought. The sound came from outside the office, somewhere deep inside the funeral home.

"What the hell was that?" asked Marshall.

"I have no idea," Jeff said, leaning back and looking toward the loading area. "I was working with the trocar, maybe it fell from the table. Let me call you back."

"No, don't. I'm heading to bed in a while. Me and the wife are gonna have some quality time, if you know what I mean. You check it out and leave a shift report on my desk."

"Okay. You give my best to the Mrs."

"I will... right after I give her my best," again he laughed. "Oh, by the way, before we hang up, I need you to look on the Case Board and give me Rabbi Feldman's telephone number. I need to give him some information first thing in the morning about the Jacob service."

Jeffrey strained, phone cord dragging, until he got to a point in the room where he could see the large, white board where all of the particulars of each case were posted. He scanned the board, found the rabbi's number, and repeated it into the receiver. After a perfunctory good-bye, he hung up. Taking a quick look at the progress his pot of coffee was making, he made it a point to reach over and turn the radio back up. If there was one thing he hated, it was to feel like he was alone in the silent mortuary. It didn't matter what the sound was—music, commercials, or even talk radio—but it was important for him to know he wasn't by himself in this oftentimes creepy place. Given the tricks one's mind could play on itself, a mortuary was not the place to let it run wild.

Satisfied that everything was ok and going according to plan in the office, he walked back across the loading area to investigate the source of whatever that banging had been. The medicinal smell of bleach coming from the washing machines at one end of the concrete loading area burned his nostrils. Most of the laundry here was blood stained and soiled with all manner of bodily fluids, and everything that got washed was done so in a lot of hot water and chlorine bleach. There was always a basket or two of laundry going. The machines worked at their loads, continually making soft chug-chugging sounds as they swirled the bed linen in their scalding water.

As he stepped through the doorway leading to the funeral home's main building, he noticed that the door to the Prep Room stood slightly ajar.

I know I shut that...

He reached out to push the door open, but as his fingers touched the painted wood, a sound of heavy movement came from deep within the funeral home. Jeffrey paused, closed his eyes, and bent his head slightly in an effort to concentrate on hearing from where the sound had come.

At first, he thought he'd imagined it and after a minute of silence he was almost sure he had, but as he once again moved to push against the door, he heard it again. It sounded like there was someone slowly moving across the carpeting. It sure as hell wasn't the sound of anyone moving with any sort of authority, but rather the hesitant steps of a person who was unsure of their surroundings, walking slowly and carefully, but not really caring whether too much noise was made.

I don't need this shit... not now... not tonight.

Adamson turned from the Prep Room door, looking around for something with which to arm himself. You know... just in case. He'd been warned by the owners again and again that some of the funeral homes in the area had been vandalized and the local police were unable to find the people responsible for the destruction. The culprits, whoever they were, had spray-painted obscenities on the walls, kicked over pews and, in some cases, took out their mindless fury on the helpless dead who passively lay in state. Jeffrey would be damned if he'd allow someone to commit such acts in this mortuary... not on his watch.

He quietly tip-toed back to the loading area and after a short search found a length of metal rebar leaning up against a wall; a left-over from the construction of the newly remodeled office which now stood where the garage and storage shed had once been. Feeling like he was something close to armed, Adamson bolstered his courage, drew a deep breath and walked past the Prep Room and on toward the doorway of the funeral home.

They are so not paying me for this...

The gray carpeted hallway stretched out before him like an empty airport runway with three visitation rooms: two on the left and one on the right. The hallway ended on the far side of the building at the foyer and jogged at an abrupt angle, bending sharply to the right, leading to the building's entryway and on toward the chapel. Jeffrey stood silent for a moment and intently listened for any further sound of movement. Hearing none, he took three steps forward and, with his heart racing, gently pushed open the first door on his left.

Inside the small room were several low platforms called biers on which caskets were laid during visitations and services, two sets of candles on ornate pedestals, and the wooden Aaron casket the funeral home received the previous day to replace the one in which Mrs. Jacob now lay. Heavy velvet drapery covered the window and the room sat cloaked in a darkness that was almost absolute. At the point where the two drapes met, a single shaft of light came through from the street lamps outside. Its beam fell coldly across the smoothly vacuumed carpet. The room held within it an air of sullen expectancy as if it were placidly waiting for the next group of mourners to come and pour out their grief like warm molasses.

Nothing in here...

Jeffrey closed the door, and as he lifted his foot to take his next step, he heard movement once again. The direction of the sound was still unclear, but that didn't matter one bit to Jeffrey's adrenal system. It kicked into overdrive the instant he'd heard that first clattering sound. His heart leapt up into his throat and took up a painful, throbbing residence. A light queasy feeling roiled deep in his bowels. His limbs burned with an almost electric feeling. Fight or flight clawed at the edges of his perception.

He stepped forward, deciding to methodically check each room one by one before venturing deeper into the dark of the building, and reached out to nudge open the door on the right. He pushed against the wood slowly and let it swing open on its own.

Leaning in, he inventoried the interior: couches sat patiently along one side of the room, tawdry landscape paintings littered the walls, as well as the dark oblong shape of a casket which dominated the front. He stepped a little deeper into the room, looking first to one side and then the other. With great care, he circled the room in an attempt to investigate every corner; reveal every nook and cranny. He soon reached the casket in the dark and peered into it, using the sparse light from the doorway to illuminate his vision.

Mrs. Devon lay in her rosewood casket patiently awaiting her service which was scheduled for late the following day. The smell coming from the large number of flower arrangements surrounding her casket bordered on overwhelming. It was an odor so sweet that it threatened to sour Jeffrey's already turbulent stomach. He turned from the casket and made his way back toward the door and walked through it into the hallway, absentmindedly leaving the door partly ajar.

Ok... two down.

His heart continued to race like an unbridled pony and his belly still felt all tight and oily as he stepped back into the dim hall. The last visitation room in the building lay just ahead and to the left. He lifted up onto his toes like a small child sneaking down the stairs on Christmas morning and tiptoed toward the final door. Jeffrey turned the knob and pushed the door open with his shoulder, just enough so he could stick his head through. The inside of the room lay much like the others: silent, still and quite empty.

Ok, only the chapel left...

He slid his body back between the door and the doorjamb, but as he did so the sound of rustling once again reached his ears. Only this time, he was able to pinpoint exactly where it was coming from—the chapel. He was sure of it now. Since the intruder was not in any of the visitation rooms, the chapel was the only logical answer. With one more quick backward glance into the visitation room to verify its vacancy, he closed the door, gripped the metal rod tighter with both hands, and proceeded across the foyer toward the chapel's doors.

Jeffrey stepped through the double doors of the chapel, pushing them all the way open with the side of his foot so that they would be held in place by the stops in their hinges. The room was bathed in darkness and lay cloaked in an almost deafening silence. Along one wall, a small garden of fake ferns and foliage sat under a row of softly colored lights recessed beneath an overhang. The pews, quiet and alone, stood in two columns with an aisle running down the middle. His shadow extended long and thin down the aisle, cast as it was by the single lamp's light which dimly illuminated the foyer.

At the front of the room sat Mrs. Jacob's Aaron which had been placed upon a bier. It looked quite austere in its simple but elegant setting. All had been prepared and was ready for her morning service which would be presided over by the good Rabbi Feldman. The woman's body arrived earlier in the afternoon and had gone straight into the casket as prescribed by Jewish tradition: no embalming, no metal to touch the body, casket made without nails to join the pieces of wood together. Once she was tucked inside, the lid was closed and held tight by an intricate mortise and tenon system. Jeffrey quickly scanned the room and to his great relief saw nothing out of the ordinary. He was about to turn and leave when he noticed that the head panel of the casket was slightly ajar, lifted just barely, almost imperceptibly.

Wait a second...

Jeffrey moved up the aisle with a cautious hesitation, scanning the shadows for any sign of either burglar or vandal. He surveyed the room, moving his head from side to side, taking in the most minute of details as an excited mind often does. Someone had left the Catholic hymnals in the pockets in the back of the

No Flesh Shall be Spared

pews. This would need to be addressed after he'd finished checking for this intruder. It wouldn't do for a Jewish service to come in and find them left behind. He also noticed that there were several empty Kleenex boxes littering the pews and they would need to be replaced with fresh ones. It was being attentive to small things like this which gave a funeral home its reputation.

So much to remember...

When he finally arrived at the side of the casket, he took a nervous look back over his shoulder. The chapel lay as it had before, quiet and empty. Turning back, he carefully slid his fingers under the lip of the lid and gently, but with constant pressure, pulled upwards. What little light there was in the room pushed back the shadows within the casket.

Mrs. Jacob's face slowly slid into full view. Her skin looked blanched of any color, her lips bleached of any shade. He used both of his hands to push the lid to its full upright position and surveyed her body. She lay in quiet repose, wrapped in a white, linen sheet with only her sallow face exposed. She looked in good shape, all things considered. Her complexion was a little drawn, but structurally she was sound as a pound. He looked down the length of her body, and it was at that moment he noticed several circles of dark blood soaking into the linen midway down her chest. He gently pulled back the cloth, hating that he had no gloves for his hands, and exposed the area. What he found was beyond any fevered imagination. Three large pockets of flesh had been torn from the woman's bound arm; large semi-circular chunks were ripped from the flesh leaving a massive amount of destruction to the tissues behind.

"You bastards!" he hissed as he cast another investigatory glance around the room. And then, as he leaned over and got a closer look inside, he whispered to himself, "These look like...bites. Who would do such a thing?"

Disgusted, Jeffrey abruptly stood upright and distractedly lowered the head panel of the casket. With his mind a thousand miles away, he turned and took a step back. His plan was to head to the foyer where an arrangement office was. There he'd make a call to the police to report the incident. As he was in the process of turning, the recognizable sound of movement on carpeting came to his ears again just seconds before he came face to face with the figure of a man standing a few feet away from him.

For fuck's sake, I almost bumped right into him!

The man, who appeared to be wrapped in some kind of shiny cloak or large shawl, stood silently staring. The dim light outlined his form, making it look as if there were a halo surrounding him. His face however, remained hidden in a constant shadow.

"What the fu...?" The curse escaped Jeffrey's lips before he could stop it. For a split second, he moved to cross himself and ask forgiveness for swearing in this place of God. "Who are you?" Jeffrey asked in his most authoritative tone. He hoped that whoever this guy was he wouldn't notice Jeffrey's knees quivering or the shiver in his voice. "What are you doing here?" He raised an accusatory finger toward him and then, pointing back toward the body of Mrs. Jacob, demanded, "Did you do this...?"

The stranger leaned forward, his face slowly coming into the subdued light. He stood there gaping back at him, his eyes empty of emotion, much less signs of intellect. Jeffrey stared into a face devoid of any semblance of humanity, an altogether empty slate. He'd seen this look on a person's face before. It was the blank face of the dead and yet here the man stood, staring malignantly at him.

With a low groan, the stranger reached out with an unbelievable speed and grabbed Jeffrey roughly by both shoulders. He pulled and drew him quickly closer. His mouth worked up and down, snapping at the air, as if he was making an attempt to take a bite out of Jeffrey; to bite wherever his lips first came in contact with bare skin. Jeffrey struggled momentarily and then having gained a solid footing, pushed against the man with his free arm and shoulder. The figure stumbled backward, almost tripping over his own feet. He came to a teetering erect posture and slowly, uncertainly, stepped again toward Jeffrey.

"Get the fuck back," Jeffrey shouted, fear casting all thoughts of forgiveness or impropriety to the wind. Pushing him back once again, he brandished the metal rebar. "Dude, I will bash your fuckin' skull in!"

The man before him gave no indication whatsoever of understanding. He just kept coming onward, opening and closing his mouth, and giving off the familiar stench of the recently deceased. Jeffrey had smelled it a thousand times and knew it instantly for what it was.

"AAAAAAAAAAH..." the man groaned as his arms reached out once again for Jeffrey and for the soft skin that lay at the base of Jeffrey's throat. In the dim light, Jeffrey caught a quick glimpse of something which circled the man's wrist. The shiny surface of the thing seemed to dance in the soft light. It was a medical wristband from St. Mary's, a local hospital. Jeffrey recognized their Holy Mother logo. As the man's hands took hold of his collar, Jeffrey was able to make out in the dim light a name typed on it: Robinson, John J.

Jeffrey shoved the dead man back once again, his brain at once understanding the wristband and its significance. With a grunt, he cocked the rebar up over his head and then brought it down straight into the center of his attacker's forehead. A sound that reminded Jeffrey of a time when he dropped a watermelon at a family picnic punched through the silence of the chapel. Repeatedly, Jeffrey pistoned the rebar up and down and John J. Robinson's skull caved inward, the bones collapsing in upon themselves. A soft jellylike substance dribbled out of the ruined cranium and coated the metal protruding from it. The man went rigid then fell, stiff legged, backward to the floor.

Silence returned to the chapel, falling like an anvil.

"What the fuck was that?!?" Jeffrey shouted, his voice climbing octaves like stairs. "Jesus Fucking Christ!"

He cast another quick apologetic glance to where the crucifix usually hung high on the chapel's wall and crossed himself. He then bent down and took a moment to examine the now still figure lying before him. He just wanted to make sure it was who he thought it was. Once he'd confirmed it was indeed Mr. Robinson, he fell backwards into a sitting position and sat, legs akimbo, trying to piece it all together.

That guy was fucking dead. I made the goddamn removal from St. Mary's myself. How the hell was he just walking around?

Jeffrey ran his hand through his hair and tried to think.

Jesus, was he just trying to fuckin' bite me?!?

Getting up on all fours, he crawled over and checked the body one more time, pulling back the plastic shroud and counting the four rectangular scorch marks that had been left when the defibrillator pads were used on the man's chest.

It was Robinson all right.

He was just fuckin' dead, goddamnit !

As he knelt there trying to figure this whole mess out, behind him, from inside the Aaron, a set of small thin fingers slid into view from under the head panel, quietly forcing it up. Mrs. Jacob's twisted features rose into view in the dim light, eyes wide and mouth moving as if she were silently gasping for air. The lid continued to move silently upward as she pushed against it. She struggled—due to the awkwardness of the Aaron's construction and the fact that she was still bound up in her shroud—to sit upright. As she moved, the linen around her fell away to reveal a frightfully thin chest on which two flat sagging breasts sat against the lattice work of her rib cage. She pulled herself to the uppermost part of the head of the casket and slid a frail thin leg over the edge. Without making a sound, she climbed out with the stealth of a seasoned predator.

Jeffrey was still sitting trying to sort through the last few minute's events. His back was exposed to both the altar and Mrs. Jacob. Suddenly the silence was broken when he heard a slight creaking of the wood behind him. He swiveled his head around and caught sight of Mrs. Jacob climbing out of the casket and struggling to stand erect.

"Uuuuuuh..." she moaned as she took her first tentative steps toward him. "UUU-uuuuuuuhhh..."

"Fuuu-uuck me!" Jeffrey sighed as he scrambled to his feet and spun to face her.

This just wasn't possible...

Without really looking, he took a small step back and reached with his hand behind him for some kind of physical mooring on which to tie his mental instability. His searching fingers found the ridges on the rebar, and with a quick jerk, he wrenched it out of Mr. Robinson's crushed skull. Using all of the muscles in his shoulders, he brought the metal rod around—Babe Ruth style—and connected with the side of the old woman's head. A sickening, wet sound reverberated through the stillness of the chapel.

Welp, if she wasn't dead, I'm going to have a helluva lot of 'splaining to do.

The old lady teetered on her feet for the briefest second like a Jenga tower. Then, with the side of her head caved in, she fell with a gut-wrenching thud. The sound of her body hitting the carpet was one Jeffrey didn't think he'd ever forget. It was so final, so utterly incontrovertible.

"OK..." Jeffrey said aloud as he looked at the scene around him, "I am outta here!"

He turned on his heel and quickly made his way up the chapel's aisle and through the open double doors. He skidded to a stop halfway across the foyer once he realized the rebar—now coated with a stew of blood, bone, brain matter and cerebral fluid—was still in his hand. In disgust, he dropped the metal bludgeon to the carpet and wiped his hands on the thighs of his pant legs. Taking a brief glance back at the now gently swinging doors of the chapel, he continued on to the hallway and its visitation rooms.

Jeffrey took the left down the corridor and his progress slowed as his mind continued the laborious task of processing all that had transpired in the past few minutes. The very fabric of what he thought possible had been torn forever asunder and he figured it would be best if he tried to gain a little perspective before executing his next move.

"Ok, so... time to recap," he said aloud and he looked up the hallway and then back in the direction from which he'd come.

For whatever reason, the dead folk in this place don't seem to want to stay dead. They're getting back up and walking around, fer fuck's sake. That much is pretty goddamn obvious. For another, they seem intent on doing me severe bodily harm. By luck or by providence, I've managed to not let that happen. I've been able to put them all back down before they could inflict any damage. How long that dumb luck will last is anybody's guess.

What was proving difficult to get his mind around were the whys and wherefores of how it was all possible. *Dead folks just don't get up after they've been pronounced dead, did they?* Something, some small sliver of information began chewing at the back of his subconscious like a rat gnawing its way through wood. Maybe it was something he'd read. Maybe it was something he'd heard. He knew there was an answer, but for the life of him, he just couldn't force the concept to congeal.

The hallway was as it had been moments before, bereft of sound and cloaked in a cover of silky darkness. The shadows played at the corners of the corridor and, given recent events, each held a promise of silent menace. Far off, the drone of the big walk-in refrigerator cycling on could be heard through the austere walls. None of it mattered much to Jeffrey. He was still busy freaking out over what just happened in the chapel. He cautiously walked down the hall toward the back of the funeral home, passing first the empty visitation room now on his right and then past the room where Mrs. Devon lay.

As he crept past the doorway of the second room, a slender hand—fingers clenched like arthritic claws—reached out for him from within the inky blackness between the door and its frame. Jeffrey tensed as the rumbling of the refrigerator ceased, but continued moving down the hallway. Suddenly, he was grabbed roughly by the back of his shirt's collar and his body was jerked to an abrupt halt. The force of his forward momentum pulled the late Mrs. Devon through the doorway and out into the hallway even as he skidded to a stop.

Mrs. Devon creakily stood near him dressed in the same olive green dress Jeffrey himself had put her in. A strand of pearls accented the outfit and a single rose corsage adorned her lapel. "Mother liked things simple," her children had told him during the arrangement conference. He'd even made a note of it in the woman's case file. Jeffrey spun around and twisted away from her with all of his might, his motion sufficient to break her feverish hold on him. Midway through, he lashed out with his closed fist.

He had to admit it... he'd really put his back into it.

When he connected with Mrs. Devon's face, his accuracy was nothing short of impeccable. He drove the far side of his fist up under the tip of her slightly upturned—suitors had once called it "coquettish"—nose. The force of the blow shattered the woman's cartilage, driving the bulk of the hardened material upward through the soft, spongy cribriform plate of her ethmoid bone and on through to her brain. The sharp edges of the cartilage punched through and bisected the lobes of her freshly awakened brain, effectively shutting it back down before it had a chance to become fully aware.

"Mom liked simple..." Jeffrey whispered, out of breath, "Mom got simple."

The woman's head jerked back with terrible force and she toppled, slamming her head into a small wooden credenza which sat on one side of the hallway. Her body crumpled to the floor like a marionette whose strings had just been cut.

Bending over, Jeffrey roughly pulled apart the front of the woman's dress, buttons popping and bouncing on the floor like Mexican jumping beans, and double checked the autopsy incisions he sewed up himself...just to make sure.

From his crouching stance, he looked up toward the door at the end of the passageway marked "Employees Only." The shadow-draped hallway beyond was the only thing visible through the small Plexiglas window set in the door at just about chest height. Further in, he could just make out the dull glow of the light coming from the office as it illuminated the ceiling from across the loading area. He stood up, took a deep breath, and resumed his now tentative journey back down the darkened hall.

Shit! Shit! Shit!

When he reached the door, he rose up on tiptoes and peered hesitantly through the window in all directions. Inside, nothing stirred. Jeffrey held his breath and again closed his eyes, willing himself to listen through the door for any sounds of movement. He tilted his head back and focused all of his attention on his sense of hearing. The soft chug-chugging of the washing machines and the distant droning voice from the radio were the only sounds that reached his attentive ears. With a soft sigh, he let out the breath he'd been holding and opened his eyes.

In the dim twilight of the hallway behind the door, he noticed that he could no longer see the light shining up onto the loading area's ceiling. The small window was completely dark. He leaned closer to try to figure out what could be obstructing his view.

Suddenly, right in front of him, separated only by the thin wooden door, an eye opened in the blackness.

"Jeez-us!" Jeffrey gasped. Another of those things was right on the other side of the goddamn door! He took a stumbling step backward away from the door just as Mr. Lodene came through with his arms outstretched and his fingers spasming.

Mr. Lodene exhaled an odor of decay and putrefaction through his stitched together jaws as he came, naked as a jaybird, through the still swinging door. As his face came into the half-light, he made an effort to pull his lower jaw into a toothy snarl. With muffled, popping sounds the stitches tore themselves loose from their moorings in the soft flesh of his gums. His mouth ran crimson with dark blood and the thin twine hung from his lips like strands of dental floss. He took two loping steps forward and clawed feverishly at Jeffrey's shirt. His mouth chewed emptiness and dribbled long, syrupy strings of saliva. Now locked in a macabre two-step, the men—one alive and the other quite dead—twisted and stumbled back down the hallway, each attempting to gain control over the other. Suddenly, the back of Jeffrey's calves bumped up against Mrs. Devon's prone body and he fell backward over the dead woman. Mr. Lodene, having no choice in the matter, fell right along with him.

The tumble put Jeffrey in an exceedingly precarious position. His legs had become entangled in the limbs of the twice dead Mrs. Devon and the nude Mr. Lodene was now on top of him, his face all fetid breath, slimy saliva, and snapping jaws. There was not a lot of time for Jeffrey to think, but one thing was abundantly clear from the microbiology classes he'd taken in college: getting bitten by one of these dead things was probably not the wisest of moves. Being careful to avoid the dead man's hungry mouth, Jeffrey grabbed him by the throat—his fingers choking and crushing flesh. It was difficult to get a firm grip on the man's neck as a result of the "skin slip," which made the flesh slimy and slippery. He finally got a solid grasp and Jeffrey extended his arms, holding the man and his ravenous jaws at bay. It wasn't that difficult to control the dead man. It seemed as if death had stolen away a lot of his strength along with his heartbeat, but Jeffrey knew that one small mistake would send those snapping jaws down to meet the yielding meat of his neck.

The sternocleidomastoidius muscle, he thought, in another of those odd moments.

This was all well and good, but it still left Jeffrey flat on his back with a newly awakened corpse on top of him. He knew he needed to be quick and to act decisively. No telling if there were more of these things wandering about... as weird as that sounded. Mr. Lodene struggled in his grasp, pushing against Jeffrey's outstretched arms, scratching at his chest and biting at the air and snarling. Inspiration struck and Jeffrey, with a sudden redirection of his energy, pulled Mr. Lodene down toward him—fast. At the last instant, Jeffrey jerked his head to the side and continued to pull the dead man past him, rolling out from under as he did so. Using all of his upper body strength, he smashed the dead man's forehead against the carpeted floor again and again, stunning him.

Jeffrey quickly wriggled the rest of the way out from under the now dazed, prone form. He quickly clambered around and took control of him from the back by grabbing two large handfuls of hair. Entwining his fingers in the greasy strands, he continued bashing the man's face against the floor; once, twice, three times. A wet spot was soon visible on the carpeting, leaving a distorted Shroud of Turin-like image. By now, Jeffrey had gained a more proper footing and yanked the dead man almost upright. Shifting directions, he hoisted his bulk up and off of the floor. He then twisted at the waist and drove Mr. Lodene's forehead down against the corner of the credenza that Mrs. Devon fell upon on her way to the floor. Repeatedly, he pounded the dead man's skull against the corner of the table. The sharp corner of the wood crumbled under the onslaught. Jeffrey finally ceased his assault when he noticed a substance which resembled grey cottage cheese covering the corner of the wood's surface. Jeffrey released Mr. Lodene and the dead man slumped downward, falling on top of Mrs. Devon.

"I am not," panted Jeffrey as he stood up, his shirt now splattered with blood and brains, "responsible for any of this shit!"

Silence once again descended on the building with a kind of finality. Jeffrey got to his feet and cautiously approached the swinging door at the end of the hall. He caught the edge of the door with his foot and drew it open cautiously. He carefully peered inside just in case there were any more surprises. Finding none, he stepped through. Everything looked pretty normal. Well, as normal as could be expected in light of recent events. The Prep Room door was open, a

consequence of
Mr. Lodene's unnatural resurrection, no doubt. The lights were still on in the room, reflecting a brilliant white from the linoleum. Jeffrey heard no sound nor saw any movement so he took another hesitant step.

No sooner did his foot touch the ground than a large shadow drifted across the doorway. Its bulk was prodigious, round and lacking in height. Jeffrey ticked off in his mind the firm's clients in a rapid succession: Robinson, Jacob, Devon, Lodene... Harvey.

Mrs. Harvey—the big woman whose heart had blown out that he'd been working on when Marshall Howard's phone call came.

"Shit!" he breathed out in a hiss.

Again the shadow drifted like a zeppelin past the light coming from the doorway. This time, he noticed an odd protrusion slanting down from the main form. At first, he was at a loss to identify exactly what it was. Mentally clicking off options, Jeffrey almost felt the light bulb go off over his head.

The trocar! She still has the trocar in her!

The thought made him sag in his own skin.

This just keeps getting better and better.

He almost considered saying "fuck it" and going back the way he'd come, but the decision was taken out of his hands when Mrs. Harvey suddenly shuffled around the doorframe and stuttered to a halt not a foot in front of him. Jeffrey wasn't sure if The Dead could register surprise or not, but the look that passed over the dead woman's face came mighty close. She hesitated for a fraction of a second and then instinct kicked in like a mule.

"Huuuuuuuuuuuuuuuu..." she screeched, her voice husky and raw. Her arms came up, hands clawing angrily at the air. Her body was even more rotund on its feet than it'd seemed when she was lying on her back on the embalming table. Rolls of fat, one on top of the other, rippled as she moved. Stretch marks glimmered in the light and highlighted the places on her skin where the flesh had been pulled beyond its limitations. Ten pudgy little fingers danced at the end of her hands, pulling at the air directly in front of Jeffrey's face. She took another heaving step toward him, closing the gap between them even more.

Just as he was about to turn and run like hell, Jeffrey felt something firm poke against his abdomen. It felt like a thick finger only more solid. He shot a quick glance downward and saw the handle of the metal trocar jutting out of Mrs. Harvey's massive belly. The butt of it prodded him firmly in the belly.

Fuck it...

With a deft move, he grabbed the metal rod with one hand and pulled it firmly from her body. Then, bending slightly at the knees, he drove the thing up toward the dead woman's face. The metal point struck her just below the lower jaw and, because of the force with which it was delivered, passed through the mouth and soft palate, lodging itself deep into the center of her skull. The woman halted briefly from the blow and then tried to take another sloppy step forward.

"Will you fucking die already?" Jeffrey shouted.

He pushed against the bottom end of the trocar with both hands and shoved the woman back, her back slamming against the wall. She tried to speak, but the sound came out garbled, like she was trying to talk with a mouth full of marbles. Her blackened tongue caressed the metal rod jutting up through the musculature of her lower jaw. Heaving with a potent mixture of muscle and adrenaline, Jeffrey pushed upward and the instrument was driven deeper into her head. Her eyes quivered in their sockets and a rivulet of blood dribbled from one nostril. Another hard push and the trocar smashed its way straight out of the top of her skull. Her massive form convulsed as the metal tip skewered bone and grey matter. Her body suddenly went rigid and then abruptly slack. Her brain now impaled, she fell, heavy and hard, to the ground.

Jeffrey's breath came in short, distressed gasps now as his tissues cried out for oxygen. Adrenaline burned like gasoline in his bloodstream and his heart beat like a drum in his chest. All at once he felt tired; really tired. The trauma of the past few minutes suddenly back-handed his reason and it was all he could do to keep his hands from shaking.

I just killed—or rather re-killed—five people.

What. The fuck.

Rushing across the loading area, Jeffrey headed toward the office. He cleared the doorway and noticed the clock on the desk read 1:48 A.M. Jesus, everything that had happened—Marshall's phone call, the investigation of the funeral home, Mr. Robinson, Mrs. Jacob, Mrs. Devon, Mr. Lodene, and that fat fucking Mrs. Harvey—everything had all taken place in just under ten minutes.

Outside the office door, loud thumping sounds were suddenly heard. Peeking back the way he'd come, he peered back into the dim loading area. A muffled, baritone moaning was added to the din coming from the washing machines to his left and the radio behind him. He looked around the loading area and saw nothing. Suddenly, he realized where the sound was coming from—the shipping container. The corpse inside was no doubt banging its fists futilely against the inside of its sealed casket, trying to let itself out. Its moans were born from a combination of rampant hunger and abject frustration.

"OK... that's it! I am done. Time to find my fucking keys and get the hell out of Dodge!"

Jeffrey surveyed the office and finally saw his keys sitting on the desk. Forsaking his suit coat on the hook on the wall, he snatched them up and headed for the door. He grabbed the doorknob and twisted. The door came open and he stopped abruptly.

What if there are more of them out here?

Cautiously, he poked his head out of the doorway and took stock of the parking lot. The area seemed empty except for his car which sat in its usual parking space at the far end under the tree. He carefully took a step out and continued to scan the lot. For a moment, his mind made every shape and shadow come alive with menace, but soon, he saw that everything lay quiet.

Thank God for small favors, eh?

He turned and quietly pulled the door shut behind him. The last thing he heard from the office as the door clock clicked shut was a voice pouring coldly from the clock radio's small speaker. Everything he heard only served to confirm his worst fears.

...every dead body that is not exterminated will rise, Ladies and Gentlemen. It will get up and, as remarkable as it sounds, it will attack. Any person that is killed or injured will do the same. Any and all dead or bitten persons

must be exterminated by destroying the brain or severing the head from the person's neck. Fire works as well. Whatever is happening must be controlled before it's too late! They're simply multiplying too quickly!!

"Yeah," he said as he headed off into the night, "no shit."

☠ ☠ ☠

The Chest

The Chest was a flat, nondescript concrete building set away from things near the back of the compound and its Firing Range. The structure lacked any adornment or sense of style. It was a cement cheese box that looked a whole hell of a lot like an exhumed bomb shelter. Its roof was flat and level with a low retaining wall which ran around the building's perimeter. Inside its thick, unadorned walls ran row after row of wooden, floor-to-ceiling storage racks. In each frame were carefully delineated spaces, each marked with a designated number that referred to a very specific piece of equipment.

It was an Obsessive-Compulsive's wet dream.

As they walked inside and out of the day's heat, the look of the place and its musty odor immediately reminded Cleese of an old warehouse job he'd had when he was a much younger man. It was just another shitty job in a long succession of shitty jobs, however, he'd quit it in a particularly spectacular fashion. One slow summer's night he nearly drowned his prick of a boss in a toilet bowl after anintellectual debate over who was the better Stooge—Curly or Shemp— had gone undecided.

And to think... some said he had anger issues.

A long countertop extended from the wall and across the front of the space, blocking off the door from the long rows of racks. A pad of paper, a pen, and a bell sat in the middle of its flat surface. The rest of the counter was empty, clean and decidedly orderly.

"Weaver!" Monk called into the dark stacks as he repeatedly hammered on the bell. "You here?"

Cleese looked at Monk and the two of them shrugged. Nothing and no one could be seen in the darkness. Monk banged on the bell some more... just to make sure.

"Weaver! Wake the fuck up back there!"

From the rear of the room, its sound dampened by the racks, came a man's deep, but jovial voice.

"You need to get the hell offa that bell or else the next time someone wants to ring it they'll have to put their hand up your ass to do it."

Monk smiled again and hit the bell three more times.

"Get your sorry ass out here, Old Man!" Monk shouted into the darkness.

"Saaaay, did somebody just shit in my Supply?" said the deep voice buoyed by just a hint of laughter. "Gawd, I seen dead 'uns that smelt better."

Out of the shadows at the back of the room emerged a big bear of a man— six four if he was an inch—with a furry, salt and pepper beard and large, round glasses. He looked a lot like Santa Claus... if Saint Nick had spent a lifetime on anabolic steroids.

"Oh, it's only you, Monk. I thought somebody'd taken a dump on my nice, clean floor." Weaver kicked at the small mounds of sawdust which made up the flooring.

Monk laughed out loud and nudged Cleese with his shoulder.

"You'll have to forgive him," and Monk winked at Cleese, "he's not been himself since Calvin Coolidge left office."

The two men smiled at one another with a genuine affection and shook hands.

"We still on for Friday Follies?" Weaver asked. Cleese learned early on of how the two friends made it a habit of hanging out on the roof of The Chest every Friday night smoking Macanudo cigars and drinking single malt scotch. It was something they'd done for a long time. Those nights were an institution and to be included was a high honor indeed.

"Wouldn't miss it for the world, Bubba. Tradition is, after all, tradition."

"This your new Cherry?" Weaver looked Cleese over with a familiar appraising eye.

Monk nodded.

"Shit, you oughtta see this guy. He fights like your mom..." and Monk again nudged Cleese and winked. "Only, if I remember right, your momma kicked a little more ass than he does... or was it that she took it in the ass a little more, I forget which."

Both men fell out, laughing; this insult game was obviously a favorite and important part of their friendship.

"You got a name, Cherry?" asked Weaver, putting on a straight face.

"Cleese. My name... is Cleese."

"Hmm..." the old man said, looking him up and down like he was breeding stock. "You're here to gear up, yes?"

Cleese nodded.

"Ok..." Weaver said as he scratched at his beard. "I'm guessin' you're about a 36 waist, right?"

A bit surprised, Cleese nodded and said, "How'd you know?"

"I've been at this shit for too got-damn long not to know a man's size at a glance, Son. You wear a large shirt, eh?"

Again, Cleese nodded.

"Not any more, Junior. People in the cheap seats want to see all those muscles you've been working so hard on. You're in a medium now and you'll do situps until you want to puke your nuts up in order to fit into it."

Weaver looked at Monk and grinned.

"Here we go..." said Weaver and he walked backward toward the shadows of the racks. "I'll send all of the shit I give you today to your crib and to your locker, but everything you get you need to care for. This ain't Macy's where shit gets replaced."

Weaver turned and, without another word, disappeared back into the shadows. Within a minute or so, he called out over the stacks.

"Shoes?"

"Huh?" questioned Cleese, looking toward Monk in confusion.

"He wants to know your shoe size."

Cleese looked down at his boots.

"Umm... Twelve."

As he looked up, Cleese heard a loud thump. A pair of size twelve, black, military combat boots was sitting, rocking slightly, on the counter. Weaver had already disappeared back into the racks. For a man as big as he was, he moved damn fast.

"Lessee... pants: black, leather, size thirty-six; socks: black, size ten to twelve; BVDs: black, size... People accuse me of being an optimist, so I'm going to say 'large.' Let's see... wife-beaters: black, medium."

He ran off the list that he kept solely in his head; pulling each item in turn from the shelves, thumping them down onto the counter, and then continuing on to the next item.

"Tunic: black, with... lessee... purple accents, size... medium." Weaver held up a shirt that glittered in the sparse light. It was made of neoprene, like a wet suit, only the sleeves were removed and replaced with what looked like chainmail. Attached at the end of the shirt's arms were what looked like leather gloves. The trunk of the shirt ended just at about the bottom of the ribcage.

Cleese glanced over at Monk.

"A fighter going out because of a small bite on the arm is bad for business. The crowds feel cheated. So, we protect your arms with this chain-mail. It's kind of like one them shark suits you see on the Discovery Channel. However, if you'll notice, it's not all about protecting your monkey-ass. We've left your belly and throat exposed so that if a UD gets a good hold of you there..." Monk shrugged. "Game over."

Cleese eyed the leather gloves and noticed that they were in fact not leather, but rather a unique kind of synthetic material. The surface was shinier and looked almost porous.

"What's with the gloves? Is that Kevlar?"

Weaver smiled.

"Good eye, kid. Those are Blackhawk Hellstorm S.O.L.A.G. gloves with a dual-layer and PittardsWR100X and Armortan treated goatskin leather."

"In the beginning, we lost a lot of fighters due to them punching on the UDs and cutting their hands on the bastard's teeth," Monk chimed in. "As it turns out, breaking the skin by getting your hand cut from a punch and breaking it cause one of the fuckers bit you is not much of a difference. Infection is infection. Weaver here came up with attaching military tactical gloves to the tunic. The man's like fuckin' MacGuyver."

Weaver gave a small bow and smiled.

"I do have my moments."

Cleese rolled his eyes toward the ceiling and laughed with a quiet snort.

Man, this just keeps getting better and better.

"Now," said Weaver as he approached the counter, grinning like a mental patient, "Let's talk a bit about weaponry."

Weaver rubbed his meaty hands together and got an evil look in his eye.

"Ok, so... Guns! Guns! Guns!"

Cleese stood a little bit straighter. Once again, he knew that this was a discussion in which he would need to pay a lot of attention. Weaponry was something Cleese had worried about from the beginning. He had a few ideas of his own regarding the things he would need to fight these unholy sons-a-bitches. He didn't want to get stuck out there with some shitty-ass gear just because he was the "new" guy.

"Sidearm... Beretta 92F... and three—count 'em—three extra clips," Weaver said with a smile.

With a heavy, metallic clunk, the pistol and magazines which were wrapped in a blue cloth marked with the League's logo were set on the counter before Cleese. The smell of gun oil wafted bitterly in the air. He picked up the pistol and hefted the weight of it in his hands. It was black as sin and had obviously been well maintained.

"Ok," he said, and nodded his head. "This'll work..."

"Now, we'll need to get you a bladed weapon..." Weaver stood behind the counter and looked at Cleese as if he were going to guess his weight. "You got a preference, Hotshot? Katana? Machete? Push dagger? Spork?"

"Actually, yeah..." Cleese said and, almost as if he were embarrassed by it, drew a crumpled piece of paper from his back pocket. "Can I get something like this?"

Weaver pushed his glasses up onto the bridge of his nose, bent at the waist, and looked at the crude sketch laid out in front of him.

"Ok... this shit just got all kindsa interesting," Weaver looked at Monk and smiled broadly.

Cleese looked at his partner and cocked his head.

"Weaver loves to make shit. He's never been a particular fan of 'off the rack,' y'know?"

Cleese nodded and turned back toward the counter.

On the small piece of paper which Weaver now held in his hand, Cleese had drawn a metal gauntlet in pencil and what the drawing lacked in technique it made up for in ingenuity. The sleeve went over the right hand and nestled against the musculature midway up the forearm. A thin leather strap was visible, wrapped tightly around the wrist and forearm, securing the contraption so that it became an extension of the arm. From the back of the hand, a shaft of steel protruded out what looked to be about eight or nine inches.

"The blade needs to be spring-loaded, and it has to lock. Also, I'll need it to be able to retract when this catch is released." Cleese jabbed a thick finger at the drawing designating the back of the hand. A crudely drawn mechanism had been scrawled there. "The point and the sides of the blade need to be sharp. The point is for stabbing. The sides are for slashing."

Monk looked up and saw the two men staring at one another with mischievous grins spreading like butter across their faces.

"Well?" Cleese asked, "What do ya think?"

Weaver winked at him and smiled approvingly.

"I think that you're one sick, fuckin' bastard," Weaver said through his grin.

Monk, who was looking over Cleese's shoulder, barked out a laugh.

"Can you make it?" Cleese asked.

"Oh, I can build this, all right." Weaver said. "I just think you need professional help is all."

Cleese looked over at Monk and smirked. He wasn't exactly sure, but he thought he saw a new measure of acceptance shining in Monk's dark eyes. It was as if this choice of weapon had proven him to be a man worthy of Monk's friendship, and more importantly, worthy of his tutelage. In this game where Life and Death were concepts easily bandied about, Cleese found a small bit of acceptance in the older man's eyes, and for some reason, that was something that mattered to him a great deal.

Weaver spoke and broke the awkward silence.

"Ok, well like I said, I'll have all this shit and this little masterpiece of yours taken to your crib when they're done," he said.

Weaver reached his hand out and shook Cleese's hand firmly.

"I look forward to seeing you work, Mr. Cleese."

Monk clapped his hand across Cleese's shoulders and pulled him toward the door.

"C'mon, Badass... I've got something you need to see."

The Holding Pen

Monk walked out of The Chest with his arm still around Cleese's shoulder. The two of them headed off across the grass field toward a large building set far from the rest of the compound. It was a structure everyone here knew and knew well yet rarely visited. Cleese looked over to Monk and raised his eyebrows in surprise.

"We going where I think we're going?"

Monk nodded. His face was now set in a grim mask, his demeanor suddenly more subdued, more reserved. After a moment, he released his grip on the younger man's shoulder and the two of them continued to walk in silence.

Cleese grinned slightly and looked down in order to hide his smile. He felt his pulse quicken as he rolled the thought of where they were going around in his head. He knew from the direction and the change in Monk's demeanor that the Holding Pen was their destination and he'd finally be able to get a look at what he'd be up against. It had been a while since he'd been up close to one of these undead motherfuckers. He'd almost forgotten what they were like: their smell, the way they looked, the unmistakable way they sounded. He knew the passage of time dulled any experience... and so could alcohol. Since the night he'd first run into Them, quite a bit of both had fallen by the wayside.

As the two men walked along, Cleese thought back to that day when the world had gone to shit and he'd seen his first walking corpse. He'd been working in The Tenderloin District of San Francisco—a notorious cesspool of aggravated assault, drugs, prostitution and gangs—as muscle for that fuckin' Stolie, a low-tier loan shark who made it a habit of taking his interest out in flesh. Stolie always got his money, one way or another. He was the kind of guy who'd turn his own mother out if there was a dollar in it for him. The guy was a real piece of work, but Cleese needed the money and figured he would make his nut and once he was solvent again bail on the gig—just like always. He'd never had to push people too hard to get his point across, never had to break much to make sure Stolie's affairs continued to run smoothly. He just made sure that promises got kept.

One night, he'd been out drinking—alone as usual—when the television above the bar abruptly clicked over to the Emergency Broadcast Network. After an hour or so of white noise, a guy in a rumpled sweat-stained shirt and skewed tie came on talking crazy.

"It has been established that persons who have recently died have been returning to life and committing acts of murder.

"A widespread investigation of funeral homes, morgues, and hospitals has concluded that the unburied dead are coming back to life and seeking human victims.

"Medical examinations of some of the victims bore out the fact that they had been partially devoured."

And then, finally, "The wave of murder which is sweeping the Eastern third of the nation is being committed by creatures who feast upon the flesh of their victims."

At that point, the steadily increasing tension in the bar broke like Waterford crystal and the bar's denizens went completely ape-shit. The last of the hardcore drunks left the bar, stumbling off in search of family or to collect whatever it was that they held dear and try to get the hell out of town. Cleese, having no family and only a pile of useless crap back at his by-the-week hotel room, instead went behind the bar in search of another drink... and then another... and then another.

By the time The Dead broke through the door, Cleese had managed to get himself pretty goddamn drunk, thank you very much. When he saw the first of Them stumble inside, he'd already picked up the baseball bat he'd found lying behind the counter, tucked a bottle of scotch under one arm, and commenced swinging. He'd been Babe Ruth, Ted Williams, and Stan Musial all rolled up into one swinging ball of drunken fury.

An uncountable number of them had come through the door and met their maker in the form of a Louisville Slugger. Cleese dimly recalled the hollow cracking sound of the hardened wood as it ricocheted off of first one skull then another, then another and another.

Forever and ever, Amen.

When he was through, dozens of Them lay around the bar, their bodies heaped on the floor like piles of diseased laundry. Cleese stumbled for the door once he realized that whatever these bastards were they were no longer coming inside the bar to get pummeled. The things may have been dead, but that didn't mean that they were necessarily stupid. Even their addled brains were able to reason that the only thing waiting behind the bar's doors was certain ruin.

This would have all been well and good except for one small wrinkle: Cleese was now three sheets to the wind and still wanted to fight some more.

And if They didn't want to come to him, he'd just have to go outside to Them.

Mountain... Muhammad... and all that shit.

He'd stormed out of the bar and stumbled to a halt on the sidewalk. It took a full minute for him to gather his wits amidst the swirling chaos. The first thing to hit his senses was the smell. The air had the odor of something between a fish market and an abattoir. Breathing in, his gorge rose and he had to choke it back or puke.

Once his stomach settled down, he raised his eyes and looked around. In all directions, the city streets were deserted like something out of one of those end-of-the-world disaster movies like *The Stand* or *The Day After*. Along the road, cars sat idling—doors thrown open. It was as if the drivers had either been yanked from their seats and dragged off or they'd just decided to get out and walk away. Innumerable radios spewed a swirling, cacophonous din as different styles of music and excited talk all clashed like drunken birds in the air.

The store fronts along the street were smashed; shattered nuggets of glass lay like glittering gemstones across the greasy sidewalk. Periodically, a person's foot or a gnarled outstretched hand protruded from under a pushed-over counter or toppled display. Beneath the sound of the city slowly dying, a low baritone moaning could be heard. It started as what seemed to be a single voice, but as more and more joined the chorus of The Dead, the sound grew louder and stronger.

Cleese stood for a long time, cradling his bat and silently cataloging all of the commotion going on around him, trying to make some sense of it all. It looked like it had a few hours ago when he went into the bar. Only now, it was as if some psychotic set designer from the movies had come in and arranged a scene to look like something out of Armageddon. As he gazed around and his eyes slowly became accustomed to the lighting, it was then that he saw the bodies. There were dozens of them. Some lay between cars, as if the person were trying to stuff himself into the smallest possible crevice in order to avoid the probing hands and snapping jaws of their attackers. Others... lay open and exposed like Death had come upon them unsuspectingly. All of it was enough to make a grown man weep.

Then from behind him a small, soft shuffling sound came to his ears.

He turned to see a young girl about thirteen, her face a tattered and twisted mess, come lurching toward him with arms outstretched and mouth drooling. Her shirt had been torn open at the neck and a bloody wound splashed its way across her throat and upper chest. As she approached, she opened her mouth and let out a soft, almost plaintive moan.

Cleese smiled a wicked little smile and then choked up on the bat.

After that, things got a little hazy. The next thing Cleese remembered, it was morning and he was walking out of the City and across The Bridge, still holding the remainder of the now-splintered, blood-and-brain-covered bat over his shoulder. His arms felt like rubber and his legs burned from the exertion of fighting his way clear of those things. But as painful as his body might have felt, it was nothing compared to the fuck-all hangover that raged like a wildfire in his head. He figured he must have abandoned the scotch bottle somewhere in the night, undoubtedly right after it had given up the last of its pungent goodness.

As drunk as he was, there must have been ample opportunity for things to go very wrong, really fast. It was a testament to either his natural fighting ability or blind luck that he hadn't been bitten... or worse.

As he looked back now on the way the whole thing went down, it seemed as if it happened a lifetime ago.

Time flies...

The two men got to within a hundred yards of the Pen when a stomach-turning odor slapped them both in the face. Cleese's attention was roughly ushered back to the present.

"Ugh..." Cleese choked, "what is that?"

"Charnel Number Five," replied Monk with a wry grin.

The odor was sickly sweet and nauseating. It smelled a lot like the training hall, only far more condensed. The stench bore a greasy aspect which threatened to invite Cleese's lunch up for a second tasting. The entire area around the Holding Pen reeked like a mass grave; a dumping ground awash in excrement, spoiled meat, and rampant disease. Even if he hadn't had a clue as to where they were going, one whiff would have been all he would have needed to figure it out.

"Here," Monk said as he handed over a small round tin of ointment which he pulled from one of his pockets. "Vicks VapoRub. Wipe a bit of it on your upper lip, under your nose. It'll cut the smell some."

Cleese took the tin and dutifully applied the greasy mentholated gel. Monk was right: it did make it a bit better, but the air out here still smelled like five miles of unwiped ass. Only now it was menthol-scented unwiped ass.

They soon arrived at a large steel door set in the side of a building that looked like the others only much, much bigger. Monk immediately banged against the metal with the flat of his fist. A hollow booming sound echoed within.

"Open up! Open up! Let me in..." he shouted, all the while grinning like the Big Bad Wolf.

He paused, took back the tin of ointment and applied it hastily. He then struck the door again with the side of his fist.

"Adamson! Answer your fucking..."

Abruptly, the door ground open on squealing hinges, as if the metal was heavy and very, very tired. Its cries were an indication of how few visitors were accepted here, nor were they ever really wanted. Out of the Cimmerian shadows drifted a man's face, long and lean, with cheekbones on which you could probably cut yourself.

"Monk...," the man sighed, exasperated. His emaciated face floated in the oily darkness. Its features were hidden by strands of greasy hair hanging before his face like oily drapes set in a ramshackle window.

Monk smiled broadly at the man, but Cleese noticed he didn't offer to shake his hand.

"I want to show my new man here around your little playpen."

Adamson looked at Cleese with that now familiar air of appraisal.

"You bring him in here and he's your problem. I take no responsibility."

"Yeah...yeah... I know. Fine. Just let us in, ok?"

Adamson pulled open the door a few more inches and then disappeared back into the gloom without a word, much less a backward glance. Monk stepped inside and led Cleese through the entryway. Once they were past the threshold, he secured the door behind them with an echoing sound.

It took a minute for Cleese's eyes to adjust to the sparse light, but once they had what he saw laid out before him was mind blowing. He could see, even in the limited illumination, that the building was nothing more than four walls and a ceiling, like an airplane hangar only a little bit smaller. Walkways extended along the perimeter and in the center was a huge square cattle pen about seven feet high and at least the size of a football field. Off to the right was a convoluted series of chutes and gangways which were all governed by hydraulic gates. These could be raised and lowered as needed in order to move the UDs toward either the training pit or to the transport trucks. Beyond that was a long passageway which slanted abruptly into the ground. Set at specific intervals, guard towers overlooked the pen. Inside each tower the shadowy forms of men could be seen manning large belt-fed guns.

Cleese recalled visiting the Chicago Stockyards with his father back before the old man left him and his mom to attend Casino school in Florida or some such nonsense. They'd never seen him again. These pens—with their slatted fencing and mazes of corridors—reminded him of that slaughterhouse. The putrid stench reminded him of his dad.

"These..." Monk interrupted, moving his arm as if he were on a game show presenting some fabulous prize, "are your opponents. The tunnel over there leads underground and to another holding pen located under The Octagon."

Cleese stepped forward and looked between the corrugated slats making up the pen's walls. Inside, in the dim light, he saw hundreds of ghostly figures milling about without purpose or reason. They shuffled and careened, oftentimes running into one another, as if their feet were held down by weights. Their heads drooped from the stalk of their necks like sacks of fetid meat as their eyes searched the shadows for something—anything—to eat. The air hung above the pen, undisturbed by any breeze or draft. It was as if even the atmosphere of this place wished to remain dark, dead and poisonous.

He leaned in closer to the fence in order to get a better look. Despite his revulsion, there was something inherently sad about the place. Each of The Dead had once been a person. They'd had family, harbored hopes and dreams, and just wanted to live. Instead, for whatever reason, they'd gotten themselves infected and all of it came crashing down around them. As Cleese looked the pen over, there was a part of him that felt a twinge of sadness for that loss.

Abruptly, something slammed itself against the space between the slats of the pen directly in front of him. Cleese jumped back, shouting out, his fist suddenly drawn back instinctively. Pressed against the railings, its features pinched into a rictus snarl, was what had once been a human face. Yellow-green teeth gnashed ineffectually against the metal and saliva dribbled down its chin, coating the fence and giving the metal a sheen that glimmered in the half-light. The thing's right eye socket was nothing more than a cavernous hole that had been punched into its skull. The other eye's pupil was clouded over, its tear duct wept a sticky, whitish fluid.

As Cleese stood there gaping at it, the thing became more and more excited as it pushed its snarling face against the fencing. Soon, its manner became down-right frantic and its furor began to affect the other UDs held in the pen. As Cleese stepped away, he caught a quick glimpse of the blood-spattered clerical collar which surrounded the thing's ravaged throat.

"Monk! Are you fuckin' nuts?"

The shout came from out of the darkness, from one of the guard towers across the Pen.

Adamson.

"Get that fuckin' idiot away from there. He's agitating my herd!"

Cleese shot Monk a quick glance and took another two steps back. The look on his face was comical: eyes wide like china plates, mouth slung open as if waiting to catch flies. He stood there grinning and offering up a silent apology.

"This's what you'll be fightin', Son," Monk said. "Never forget how that one snuck up on ya. This ain't San Francisco, Sparky, where you'll see 'em all comin'. Here, they'll bag ya and tag ya when you least expect it."

He dropped his arm back across Cleese's shoulder and led him back through the darkness and toward the exit.

"Always remember..." Monk said quietly in Cleese's ear, "it's not the one you hear that'll get you. It's the one that you don't."

Cleese nodded and tried to swallow his heart which had leapt up into his throat and thumped there like a trapped rabbit's. Together, they walked back they way they'd come and then out of the door of the Pen.

Soon, they were heading back across the field toward the Training Hall. As they walked, Monk remained silent, leaving Cleese to his thoughts and to again question what the fuck he was doing here.

☻ ☻ ☻

The Lay of the Land

Fluorescent fixtures shone down brightly over row after row of cafeteria tables. Their flat laminated surfaces reflected the light back onto the ceiling as small irregular squares of illumination. The bulbs that were set into the assembly gave off a low, buzzing sound like angry houseflies caught in a Mason jar. Each fixture hung from two conduits set in the acoustic tiles. Each tile was peppered with tiny holes.

The room was painted a soft, off-white. Its flooring was scarred industrial linoleum. Along one wall, floor-to-ceiling windows displayed the large expanse of grass which surrounded the building and framed the rest of the compound. Far off, the Holding Pen stood brooding; a constant reminder of the true nature of this place. Even with the open view, the room had a bland and institutional appearance, as if it were constructed solely to be used for feeding the hungry and then quickly abandoned. Because of the acoustics, any sound echoed hollowly making the room seem far emptier than it was. As most dining rooms were warm inviting places, this was quite the opposite.

At the far end of the hall was a kitchen from which emanated savory smells. Just stepping into the space and taking a whiff was enough to make your mouth water. Several Asian and Hispanic women, hair tied back and encased in spidery nets, could be seen through a small pass-through as they moved about, working diligently behind the gleaming metallic counters. Large bins overflowing with food were set in the slots of the steam table. Ethereal vapors swirled over the food and coated every morsel with a glistening patina. The sheer bounty of it all was awe-inspiring.

The League fed their fighters well and even though the food was dispensed in a cafeteria-like fashion, its quality was of the highest caliber. The men who toiled here needed sustenance and their requirements were very specific. Nutritionists had designed each menu to give maximum caloric benefit with a minimum amount of fat. Lean buffalo steaks could be both seen and smelled as they sizzled behind the women while large, sumptuous filets of salmon were grilled off to the side. Brown rice and mashed sweet potatoes sat in large pots near a carving station of the leanest prime rib. Bins of romaine lettuce and a literal garden of vegetables completed the mouthwatering tableau.

The doors leading into the building had only just been unlocked, but already there was a line of hungry people waiting to get in. The stomachs of the compound's population were more reliable than any Swiss timepiece and their grumbling would let them know when it was time to eat before any clock. When you pushed your body as hard as the fighters here did, food was second only to air in its necessity. The majority of the residents had by now lined up and was slowly working their way through. The others would surely be coming before long.

Monk and Cleese walked into the room and each grabbed a tray and a fistful of metal utensils which were made available in large plastic bins just inside the door. Taking their time, they quietly circled the room and stepped up to the back of the line. Monk motioned with his head for Cleese to look around. Since Cleese was still getting to know the lay of the land here at the compound, Monk said it was a perfect opportunity for him to size up the competition.

"Pay attention," Monk all but whispered as he leaned in close. "Knowing who's who—who you can trust and who's a complete asshole—could one day save your ass."

In loose cliques, several social groups had already coalesced at sporadic intervals around the tables. On the far right, near the window, the man known as Robinson sat hacking away at a Fred Flintstone-sized steak. Next to him sat his pal, Murray, who was busy talking and shoveling food into his mouth without even looking to see what it was. The two black men were as big as they came; each with shaved heads and tiny pencil-thin moustaches. They looked like brothers from different mothers. For the most part, these two kept to themselves and had come from a background of mostly streetfighting. Their technique, from what Cleese could see, was raw but effective.

"Look, it was just a dumb fuckin' move is all I'm sayin'," Cleese overheard Robinson comment. "That dead bitch made more noise than your momma gettin' gorilla fucked and you didn't hear her comin'. If I hadn't've yanked her goddamn lead back, she'd have fucked your ass up for shore."

"Shit, man," Murray sighed. "I had 'er in my sights. There was no need you worryin'. I was gettin' to 'er."

"You were getting' to jack shit. What the fuck you doing, pacing yourself? She was on your ass, Bro. Weren't no gettin' ta nuttin'."

Cleese smiled at the exchange. Monk had already chastised him for doing some of the same shit. It made him glad to hear he wasn't the only one making mistakes out there on the sand.

Across the room were Rustici, Andrews, and St. George: big Eastern Europeans who had fists like bricks and heads twice as hard. Rustici and Andrews had been following St. George around like they were puppies because of his supposed history as a champion Savate fighter back in the day. Whatever St. George had, it had helped keep him alive for the time being and that was good enough for Rustici and Andrews.

Toward the center of the room was a guy called Lenik who sat with his trainer, Cartwright. Cartwright was about Monk's age and reminded Cleese of that farmer guy on Captain Kangaroo. He had a look of someone who'd seen a fair amount of shit in his time. He also looked perpetually tired. It was an affect that a lot of the older fighters had.

Not Monk, though. He was different in that respect. Although he had some grey in his hair, there was still a young man who stared out at you through his eyes.

Monk said he'd known Cartwright awhile and him being here... Well, it had begun to wear on him. He went on to explain that when a mentor showed that kind of wear, it was never a good thing and was usually a forerunner to the guy making a big fuckin' mistake. And, as had been made clear time and time again, mistakes meant your ass.

Lenik was in his late twenties with a splash of blonde hair and a complexion like that of a Sydney Pollack painting. He was in the middle of some diatribe, waving a fork around like a conductor's baton. Four of the younger fighters—Cloverfield, Shenkel, Gonzales and Llewellyn—were sitting near him and lapping up what he said as if they were his fucking apostles. They all had that "destined to die" glow about them and it just seemed sad. The majority of the other men in the room kept their distance from that clusterfuck.

Lenik was either too driven by his own ego or too stupid to notice.

Or maybe... C: All of the above."

"The thing to remember, Boys," Lenik's voice rang out above the din, "is to always keep your eyes open. You can bet the rent on one thing and it's that these sonofabitches are totally brain-dead. They live to eat and they'll take any opportunity to do so." As he concluded the thought, he stuffed a forkful of food into his yapping mouth.

Except for taking notes, the younger men were doing everything they could to commit these pearls of rather obvious wisdom to memory. The group of them nodded like those dogs you sometimes see in the back windows of cars.

Cleese looked at Monk and cocked an eyebrow.

Monk said nothing. He merely pointed with his index finger to one of his eyes and then pointed back to the crowd as if to say, "pay attention."

"Jesus, that guy's a fuckin' weeping sore," said the square-jawed man in line in front of them. Cleese had seen him around and knew his name to be Hanson. The guy was in The League for some time and his gravelly voice sounded weary and had a hard, bitter edge to it. According to the grapevine, he'd been brought here from what used to be a Muay Thai camp in Thailand. The dude seemed to take great pride in being referred to as "Farang Ba" which, according to Monk, meant "crazy white foreigner." Word was he'd leveled more than his share of zombies back when the shit got shook.

"The man's a fuckin' menace," Hanson growled.

Cleese nodded to him and looked back over the crowd.

In front of Hanson, stood Jenkins, Parrish and Borden who, as one, nodded in Lenik's general direction and made "jack off" motions with their fists. The three men laughed and clapped one another on the back. This exchange, it would seem, was the height of hilarity for them. To be fair, they were fighters Cleese said he needed to keep an eye on. They all trained in the Greek art of Pankration and their training was second only to The Budo Warriors in severity.

Well, not counting Monk's, that is.

Cleese noticed that none of the Budo Warriors was here and thought that odd. He'd heard Chikara kept them on a cruelly sparse diet and they'd been allowed to schedule a different time to eat. Rumor was that the diet she'd concocted for them was mostly brown rice, lightly cooked fish, and green tea. He'd heard one of the Warriors say that it kept them focused. Cleese mused that eating like that would only keep him pissed the fuck off. Focus could never be found at the end of a fork... or the lack thereof.

The line for food moved incrementally forward, and as Cleese moved with it, he glanced over his shoulder toward the door. It was then that he noticed the imposing figure of Masterson looming like a gargoyle in the corner. As usual, he was dressed in another one of those suits, his arms crossed behind his back in a loose "parade rest" stance. The position seemed to strain the seams of his nicely tailored jacket and make the lapels slightly pucker. His eyes drifted over the crowd appraisingly until they finally connected with Cleese's and he nodded slightly. His expression never changed, his head just dipped and returned to its former position.

Soon enough, they'd made their way to the start of the metal counters of the kitchen and Cleese made a note of what Monk piled onto his tray. Every day it was exactly the same. A huge salad with a large ladle-full of Italian dressing, a large side plate of steamed vegetables, a couple of hot rolls, and an immense cut of salmon were unceremoniously stacked on plates. Then, a chicken breast or two to fill in any gaps. Protein and fiber seemed to be the general theme of the meal. Three twenty-ounce bottles of water were tucked into Monk's pockets and he was done.

Damn, Cleese thought, this old fucker could eat.

Cleese did his best to keep up, but he knew he'd never be able to eat all that, so he adjusted the portions to fit what he knew his stomach's capacity to be. As the two of them stepped out of line, Monk motioned for them to take the extra trip and find a place far away from the cliques of people.

"You want none of this bullshit, Son," he said. "Most of these motherfuckers are nothing more than statistics. Half of them will be in a box before the close of the end of the month's business day."

Cleese nodded and followed Monk to a more or less deserted part of the Mess Hall. They made their way through the tables and chairs until Monk felt that they were far enough removed from the madding crowd.

"These assholes will talk your ear off about how you should fight your match," Monk continued saying as they walked, "and if you want to listen to them, fine. I'll go do a fuckin' crossword puzzle. But, if you want to stay alive out there on the sand for longer than five fuckin' minutes, you'll sit here with me. The only thing those idiots can do is cloud your thinking, and, as we've already covered, clouded thinking will lead to you having a very fucked up day."

Cleese smiled and continued to follow Monk.

"Lay on, Macduff," Cleese said with a bow.

Once they'd gotten themselves seated, they ate in relative silence. Periodically, Monk would comment on one thing or another, but it was almost as if he felt that the silence itself was an important aspect of his brand of training. The old man once commented that what was not said between trainer and trainee was almost as, if not more important than what was said.

"In the silence," he had said, "is where each of you can learn the other's rhythms."

And so, they ate without saying much of anything.

Soon, Monk leaned back in his chair and belched loudly, signaling that he was done.

"So," he said raising and lowering his eyebrows as he picked at his teeth with the edge of his fingernail, "you want to go look at more training tapes, my young prodigy?"

"Sure," Cleese said and stuffed the last bit of a roll into his mouth. "As you know, I live for that shit."

They got to their feet and quickly bussed their trays. The conversation in the room had more or less died down to a dull roar now that almost everyone had eaten. There were still bursts of laughter as well as some hooting and hollering going on, but for the most part things became a lot more quiet. For the majority of the fighters, this meal signaled the end of another tough day of training. The only thing left to do was unwind, soothe tired muscles and try to get some sleep in order to be rested enough to do it all again tomorrow. These were the fighters who took things seriously enough to adhere to a regimen and because of that, they stood a better chance of surviving.

The rest of them would drink, shoot pool in the Administration Building and try not to go stir crazy. These men were the ones who'd come here carrying a lot of personal baggage. They were the ones who'd been recruited from biker and street gangs and raising hell would always be their primary vocation. Cleese understood the mindset all too well. He often wondered which group he would have fallen into had it not been for Monk, who believed in a happy medium between the two.

Monk and Cleese dumped what little remained of their meals into one of the big rubber trashcans near a back door and left their trays in a bin nearby. They walked the periphery of the room and, as they approached the exit, Cleese saw Masterson moving like a shark toward them.

"Ah, shit," Monk said turning his face away so Masterson couldn't see it. "Keep walking."

"Monk," Masterson said as he intercepted them at the door. "Cleese."

"Masterson," Monk said and smiled a mirthless smile.

Cleese just nodded.

"How are things going with our new man here?"

"They're ok. I still think he's too old and he doesn't listen too well, but... Give me enough time with him and he shouldn't get himself killed too quickly."

"Hey, man..." Cleese said feigning insult, "that shit hurts my feelings. You wound me, Monk. You really do."

"Yeah, well... if you're looking for sympathy, it's in the dictionary between 'shit' and 'syphilis.'"

Masterson smirked and nodded.

"I see things are indeed going well. Well, welcome again, Cleese. We're happy to have you here with us."

Cleese raised his eyebrows in surprise. Masterson didn't seem the type to give out compliments or warm greetings. This was not the same guy who'd kicked him out of bed not so long ago. For the life of him, Cleese wasn't sure whether it was a sign that things really were going well or that Masterson was merely blowing smoke up his ass.

He hoped it was the former because he hated the latter.

"You aren't going to get all mushy on me are you, Masterson?" Cleese said. "You know how I hate it when you get emotional."

"I think it's a safe bet to say, 'No.'" Masterson said, coming as close as Cleese had ever seen him to genuinely smiling.

"Well, we'd love to stand around talking all night," Monk said, "but we were just on our way to the Tape Library to review some of the last Live Event matches."

Monk moved toward the exit.

"Come along, young squire."

"Yep," he said, and took a step away, inwardly glad to be away from the conversation since Masterson—from the day they first met—made him feel skittish. Every fiber of Cleese's body told him not to trust the guy. Maybe it was the memory of their first contact when Masterson demanded he get onto that Blackhawk. Maybe it was the way he never felt he knew what was going on behind that dark suit and those even darker eyes. Maybe it was just simply that viper-like smile. Cleese didn't know and, quite frankly, he didn't want to know. He knew that he couldn't be trusted and that he wanted to always keep a little distance between Masterson and himself.

"Hold on one second, Cleese," Masterson said. "Monk, Cleese will catch up with you in a moment."

Monk shot a glance back and locked eyes with Cleese as if to say, "Watch yourself."

Masterson pulled Cleese over to the side of the door.

"Son," Masterson said in a tone that was almost conspiratorial, "I was asked by Corporate to let you know that some very important people have been watching the training tapes of your sparring with Monk and we're all very impressed. We see big things in your future if you continue to do as well as you have been."

Cleese looked at him for a moment and wondered, what would make someone who couldn't have cared less if he'd lived or died a few short weeks ago suddenly start sucking his dick like this? It just didn't make a whole lotta sense. While he considered it, he decided to dole out a little more rope to see if Masterson would hang himself with it.

"Well, thanks. I'm actually enjoying this more than I thought I would."

"That's good to hear, Cleese," Masterson said with that snakey smile again and all the while staring at him. After pausing for effect, he continued talking, "You don't know how close you came to being booted outta here after that piece of business with Michaels in the weight room." He paused as if to make his point and then, "We want to see you do well here. If there's anything you ever need, you let us know, ok?"

Little alarms starting going off in Cleese's head. The feeling was like termites eating their way into the back of his skull. He couldn't quite put his finger on it, but something suddenly felt more than a little bit hinkey to him. A voice in the back of his head urged him to move along; to get as far away from this slimy fuck as possible. It was a voice that Cleese was used to listening to and he couldn't comply fast enough to suit him.

"Well, golly…" Cleese said, his voice spiced with just a hint of sarcasm. Despite the creepy feeling he got from Masterson, there was still a part of him that took a bit of pleasure from fucking with him. "I really appreciate you saying that, Buddy, but I really should go and catch up with Monk."

Masterson's shoulders almost imperceptibly bunched up, but he quickly regained control of himself and smiled that unnerving smile again.

"We'll talk again, Cleese. We're looking forward to seeing what you can bring to The League."

Cleese nodded and stepped away from the conversation. He smiled slightly and slowly walked toward the door.

Almost dismissively, Masterson returned his gaze to the crowd in order to continue his observation of the fighters still left in the room. After a moment, he turned to eye Cleese suspiciously as he disappeared through the doors.

💀 💀 💀

Communion of The Dead

Before...

> But now is Christ risen from the dead, and become the first fruits of them that slept.
> For since by man came death, by man came also the resurrection of the dead.
> For as in Adam all die, even so in Christ shall all be made alive.
> - *I Corinthians 15:20-22*

The first rays of the sun broke through a dense cloud bank and fell upon the city as the bells of St. Joseph's Catholic Church rang out into the crystalline morning. The once bustling metropolis around the little church lay, as it had for weeks now, not merely sleeping, but quite literally dead to the world. Newspapers with headlines which proclaimed "The Dead Walk," "National Guard Overwhelmed," and "President Declares State of Emergency," blew about the deserted streets like origami tumbleweeds; detritus from a world gone terminal. Packs of what were once domesticated dogs roamed the desolate streets and avenues and searched for whatever food might have been left behind. Their masters, who were now far beyond caring about much of anything except the unrelenting hunger burning in their gullets, searched alongside them although their goal was for a far more elusive prey. The skyscrapers and office buildings of this slain city towered above the tiny, masonry church and cast its painted edifice in a continual shadow. The heavy, wooden doors of the parish stood propped open in welcome and, one by one, the reanimated dead were slowly finding their way inside.

The interior walls of the church rose up majestically toward the heavens, adorned in the consecrated imagery of faith and forgiveness; portraits of repentance granted and redemption won. What little light there was inside had seeped into the building through two large, stained glass windows set in the masonry walls on either side of the gilded altar. The ornately decorated Sanctuary loomed at the far end of the church. Above it, a domed apse loomed high and was painted a soft sky blue. Statues carved with an obvious reverence stood regally on either side of the expansive nave where the congregation would sit and bear silent witness to the downfall of an over-confident and sinful world. The light of the fluttering candles at the feet of the sculptures added minutely to the sparse illumination within the room. Once, this place of worship had as its guests king and pauper, billionaire and bum. These days, only the shambling multitude came to hear the Word of God, for they were all that seemed to be left.

As the sun pressed its way through the clouds and continued its rise in the eastern sky, the lumbering host straggled in through the church's doors for that morning's mass. The Dead had come in all manner of creation—or disintegration might be a more apt term—held together despite the ravages of Time and her twin sister,

Decomposition. But come they did for this was once a holy place in their minds and therefore held great import in their lives. They would come and continue to come, no doubt, for as long as their slowly putrefying bodies were able.

An uneven hush settled over the assembled congregation as Father Handel entered the church proper through a side door. He approached the pulpit at a languorous pace, carefully orchestrating his arrival's sense of drama. Tall and once considered to be good-looking, the priest moved slowly across the Chancel at the front of the room, his gait betraying both his stress and his advancing age. What remained of his once dark hair had gone silver and now laid slicked back across his rapidly diminishing pate. The white vestments of his station hung from his bony shoulders like a flag on a windless day. His manner was that of an already fatigued man pushed far beyond his limits of endurance. It would have been obvious to anyone looking into the church that these last weeks had been an exhausting ordeal for him. Unfortunately, there wasn't anyone in the vicinity left alive to witness his deterioration, so that point was a moot one.

Silence settled erratically over the crowd like a flock of nervous pigeons as he took his place at the lectern. Father Handel quietly waited for the crowd to completely calm themselves before looking up and addressing them. He was confident that there would be none of the disruptions that sometimes interrupted his services of the past. For this was St. Joseph's and those gathered, despite their advanced state of decay and murderous recent history, instinctively knew that here—now— propriety would still rule the day. Father Handel had seen to that, gently but insistently. This almost civil behavior was one of the small accomplishments in which the priest felt he could take a slight amount of pride. He'd managed to make contact—to really connect—with these dead souls and impart to them a concept they'd actually been able to understand and one with which they could comply. Yes, there were odd disturbances here and there, but for the most part, things went according to the church's preordained liturgy.

As the priest looked up from his podium and formally addressed the congregation, the group rose clumsily as one to their feet. Some did so awkwardly, rocking from foot to foot like they were drunk or mentally ill. While others stood in stillness, blindly following the group, staring gape-mouthed straight ahead. Hair mussed, clothes torn and spattered with blood, they stared with wide eyes and open mouths at the altar, awed as if by the presence of God himself.

There was Mrs. Roselli in her usual pew. The heavy Italian woman who once wore her piety like a shawl now stared blankly up at the Corpus Christi and reacted as if she were seeing the sculpture for the very first time. A bit of her husband's half-chewed and decomposing lower leg, which she still held lovingly in her arms, fell unnoticed from her torn lip and hit the floor with a sharp wet sound. A small toddler with blue-tinged skin crawled about the floor under her seat and quickly retrieved the fallen morsel. Eagerly, the child stuffed the meat into her toothless mouth.

Despite the service beginning around him, The Honorable Judge Harris sat wearing his pajamas in the centre aisle, legs splayed akimbo, trying in vain to form a cross with the two matted femur bones he'd brought along with him. He continually looked from the crucifix on the wall to the bones in his hands as if unsure of how he might make one become the other. Soon his attention wandered and his gaze came to rest on the thing he'd set lovingly in his lap. The crimson lump was now a highly valued thing in his undead world and one that he considered to be of the utmost importance. He'd torn it unceremoniously from his wife's chest as she slept. Now the chambered muscle lay cold and still in his hands. He cradled the treasure protectively for it was to be his offering for the service's expected collection plate.

Along the main aisle near the back of the room sat little Julie Brown, a raven-haired girl to whom Father Handel had given First Communion only a month or two earlier, in a time just before the world unraveled. As she fingered a small hole in her torn and darkly matted dress, one of her bright blue eyes hung limply from its shattered socket. When Father Handel's gaze fell upon her, she smiled. Her grin was at once wide and malignant. Her mouth held splintered teeth and clotted blood; clumps of human flesh caught between the shattered dentition.

It was evident from the empty gazes and confused stares that most of The Dead could not remember how they had come to be what they were. None could recall the cataclysm which had brought them this state of decrepitude. They only glimpsed ghost-like shadows of their past on the ragged curtains of their minds. Knowing nothing else, the multitude was forever compelled to try to recreate their dimly remembered lives. It was why many of them were here today.

Father Handel placed his tired, worn hands on the pulpit and bowed his head. The congregation fell back clumsily into their seats. He waited patiently for silence to once again return to this, his undead fold. In that short time his mind wandered and he was free to momentarily consider his present circumstances.

In the first few days of The Dead's return the priest would have been very much opposed to the idea of willingly walking into a room full of "Shufflers," as they were called by those who were still living in the fortified encampments outside the city. He'd heard some of the refugees talking on the short wave radio which kept him company through the long nights in the empty rectory. At first, he'd begged them repeatedly to come to his aid, but it soon became apparent, due to the overwhelming numbers of The Dead still left in the city, that any such rescue mission would only end in all of their deaths. Father Handel soon came to accept himself as a sort of Robinson Crusoe who was marooned amidst a lethal and yet lifeless sea.

And so, he listened. He listened to the chatter, listened to the cries for help, listened to the denials and justifications, listened to the soul-crushing reports of how things were going elsewhere in the world. Slowly, he began to get an idea of the enormity of the situation and how dismal it looked for everyone. From the stories he heard the priest knew his situation was hopeless and that was something he could not bear to let roam his conscious mind. For sometimes even a holy man such as he could not exempt himself from feeling a sense of futility and a deep and abiding loathing for the horrible and unforgiving things which had slowly, but inexorably, taken over his world.

However, he'd taken an oath—a sacred and holy mandate—and sworn to himself and to the Heavenly Father to lead His children to salvation. And, like it or not, these terrible creatures which now sat staring gape-mouthed before him were still his fold and, more importantly, His flock. Father Handel looked down and as he steeled himself for the impending service his mind continued to recall how it all had gone down.

After the initial outbreaks had been reported by the news services it wasn't long before the numbers turned and the shambling minority became the moaning majority. All too soon, it was apparent that he would be unable to escape the city due to the sheer magnitude of the dead and so it seemed prudent for the priest to figure out some sort of purpose for himself to show this undead occupying force, if only so that he would be allowed to continue to live.

...and to preach God's word, of course.

He could still remember how desperate the times had been when the first reports started coming out of Butler County in Pennsylvania. Soon the "phenomenon," as it was being called by the radio and television, had spread across the country like one of the plagues from the Bible itself. It wasn't long before everyone had lost someone and the final days of the contagion were only just beginning. The thought of it... Well, it all seemed so utterly outrageous. Who could have ever believed the things they'd been hearing coming from their television sets: "Armies of the dead", "Human cannibals" who wouldn't stay dead unless you destroyed their brains, "Lock your doors", "Dispose of your dead immediately"? No one had ever imagined that something like this was possible; that something like this could ever happen outside of a fevered imagination. It was that error in judgment that cost humanity its initiative and therefore its hope and future. When a respected network anchor came on the *Nightly News* and devoured his co-anchor just before the Weather and Sports, the world at large realized that all was lost.

Humankind was quick like that.

It wasn't long before The Dead had more or less taken control, their rapidly increasing numbers saw to that. They made sure that every human they encountered was either stripped as a food source or became one of the "converted." In no time, they became a horde of walking pestilence; an army with only hunger as their coalescent dogma. All that they had were the echoes of lives passed, routines dimly remembered and patterns they were compelled to repeat.

They'd needed some sort of guidance, a unifying force.

...a theology.

And so... When The Dead finally began banging on the door of St. Joseph's, Father Handel had been ready for them with a plan in hand. He would attempt to awaken Them, much like Jesus had done at the tomb of Lazarus. He would give them a brilliant flash of the evangelical memory that had once shaken them to the very core of their beings. His message would be simple: "You are all still God's children. You will always be God's children. He still loves you. And only through Him" (and Father Handel, of course) "can you find absolution and an end to this pain and suffering." If it worked, it would buy the priest some time until help could arrive.

The only thing was... help had yet to arrive.

His plan worked like the proverbial charm, the Lord had seen to that. The Dead quickly came to accept him as their Shepherd, a leader that God Himself had sent to guide His malignant Flock to Paradise. However his life as a captive, while in many ways safe and secure, was not without its hazards. Several times he'd been careless and come dangerously close to being bitten early on. But now as The Dead had come to think, in their limited capacity, of Father Handel and their dimly remembered God as synonymous, his life seemed spared. He was cared for and allowed to eat from the larder of food left behind by the city's now deceased residents. None of The Dead made attempts to eat him any longer and that was a plus. It looked, for better or for worse, as if he'd been allowed to survive and would continue to do so for as long as he preached to the Living Dead their version of the Gospel.

Father Handel rationalized to himself that he must do whatever he had to in order to stay alive so that he could guide these murderous children back toward God's salvation. It was the very definition of his role as priest. But there were downsides to this plan of his. The service he was about to conduct would have once been considered an abomination by the Church and therefore unthinkable. However some of the more lucid Dead had been quite insistent upon it being conducted. They'd silently made their wishes quite clear. In fact, it was the one thing they seemed determined to have him do since it was a seminal rite in their religion. He'd agreed to do it, but only once he saw how passive they were after he had performed it.

The crowd before him had by now grown restless and the motion from their impatient movement brought Father Handel back from his reverie. He cleared his throat, looked around with his most benevolent expression and spoke from the Missal.

"Blessed are you, Lord, God of all creation," Father Handel began, his voice a low monotone. He was careful not to raise his volume too abruptly or too sharply since he didn't want to risk exciting the throng assembled before him. The priest was still learning just how far they could be pushed before civility was cast aside and blood was spilled. The last thing he wanted was to incite a feeding frenzy where he would well become the center of attention. "Through your goodness we have this food to offer, which earth has given and human hands have made. It will become for us the Bread of Life."

A silence fell across the faithful as final as any death shroud and Father Handel shifted anxiously on his feet as he waited for what he hoped would follow, their dutiful response. His heart felt heavy and his blood was slowed by the fear. Fleetingly, he wondered if today was the day that The Dead had finally come to St. Joseph's serving a more sinister purpose.

After a short silence, the throng stood and drew a collective breath. As one, they mechanically opened their mouths and moaned, "Blesssss beee Gaaaa' forrr e'er."

Father Handel sighed softly in relief, then smiled so that the congregation could see his approval. Lowering his gaze, he continued reading, "Blessed are you, Lord, God of all creation. Through your goodness we have this wine to offer, fruit of the vine and work of human hands. It will become our spiritual drink." He paused for effect and took the time to look up from the heavy, leather book which he held open in his hands.

The throng stood wide-eyed and, for an instant, the priest felt as if he'd caught a glimpse of the people they once were, caught just an all too brief image of the lives and the memories which were held captive behind those clouded eyes. And it was in that moment that he was convinced, now more than ever that he'd been correct. These shambling abominations truly were his flock and they all looked to God, and to him, for a sense of security and an unwritten guarantee of their exemption from Hell's all-consuming fire.

While it was true that they had become a congregation of monsters, like something out of a dime-store novel, it was also true that it was only through His word they could find redemption. And while they were now no much more than beasts who gave little thought to the act of killing as well as to the ingestion of human flesh, they could still be granted Salvation through His Grace. Now that they'd been held safe in the cold yet comfortable embrace of the Elysium which laid behind Death's exclusionary door (even if that door had needed to be thrown open, creaking on hinges lubricated by the blood of the fallen, to do so), they knew better than anyone the glory of Heaven and of the majesty of His plan.

As one, the parishioners sucked in a collective breath and groaned, "Blesssss beee Gaaaa' forrr e'er."

An odor of mold and of the grave swirled about the room as the fetid air held within their stagnant lungs was expelled. A stomach-turning smell drifted across the room and up to the podium. The priest, his stomach lurching suddenly, set the leather bound book in his hands down on the lectern and ran his index finger across the underside of his nose. He knew that the smell of the incense which lay trapped in the folds of his sleeves would mask the putrid stench. It was a small trick he'd learned early on. He knew instinctively that vomiting before Them—and because of Them—would absolutely send the wrong message. So steps were taken, adaptations were made.

"Pray, brethren, that our sacrifice may be acceptable to God, the almighty Father," continued Father Handel, raising his voice just a notch. He spread his arms out, mimicking the figure hung on the cross behind him, and bowed his head. From the look in the crowd's glassy eyes, the posture achieved the desired effect.

The congregation was in full recollection now and the words flowed, albeit clumsily, over their swollen tongues and blackened lips. "May ah Lo-o-or' accep' aah sacrifi...aah yor han's fah ah pra-ase aah g'ory ah hisss na-a-ame... ffah argh goo' ah daa goo' of ahhl hisss Churrrrsh."

Father Handel allowed a full smile to drift across his face as he thought of all the progress his fold had made. When they'd first started arriving at his door, they could barely focus their attention on one thing for any length of time without trying to put their mouths on it. Now, through their continual repetition and his dogged persistence these past few weeks, they were almost understandable. He looked back to his book and continued, "Lord, make us worthy to celebrate these mysteries. Each time we offer this memorial sacrifice, the work of our redemption is accomplished. We ask this in the name of Jesus the Lord."

Another stuttering breath was drawn by the crowd and they spoke as one. "A-a-a-a-mennnn." The word, which once had been the very personification of the devotion of the faithful, now sounded hollow like the echoes of sanctification long lost and forgotten.

As the priest continued reciting the ritual, he noticed more of The Dead trying to gain entrance to the church. There were just so many more of them these days. All of them lured here by either a memory of the forgiveness offered or drawn by the rumor of what was freely given in this macabre communion. Since all of the seats of the cathedral's pews were now filled, the others were forced to stand awkwardly at the back or were left to aimlessly roam the aisles.

A few of the newer Dead, those having come bewildered into their new state of being, clawed at the feet of the carved statue of the Holy Mother which stood on one side of the room. It was as if they believed that anything even remotely human in form would yield some form of sustenance. Father Handel drew his arms back toward his body and slowly raised his right hand in a replication of the Sacred Heart. He drew a stuttering breath and continued the ritual.

"Bless and approve our offering; make it acceptable to you, an offering in spirit and in truth." He raised his voice even louder now, feeling the power of the words and forcing—by shear potency of will—the crowd to feel their power as well. "Let it become for us the body and blood of Jesus Christ, your only Son, our Lord."

"Throoo Chrisss' aah Lor', A-a-a-a-mennnn."

The congregation fell back heavily into their seats and waited as Father Handel closed his book and left it on the podium. Forlornly, he looked out over his fold and walked to the middle of the altar. There a silver tray lay on the heavy cloth Corporal which completely covered the table underneath. In the center of the elaborately engraved platter, a silver knife and a chalice covered with a dark purple cloth commonly called a Purificator was set. The exposed metal gleamed in the half light and the priest briefly touched it, meticulously adjusting its placement on the pall.

Off to the side of the Chancel, Father Handel heard the door to the sacristy open. Almost immediately, he sensed the congregation's concentration waver and he knew he would need to hurry the service along. He would be only able to hold The Dead's attention, and by extension of that, their civility, for a short time once the Offering was wheeled in. It was, after all, the thing for which a lot of Them had come. Well that and for their absolution, of course. He looked out of the corner of his eye and indeed saw the hospital gurney being pushed into the room by Javier, the young Hispanic boy who'd been serving as his acolyte these long weeks.

On the small metal table a young boy lay gagged, his hands securely strapped to his sides. There were a number of loosely wrapped, yellow tinged bandages covering several large bites which had been taken from the child's torso and upper arms. Each bite in and of itself would have sealed the boy's fate, sentencing him to a slow degeneration into one of the very Dead who now filled this church. It was now the order of things.

The wounded child's gasp was audible through his gag as he caught his first glimpse of the congregation sitting attentively in the church. Weakly, he wriggled against his restraints. The horrified look of betrayal in his eyes was unmistakable. A small cry of fear escaped from beneath the cloth around his mouth and the sound of that cry broke Father Handel's heart.

A palpable ripple went through the crowd as they all became aware of his presence, for even the ones who still clung to their faith became agitated as the living body was brought in. Yes, the priest thought, he would indeed need to hurry or this service would deteriorate into a scene from which he surely would not be able to escape.

The priest looked into the child's frightened eyes staring up at him and despite the heart-rending empathy he felt, he tried to separate himself from the desperate emotion which lay trapped there. He stroked the boy's messy auburn hair and bent over him, tenderly laying his lips upon the boy's forehead. He paused and whispered, "My child, I absolve thee in the name of the Father, and of the Son, and of the Holy Ghost of any and all sins of this life and I send you to sit at God's side knowing that it is a far better place that you go to now than the one where you have been. May God have mercy upon your soul," and he paused, then whispered under his breath, "and mine."

The boy's eyes darted about, unsure of the priest's full meaning. Violently, the child shook his head back and forth as if saying, "No! No, you don't have to do this!" He watched amazedly as the priest standing over him made the sign of the cross and touched his hand to his forehead. Finally tired from the extent of his exertions he fell still; panting rapidly. Tears slowly rolled down his dirty cheeks leaving wet discolorations in the filth.

Father Handel stood to his full height once again and gently picked up the silver knife on the table before him. He grasped the chalice and raised his voice to the throng. "The day before He suffered to save us and all men, He took an offering in his hands and looking up to heaven, to you, His almighty Father, He gave You thanks and praise. He took a glass, gave it to His disciples, and said: 'Take this, all of you, and drink it: for it is the blood of the new and everlasting covenant. It will be shed for you and for all so that sins may be forgiven. Drink ye all of it; For this is my blood of the new testament, which is shed for many for the remission of sins.'"

Feeling the power and majesty of the scripture himself, Father Handel pointed with the blade's tip out over the heads of the crowd as if it were the very Flaming Sword of Uriel. "Let us proclaim the mystery of faith: Father, we celebrate the memory of Christ, your Son. We, your people and your ministers, recall His passion, His resurrection from The Dead, and His ascension to glory; and from the many gifts You have given us we offer to you, God of glory and majesty, this holy and perfect sacrifice: this child of God who has now become the body of Christ and the cup of eternal salvation which is His life's blood."

For the briefest of moments, the boy and the priest locked eyes and an impassioned, but wordless exchange passed between them. The boy's eyes pleaded for help and release. The priest's cried out for forgiveness. The emotion that clouded the doomed child's eyes was one that shook Father Handel to his very core. He gave the child the smallest of smiles in the hope that it would make the next moments more tolerable. Somehow though, he knew it would not. Abruptly, he dragged the glistening blade in his hand across the soft flesh of the young boy's throat. Blood pulsed out of the gaping wound and pooled like oil onto the vinyl padding of the gurney. The child made a frantic gulping motion as his life pumped out of him in thick, syrupy surges. The priest quickly placed the chalice under the pulsing torrent at the boy's throat, filling it with the hot, crimson fluid. An impassioned sigh ran through the crowd as the air became charged with the coppery scent of plasma.

Within moments, the boy stopped moving.

Father Handel set the now nearly full chalice aside and raised the now bloody knife into the air. He raised his gaze and once more looked out over the crowd.

"It was then that He, who is the one true messiah, looked to his faithful and, as they were eating, Jesus took the bread, and blessed it, and broke it, and gave it to the them, and said, 'Take, eat; this is my body. Do this all in memory of me.'"

The priest turned back to the gurney and, with a sawing motion, he sliced deep into the meat of the boy's exposed upper leg. The milky, white skin split and parted, exposing bright, yellow nodules of fat and the grey-red fibrous muscle tissue beneath. Once the initial cut was made, the priest discreetly handed off the knife to the boy, Javier, who had come up to stand quietly next to him.

Father Handel would leave the rest of the cutting for the boy to finish. The acolyte dutifully began slicing away small pieces of flesh and stacked them on the silver ciborium which sat next to the now dead boy. Javier busied himself with the task making sure, as he'd been told, to keep the pieces out of sight of the faithful who sat moldering in their pews. Father Handel picked up few of the first stacked morsels and deftly palmed them. His vision was now blurred by the tears coursing down his cheeks, but he knew that since he'd come this far,going the rest of the way was a given. He held the blood-covered morsels in his blood-soaked hand and reached over to retrieve the goblet.

He turned back to the congregation and motioned for them to begin their approach to receive this most unholy of communions. The crowd stood and began their protractedly shuffling, one by one, toward the altar.

Father Handel took a moment and reminded himself that this was a most precarious time. A large crowd gathered. blood in the air and fresh meat on display made his situation all the more dangerous, to say the least. He reminded himself with a castigatory thought that one mistake, one bite from one of these Dead, would seal his fate just as it had for the boy whose body was now being prepared as the communion host. The contagion or whatever it was that had made these creatures crawl out of their graves, would course through his body and in time make him one of Them. He'd nursed dozens of people suffering from such bites and he knew that once bitten the victim's death decree had been irrevocably signed with the black ink of affliction.

The first supplicant came forward, the thing's eyes staring blankly straight ahead. It dropped clumsily to its knees in front of the Father and raised its head. The man's face was horribly mangled from a mixture of ante-mortem wounds and post-mortem nibbling. Long, raking furrows were torn from his left eye across the place where his nose should have been and dug deep into the meaty flesh of his right cheek. The man dutifully opened his mouth and Father Handel carefully dropped the meat onto his tongue. The mangled face worked the morsel over; the man's jaws chewing as a rapturous expression spread across what remained of his features.

The priest held the cup by its stem and offered it to the man. He placed it onto the man's torn lower lip and gently tilted it. The dead man slurped up the viscous liquid like someone who had been lost in the desert and was dying of thirst. As the priest pulled the goblet away, the woman next in line pushed the first man so that she might receive her sample of what was now in her necrotic mind the Blood and the Body of Christ.

And so it went, hundreds of The Dead came and took their mouthful of flesh and their swallow of blood. Some were unsatisfied to get only a small piece of the boy, but The Dead had by now made their own rules and the jostling and non-verbal reprimands of the others made for a more-or-less smooth ceremony. The flock came and went in a cortege of putrescence and when the last of them had received their communion Father Handel instructed that the church's doors be shut and barred.

As Javier moved away from locking the doors of the church, the priest gazed down at his now blood-stained vestments and abruptly sank to his knees on the steps of the altar.

It is all so difficult, Lord, and I am so tired.

How many times must he go through this before God would end this madness? From what he was continually hearing on his radio The Dead were still increasing in their numbers and still no hope was in sight. The voices on his radio at night sometimes spoke about people mounting a counter-offensive against The Dead and taking back the world. Some even spoke of how the Army was planning their own solution.

But so far, Father Handel saw little progress on either front.

As he sat trying regain his strength and hold back his tears Father Handel tried to imagine, as he had many times before, what had humanity done? What could the severity of their sin have been to bring about His wrath and in this magnitude?

Was this to be a cleansing as Sodom and Gomorrah had been?

Why had He turned His back on those who might serve Him?

The priest looked up toward the carved face of the figure hung from the cross for some assurance that this was all a part of His plan.

Where was the divine justice in any of this?

His supplication, as usual, went unanswered.

Now all that Father Handel had left was to continue teaching His word and to hope that God, in His eternal wisdom, would look kindly upon his acts. After all, wasn't he merely trying to do that which he was meant to do as a part of His design? Had he, too, gone astray? He felt in his heart that God would surely look upon his acts with a certain amount of clemency, since the priest had acted in His name so that he could continue to teach His word.

Right?!?

He looked over at the body on the gurney and saw that there was hardly anything left of the bound boy now. His corpse had been practically picked clean. Father Handel looked up again to the carved representation of Christ above the altar, hung his head and wept quietly. His shoulders shook from his heaving sobs. His body was wracked by the depths of his sorrow. He sensed rather than saw Javier walk up softly and stand next to him. The boy waited patiently for the priest's outburst to abate. Once Father Handel's tears subsided, the priest felt a small hand gently touch his shoulder.

"Padre," the boy said in the quietest of voices, "I take you to your room now. You shower and change clothes. I clean up here."

The priest, who was still only just a man, painfully stood and nodded wearily.

"Bless you, My Son," he said in a hushed tone.

"Padre?" the boy asked sheepishly as they began to walk.

"Yes, Javier?"

"Will La Muerte stop coming one day?"

"I don't know, My Son. I just don't know. I've heard on the short-wave that the Army may be coming. Perhaps they will be able to get a handle on things. Honestly, I had thought The Dead would have all rotted away by now, but... they still come. We must remain patient and trust that it is all a part of God's will."

The boy walked and considered this. Absentmindedly, he wiped the blood on his hands on the seat of his pants. Deep red stains appeared on his already blood-spattered clothing.

"Padre?"

"Yes, Javier?"

"If La Muerte stops coming, who will be left for you to preach to?

"If The Dead were to ever stop coming, Javier, you and I would leave this place. I promise you that. We'd go and find ourselves someplace nice, someplace sunny and warm..." The priest raised his hand and gently mussed the front of the boy's hair, "...someplace safe." The old man looked into the deep brown eyes of the boy. "How does that sound, eh?"

The boy broadly smiled up at the older man and nodded aggressively.

"Muy bien, Father," he said with a wide grin, "I would like that."

Father Handel smiled and sighed quietly. He leaned gently against the boy, dropping his arm around the younger man's shoulders for additional support. The boy shouldered the older man's weight and led the way into the stygian shadows of the church.

☠ ☠ ☠

Chikara

Cleese stepped out of the Training Hall and walked onto the large expanse of grass which separated the gymnasium from the fighter's cribs. After a few minutes of walking, when his view was no longer obstructed by the surrounding buildings, he stopped and took in the setting sun. The slowly descending orb hung just above the horizon and bled the entire sky a deep red. The sight of the sun going down always filled him with a sense of wonder, as it had for his entire lifetime.

Some things in this oftentimes rotten life could be so beautiful.

He slowly ran a hand through his hair and pulled it back from his face. A small spasm twitched in his back and he stretched the aching muscles with a sigh. He straightened his legs and methodically bent over at the waist to touch his toes. His hamstrings burned and felt as if they were made out of razor wire. After a couple of bounces to pull the muscles loose, he stood up, spread his arms and arched his spine until he heard it crack. The pain he'd been feeling from all of the training created a fiery sensation down deep in his muscle fibers. Every movement he made now caused his muscles to cry out in a symphony of suffering.

He felt tired—damn tired—but in a good way. He was damn near dead on his feet, yet conversely felt like a million bucks. Pain was, after all, just weakness leaving the body. Or at least that was what Monk had told him. Monk was full of shit like that, little aphorisms that sounded like they'd come straight out of a Shaw Brothers movie.

"Pain is inevitable. Suffering is optional."

"Pain is temporary. Pride is forever."

To Cleese's ears it was all "snatch the pebble from my hand..." -type bullshit, but it had a way of sticking in your head like gum.

A sudden stinging sensation buzzed high on his left arm. He swatted at its source only to find that a mosquito had landed and just bitten him. A small smear of blood and bug guts greased his upper deltoid. He wiped the goo off and spread it on his pants. It was a little surprising how firmer his body felt even after only the short time he'd been here. He poked at his bicep and liked what he saw.

He'd packed on some pounds and dropped literally an ass-load of body fat since arriving here. As his body started to slim down, he'd felt a lot of the speed and alertness of his youth return. Before stepping out of that helicopter, he would've been lucky if he could have walked a mile. Now he was clearing the "four minute" mark. At Monk's suggestion, the blunts and alcohol stopped the minute Cleese had seen what he was going to be up against. Him being high as fuck had been fine for pulling his meat out of the grease before, but given the current situation he figured a straight head and a clear throat would be better if he wanted to keep his noggin' on his neck.

A sudden, sunset breeze blew coolly across his face. He turned his head toward it and breathed in deeply. The chilled air felt good as it swirled deep down into his lungs. It sure beat the hell out of the salt and urine smell of The City that was for sure.

Cleese looked around and decided that since Monk had been called away for some face-time with Corporate and he had some free time to kill, he would take a little walk around the compound to check out some of the sights he'd not had a chance to see. He welcomed the alone time and the chance to clear his head. So much had happened so quickly since he'd arrived here he felt as if he needed a little perspective. Oftentimes perspective could only be achieved with time, distance and solitude.

He walked aimlessly across the grass, heading in the general direction of the shooting range. He could hear what sounded like somebody popping off rounds, but the noise now coming from the range was nothing like it was during the busy time of day. It was a given among the fighters that being proficient with a gun was not a matter of choice, but of necessity. Being good with a weapon—be it fists, blade or gun—was second in importance only to the "Don't Get Yourself Bit" credo.

For a few minutes he walked and did nothing but look at the sky and let his mind clear. Breathing in through his nose and out his mouth helped aerate his brain and calm his jangled nerves. He was nearly halfway to the range when, out of the corner of his eye, he caught sight of some movement off to his left; at the top of one of the hills that butted up against one side of the range. He tried to focus on it, but given the distance, couldn't see much of anything. Whatever it was, it was low to the ground and looked like a pile of large stones. He was about to dismiss it as nothing more than a trick of the light, but then saw it move again. Almost instantly his curiosity was piqued.

Without giving it too much thought, he decided to wander in that general direction if only to satisfy his own inquisitiveness. Besides, it wasn't as if he had anything else to do much less anywhere to go. After a few more minutes of walking in that direction, he was finally able to make out that the pile of rocks he'd seen was in reality a slight figure sitting under one of the Wisteria trees planted at the crest of the hill. His interest now fully engaged, he thought he'd forego the visit to the range and just see who felt he needed that kind of privacy.

He made his way toward the rise at the base of the hill and did his best to keep out of sight. He figured he'd get a look-see at whoever it was up here and, if it proved to be someone of no interest to him, make his way back down and then head back to the Firing Range. As he climbed, his hamstrings again cried out in pain and resisted the call to strenuous exercise. After everything they'd already been through during the day's training, the last thing his muscles seemed to want was a round of hill-climbing. Setting his resolve, he pushed past the discomfort and his muscles soon relaxed, making the climb easier.

About midway up the hill, his calf got tight and gave the first indications of cramping up. Pausing to flex it out, he turned and looked back toward the compound. He knew that the place was big, but now it was obvious that it was a lot bigger than he'd initially surmised. He'd known that there were wide fields separating the large, squat buildings, but now he could see the extent of the Compound's acreage. Cleese could see what looked like miles of cyclone fence running around the vast complex. He squinted and was able to make out a thin line of electrical wire threaded through the diamond-shaped spaces of the chainlink. Above the fencing, razor wire twinkled in the diminishing sunlight. Beyond the formidable fencing, there was nothing but mile after mile of empty countryside.

He turned and looked back up to the top of the hill. He still had a ways to go, so he lowered his head and returned his attention to the laborious climb to the top of the hill. His efforts soon brought him to the crest and put him just to the right of where the mysterious figure sat like a Buddhist monk: legs crossed, hands lying loosely in his lap.

He continued on, moving quietly.

By now he'd gotten to within a dozen or so yards away and was able to ascertain that the figure in the shadows of the Wisteria was that of a woman. He could see that her build was smaller than that of a man and her posture was nearly perfect; back straight, head held high yet relaxed. Most of the men here moved like apes, but she had an air about her that was almost angelic. She seemed to take up a hundred percent of the space she occupied. Her body exuded diametrically opposed energies: totally peaceful harmony and complete deadly menace. Even though she was relaxed and off-guard, her body gave the impression that with the proper motivation all that could change... and that change would be very dangerous indeed.

It didn't take a genius to figure out this woman's identity: Chikara.

Surreptitiously, he'd learned as much as he could about Chikara as soon as it was possible. After hearing the stories, he'd sneaked off whenever he could and viewed her tapes. The more he saw, the more he was interested in her, her Warriors, and her unique fighting style. He'd never met a woman who could hold her own in a full-on fight, but this one... This one was different. Much like Monk, she'd taken what Life had given her and turned it into something undeniable. This was a woman who did what few others could.

She kicked ass and took names.

And when the asses got kicked and the names had been taken the end result usually meant a lot of bodies hitting the floor.

Cleese remembered one specific tape he'd seen. It was late in her match and she was obviously tired. Covered in blood and bits of meat, she'd stood quietly and allowed herself to be surrounded by a group of UDs. She'd batted their advances aside when necessary, but for the most part she simply let them get inside her strike zone. After giving the television audience their fair share of anticipation and dread, it became clear by the change in her expression that she'd had enough. Then in a blur of punches, kicks and whirling swordplay, she'd dispatched them all in seconds. One moment she was surrounded and things were looking grim, the next it appeared as if someone had turned on a blood sprinkler. She literally became a whirling dervish of death. When things finally settled down, there she was, panting from the exertion, standing over a pile of bodies and grinning like a demon from Hell.

It was, to say the least, impressive.

It was also, at least in Cleese's opinion, sexy as hell.

From afar he took a moment to look at her, quietly cataloging her appearance. She was pretty beneath all of that bluster and violent retribution. She wore her hair short and kind of spiky which was something that a lot of fighters did. The UDs could sometimes entangle their clawing hands in a combatant's hair and that could create some major problems. It was just easier to keep a short haircut. Even Cleese, who wore his hair long, kept it tied back tight to his head in a ponytail.

From this distance, he noted how well-defined and leanly muscled her upper body was: firm musculature having been augmented by exceedingly low body fat. In the dying light, Cleese saw the thick cabling of her vascularity as it accented each individual muscle group. There was no denying that this was a beautiful and powerful woman. Silently, he wondered how she'd do in a sparring match both in the Pit and in bed. He made a mental note to try to find out should either opportunity ever present itself.

"Do you often sneak up on people and stare at them, Cleese?" Chikara asked abruptly, eyes still closed. Her voice almost tinkled on the blossoming night's crisp air.

"No. I...uh..." he stammered and then chuckled. "I apologize. I was just out walking..."

She slowly opened her eyes and languidly turned her face to meet his.

Cleese hesitantly walked the rest of the way over to where she was sitting.

"I hope I'm not interrupting," he said. As he got closer, he noticed that this woman was a lot prettier than he'd initially thought. Her bone structure was sharp and her mouth wide. Her lips were full and generous. He looked down and met her gaze. He was brought up short when his gaze finally came to a rest on her eyes. They say that the eyes are the window to a person's soul. These were dark piercing orbs that sent a cold chill down your spine. They were eyes that had seen a great deal of loss and endured unfathomable amounts of suffering.

Cleese felt that adversity tempered the spirit. Nietzsche said, "That which does not kill you, makes you stronger." If that were true, then this woman was carbon steel.

"Well," she responded, "I was in the middle of my meditation. However, I have been meaning to talk to you."

"Oh?" he asked and he cocked an eyebrow. He'd been trying to keep a discreet eye on Chikara and her Budo Warriors since he'd first arrived. He had no idea that the fascination had been mutual.

"I have. Here..." and she patted the grass next to her, "sit with me."

Cleese made his way over and sat down heavily. Despite his best efforts to the contrary he groaned as his quadriceps screamed out in their distress. After a bit of painful adjustment he settled in and made himself comfortable. All the while, he never noticed the smirk that slid across Chikara's lips.

"Sore?" she asked, looking away to hide her still grinning face.

"Ha-ha..." he said wincing. "I feel like I've been hit by a bus. Twice."

Smiling fully, her eyes returned to the tableau before her.

Cleese took a moment to drink in the view from this vantage point and was amazed. It was stunning the way the final orange and purple rays of the sun slashed across the sky and threw long, skeletal shadows upon the fields of manicured green. He was surprised it had taken him this long to find the place.

"Wow," Cleese said with a sigh as he got himself comfortable, "this is a nice little spot you have here."

"It is preferable to the last place I used which was next to the Holding Pen," Chikara said, her voice ringing out sweetly in the air.

Cleese looked at her and realized that this was the first time he'd caught her smiling.

"I'll bet," he said. Then after a moment, "So... What did you want to talk to me about?"

Chikara drew her index finer around her right ear where two piercings twinkled in the light, and pulled the short bristly hairs back behind her ear. The movement made Cleese's pants feel funny; funny in a way that they'd not felt in a very long time.

"We have been watching you, Cleese," Chikara began.

Cleese involuntarily raised his eyebrows in surprise.

"So far, we like what we see," she said finishing he thought.

"We?"

"Yes, we..."

"I'm flattered."

"You should not be," she said with a slight sniff. "We—and by 'we' I mean the Budo Warriors—have been watching you since you first arrived. In fact, it was one of my Warriors who first brought you to Masterson's attention."

"Hmmm... so, I have you to thank for this little adventure."

"In a way, I guess... Yes. We heard about you and thought you would do well here. Now that we have seen the genuine article, it is evident that we were correct in that assumption.

"Hmm... well, thank you," he responded. "I'm guessing there's more..."

Chikara smiled again and turned to look him in the eye.

"We were hoping you would join us."

"Join you? Join the Budo Warriors?"

Chikara nodded and looked off serenely into the distance as if, her request now made, she'd returned to a peaceful place in her mind while she awaited her answer.

Cleese stared at her for a long time as he pondered the real meaning of what had been said. He was honored. Hell, who wouldn't be? Still... Cleese had never exactly been a "team player" and the idea of joining the ranks of any organization—no matter how loosely compiled or prestigious—sat like a turd at the back of his throat.

"Well..." he said, "while I am honored at the invitation, I'm not so sure that would be a good idea. I'm not exactly someone who is able to tow a line, you know? And in case you haven't noticed, you tow a pretty stern line."

Chikara grinned and nodded. Cleese found that, despite himself, he respected this woman. She'd no doubt suffered a lot in order to bring her to where she was today, fought her way through competition and adversaries alike and had come out on top. In many ways she was a lot like the other fighters that were here, but in other ways—more important to Cleese's way of thinking—she was quite different. She gave off an air of great strength and yet there was a deep compassion and sensitivity evident in her.

"Somehow," she said finally, "I knew you would say just that."

Cleese smiled and leaned back against the tree.

"Well, I aim to please."

The two of them sat quietly as the sun slid below the horizon. Cleese periodically looked over at Chikara and was amazed that she'd returned to her meditation, effectively shutting him out. He took the time to look her over once more. Sitting this close he noticed some small ragged scars across her upper arms and neck. He leaned in just a bit closer and saw that they were several matching sets of four scratches; one scratch for each of what must have been a UD's jagged fingernails.

He figured that the scratches were a result of the way Chikara got in so close during her matches. A fighter couldn't let that sort of shit happen as much as she did and walk away unmarked. Luckily, no one had ever become infected as a result of a scratch or two.

No, for that, it took a bite.

"You are staring..." Chikara said with a slight smile, eyes still closed.

Cleese was yanked out of his reverie and realized that he had been staring—pie-eyed and open-mouthed—just a couple of feet away from this woman. He felt his cheeks grow suddenly hot and flushed.

"Oh... uh... sorry," he apologized.

Chikara smiled and seemed to rise like a marionette; her strings lifting her effortlessly to her feet.

"Come. We should get back." Then, "I would like it if we were able to talk more sometime later."

Cleese smiled and nodded.

"I'd like that as well," he replied and, with another groan, he got stiffly back to his feet.

"Well, good," and she graced him with another one of those smiles.

"Jesus..." he said with a wince once he'd gotten fully to his feet. He bent his back and it made another painful cracking sound. "I feel like shit."

"Lactic acid has built up in your muscles as a result of all of this exercise. It is just making them stiff. An interesting side note for you... lactic acid is very similar in chemical composition to something found in the UD's metabolism—something called Sarcolactic Acid. In The Dead, Sarcolactic Acid or Paralactic Acid is the chemical that causes Rigor Mortis. So, in essence, what you are feeling right now is nothing more than ante-mortem rigor. Stop by my crib later and I can give you an herbal tea that will ease some of the pain a bit."

"Man, lookit you..."

Chikara laughed aloud, her laughter sounding light and almost care-free on the evening air. She looked up at him and, after a moment, looked away. In the diminishing light of the day, the blush that flushed her cheeks went unnoticed.

"Well," she said, "I, too, aim to please."

As they made their way down the hill and across the grass, Cleese stared at her for a long time. Again, something primal stirred deep within his belly. It'd been a long time since a woman made him feel the way Chikara did; too long. As he smiled to himself, he decided that he liked this feeling and wanted to explore it further.

They walked together in silence until they'd reached the outskirts of the compound's buildings. Abruptly, she stopped and reached out to lightly tug at the bottom hem of his shirt. Almost as suddenly as she'd done it, she pulled her hand away. A wave of embarrassment washed over her face as if her body had betrayed her and done something she'd not meant it to. Her gesture was something from another time and another place. It was like a distant echo from when she'd been another person. It reminded her of how long she'd kept that person locked away from the world. For some time now, she'd not allowed herself to feel like a woman. Doing so had proven itself to be far too dangerous here. Cleese, though, was able to let her be who she was and not make her feel like that was to her detriment.

She silently feared the repercussions should she let the Woman influence the Warrior.

"I have enjoyed finally meeting you, Cleese."

Cleese smiled broadly and ran his hand through his hair. The motion was something he'd tried to control for a long time. It was his "tell." And what it told was that he was interested or embarrassed. For some reason, none of that mattered to him now.

"Believe me... the pleasure was all mine."

The two of them stood looking at each other, each silently not wanting or knowing how to disengage.

"Come by before you turn in for the night," she said, breaking the awkward silence. "I will give you that tea."

"Yeah, thanks," he said and his hand once again ran through his hair. "I'd appreciate that."

And without another word, the two fighters walked off toward the center of the compound; each of them lost in the whirlwind of their own thoughts.

Last Rites

As the moon slowly rose to its apex over the relative quiet of the compound, the temperature within the Holding Pen had begun to slack off and the heat of the day finally started to dissipate. Shadows, a constant commodity in this forsaken place, covered the ground as heavy and thick as spilled oil. The incessant gloom arrested the sparse illumination and gave the space a muted tone, making it seem even more menacing that it already was. The darkness was just something you got used to if you spent enough time tucked away here. It was something that usually happened shortly after you got used to the never-ending moaning of the dead.

Getting used to the smell...

Well, that took a whole lot longer.

Adamson no longer noticed any of it. He'd been looking after and caring for the dead for so long that the gloom and the smell had become integrated into the fabric of who he was. As for the sound, where others heard the horrifying cacophony of death and fear, he heard a mournful aria of loss. To his ears, the dead were not calling out in warning, but rather they cried out to the dark for some kind of understanding, a desperate plea for compassion made to a god who no longer listened, much less cared.

He'd cared about them before their resurrection and he continued to care now.

It was who he was.

Watching over The Dead was a business and it was one that Adamson knew well. The containment and control of the reanimated dead was something he understood down deep in his bones. His ability to feel compassion for them—even when no one else here did—was what made him so good. In more ways than one, he felt as if he knew the dead (and liked them) a hell of a lot better than he did the living.

Adamson walked around the large pen where the hundreds of UDs were stored. The sound of their movement was a constant thing, a steady and unvarying tone which was heard as the dead milled about in their never-ending search for food.

While the building was large, most of its floor space was taken up by the cattle pen-like enclosure. The air was kept cool by large refrigeration units housed on the roof of the building. Their use was nothing more than a token gesture to try and slow the inherent decomposition of the dead, but it did little good. Time would have its way and there was little anyone could do to slow it. Like fragile flowers, the dead too would wilt and fall into corruption and decay. It was another one of those immutable laws of nature; an edict that offered neither appeal nor demurral.

Seven foot high walls made of chain link and corrugated metal formed the large rectangle of the Pen, the enclosure which housed the League's most important—and dangerous—resource. At each corner stood a guard tower, giving the place a concentration camp-like appearance. Sitting high in the towers overlooking the meandering dead, guards manned large caliber United States Air Force issue GAU-2/A miniguns. An electrically powered Gatling gun capable of delivering over three thousand 7.62mm rounds per minute, it could reduce a crowd of UDs (or people for that matter) to mashed potatoes in seconds. Adamson considered the guns his fail safe. If his herd were to ever break out of their enclosure, the mounted artillery (as well as a few more portable XM214 Microguns) would stop that shit before it ever got too out of hand.

Adamson approached the furthest guard tower and, laying his hand on the railing to guide him, walked up the gangway to where the guard stood watch. As the clock rapidly approached midnight, it was almost time for a change of the guard shifts. As part of his unending job description, he made it a point to dismiss and greet each and every one of the guards at the beginning and end of their shifts. While it seemed like a formality, the ritual served a couple of purposes. One—it made each man feel connected to the whole, made him feel as if his oftentimes boring work was appreciated. Two—it was a chance for Adamson to look each guard in the eye and silently assess him for cracks in his veneer. The job these men were being asked to perform was both exceedingly boring and exceptionally dangerous. It was boring in that they ended up watching over an area where literally nothing happened... until the time came when something happened and life got real hazardous, real fast. The gig went from mind-numbing boredom to critical mass like that.

It was not a job many could perform. A lot of men were lazy and undisciplined— a dangerous combination that meant death for them and potentially everyone else. If that happened, it was a situation where the Watcher could potentially become the Watchee. Even though The Dead seemed dim-witted, they were forever vigilant having all the time in the world to watch and wait and scheme. Death was a finality that no longer mattered in their world. It was a concern that had been quite unceremoniously wiped from the table.

Now all they had was time; time and their ever-present hunger.

As he stepped into the relative cool of the tower, Adamson saw the guard on duty turn to greet him. Miller was the guy's name and he was a trusted employee who'd managed to adapt to the job's requirements and make it work. A kid in his late twenties with short-cropped hair and a reddish complexion, he had this open-eyed gaze like he was in constant amazement at what Life had to show him. Adamson liked the dude and considered him to be someone he could trust.

"Miller," Adamson said in lieu of a more formal greeting. "How're things?"

Miller smiled that dopey smile of his beneath a set of standard issue night vision goggles. Realizing they were there, he reached up and pulled them off. Once they were clear of his face, he set the bulky headpiece into the frame mounted on the wall to the right of the minigun.

"Everything's a-ok here. The dumbfucks are doing what the dumbfucks do best," Miller said. Even though Adamson disliked the term "dumbfucks," he knew that there were worse euphemisms used by the guards for the UDs. He also understood that the use of those types of things were coping mechanisms which were necessary for the men to distance themselves from the reality of their occupation.

"Next shift is gearing up now," Adamson explained, "your relief should be along in a second."

Adamson stepped up beside Miller and looked out over his pen.

Spread out before his eyes was an undulating sea of dark motion made up of hundreds of roaming bodies. There were eddies and slipstreams within the mass as the crowd aimlessly moved about inside the enclosed corral. It was a tide of the undead that, at one time, would have meant certain death for anyone unlucky enough to come up against it. Now it was just an ocean of reanimated meat. A low chorus of moaning acted as white noise and seemed to come and go like the soft crashing of waves against the shore.

As Adamson looked out over the darkened corral, it never ceased to astound him how many there were or how tenuous the balance of power remained.

"In so many ways, these are my children," he said softly. "They're all I have left..."

"Excuse me, Sir?" Miller asked.

Adamson was shaken out of his reverie and looked up as if embarrassed. He quickly shook it off and returned to business.

"Nothing... anything going on that you think I should know?"

"Well, I wasn't going to mention it, but..." Miller said and looked back out over the heaving crowd.

Adamson turned and looked at him sternly.

"If there is something going on that I need to know, Miller, I need to know it. Out with it, please..."

Miller took a quick, almost nervous look around the small space within the guard tower and lifted his gaze to Adamson's. He looked like a kid who was about to tattle on a sibling.

"Well, the priest has been coming around a lot lately and doing his thing near the pens."

"Handel?"

Miller nodded and stared down at his feet. "He comes in like this, usually late at night, and hangs around toward the back of the building in the walkway there. Some of the guys are saying they hear him," and he raised his obviously concerned eyes to meet Adamson's, "talking to the UDs."

Adamson knew the man well. He'd come to the League a few years ago after having spent his life as a priest in some place Adamson couldn't remember. There were rumors of him having gotten into some kind of trouble with the diocese for reasons no one ever talked about. He'd come onboard as a Psych Counselor and was supposed to help the fighters come to terms with the reality of what they were being asked to do here, but he still carried himself like a priest. He was a guy who looked a lot older than his already advanced years, but that wasn't too terribly abnormal. After everything that had happened in the world, who didn't have a few extra wrinkles and grey hair?

Adamson took a moment to look deep into Miller's eyes, plumbing the man's depths for any hint of malevolence or manipulation. Finding none, he turned and directed his gaze toward the back of the building. Beyond the undulating crowd and the ever-present fencing, he could just make out some movement deep within the veil of the shadows.

"Ok," he said with a sigh, "I'll check it out." He patted Miller reassuringly on the shoulder.

Miller nodded and stepped up to retake his position on the minigun. Slowly, as if deep in thought and already feeling bad about reporting the priest's activity to management, he lifted the night vision goggles from their stand and pulled them on.

Adamson took a couple of steps toward the walkway and stopped.

"Miller..." he said paternally, "you shouldn't feel guilty about telling me when something's happening that's out of the ordinary. If someone is fuckin' up he puts all of us in danger."

Miller nodded and smiled with relief.

"We clear on that?"

"Yes, Sir. Clear as crystal."

Then, it was Adamson's turn to nod and he turned and walked back down the walkway and into the gloom.

Father Handel stood with his small briefcase in hand in the shadows behind the Main Pen and carefully looked between the slats into the dimly lit expanse of the enclosure. Dark figures swayed in the half-light, rocking back and forth, moving from side to side. As always, the acrid odor of death was pervasive in this place, but every so often an extraordinary wave of putrescence would waft between the corrugated lengths of metal and assault his senses anew. This was an odor he'd come to know well ever since the dead had risen. God knew, he'd lived with it long enough at St. Joseph's. It had become inextricably linked to what he considered his mission.

As he gazed into the undulating crowd, the face of a child pressed itself up against the chain link. It was a small boy, no more than nine or ten, who stared out at him with an unnerving mixture of open-mouthed wonder and abject hunger. His face was an utter mess. Long raking slashes tore down his right cheek, the white of his skull visible through the coarse separations of his anatomy. Coagulated blood was splashed and caked across what was left of his ruined features.

"Dear God," Handel softly whispered, "so many of Your children. So many... and so lost."

He pulled himself away from the boy's unwavering gaze and with renewed vigor got back to the bit of business which brought him here. He set his valise on the ground and carefully opened it.

"O Lord," he intoned in a hushed voice, "who has said, 'My yoke is sweet and my burden light,' grant that I may so carry it as to merit Thy grace."

The priest removed from the case what looked like a thick crimson scarf. The material was deeply colored and had a cross embroidered in gold thread at each end. Holding it aloft, he kissed each end where the cross was stitched and held it to his forehead.

"Protect me, O Lord, so I may resist the assaults of the devil and cleanse my heart with the Blood of the Lamb so that I may be deserving of your eternal reward."

He laid the scarf around his neck so that it draped down his chest. Softly, he whispered, "Restore to me, O Lord, the state of immortality which I lost through the sin of my first parents and, although unworthy to approach Thy Sacred Mysteries, may I deserve nevertheless eternal joy."

He then withdrew a small bottle filled with Holy Water and held it gingerly in his hand.

Now, more or less prepared for the ritual to come, he turned his back to the pen and carefully ran his hand along the wall, searching for the small nail he'd placed there on a previous visit. Finding it with his fingertips, he reached into his case once more and pulled from it a silver crucifix. He kissed the figure on the cruciform and gently hung it from the nail.

He returned his attention to the pen and noticed several more of the dead had gathered around the child, all staring out at him from between the slats of the fence. They must have caught wind of him and that was what drew them to the spot. His body's odor had undoubtedly acted as a lure which enticed them one by one to come to where he now prepared to cleanse them of their sins. He knew he'd have to be both quick and careful if this was going to go as smoothly as it had in the past. His primary concern, of course, was that he not get himself bitten. Thankfully, he had some experience in this regard so he wasn't too worried. Secondarily, he knew Adamson and his people did not fully understand or approve of his reasons for being here now, doing what he was about to do. Well, maybe Adamson. There had been some discussions regarding The Dead's salvation before. He might be willing to overlook it, but The League would surely have taken a dim view.

But that was a concern best left to another time.

He carefully poured the Holy Water into his hand and splashed it as best he could onto the faces of the gathered dead. Then, he did it again. Most of the fluid landed on the fence and softly reflected in the dim light, but some of it made it through and hit the open-mouthed faces of his intended targets.

"Is any among you sick?" he said, quoting from the Book of James, in a subdued voice. "Let him call for the elders of the church, and let them pray over him, anointing him with oil in the name of the Lord; and the prayer of faith will save the sick man, and the Lord will raise him up; and if he has committed sins, he will be forgiven."

In the half-light, the dead continued to stare at him hungrily.

"Oh, Heavenly Father," he continued, "we call upon you to heal the sick, cleanse the lepers, raise the dead, cast out devils: freely ye have received, freely give." The irony of the "raise the dead" line was not lost on him, but by now the words were flowing freely from his lips and could not be stopped.

"And into whatsoever city ye enter, and they receive you, eat such things as are set before you: And heal the sick that are therein, and say unto them, the kingdom of God is come nigh unto you."

One of the dead, an older man of about fifty, pushed his way through the crowd gathered at the fence and pressed his face against the chain link. He mashed his features against the metal and let out a sigh that reeked of the tomb, a smell of decaying anatomy and of blood freely spilled. His grue-stained fingers wound their way between the links and gripped the metal fervently.

Pausing briefly, Handel looked the man in the eye, the pupils cast opaque and milky in the faint luminosity. Slowly, the man opened his mouth and pressed himself even tighter to the fence, as if he was trying to push himself through the grating. His blackened tongue raked across swollen, bloated lips and he painfully pulled air into his lungs.

"A-a-a-a-a-a-a," and he paused and then breathed out, "me-e-e-e-e-ennn."

Father Handel smiled to himself and continued to give The Dead their Last Rites.

Adamson came around the far end of the pen and heard Handel whispering long before he ever saw him. Through the shadows, he was able to make out his silhouetted form lit by the sparse ambient lighting. Moving forward he walked slowly, hoping to get an idea of what the priest was up to and why he was going about it with such secrecy. From some of their past conversations, he thought he might have a pretty good idea. As he got closer, he heard Handel's low voice drifting out of the blackness.

"And they cast out many devils," Handel said, "and anointed with oil many that were sick, and healed them."

Adamson then saw Handel pour something into his hand from a bottle and toss it at the fence. He punctuated what it was that he was saying with this motion again and again. From where Adamson was, it appeared as if the priest was splashing the liquid onto the fence as well as whatever lay beyond. It was then that Adamson caught sight of the crowd of UDs that had gathered on the other side of the barrier. There must have been a dozen or so huddled around where the priest stood. The weird thing was that they weren't acting excited or aggressive in any way. They simply stood and stared as if transfixed. One of them pressed his face against the chain link and Adamson could just make out the thing's lips moving, almost as if it were trying to speak.

Whatever was going on here was weird and Adamson didn't like it one bit.

"Handel?"

The priest turned abruptly at the sound of his name. The bottle he was holding slipped from his grasp and hit the floor with an eruption of liquid sloshing out from its open mouth. The expression on the man's face was like that of a kid who'd been caught stealing money out of his mother's purse—embarrassment and guilt all wrapped in one wide-mouthed gape.

"A...A... Adamson," he said and his voice quivered nervously.

"Mind if I ask what you are doing here?" Adamson inquired, having come closer to view the makeshift altar that had been created. A silver crucifix hung from a nail driven into the wall behind where Handel stood. The priest was dressed in an elaborate clerical gown and a small leather bag laid on the ground at his feet. Whatever he was up to, it was obvious he'd put a lot of planning into it.

"I... uh... I..." he stammered and then abruptly regained his composure and stood erect. "I am giving them..." and he looked around as if unsure of exactly how to explain... "the Last Rites."

"You're... what?"

"We've talked about this before, Jeffrey... These are still God's children and they deserve some level of our sympathy. The League refuses to acknowledge that. I cannot."

The two of them had indeed had discussions about Handel's theories on The Dead and, every time they did, Adamson found it difficult to believe what he was hearing.

Sympathy?

From all of his time working with The Dead, Adamson had learned one thing—these were dangerous and unpredictable creatures with no sense of humanity left in them, much less a soul. They were, in many respects, like tigers that had developed a taste for man's flesh. They could appear docile, but it was only because they were looking for an opening through which to get their claws into something. Something solid. Something wet. Any semblance of their humanity had been stripped away long ago.

"Do you know the trouble you could get into—the trouble I could get into—if you end up getting yourself injured... or worse? If someone were to find you here they'd think you'd gone nuts."

"I know. I know. But these are—these were—still people, first and foremost. They are not monsters. They are people who have been changed, transformed if you will, but they still deserve to be given absolution by the Lord God."

"Father... with all due respect... Are you out of your fuckin' mind? Yeah, ok... They were people... once... but whatever they were, whatever it was that made them them, was burned away a long time ago." Adamson ran his hand over his face in exasperation. "Dammit, how many times must we go over this?"

Handel shook his head in disgust. He simply refused to believe what he was hearing. He'd seen it, seen it with his own eyes. The Dead... they understood, they remembered. Hadn't one of them tried to speak to him just a moment ago? What he'd heard was not some random vocalization. It was the completion of a prayer... which suggested comprehension and context.

"Look, Father..." Adamson continued, "back in the day, I was holed up in a restaurant's store room for a few days. One of these things broke in and stumbled around the kitchen for a few hours. It rattled pots and pans, it broke open the door on one of the walk-in refrigerators, and from the sounds of things, it was making itself quite the little banquet. When I finally got up the nerve to sneak a peek into the room I saw it hacking away at its own hand with a meat cleaver. The fuckin' thing chopped off one of its fingers and was stuffing it into its own damned mouth."

Handel looked away and stared at the group of UDs through the fence. Their open and empty expressions met his. The one who'd spoken was now stupidly chewing on the metal wire of the fence.

"These are not intelligent beings, Father," Adamson said with as much sympathy as he could muster. "They are mindless killing and eating machines. No offense, but God turned his back on them a long time ago; back when they all went flat-line."

"No... you are wrong."

"No, Father... I am right. These creatures are without both intellect and soul. They are empty shells which act like people for only as long as they can get their filthy hands on us. The sole thing keeping them from ripping you apart right now is that they can't figure out how to get through that fuckin' fence."

Handel silently stared at Adamson for a long time and a range of emotions washed over his face as he did so: sorrow, regret, contempt, fear, condescension... It was obvious to him, as it had been since their first discussions on the topic, that this was not a battle he would ever win. Adamson, much like many others, had made his mind up with regard to The Dead. Nothing could change that. The best Handel could hope for was a stalemate; a philosophical détente.

Handel suddenly smiled and nodded. If he were to be able to continue his work, he'd have to get Adamson's... agreement, if not his blessing. A new tact may be in order.

After all,there was more than one way to skin a cat.

"Look, you're probably right. Perhaps they are unable to understand, perhaps I am truly just wasting my time. But then again it's not like I'm hurting anything, right?"

Adamson regarded the priest with a puzzled expression. It was true no one was being harmed by any of this. If the old man wanted to splash some water on the fence and think he was saving some souls, where was the real harm in that? Besides, a part of Adamson felt as if some small act of benevolence was missing in this place. So much brutality was directed at the UDs on a daily basis, some slight bit of consideration wasn't completely out of the question. After all, wasn't that what laid at the heart of everything he'd been taught and had tried to do during his funeral director days? Provided the old guy didn't get too close to the fence and get himself tagged, there really was no harm done.

"Look," Adamson said and he stepped slightly closer to Handel in an almost conspiratory manner, "I might be willing to turn a blind eye to what you're doing here, but..."

He ran his hand through his stringy hair making it lay flat against his skull with a wet look. There was no workable solution to any of this. He knew The League would be pissed if they ever caught wind of any of it. He also knew the depths of Father Handel's convictions. Over their past discussions, he'd become convinced that the priest thought he was doing the right thing; that he was indeed doing God's work. Even if Adamson forbade him from pulling this shit ever again, he knew that it would do no good. Handel would find a way to make it happen one way or another. By hook or by crook, the priest would make his way in or even bribe one of the guards to allow him to do just what he'd been doing all along.

Adamson looked at Father Handel and saw the passion burning within the man's eyes. Who was he to stand in the way of that? After all, maybe there was a God up there somewhere and all of this shit was just another stage in His master plan?

Who was to say?

Adamson sighed in resignation. "Look, Father, I've got a shift change to co-ordinate. I want you to pack your gear up and leave—for now. We'll talk about this some other time, ok? In the meantime, I'll promise I'll check with Corporate and see if I can get you some kind of special exemption. Maybe have you go through the same training our guards receive."

Adamson looked at the priest for a hint of compliance.

The priest smiled and nodded.

It wasn't the resounding concurrence Adamson was looking for, but it would have to do.

And with that, Adamson reluctantly turned and left. Over his shoulder he called back, "I'll be returning in about twenty minutes. I don't want you here when I come back."

"Twenty minutes. Got it."

Handel watched Adamson as he walked away. When he was out of sight he bent to retrieve his Holy Water and poured more of it into the palm of his hand.

After all, it was the only Christian thing to do.

Braggadocio

The Octagon looked bleak and decidedly inhospitable as it sat in the darkness at the far end of the nearly empty Training Hall. Residual steam rose in swirling clouds above the fighting space; smoky tendrils reaching out for purchase in the open beams of the ceiling. Lights blazed from above, hot and suffocating, illuminating every inch of the pit. The shadows had been effectively pushed back and dared not battle the light in this place.

Down in the Pit, Monk stood with his feet planted firmly in the sand. He held two reins out in front of him, caressing them as if he were running his fingers through a lover's hair. Standing roughly six feet behind the harnessed UD, he held the thing on a short, but very effective lead. Headgear was strapped tightly over the thing's head; lengths of leather bound by dull, metal clasps. A short baton of hard rubber acted as a bite block. The setup prevented the diseased mouth of the UD from getting a grip on anything or, God forbid, actually getting a hold of anyone. It wasn't pretty, but it made handling them more or less safe. Despite all of the preventative measures and specialized equipment, Monk still kept a fully loaded shotgun propped against the wall... just in case.

The dead thing at the end of the reins shuffled and stumbled its way across the sand, intently focusing its gaze on Cleese as he crouched before it. While its gait was off-kilter to begin with, its present lack of coordination was mostly due to Monk pulling on the lengths of leather now and again, dragging it off balance. You know, for safety's sake. The thing reached out its hands pleadingly for Cleese like a child asking for a beloved toy. Its fingers were splayed and pumping. An anxious look of expectancy lit up its slackened features.

And all the while, its jaws were working. Its mouth ground back and forth and drooled, hungering for just a taste of the living meat which danced before it just out of reach.

Even though Monk heard all about how Cleese was some sort of prodigy and had even seen a bit of his talents for himself, he was still mighty impressed. The kid was a little unsure here and there, but all in all he was as close as Monk had seen to a sure-as-shit natural. He flowed when he should, stood firm when he needed to and he didn't make too many stupid mistakes. He fought with a Zen-like calm that was not too different from the way some of the Budo Warriors did, only Cleese brought a shitload more power and aggression to the party. There was none of that "bend like a reed in the wind" shit in him.

Nope. None at all.

The way Cleese worked was nothing short of inspired. Whenever he went to the inside, the UD would reach out to strike and as if by magic Cleese would no longer be there. It was as if he'd vanished into thin air only to reappear on the thing's flank—on its weak side. It was then, when he was safely in the dead thing's blind spot, that he'd strike with a devastating impact.

Monk couldn't imagine what this kid was going to be like once he got used to being around these things and they put him into Live Combat. He mentally noted a need to talk with Adamson about increasing the number of UDs they kept in The Pen. This kid was going to send a lot of them out of here in pieces.

Despite his natural acumen, mental acuity and physical superiority, he was still holding back. It was like he was there in body, but his spirit was off lurking in some darkened nether region of his brain. Monk almost got the impression that Cleese didn't want to hurt the damn things. Silently, he wondered if maybe he ought to give Cleese a bottle of hootch just to help him recapture a bit of the mindset that brought him here.

Monk smiled almost imperceptibly as he watched Cleese wrestle with what was left of his conscience. At first he was all gung-ho. Then you could see the seed of his scruples sprout. After that, his consternation was evident from his furrowed brow and lack of commitment. After a bit, Monk decided it was time to cut the crap.

"Listen you stupid shit," Monk shouted as he jerked the UD back around. "You really need to hit 'em harder. It's what they're fuckin' here for. They're goddamn training aids."

Monk wrenched the leads violently and threw the UD so far off its balance that it pitched over sideways. Blood dribbled out of its mouth and landed on the sand dyeing it a deep maroon.

"What the fuck are you holding back for? For fuck's sake... It's not like they're gonna get pissed atcha. I mean... goddamnit ! They're not even human any longer. They gave up being that a long time ago."

Cleese looked at him and frowned. He took a long look at the dead woman in the harness staggering to her feet. Her face was an angry, hungry grimace; her body a horribly ruined shell. Still though... she'd been somebody's wife once... or some-body's mother or....

Slowly, he dropped his hands to his sides.

"Man, that's just despicable. She was a person once... What about her? Huh? What about her family? Do they even know what's happened to her?"

Monk let the reins slip through his fingers a little and the short fat woman in the soiled housecoat who looked like she might have been somebody's grandmother jumped Cleese. The two of them fell to the ground in a mass of flailing arms and kicking legs. Her hands clawed and scratched their way across his chest. Her jaws opened and snapped shut as they descended with a remarkable quickness toward his throat.

Abruptly, Monk yanked her back, sending her sprawling onto the sand.

Cleese looked up from flat on his back.

"Motherfucker..." Cleese gasped.

"Never forget why you're here, Captain Fuckin' Sensitive."

Cleese quickly ran his hands over his torso, obsessively looking for any lacera-tions.

"These things will eat your fucking liver just as soon as look at you," Monk shouted, "and don't you ever fucking forget that!"

Monk yanked the woman roughly to her feet by tugging on a strap at the back of the bridle. He quickly released her and, planting his boot in the small of her back, kicked her toward the center of the pit.

"And you know what? Fuck their families!" he shouted. "They've all been well compensated. You don't need to worry about none of that. All you need to remember is the shit I tol' you: 'grab—kill—and move on.' You got me?"

Cleese looked at him angrily.

"Huh?!?" Monk repeated. "Do you fuckin' remember having that goddamn conversation? Look, you do what I taught you, you dumb sonofabitch. Do it or I let Granny Clampett here eat your dick on a toasted Hoagie bun. Are we fuckin' clear, Cherry?"

Cleese unhappily nodded his understanding.

"Now," Monk said, pulling the woman back to her feet by her reins and wheeling her around, "pretty please... will you fuckin' punch this cunt?"

Cleese scrambled back to his feet and strode toward his target, his hands coming up into an open-handed, ready position. The closer he got, the more determined he looked. With his brow set and his mouth firm, he lowered his chin toward his sternum and came on like a freight train.

Briefly, even Monk was taken aback by the look on his face. For a second he almost felt sorry for the dead thing at the end of the lead. She was standing at Ground Zero and her jacked-up brain didn't even know it—but she was sure as hell about to find out.

The woman reached out for Cleese the instant she saw him; moaning coarsely and salivating over her bite block. Monk gave her a little more of the lead and she staggered hungrily toward Cleese. As she closed in, another rope of blood and drool dribbled past the bite block and hit her chest. Now within just a few feet, the woman raised her arms and reached out hungrily.

Cleese responded in an exquisite fashion. He ducked under the grab, bobbing briskly, and then hook-punched her—hard—in the chest. Muhammad Ali himself would have been proud. With the force of the punch, the woman's ribs caved in with a sickening crunch. A splinter of bone carved its way loose and proceeded to tear through one of the lobes of her lungs. Any further attempt she made at vocalizing suddenly sounded raw and painful.

As her body bent from the blow, Cleese delivered a fast Muay Thai knee strike to the right side of her jaw setting it to hang loosely from her skull. Unceremoniously, he threw the thick musculature of his back into a savage palm—strike directed at the back of her head. Monk tried to pull her out of the way, but Cleese's blow came too damn fast. Her skull made a hollow "clu-chunk" sound; like an over-ripe melon being dropped. Her occipital bone fractured and shards of skull tore through the spoiled grey matter beyond. Her face abruptly went slack as if the very life had been kicked out of her, and it had. She took two drunken steps forward and fell face first into the sand where she didn't move again.

"Ooooo-k, shit..." Monk said, dropping the reins to the ground in disgust. "That was pretty goddamn effective, but still utterly useless for our purposes here today. You're going to need to learn some control, my friend. You need to learn to dole that shit out like it was medicine. Now, we'll have to go harness us up another one."

"Not today you won't..."

A voice from the pit's entrance punctuated the sweltering air.

"It's 1900, Monk, and my time in the pit."

Lenik walked out onto the sand with Cartwright trailing behind him like a scolded puppy. Cartwright carefully shut the hatch behind them and dutifully followed after his partner. The fighter came toward them, walking as if he owned the place. With his chest pushed out and his shoulders squared back, he looked like he thought he was really something special.

Monk, Cleese, and every other fighter—with perhaps the exception of Cloverfield, Shenkel, Gonzales and Llewellyn—knew better.

They'd already talked about how doomed Lenik and Cartwright's relationship was. Cartwright was an experienced fighter, but Lenik had the stronger personality and the bigger mouth and when an inexperienced student usurped a competent teacher it always ended in disaster—for them both.

"You ladies'll have to go play elsewhere. It's time for you to let a real man work." Lenik said, nudging his mentor. As he walked past Cleese, Lenik looked at the dead woman in the sand and hissed, "Real nice…" as he rolled his eyes.

"No problem. We were just leaving," Monk replied casually. "Say, be a sport and clean this shit up, will ya?" He waved his hand over the dead woman. "I mean, it is your time in the pit after all."

"Hey fuck you, Monk!" Lenik whined. "I ain't cleaning this!"

"Heya, Cartwright," nodded Monk as he passed the older man.

Grabbing up his shotgun, Monk walked out without looking back.

Cartwright stared back at Monk and said nothing. His face was set, but his eyes told a different story. For a brief moment he almost seemed embarrassed by Lenik's behavior. Slowly, he walked over and pulled the dead UD by her headgear toward the side of the pit.

Cleese smiled broadly at the two men and followed Monk out of the pit and up to where the older man was stowing his shotgun in a rack just outside the door. Beyond that, the cool calm of the grandstands waited like an oasis in the desert.

"That sonofabitch," Monk hissed as the two of them sat cooling down in the stands.

Cleese leaned back, resting his upper body's weight on his elbows. He was busy trying to get his heart rate and body temperature back to normal after his exertion in the pit, but Monk… Monk seemed intent on raising his high enough to give himself a stroke. If Cleese had learned anything since meeting the old man, it was that he was prone to explosions of anger. After he calmed down he'd forget all about whatever it was that he felt slighted him—whether real or imagined. Then it would be business as usual and he'd return to his normal cantankerous self.

"I oughtta go pop that young punk right in the fuckin' mouth," the old man grumbled.

"Easy there, Trigger."

"You know I'm going to hear all about that shit from the suits upstairs…" he jerked his head back toward the pit. "But…" and he chuckled guiltily, "I couldn't resist."

"Would 'sorry' help?" asked Cleese, feigning embarrassment.

"I mean, look at him," Monk said, ignoring the interruption. He pointed back toward the lights of The Octagon with a stubby finger. "What a fuckin' asshole!"

Lenik was standing down on the sand in the middle of some defensive drills. Easy shit mostly, just getting in close and batting advances away with his protected forearms. Cleese had learned that kind of crap a long time ago, back when he was a kid and had to fight off the older kids for what little lunch money he'd been able to scrape together. As he watched the fighter before him, he took a minute and and evaluated his potential.

Now that he had an opportunity to see him in action, Lenik was—in Cleese's considered opinion—more of that cannon fodder he'd noticed when he first arrived. The man talked some shit, but when it was all said and done he had a nasty habit of leaving his right side exposed time and again. He was ripe for an attack from his blind periphery or even from behind. He was over-confident and stupid and he would no doubt be carried out of here on a litter.

By now Monk managed to calm himself down and took an interest in what it was that Cleese was looking at in the pit.

Cleese saw him out of the corner of his eye and nudged him.

"Toes up..." Cleese said, nodding toward the pit.

Monk nodded in return.

"Ain't that shit the truth?"

"Hey, Cleese...!" came a sudden and unexpected shout from under the lights.

"What do you want, Lenik?" returned Monk.

"Let me show ya a thing or two... Something that old man of yours would never demonstrate in a million years!"

Out of curiosity, Cleese sat up and focused his attention down onto the pit's floor.

Lenik sauntered over to the UD (a male about forty-five in a soiled button-down business shirt and tie) and, in one a fluid motion, tore off the headgear and tossed it aside. Mr. Shirt-and-Tie stood dumbfounded for a second, rolling his head about in drunken circles. Lenik backed away from the man and drew the machete he wore strapped to his thigh.

Cartwright moved across the pit, shaking his head at his partner's actions, to retrieve the harness. It was pretty clear that Lenik did this kind of showboating all the time.

"Stooopid shit..." Monk groaned as he rose to his feet.

Lenik crouched, waving the weapon in front of him as if it were a magic wand.

The UD stood still for a second, grabbing hold of what little bearings its dead mind could muster, and took a tentative step toward Lenik. Then it stopped and looked up toward the lights. It stood still for a second, sniffing at the air as if trying to sort it all out. Then, abruptly, the dead man lunged screeching toward one side.

It grabbed a very surprised-looking Cartwright from behind, knocking him forward and off his feet. The old man never saw it coming. Both Cartwright and Mr. Shirt-and-Tie fell face-first to the sand with a grunt. The UD's face bounced off Cartwright's back. Long goblets of saliva left puddles of mucous behind in a circular pattern. The thing quickly angled its head, moving as if by instinct, toward the exposed nape of Cartwright's neck.

Cartwright only had time to marvel at the speed with which the dead man moved before his blood ran in thick streams down the back of his tunic.

Surprised, Lenik shouted and did the unthinkable. He jumped on top of the two men.

Cleese almost had to laugh out loud at the sheer stupidity of the man. It knew no bounds! Any fighter worth his salt knew that you never jumped into a brawl that was already on the ground. Your legs often got tangled up in the multitude of flailing limbs. You slipped. You fell. You spent the rest of your night getting to know the tip of some guy's (or a group of his friends') boots as he tried to kick in your sternum.

Cleese and Monk reflexively came off the benches and sprinted around the railing and toward the pit's entrance. They instinctively knew that whatever was going to happen in the pit would already be decided by the time they got there, but that didn't stop them from trying. Lenik would have either hacked Mr. Shirt-and-Tie's head from his shoulders with his pig sticker or the dead man would be sucking up Lenik's blood like gravy. There just wasn't a lot that they could do to prevent the outcome.

It was safe to say that Cartwright got tagged. From the way they went down and with Lenik now in the mix to further fuck up the situation, this was not going to end well. The last image Cleese could recall of the scene had a lot of crimson in it, and that was never good.

Not in this game.

The two men made their way rapidly along the gangway, rounded the stairwell and burst through the door to the pit. As they came running through the hatch, they saw Mr. Shirt-and-Tie bent over Lenik happily chomping away on a chunk of the man's exposed stomach. A wet, smacking sound echoed hopelessly within the emptiness of the pit.

Monk, who'd forgotten his shotgun in his haste, came up behind the zombie and deftly slid his protected right arm under the thing's gnawing mouth, just across its throat and under the jaw. He braced his left arm behind the thing's head and clamped down like a vice.

He quickly glanced downward and found himself staring into Lenik's eyes. Despite the fact that the guy was an asshole, Monk was saddened as he watched the fighter's life drain out of his gaze and his breathing stutter to a stop. As he died, his mouth quivered and one eye drifted closed.

Monk wrenched his gaze away and torqued down on the UDs neck, making sure he felt the cervical vertebrae tighten and bind up. Then, he bore down with all of his strength.

The crunch of the thing's neck breaking was almost silent. Cleese had cracked his knuckles and made more noise. It sounded almost like it would have been a relief, like when a dislocated shoulder popped and the bone fell back into place.

Mr. Shirt-and-Tie made a small sharp snort and then his body just sort of deflated into itself. Monk threw his body aside like it was a sack of shit and quickly bent over to check on Lenik. It was pretty obvious from the extent of the wound and the amount of blood splashed about that the man was truly dead.

Monk's shoulders sagged and his head dropped in frustration. No matter how many times he'd seen fighters die, it always broke his heart, even an asshole like Lenik. He suddenly jerked his head to the side as remembered Cartwright. He swiftly looked up at Cleese.

"Check him," Monk commanded and he pointed at Cartwright.

"Check him?" Cleese asked dumb-founded. "Check him for what?"

"To see if he's still alive."

"Are you fuckin' crazy? His throat's torn out!"

"What...?" Monk's face screwed up and he squinted. He looked over at Cartwright and, as if seeing him for the first time, noticed how badly the man had been hurt.

"Ah, fuck..."

☠ ☠ ☠

Chivalry

Before...

    A murky haze hovered over the campground that had been set up high in the hills of the Golden State National Recreation Area. The dense fog blanketed the assorted tents, trailers, and mobile homes in a thick, swirling miasma and gave the place an ethereal, dream-like quality. The mist carried with it the sweet smell of the dew-moistened foliage as well as the throat-clogging scent of burnt wood. The odor left everything smelling like a campfire doused by a sudden rain. Groups of people milled about the compound, some in search of food or water while others scoped out places to get medical attention or some much needed sleep.

    Everyone in the camp went about their business, but they all had that wide-eyed look of someone who'd survived something dark and terrible. With eyebrows perpetually raised and the whites of their eyes visible around an open-irised glare, their gazes flitted about nervously, as if expecting whatever it was that had spooked them before might return to wreak havoc again. The more resilient and well-grounded of them had been able to quickly adapt to their new lives here in the camp over the last few weeks. A few had even managed to rediscover laughter and the easy manner in which people were able to become friends. Others though... They would forever wear the emotional and, in some cases, physical scars of what had been carved into them by seeing and doing things they were still only barely able to articulate.

    Off to one side of the main area sat a couple of large tents where several husky men cleaned and repaired the vast array of guns which had been found or brought to the camp. Boxes of ammunition scavenged from a nearby National Guard base lay stacked on large wooden pallets toward the back of the tent. The ordnance had been liberated by a few of the foraging crews routinely sent out on midday runs into the once bustling metropolis at the base of the foothills. These teams had even been able to pick up a few Guardsmen found barricaded in one of the rooms on the base. The soldiers had come in real handy, acquainting the gunsmiths with some of the more exotic weaponry found in their armory. Hastily nailed together wooden racks of Rugers, Berettas, Colts, Brownings, Mossbergs and even a few compound bows were lined up inside the tent while the hardware being worked was spread out on tables in the early morning light.

    The gunsmiths talked and laughed, but mostly just bullshitted with one another as they adeptly refurbished and reassembled the guns before them without giving them much of a verifying glance. If they hadn't already had a comprehensive knowledge of the armaments when they came here they did now, if only through the sheer repetition of constant maintenance and repair. The ability to field strip, oil and reassemble a weapon—or quickly learn how—was an essential skill here. It was the only thing keeping them from being drafted into doing the "snatch and grabs" that the other—less knowledgeable—men were doing. These excursions into the highly dangerous surrounding areas were not something anyone wanted to be a part of. Out there, it wasn't a matter of if you'd get hurt, it was a simple matter of when.

In the center of the camp, around which most of the activity took place, two "roach coaches" were parked back to back. Plumes of greasy smoke billowed from the exhaust vents on their roofs. In the cramped space between them was a makeshift larder where vegetables and assorted dry goods were prepped for cooking. Off to one side, a gas powered generator hummed as it fed a series of freezers, where the meat was kept, and refrigerators which were used to store dairy, eggs, and some medicines. Teams of men and women in oil-spattered clothing worked diligently, making sandwiches, hamburgers, hot dogs and lots of hot coffee. This was an army now and, as any soldier knew, a successful army ran on a full belly. It was these folks' job to keep the group fed and it was one that they took pretty seriously. Even though they were forced to play things a little bit on the frugal side when it came to rationing their stores, there was still enough in the larder to keep them all sufficiently nourished.

Around the armory and food supply, a dozen mobile homes were arranged in a loose circle. Around them, various styles of tents clustered like newborn pups around their mother. Along the outer edge of the perimeter—on hunting stands mounted in the trees—sharpshooters sat silently whiling away the time with Sudoku puzzle books or water-damaged porn magazines. Each guard made sure to keep his eyes moving in a vigilant triangle: left side, right side, magazine. If anyone or anything was so unfortunate as to venture into his eye-line and did not move with the stride or purpose of a living person, it would soon be greeted by some very precise bullet placement. The men in the trees were put there for a very good reason. Lifelong hunters, they'd proven themselves time and again and could shoot the balls off of a flea at a hundred yards.

All in all, these folks had become an efficient and well-honed survival organism. They'd had no choice but to do so. After experiencing some of the things they had recently, they'd needed to come together quickly and luckily their cohesion had met remarkably few speed bumps. Yes, there were a few of your garden variety personality conflicts and even fewer vain attempts at "power grabs," but for the most part things were going smoothly. Cataclysm had a way of doing that—of forging alliances between the most unlikely of parties. Whether a person was young or old, rich or poor, Democrat or Republican, these folks instinctively knew that they would need to put their differences aside if they were to all survive. They'd been given a role and a purpose and each was imminently aware of the fact that survival depended on them doing exactly what they'd been asked to do. If one of them was lax in his duties, then all of them potentially would suffer. And now that the world was getting spun on its collective ass, suffering meant a hell of a lot more than some hurt feelings or a few skinned knees.

As the group went about its business, a sudden shout erupted from the tree-line on the south side of the encampment. Talk of the alarm and what it might mean rippled quickly through the crowd. This isolated place had been chosen on purpose and any encroachment from the outside was news. As a result, any word of what was happening in the real world was both welcomed... and feared.

A teenage girl who'd been delivering food and thermoses of coffee to the sharp-shooters out on the perimeter came sprinting through the tents and RVs and into the center of camp. She wore a pair of faded denim overalls, a cream-colored thermal shirt and had her hair pulled up in high pigtails which accentuated her face. She was barely eighteen, but there was a beautiful woman blossoming there and more than a few of the men in camp were beginning to notice. The girl ran—sidestepping people and jumping over obstacles—without stopping until she reached the armory tents. Her gait stumbled to a stop and she fought to catch her breath before trying to speak.

Bob Wolf, head gunsmith and the unofficial leader of this militia, set the Browning BAR Safari he was working on aside and walked from around his worktable. He approached the panting girl and held his hand out to offer her some stability. Wolf was a big man with long graying hair and a full salt-and-pepper beard. Even though he was a little thick in the middle he still looked like one tough customer. He was the kind of man who, due to his past as both a decorated veteran and an ex-biker, led naturally. His history and level of experience gave him an unquestioned air of authority. When he talked, people listened. It was a large part of the reason why they'd turned to him when the rules of the world got abruptly changed. He was younger than one might expect, given the responsibility he now shouldered, but he wore the mantle of leadership well. The red in his eyes, however showed he was also a bit overwhelmed by the present situation.

"Jenny?" he said paternally, putting his hand on her shoulder and steadying her. "Catch your breath, honey and tell us... what's the matter?"

Jenny Maguire panted and drew heaving lungfuls of air into her chest. She looked up at Wolf excitedly. When she tried to speak, her voice came out in asthmatic gasps.

"Take it easy, child," Wolf said, his voice sounded grizzled but still holding a sense of reassurance. The gathered crowd leaned in as one to listen to what the girl had to say.

"A...a...a..." Jenny barked, "a man."

"Where?"

"At... at the northwest tree-line."

"They found some people?" someone in the crowd asked.

She shook her head back and forth, tossing her hair about like kite tails swirling in the wind.

"No... just... one... one man."

Cleese sat at the end of a long picnic table, aggressively wiping slices of bread across the plate in front of him. His eyes roamed over his surroundings warily as he stuffed fingers full of food into his mouth. It had been a while since he'd eaten actual cooked food and the fare these people were serving up warmed his stomach and stuck to his ribs.

With every mouthful, his head became clearer and thinking back, the last memory he had of a full meal was the one at the bar, before everything went to shit. He'd just finished eating and was about to settle down to spend the evening indulging in his favorite sport—competitive drinking—when things got hazy. He had a dim recollection of some commotion that had started after something had been broadcast on the television, a foggy memory of people talking excitedly about some crazy shit.

The bits of conversation he was able to pull from the sludge of his memory seemed like something out of a horror movie more than anything else. Then there'd been the sound of wood splintering and his memory of the night blurred into visions of pale faces with gnashing teeth, punches being thrown, and the sticky sensation of blood on his hands.

The next thing he knew, he was walking in the early morning sunshine and nursing one hell of a hangover. After that, it had been what seemed like days and days of running and fighting and the constant struggle to make his way through the city and across the bridge. The memories of that time were not anything he wanted to hold onto. He preferred to let them lurk at the furthest periphery of his thoughts, for they offered him little solace. Once across the bridge, he'd decided the best plan was to put some distance between him and where he knew the dead lurked by heading into the woods. He could figure things out once he had some time to rest and get an idea of exactly what the fuck had happened—and how bad it all was. That little plan was interrupted when he was stopped by Wolf's heavily armed men.

Flash forward to the present and Cleese finding himself here.

After a quick but welcomed shower, change of clothes, and food, he was ready to have some of his questions answered. Unfortunately, the things he was hearing didn't make any more sense than his memories did.

Wolf sat across from him and was just finishing his explanation of what was now what. Cleese listened carefully as he polished off a heel of bread coated with the last remnant of his meal. On any other day, he would have called the man a "bullshitter" if he was being nice or a "fucking liar" if he wasn't and then sent him packing. Today though, some core of his intellect, some small shard of his drunken memory, was able to vouch for the veracity of the man's story; no matter how far-fetched.

"So," Wolf concluded and sat back in his seat, "that's where we are. The dead aren't exactly obliged to stay dead any longer, and as you well know it's pretty dangerous out there."

The young girl in ponytails suddenly appeared at Wolf's side and set two cups of steaming coffee before them. She cast a quick, yet surreptitious glance at Cleese.

"Thank you, Jenny," Wolf said and smiled at her in gratitude.

Cleese half-stood and thanked her with a reflexive slight bow. The girl looked at him and smiled. Then, as quickly as she'd come she disappeared back into the crowd.

Cleese grinned as he sat and looked at the steaming cup. Picking up the Styrofoam cylinder, his hands were instantly warmed by the hot smoky fluid within. The first sip sent cascades of warm flavor down his throat. Cleese kept the cup at his lips and blew across the rim. Breathing in the rich aroma, he cast his gaze into the surrounding crowd. His eyes were met by a small sea of normal—albeit frightened—faces. The interesting thing was not one of them stood out as exceptional. These were not soldiers, not by any stretch of the imagination. What he saw was the run-of-the-mill faces of grocers, students, delivery drivers, businessmen, and cashiers; all of them just regular people who'd been thrust into a nightmare far beyond their wildest reckoning. Hot on the heels of that thought came the realization that unless things radically changed in the world, the vast majority of them would be dead inside of a month.

"We've managed to make a safe place for ourselves up here," Wolf continued, "but it's still pretty touch and go. We have supplies. We have food and ammunition. But we know all too well that one—just one—of those things getting inside the perimeter would mean the death of every one of us."

As Cleese drank his coffee and pondered all that he'd been told, a pot-bellied man stepped out of the crowd and sat down uninvited next to Wolf. The guy gave off a bitter vibe due mostly to the perpetual look of disgust on his face; the expression of someone who'd just stepped on a slug in his bare feet. From his build, Cleese could tell the guy had some muscle on him back in the day; probably from playing high school ball. These days though, he was just another fat guy who was way past his prime, laboring under the misconception that he was a whole lot harder than he really was.

"Enough of this shit, Bob," the guy interrupted. The man tried to look Cleese dead in the eye and push his dominance. Cleese stared back unimpressed. In his day, he had given hundreds of fat slobs like this the bum's rush; tossing them onto their asses out of the back doors of more bars than he could count. In the end, it wasn't Cleese who looked away.

"Cleese," Wolf said as a way of introducing this pudgy asshole, "this is Fred Bartlett. He's been helping out with scheduling the security watch around the camp and leading some of the recon runs into town."

"Charmed," Cleese said to Bartlett and, as if in dismissal, returned his gaze to Wolf.

Bartlett returned his gaze to Cleese for a moment and his sneer intensified. He snorted in what passed for disgust and then went back to his obviously prepared bit of bravado.

"So, tell me... Cleese was it?" he said with an exaggerated smirk. "How is it that you—all alone—made it out of the city in one piece? Everyone we've run into out there has been either severely injured or infected. Yet, here you are... neither one of those things."

"What can I say, Fred?" Cleese responded wryly. "I'm a talented motherfucker and a mean, mean man."

Bartlett turned and rolled his eyes exaggeratedly to the obvious appreciation of his collected short bus of sycophants off to the side. There was the bespectacled bald guy who looked like a pharmacist, the Polack with the big nose and clown hat of hair on his head, the ex-corporate suck-up who was now playing at survivalist tough guy, and the dark complexioned dude with the even darker circles under his eyes. This confederacy of dunces watched over Bartlett like he was their own personal Jesus.

Something told Cleese that these dopes would soon become a major sore in his ass. He chalked it up as little more than a hunch, but if experience had taught him anything, it was that his hunches were rarely wrong.

"Well, I don't know about any of that, but..." Bartlett said, looking back incredulously, "I'm of the opinion that you're either one of the luckiest men on the face of the earth... or, and this is much more likely, that your story is full of more holes than a block of Swiss cheese."

"Well, shit, Fro-derick... that just plain ain't nice," Cleese responded with a slow smile. "You wound me."

As this exchange was transpiring, Wolf's gaze drifted over the assembled crowd, judging their mood. He quickly realized that this avenue of bickering and macho posturing was proving to be a fruitless one and would, in the end, be antithetical to them continuing to work together as a team.

"Well, whatever..." Wolf interrupted. "You know as well as I do, Fred, we all have our stories and maybe Cleese will share his one day. Right now though, we still have a schedule to keep and there's enough of the day left that we can do that run into the 'burbs and recon that strip mall we saw last time out. I'm convinced that pharmacy has some shit we can use. Agreed?"

Bartlett cocked a sideways grin and nodded. He figured that whatever Cleese's story turned out to be, they would get to the bottom of it soon enough. They'd all see him for what he was—a fraud—and they'd see that he'd been lying about where he'd come from and what he'd done. Awkwardly, he stood up and took a step away from the table.

"Cleese," Wolf continued, "you're welcome to stay here for as long as you'd like, but we'll need to find something for you to do, some way to contribute. No one rides for free around here and you look pretty able-bodied."

Cleese nodded. "I'm happy to help in any way I can."

Bartlett, who'd taken another step toward the crowd, stopped and looked back over his shoulder. A wide grin of smug self-satisfaction spread across his face. It was pretty obvious he'd done himself a bit of quick thinking.

"Hey, Wolf... How'z about we get Mr. Talented here started by having him come with us to check out that drug store?" Bartlett suggested. "We'll get him a gun and I can show him the ropes."

Both Cleese and Wolf saw the idea for precisely what it was—an opportunity for Bartlett to establish a pecking order with the New Guy. It was a move that would by definition put Cleese in a subservient role.

Bartlett figured to use it as an opportunity to put Cleese in the shit and when he went pussy, he'd be exposed for what he was—a phony and a coward.

Cleese knew it would be fine and perhaps even shut this fuckin' idiot up once and for all.

Wolf shook his head and was about to shoot the idea down, but Cleese quickly interrupted him.

"That sounds like a swell idea, Freddie Boy and maybe, while we're out there, we can get us some matching tee shirts. You know... his and hers."

Wolf looked at Cleese and thought that there just might be more to the guy than what met the eye. Sure, he had the look of someone who had been in some scrapes, but his relaxed manner said there weren't a lot of situations he felt he couldn't handle. If nothing else, a couple of things would become apparent. First, they'd get a chance to see how well Cleese handled himself under pressure. Second, Cleese just might take Bartlett down a few notches. It sounded like a win-win to Wolf.

Wolf looked at Cleese and gave him an appraising stare.

"Listen, friend..." he said, "right now, the Asshole-to-Good Guy ratio is at an all-time low around here. I'd like to keep it that way. Now, I don't know you from Adam, but you strike me as someone who can handle himself and may just come in handy."

Wolf stroked his beard and stared more intently.

"I'm going to put a modicum of trust in you in the hopes that you don't fuck up and make me regret it. Sound fair?"

Cleese shook Wolf's hand and said, "Fair enough."

Wolf nodded to him and then looked over at Bartlett.

"Go get your team ready, Fred. I'll get Cleese a gun and have him ready in twenty."

Through the binoculars, the drug store they'd come to recon sat like a monolith at the far end of the lifeless parking lot. As he sat in the passenger's seat of a mid-sized Self-Haul truck, Cleese lowered the eyepiece and looked over at Bartlett. Seeing the human facial equivalent of a dial tone, he shook his head in disgust and raised the glasses back up to his eyes to get a more comprehensive look at what they were up against.

Past the trees and down the hill, the pale cement and red brick of the store's geometrically designed façade gave the building a cold, sanitized appearance. A large blue and white sign which read "Accinelli's Drugs" hung from the flat face of the building, its vivid color a bright and contrasting eyesore. Across the sweltering tarmac, two buildings were set at right angles, half-framing the parking lot around the pharmacy. Their retail spaces were a mixture of small specialty shops: a beauty shop, an Indian restaurant, a sandwich joint, and a mailing store. A few cars were sporadically parked about the lot, abandoned by their owners back when things went south. Some still had their doors open from when the occupants either abandoned their vehicles or were pulled from behind the wheel, but a few—the ones toward the back of the lot—were shut tight. Near the front doors of Accinelli's, a beat up old Honda 650 laid on its side like a horse left to die in a waterless black desert. A rainbow-hued mixture of oil, water and gasoline pooled beneath it.

Oddly, there were only a few of the dead roaming around and they were busy moving about the dumpsters at the back of the lot near the Indian restaurant. The rotting garbage drew them in as they continued their never-ending search for food.

Cleese lowered the binoculars and again looked at Bartlett.

"Looks ok to me. There are a few of them, but they're pretty spread out or busy with that dumpster."

"Well, then... by all means, if you say we're good, we're good. Let's go check it out," Bartlett responded and put the truck into gear. The guy acted pretty much like a dick when they first met and his mood had only gotten dourer as the day wore on. Not that Cleese gave much of a fuck. He'd pretty much written the guy off as a waste and was now only following his lead in order to secure a place in the compound. Against considerable odds, Wolf and his people had managed to pull a good thing together in the crush of it all. Cleese was willing to help out for as long as he could. Or as long as it suited him. Truth was... while things looked good now, he knew how quickly shit could go south and so he probably wouldn't be sticking around for long. He'd help them out while he could, but he wasn't exactly the type to go all in.

It just wasn't how he was wired.

The truck pulled into the lot and drove around the perimeter in a wide arc, moving indirectly to the front of the drug store. Bartlett was obviously doing his best to keep them out of the sight of the few dead that were milling around. There was no sense in broadcasting their presence if it wasn't absolutely necessary. When the truck came to a stop, the back door slowly rolled up so it made as little noise and possible and four figures jumped out. Bartlett and Cleese climbed out of the cab and the group was soon gathered at the back of the truck. All of them moved assuredly, holding their rifles tightly to their chests. Leaving the back door of the

Self-Haul open, the men cautiously approached the building.

Coming back into the city from the safety of the compound was never fun nor was it ever easy. Inherently, the excursion was dangerous and, though everyone was called upon to do it, it was not an activity anyone relished.

Well, not anyone sane that is.

Cleese shouldered the heavy SIG 556 SWAT rifle Wolf gave him and directed his gaze at the spot directly in his line of fire. With every step, the weight of the 9mm in the shoulder holster he wore thumped against the soft flesh of his armpit. As he moved carefully across the sidewalk in front of the store, he took the opportunity to give Bartlett's crew a closer look, summing them up. Cleese believed that knowing your cohorts—what their pros were, what their cons were, and being able to make a guess on which way they'd fall if a bad wind were to blow—was essential to remaining an upright and breathing member of the human race.

After giving them the once over, he was disheartened to arrive at the conclusion that these guys were all jolly-timers and were likely to get him—and themselves— killed in short order. They were total amateurs playing army. They'd been given a shot of courage after they'd come up victorious against a distinctly brain dead enemy. They were, at least to Cleese's mind anyway, little more than walking liabilities.

As they'd geared up back at the campground, Bartlett had done the formal introductions and Cleese made it a point to take some mental shorthand on each of them. There was Hines (who, as it turned out, was a pharmacist, so he'd made a good call on that one). His beady eyes peeked out from behind a pair of thick-rimmed glasses which constantly slipped down his nose. His bald head reflected any offered light. Next up was Pugnowski. The guy was a goof with the big nose and a volcanic eruption of red hair coming out of the top of his head. Harrison had, once upon a time, been an executive or some shit. Now he was Rambo on a fuckin' day pass. Finally, there was Del Castillo, a Spanish dude with a paunch and an annoying habit of calling everyone "Bro."

Looking them over, they reminded Cleese of a heavily armed Our Gang.

Overhead, the sun had already begun its descent from the noonday sky, but its warmth remained. The group carefully made its way to the electronic front doors, grateful to be out of the heat and in the shade. Cleese put his hand up to the glass to cut the glare and peered inside the dark of the store. Row after row of shelving extended into the blackness. Signs that hung from fine filament declaring "Sweet Summer Sale" twisted in the air like the bodies of hanged men.

"Harrison..." Bartlett said breaking the expectant silence, "blow the door."

"Wait! What?" Cleese asked, turning and staring dumbfounded. "Why?"

"We need to get inside."

"So...?"

"Power's been cut. We'll smash the glass and get in."

"Are you fucking retarded? You bust this glass and if there are any more of those things around than what we saw, they'll hear you. You might as well stand up on the roof and ring a goddamn dinner bell."

Bartlett looked at Cleese and sniffed in contempt.

"You got a better idea?"

"Maybe. Just let me try something before you go shootin' the doors off the place, ok, Wyatt Earp?"

Cleese slung his rifle behind his back and stepped up to the two sliding doors. He half-expected them to open on their own once he stepped onto the activator pads. When they didn't he raised his arms, slid the tips of his fingers into the crack between them, and gently applied increasing pressure outward. As he'd predicted, the doors weren't locked, just closed and unable to move now that the power was shut off. With a slight squeaking sound, the two heavy panes slid in their rails and opened.

"Open says me." Cleese said and extended a hand with a flourish toward the now open doors.

Immediately, Del Castillo and Harrison stepped through the entryway, sweeping the barrels of their guns from side to side as they'd no doubt seen so many times in movies. Once the front of the store was secure, Pugnowski and Hines followed. Cleese waited for them all to enter before closing the doors behind them. He hung back a bit allowing Bartlett to get well ahead of him. There was something that told him he didn't want the man behind him, especially not with a rifle in his hands.

The men fanned out and quickly checked each aisle for hostiles. Pugnowski scuttled toward Cosmetics and found a young dead woman (who'd probably been an employee) sitting on the floor behind a counter slowly eating one tube of lipstick after another. Her face was a kaleidoscope of color and she looked like she'd just blown a clown. He managed to get behind her without being noticed and placed the barrel of his .22 pistol against the back of her head. When he pulled the trigger, her skull acted as a silencer and only a soft popping sound was heard. She slid to the ground, her bulging eyes bloodshot from the pressure change caused by the expanding gasses from the firearm going off inside her head.

Hines ran down the main aisle, took a quick left, and ended up in the aisle where kids' toys were kept. He found a stock boy there standing next to a comic rack, retardedly spinning the wire frame around and around. As Hines came around the corner, the kid heard him and slowly turned toward the sound. The second the kid caught sight of the living man, he bared his teeth and came running. To Hines' credit, he didn't panic or freak. Instead, he took the brunt of the kid's charge and hip-tossed. As the kid's back slammed to the ground, Hines smashed the butt of his shotgun against the boy's forehead repeatedly. Soon, the floor was covered in what looked like marinara sauce and cottage cheese.

The rest of the team's searches came up empty.

When the store was given the "All Clear," each man immediately went about gathering items from the list of things he'd been assigned. Hines pulled a couple of foldable gym bags from his rucksack and went off at a run toward the pharmacy. His mission was the real reason they'd come to check the place out. There were a growing assortment of people at the compound and they all had needs: diabetics needed insulin, some people needed thyroid medication, antibiotics were always a necessity, hell, even pain killers would be worth their weight in gold should the need arise. Hines leapt over the counter and started gathering shit from his mental shopping list.

The rest of them made their way through the aisles and systematically pulled items from the shelves. Cleese was busy grabbing as much prepackaged beef jerky, Spam, candy, nuts, cookies, and crackers as he could and stuffing them into the bags he carried. Harrison and Del Castillo made hurried trips back and forth shuttling cases of soda, bottled water, beer, and powdered milk. In no time at all, they'd pretty much emptied the entire drink aisle as well as the cold cases. They soon had a substantial stack of goods piled near the front door. Bartlett and Pugnowski repeated the same routine only their booty was as many packages of toilet paper, paper towels, sanitary napkins and diapers as they could find.

Cleese decided not to point out the irony of Bartlett grabbing these particular items. Things were already rough between them. The joke just seemed too easy to make.

They'd stripped the store of anything of value and were soon reassembled at the front doors. Cleese took a quick look around outside and then, finding it clear, pulled the doors back open. The group quickly formed a fireman's line and silently passed items to one another. In time, the truck was filled to near capacity. Finally, when everything they'd collected was loaded on board, Harrison eased the back door of the Self-Haul almost closed and they were ready to roll.

As he stood outside, once again feeling the heat of the day wrap its arms about him, Cleese was surprised at how smoothly it had all gone down and was almost impressed. There wasn't a lot that could change his original opinion of these guys, but this was certainly points in their favor. In the end though, they were what they were... and what they were at the moment was a bunch of monkeys who'd done a good job of learning how to pull this particular lever for this particular treat. He knew that if they were to be dropped into a different situation with a different dynamic, things might not go so smoothly. Silently, Cleese wondered how many people had died for them to learn how to do this kind of thing with this level of proficiency.

"Ok, so..." Cleese said, "we're done, right?"

The guys moved their heads like bobblehead dolls.

"We're good," Hines said.

"Wait... where's Bartlett?" Del Castillo asked.

Cleese looked around and quickly counted heads. Sure enough, they were one short. Suddenly, the sound of a rifle shot cracked from inside the store. Then, another. Across the parking lot, several of the dead near the dumpster raised their heads at the sound. Seeing nothing, they returned to digging in the trash.

"Fuck!"

Cleese was running back inside before he even realized he was doing it, the SIG 556 locked and loaded at his shoulder. He heard the footsteps of the other men coming up behind him as he moved down the aisles; their heavy boot falls echoing in the silence of the darkened building.

Nearing the back of the store, Cleese saw no sign of Bartlett. The aisles were empty with only the bodies of the dead they'd taken down earlier. Suddenly, the crashing sound of a struggle was heard coming from a side hallway leading to the bathrooms. Bartlett stumbled into view, making his way down the hallway and into the half-light with someone clutching at him. Cleese figured that he must have gone back inside to take a quick squirt and found more than a waiting urinal.

As the two bodies fell from the shadows of the enclosed hallway and into the dim light, Cleese could see that the thing holding onto Bartlett was a young kid. He couldn't have weighed more than a buck fifty and was dressed in jeans and a blood-spattered leather jacket. His face was obscured by a full face motorcycle helmet. Underneath the jaw-line, at the point where the strap buckle was visible, you could just see where a large bite had been taken out of his neck. Cleese figured that the toppled Honda out front must have been his.

As the two of them continued to fight and thrash about, their legs slammed into a low-lying display and they fell into a heap to the ground. Bartlett pushed the kid away and Cleese saw two bullet hits on the brow of the helmet. Amazingly, the insulated brain bucket had held firm and deflected both shots.

Cleese had to smile as he imagined the look of surprise on Bartlett's face after shooting the kid dead center in the forehead and him not going down. Man, he must have shit his pants. The funny part was that the very thing that had protected the kid from the rifle rounds was also what was keeping him from being able to take a bite out of Bartlett. The full face helmet not only covered his skull, it also covered his jaws and kept him from being able to sink his teeth into anything. The thing possessed—quite literally—all of the bark of the undead, but none of the bite.

By now, the rest of the men had arrived and could see what was happening. Behind him, Cleese heard Pugnowski raise his rifle and click off his safety. Cleese reached out and put a gentle hand on the barrel of his gun. He shook his head, silently reminding him that it was too dangerous to just start firing blindly. Bartlett was in no real danger and it would be too easy to hit him in the ensuing hailstorm of bullets. Not to mention that the noise would bring every zombie within a thousand yards running.

With Bartlett screaming and thrashing about like a stuck pig, Cleese stepped up behind the two fighting figures and brusquely grabbed the kid by the collar of his leather jacket. Putting his legs into the lift, he yanked the kid up and off Bartlett and casually tossed him aside. The kid hit the ground on his back and immediately scrambled back to his feet. Once mobile, he quickly moved back in the direction of the downed man. Cleese stepped into its path and slammed the butt of the SIG into his helmet's windscreen. The force of the blow spider-webbed the visor and knocked the kid back. Cleese spun at the waist and kicked him in the sternum with a reverse round house. Stale air came rushing out of his chest in a muffled "whoof!" Dazed and hurting, the kid crumpled to the ground.

Suddenly, a shot rang out and blood erupted from one of the kid's knees. Meat and bone splashed across the linoleum. The kid gave a piercing cry of pain, its voice sounding hollow from within the tightness of the helmet. Then, another bullet slammed into the other knee. Cleese turned to see Bartlett holding his still smoking rifle.

"Christ, Bartlett," Cleese said exasperated. "You sure as shit are making enough fuckin' noise. If you're gonna kill it, kill it, but don't fuck around torturing the damned thing."

"Shut up, Cleese!" Bartlett shouted and fired two more rounds into the dead thing's chest. Blood blossomed like red flowers on the shiny surface of the kid's leather.

"Oh, come on... I know it surprised you, but look at it. It can't bite you. Just fucking put it down, Man."

"Shut. Up!" Bartlett repeated and angrily turned, pointing his rifle at Cleese.

Cleese glowered and his demeanor immediately turned serious; deadly serious.

"Bartlett..." his voice slid from his mouth like venom. "Get. That. Fucking gun. Out of my face!"

Bartlett took a step forward and kept the rifle pointed at Cleese.

"Or what, Tough Guy?"

Instantly, Cleese slapped the barrel up toward the ceiling and spun at the waist. He quickly grabbed the rifle and, with a quick tug, yanked the gun away. Behind them, the kid could be heard trying to get to his feet, but his wounded legs wouldn't support him. Without a second thought, Cleese flipped the gun around in his hands and slid the barrel of the rifle up under the kid's helmet just at the jaw line. An explosion of blood, brain, and bone erupted against the fractured surface of the kid's visor.

"You're making too much fuckin' noise, man," Cleese said, "and I won't have you endangering us all just because you want to get your rocks off torturing this thing." He pulled the clip out of the rifle and ejected the chambered round. The discarded brass tinkled brightly as it hit the ground. Cleese raised the rifle so that it could be seen. "And you'll get this back at the end of the semester, young man!"

Bartlett shot an angry look at his back as Cleese walked back down the aisle and toward the front of the store.

"Fuck you!" Barlett barked.

"Oh and point another gun at me, Fuckstick, and I'll drop you like the sack of shit that you are," Cleese called back over his shoulder.

"Don't threaten me, Cleese!" Bartlett shouted after him.

"I don't threaten, motherfucker," Cleese's voice came slithering out of the darkness, "I offer up prophecy."

The ride back to the compound was a quiet one. Cleese decided to sit in the back of the truck with Del Castillo, Harrison and Hines. They'd rearranged boxes and made little cubbyholes to sit in between the stacked fruits of their labor. Cleese noticed that there was a distinct separation between theirs and his.

Whatever...

It wasn't like he was ever looking to make friends.

As the truck rumbled along, he could hear Bartlett and Pugnowski as they talked in the cab. He caught muted mumbling that, from their tone, had all the earmarks of bitching and posturing. Cleese had heard it time and time again, usually from some propped-up tough guy who'd just had his social standing diminished by someone tougher and smarter.

Cleese leaned back and got as comfortable as he could given the constant rocking of the truck as it rumbled down the road and back up into the mountains. He grabbed a package of toilet paper and set it under the back of his head as a pillow. He knew he'd not heard the last of Bartlett and his empty-headed cronies, but it wasn't like he was worried. If there was ever going to be a serious altercation between them, it would have happened at the drug store when they were all alone and everyone was well armed. Instead, Cleese had walked away without so much as a tussle.

It told him everything he needed to know.

Spines of water.

As he settled in deeper and tried to get comfortable, he took a glance over at the three men riding with him. As he met their gaze directly, they looked away or into their laps.

Cleese smiled to himself, closed his eyes, and promptly took a nap.

Back at the compound, Cleese turned in the SIG, but asked if he could hold onto the nine mil. Having a pistol in this day and age just seemed like a pretty good idea to him.

Luckily, Wolf agreed with him.

He felt almost like himself after his nap in the truck and as the sun slowly set he decided he'd go and dig up some chow. The smell of food being prepared caught his attention the second they'd made it back to camp. He figured now that he'd done a little something to earn a place here, he'd reap himself some of the benefits in the shape of a full stomach.

As he made his way through the encampment and toward the roach coaches, he saw that a line had formed and it suddenly occurred to him how many people had come under Wolf's protective banner. Dozens of men, women, children, the handicapped and the elderly stood waiting patiently for their food. Even though they'd all faced a pile of shit, they were an orderly bunch; surprising since it'd been only a short time since what many had come to refer to as The Fall. A few of them still had that "What the fuck?" expression on their faces, but they all looked like refugees from some foreign conflict. What made it worse was that they were Americans who'd suffered while on American soil. Theirs had been a life of entitlement and plenty. None had experienced any calamity of note before, especially not "up close and personal" like this.

Never mind coming to grips with the whole "dead guy getting back to his feet and trying to eat you" thing. That shit was too fucked up to get a handle on for even the hardest of them. Shit, if the military lost their motherfuckin' minds over it, what chance did John Q. Public have? Some things were better left alone. Others were best left not even being considered.

Abruptly, a disturbance became apparent toward the front of the line. Cleese leaned out and saw the pony-tailed girl, Jenny, waving her arms and gesturing wildly. She repeatedly pointed her finger at someone as if in accusation and then another more heated exchange took place. Whoever she was talking to, it was pretty obvious that she was pretty pissed at them.

Then suddenly, the object of her ire stepped out of line and made himself known.

Bartlett.

Man, that guy just has no skill at making friends.

The crowd around them was starting to become visibly agitated, due primarily to the fact that whatever was going on was keeping them from getting their dinners.

"What's that all about?" Cleese asked the small dark-haired women standing in front of him. She held a fidgety two year old boy tucked under her arm and her face was covered with a thin layer of dirt.

"Someone's jumping the line," she said, brushing a lock of hair from her boy's tired eyes. "It happens... especially when the Scavenger Squads come back with supplies. Some of them feel like, since they took all the risks, they deserve first dibs."

"Some of them, eh?" Cleese quietly excused himself from line.

With an amiable gait, he slowly made his way up alongside the queue. As he got closer, he was able to make out bits and pieces of the conversation.

"Look, we earned a place at the head of this line, Jenny," Bartlett said in his most cocky manner. "I didn't see any of these people out there with us... when we were risking our lives!"

"Don't make me have to go get Wolf, Fred. You know what he'd say about this kind of bullying."

By now, Cleese was close enough that he could be seen by Jenny. She nodded slightly, but didn't acknowledge him. She had bigger problems.

Bartlett stood with his back toward the line so he therefore had no idea Cleese was coming up behind him.

"Go get him! I don't care!"

"These people are just as tired and hungry as you or any of your men. The line moves quickly. You know that. Just show a little patience."

"Honey, we risk our asses to get this shit while the rest of you sit up here and do nothing."

"When exactly did you risk jack shit, Freddie?" Cleese interrupted as he stepped up behind Bartlett. "Before or after Motorcycle Boy got the drop on you? The only thing I seem to remember is when you were rolling around on the ground with him, screaming like a bitch."

A wave of snickers rippled through the crowd.

Bartlett markedly jumped at the sound of Cleese's voice and quickly turned around. His expression spoke volumes as to how unwelcome Cleese's involvement was in all of this. A pain in his ass since he first walked into camp, Cleese somehow managed to yet again show up and make him look like a fool. Bartlett looked back and forth between the diminutive girl who had stood up to him and the newcomer who'd managed more than once in less than twenty-four hours to make him look stupid and ineffectual.

Visibly angry, he mumbled a quick "fuck you both" and strode off sullenly toward the tents and campers which surrounded the Mess area. His boneheaded coterie was quick to follow close behind him.

Jenny sighed and stepped closer to Cleese.

"Thanks for that," she said diplomatically and then shrugged in resignation. "Fred's a decent enough guy... I mean... He means well, but..."

"Sister, Fred's an asshole and could use a good paradigm shift, but... No problem," Cleese responded and turned to go back to his place at the end of the line. "Rest assured though... he's not going to let this go."

Jenny stared at Cleese as he stepped away, her eyes sparkling brightly in the diminishing light.

"He's someone who's fueled by his ego. And that ego now has a pretty big dent in it thanks to you and me. If I'm any judge, he'll be looking for an opportunity to regain some of his sense of self."

"Are you saying that he's dangerous?"

Cleese looked over his shoulder and grinned. "Hell, who knows? In the last few weeks, I've seen things that I thought were incontrovertible suddenly get turned upside down and become something out of a nightmare."

Knowing all too well what he was talking about, Jenny grinned and looked down toward the ground. She reflexively slid her hands into her pockets.

"All I'm saying is..." he said walking away, "that you should be careful."

Jenny nodded more to herself than anything and watched Cleese's broad back diminish in size as he walked away in the fading light.

The midnight moon shone down over the silent compound, bathing everything in a cool and subdued light. Lanterns were lit inside many of the tents and RVs where the camp's citizenry lay settled in for the night. The lamps gently pushed back a little of the darkness and made the meager domiciles almost feel like home.

Almost.

High up in the trees, the overnight sniper watch shift settled into their spots with their thermoses of hot coffee, a sandwich or two, and high powered scopes equipped with night vision. Their prying eyes continually roamed the surrounding countryside, vigilant for any out of the ordinary movement or disturbance. So far, the night had been a quiet one.

Thankfully.

Cleese left the armory tent, having bid Wolf a good night after a few too many shots of whiskey and a few too many rounds of chess. The whiskey had come first and, once a mutual interest had been discovered, the chess soon after. You could say a lot of things about Wolf, but he wasn't dumb. His playing had been some of the best Cleese had ever seen. Not that he was any kind of master chess player, but Cleese had learned a thing or two about the game from some of the faculty of the rec center he'd frequented as a kid back when his mom was busy working. While he wasn't going to give Kasparov a run for his money anytime soon, he was no slouch when it came to the game of kings. Wolf was a solid player and, to Cleese, that spoke volumes as to the kind of man he was.

Winding his way through the assorted tents and recreation vehicles, Cleese felt the cold night air against his skin and was grateful for it. The crisp, biting chill in the wind meant that the seasons were changing, and despite all that had happened over the last few weeks, Life went inexorably on no matter what the machinations of Man were.

As someone far better than he once said, "And so it goes..."

It was still a little too early for him to try to get to sleep, so he decided to take a stroll through the campground and get a sense of the place after the majority of people had hit the hay. It was a habit he'd picked up early in his life: roaming through the house in the early morning hours, making sure everyone was safe and snug. Sleep had always been a ghost he chased but only caught for small bits of time. Wherever he ended up living, he could oftentimes be found walking the halls in the dead of night, watching over the house and making sure the doors were locked, the windows were secure, and everyone was covered and warm beneath their blankets. In many ways, the feel of a place late at night gave him a better sense of itself than it ever could when there were people around to confuse the issue. When it was quiet the house would speak to him, telling him its secrets.

As he walked, a voice from his past came echoing from the recesses of his intellect. "The night hath been to me a more familiar face, than that of man; and in her starry shade, of dim and solitary loveliness, I learned the language of another world." It was a piece of a Lord Byron poem, one of his mother's favorites, that had stuck with him over the years. His brain couldn't recall what he'd had for lunch the day before, but the important things—the things that nurtured his soul—he always seemed to remember.

Earlier, he'd met a few of the men who kept the line outside the compound safe as they collected their weapons and ordnance. He felt a lot more secure having done so. They were, to a man, capable and well-equipped. After meeting them, he'd been satisfied that they could put down anything that might encroach on the camp from outside. Anyone with a keen eye could see that they had a bold combination of vigilance and duty in their eyes. It seemed like an almost sacred obligation that they'd undertaken, each being well aware of the fact that the safety of them all depended on their attentiveness. Every so often throughout the long cold night a muffled rifle shot would be heard when one of the snipers caught sight of something making its way through the surrounding forest and toward camp. After a while, people didn't even notice it. The random pop and crack sounds soon became part of the soundtrack of the camp.

If more than a few were heard, however, the group would take it as a signal that something was up and they'd all grab their firearms and go to Full Alert. The residents had their own posts specified where they were to report should something untoward occur. It had, from the beginning, been of one Wolf's highest priorities that everyone in the camp remained well trained and ready.

It was another one of the things that made him a good leader.

The thing that gnawed at the back of Cleese's mind now though was the multitude of unsavory things that might potentially take place inside the compound. People were people, after all, and people... sucked.

And it was that thought that brought up the mental image of Bartlett. Cleese couldn't shake the bad feeling he had regarding him. The guy had been an asshole when they'd first met, and after the incident at the drug store and the face-off with Jenny in the mess line, he was someone who Cleese knew he'd need to keep a watchful eye on. His years of dealing with the drunken public had given him a sixth sense when it came to such things. Both Jenny and he had made that fat fuck lose face in front of the local populace and that was a recipe for trouble. Bartlett was someone who harbored a deep-seated hunger for power and now he'd gotten a taste of it. He wasn't going to give up even a small amount of it without a fight. For anyone to take the spoon that fed that desire away from his ravenous mouth was to deny him his drug of choice.

And to deny any junkie his dope was always a dangerous proposition.

By now, he'd found himself near the roach coaches and saw that the metal doors covering the serving windows were pulled down and closed up tight. The smell of cooked meat lingered over the area like an aromatic pall as did the rich odor coming from the large canisters of brewing coffee which seemed to be constantly percolating. Alongside them on a small table plastic containers sat with pre-made sandwiches inside. The cooks made sure to always have some sort of food available during the night. It was important to keep the watch shifts caffeinated and fed.

He walked past the Mess area and continued on to the RVs, heading toward the tents on the far side of the campground. Cleese cast his gaze skyward and saw through the trees a large moon suspended in the sky. Strings of clouds moved lazily across its bright yellow-orange face, giving it a veiled, sad look.

Far off, a coyote wailed mournfully.

Strolling along, leisurely enjoying the feel of the night air on his face, Cleese caught the sound of several hushed voices whispering excitedly in the darkness. He almost dismissed it and continued on his way, but then a loud slap punctuated the exchange. Changing the direction in which he was heading, Cleese soon found himself near the far perimeter of the camp. There a large family-sized tent sat, looking bluish-grey in the moonlight. He stopped and listened intently. He cocked his head to one side and closed his eyes as he tried to pinpoint the source of the slap. This far out, it could have only come from inside the tent. As he ambled over, he saw two men exit the tent, both shaking their heads in what looked like disgust. The moonlight threw a cold light across their faces as they headed off into camp.

Hines and Harrison.

Now obscured by the shadows at the side of the tent, Cleese turned his head and looked through the uncovered mesh window. Inside, he saw a group of broad figures, cloaked in varying shades of shadow, standing inside hunched over something curled up into a ball on the ground. He was just about to step away figuring it was none of his business when the thing on the ground spoke.

"Fred... please. You don't want to do this."

Jenny.

"Shut up, bitch! You don't know the first thing about what I want to do."

Bartlett.

"Yeah, but she's soon gonna learn, right?"

Pugnowski.

Cleese didn't wait to hear any more. He drew the flap open and stepped into the cramped tent. Once inside, his added bulk made for some very confined quarters.

"Gentlemen..." he said, his voice dripping with menace. "Is there a problem here?"

As one, what remained of Bartlett's men stepped backward and pressed themselves against the side of the tent. Like little boys who'd just been caught with their hand in the cookie jar, their faces betrayed not only their guilt, but also their intent.

Bartlett was the first to step forward.

"Get the fuck outta here, Cleese," he growled and then did the unthinkable. He poked his left hand's index finger against the center of Cleese's chest. Not once, but twice.

Cleese was someone who was not exactly fond of being touched by people he didn't know. In fact, he absolutely hated it. The only thing he hated more was being touched by people he didn't like. That feeling, coupled with what was obviously going down in the tent, provoked an immediate response. With blinding speed, he caught Bartlett's index finger in his fist and twisted it roughly. The sound of bones breaking was painful in its tenor. Cleese then pushed the shattered appendage back toward Bartlett's wrist, hyper-extending it. Bartlett fell to his knees before he knew what happened. His cry of pain was a welcomed thing to Cleese's ears.

"Jenny," Cleese said gently, but firmly, "get up and on out of here."

Jenny slowly climbed to her feet and ashamedly tried to arrange her twisted clothing about her. From the look on her face, things had already gone well past the point she felt comfortable. Looking down toward the ground, she did her best to pull her hair back and into something less disheveled. As she passed, her eyes were wet with tears.

Cleese counted himself fortunate to have happened along when he did.

"This ends now!" and he gave Bartlett's finger another twist.

Bartlett cried out and then cursed under his breath.

"Don't make me tell you again."

Cleese let go of Bartlett's finger and stepped back toward the tent's flap. He bent slightly and, never taking his eyes off of the men before him, ducked out of the tent. Once back in the night air, he turned and gave Jenny the once over. She was clearly—and justifiably—upset and her clothes bore the marks of where she'd been grabbed by Bartlett and his crew. One side of her face burned a bright red in the half-light from where Bartlett had clearly slapped her.

"Are you ok?" Cleese asked gently resting his hand around her shoulder.

She nodded and, now feeling safe, immediately burst into tears.

Just then, the tent's door flap was roughly thrown aside and Bartlett came storming out into the moonlight. His face was flushed and he was holding his left hand protectively to his chest.

"You son of a bitch! I am gonna kill you!"

At a different time and in another place, Cleese would have fed this fat dolt his teeth, but as he held Jenny and felt her warm tears against his chest, he thought it best to get her clear. He'd tell Wolf about all of this later.

"Hey, motherfucker! I'm talking to you!"

Then again, talking to Wolf could probably wait a few minutes...

Cleese let go of Jenny and gently eased her behind him. Once she was more or less protected, he turned on the enraged Bartlett.

"No..." Jenny said softly, touching his back, "It's not worth it."

By now, Bartlett's clique had followed him out of the tent and had adopted an aggressive stance; flanking their clueless leader. Cleese hoped they'd be smart and not push the issue. He'd really hate to have to hurt anyone.

Ok, he was lying about that last part.

The truth was that a part of him really wanted to put a hurt on these fucks just on general principles. Another part, wanted to jack their shit up if only for what they'd done to the girl.

Still... First things first.

And the first thing was to get Jenny out of harm's way.

Pugnowski came up next to Bartlett as if offering his support. Despite his posturing, Cleese was convinced the fuck would go down like a shooting gallery target the minute shit got tight. Surreptitiously, he checked on Spanky and Alfalfa. In their faces, he saw the very things he wanted to—fear and misgiving. Whatever had transpired inside the tent, it had now blossomed far beyond what the other men were comfortable with. Sure, they were onboard when the coast looked clear, but now... Now that there looked to be storm clouds ahead, they weren't so sure. Cleese met their gaze and pushed his intent.

Thankfully, they backed down.

"Jesus, Fred..." Del Castillo said under his breath, "Let's just go, Bro."

"Fuck you!" Bartlett shouted. Now that some smart part of his intellect had fired up, it was obvious how big this fuckup was. Wolf favored Jenny. Always had. Knowing him, he'd probably be pissed enough to throw them all out of the camp no matter what their perceived worth might have been. Even with a rifle or two, they'd all be slaughtered by the multitudes that still swarmed the cities. Their deaths would not only be grisly, but they'd be met in short order.

"Yeah, Fred," Cleese said and smiled a malevolent grin, "just go."

"Fuck you!" Bartlett repeated and then, suddenly, Pugnowski's rifle was in his hands. The barrel waved erratically in the air, but its business end was pointed directly at Cleese's chest.

"What did I tell you about that pointing a gun at me, Buddy?" Cleese asked, his eyes narrowing slightly. "One might come to the conclusion that you don't listen."

The sound of the rifle's safety clicking off was as loud as a cannon.

Cleese stared intently at Bartlett and tried to second-guess if he was really going to pull the trigger and, more importantly, when. At this point, Bartlett had nothing to lose and probably thought if he could just shake the Etch-a-sketch hard enough things would somehow return to the way they'd been.

Simple fuck.

"Now, think, Freddie-boy... Think hard. D'ya really want to do this?"

Cleese slowly rose up onto the balls of his feet and prepared himself for the movement he hoped would get him out of the way of the bullet. He knew his timing would need to be perfect, but given how close they were to one another, it would be tight. Seeing how worked up Bartlett was, he figured negotiation was now out of the question. He'd just have to hope the man had enough of a "tell" that he'd have time to get out of the way.

At least that was the plan.

Time seemed to slow and milliseconds seemed like minutes. Behind him, Cleese heard the soft sound of feet moving in the dirt. From the length of the stride, he could tell that Jenny had taken advantage of the shift of focus and was now off and running to get help. From the rhythm of her steps, she was moving pretty damn quick, too.

It was at that moment, Cleese saw Bartlett's brow constrict and a small wince cross his features. Then, a minute tightening of his shoulders became evident and his right bicep constricted. Suddenly, the rifle fired and Cleese threw himself backward like a limbo dancer. Standing as close as he was, the concussion of the rifle was deafening. Cleese felt the air split just over him as the bullet tore through the atmosphere. As he fell, he caught a glimpse of Jenny as she ran for the safety of the surrounding tents a few yards away.

Then, to his horror, the back of her head erupted in a splash of red. A piece of something skipped off of her skull and sailed into the bushes next to the trail. He heard a pained grunting sound and then what remained of her head was slapped forward. Her body fell lifeless to the ground and bounced against the dirt on impact.

Rage swept over him like a violent storm, darkening his vision and setting his blood to boil. In a blink of an eye, Cleese was back on his feet and had crossed the distance between Bartlett and himself. Bartlett's face slowly expanded into the classic "Oh, fuck!" expression and then his vision ratcheted down onto the big man standing in front of him. He tried to lift the gun and point it at Cleese, but he was already too close. Cleese slapped the barrel away with one hand and followed up with a vicious uppercut. The blow smashed into the front of Bartlett's throat.

Bartlett's grunt of pain was cut short, halted by the knuckles of Cleese's fist.

Cleese quickly raised his hands overhead, and brought both fists down onto Bartlett's collarbones, putting all of his upper body strength into it. A sickening crun-crunch sound echoed in the darkness. Between the searing pain which exploded across Bartlett's chest and the rapidly bruising tissue in this throat, it was impossible for him to catch a breath. Every time he tried, it felt like daggers were being pushed deep into the meat of his neck and shoulders. There was a sudden constricting sensation in his chest that felt like there was an elephant sitting on it.

As for Pugnowski and Del Castillo, they'd fallen back several steps once the gun went off. What had started out as a pursuit of a good time had now gone terribly,

terribly wrong and they knew it. It was bad enough that Cleese saw what was going on in the tent, but now Jenny was dead. There was no way around it, all of them were utterly fucked. It was a situation none of them ever imagined they'd be in, but here they were. And from where they now stood, it was not an enviable place to be. Both of them slowly stepped back and tried to appear as small and unthreatening as possible.

Bartlett fell to his knees; his breath labored and wet sounding. Pugnowski's rifle had fallen from his grip and it laid there like a eunuch in a whorehouse. Bartlett clutched both of his hands over his chest, impotent and unable to protect himself from any further damage. His pain-wracked face lifted skyward as he begged the ever-silent moon for forgiveness.

It was then that the light of the moon went out and Cleese fell upon him.

Cleese landed on him and drove his shattered body to the dirt. With wet, packing sounds, he vented his anger on the man with a flurry of hacking punches and brutal twists of Bartlett's already damaged anatomy. An ear-piercing shriek broke the stillness of the night, its timbre was high pitched and desperate.

And then, the sound was abruptly cut off as if it had been stomped on unmercifully.

Finally, his fury now spent, Cleese pulled himself off of Bartlett. The body on the ground before him lay broken and distorted in ways that defied both logic and reason. Bartlett's decimated corpse sprawled on the ground, his limbs bent at odd angles, his head turned savagely facing the wrong direction.

Once back on his feet, Cleese stood panting in the night air. Soft plumes of fog streamed out of his flared nostrils. From his hands to his elbows, his arms seemed to be coated in a thick substance which appeared black in the sparse illumination. He turned to face Pugnowski and Del Castillo and stared at them, his eyes burning with a fierce intensity. They both looked as if Death itself had come to claim them.

Already, the killing of Bartlett was a fading memory in his mind. He'd killed people before—when they'd deserved it... and, let's face it, some people deserved to die—but this... This was a killing that needed to happen. More than any others before him, Bartlett was someone who had literally signed his own death warrant. He'd done so the minute he'd forced Jenny to go into that tent. His shooting of her... well, that was him making sure the ink was dry.

With the sound of a rifle being shot within the confines of the compound, a general alert had been sounded and people were already running to investigate. The tableau that greeted them was one that both broke their hearts and turned their stomachs. A few of the women moved to cover Jenny's body, but left Bartlett's out in the open, ignored and unattended.

Cleese stood over Bartlett's corpse, lost inside the whirlwind of his thoughts; his blood still boiling, his anger remaining unabated. He continued to glare at Bartlett's crew and silently wished for one of them to say something, anything. Even with Bartlett's blood on his hands, his retribution was far from sated and therefore incomplete.

A hush fell over the crowd as Wolf stepped out from the fold and into the clearing between the tents. What he saw before him made his flesh turn pale. Cleese met Wolf's gaze, shook his head, and looked away.

"What the fuck's happened here?' Wolf asked, his voice cracking with anger.

"Ask them," Cleese responded and jerked his thumb toward Pugnowski and Del

Castillo.

Wolf turned to face the two men and saw the guilty look on their faces immediately. They'd been drinking, that much was obvious. He could tell that from the redness of their cheeks, their open-mouthed breathing and their heavy-lidded stares. Wolf knew instinctively that the rest of the story was not going to be one he was happy with. It was then that he noticed the front of Pugnowski's pants and his unzipped fly. Wolf looked over at Cleese and recognized the anger that still burned in the man's eyes.

Slowly, his gaze wandered over the scene before him and nothing he saw made much sense. Bartlett's crew stood there like a mouth-breathing Greek chorus, looking guilty and ashamed. Bartlett's battered body spread out in the dirt like a rag doll that had gone through a lawnmower. Cleese stood hovering over his dead body like an avenging barbarian whose vengeance was something no possible amount of blood or sorrow could sate.

And then... and then he saw Jenny.

Wolf closed his eyes and tried to push back the tears of grief and frustration.

Against the blackness of his eyelids, a waterfall of images of the young girl came flooding into his mind. He saw flashes of her warm and reassuring smile, the moments of tenderness she always seemed to have for the frightened children or the injured, and then there was the scope of her potential as a person—and as a woman—if she could only survive these dark and dangerous days.

And now...

Now, her young body lay face down in the dirt, unmoving and growing cold in the midnight air. Her smile now stilled forever. Her kindness offered up as compensation for her sin of naïveté. Her limitless potential now leaking from her body in the form of her life's blood, reparation paid to a gutless egomaniac who'd decided to dole out his own idea of heavy handed retribution for her crime of slighting him.

"Shit..." and then the tears came.

The next morning, after a sleepless night in which he'd gathered several versions of the same story, Wolf thought he had a pretty clear idea of what had gone down. The bottom line was that there were now two people dead in his camp and two more who would have to leave if for no other reason than for the good of the camp. There was no other way of handling it, from what he could tell.

No matter how you diced it up, it was a shitty proposition. From the loss of innocent life to the inevitable deaths of those who would have to be sent away, it pained him to know that it was avoidable on all fronts.

And then there was Cleese. Yes, he'd killed Bartlett, but no one really held that against him. The consensus amongst the camp's inhabitants was that Bartlett got exactly what he'd had coming, given his crime. Cleese only did what everyone there wished they could do. Plus, in the short time he'd been here, Cleese had proven himself to be a substantial asset. He was good with gun, concerned about the others, and he didn't seem to mind putting himself in harm's way for the good of the cause. All of that meant something around here.

But then again, from the looks of things, he was also something of a shit magnet.

Wolf decided he'd have a talk with Cleese before making any hard and fast decisions in his regard. Truth was... he'd hate to lose him. Not only was he a good addition to the team, but he played a mean game of chess.

Wolf left his tent and headed for the roach coaches. He figured he'd get himself some coffee and maybe something to eat, then he'd pass along the judgment that he hoped would set things right.

God knew... after he did, he would probably not want to eat again for a very long time.

Far off, on a cliff that overlooked the camp, Cleese watched the compound come to life. He stood quietly and thought about how Wolf had a good thing going here. He was a good man and a competent leader and Cleese hoped that some of them would survive if and when this all got sorted out.

No sense in me fucking that up for him any further.

It was better for everyone involved if he just climbed back under the rock where they'd found him. Maybe someday he'd be able to sort out what the fuck happened here... but that day was not today.

Luckily, no one had seen him in the early morning hours as he helped himself to some ammo and the newly oiled SIG which laid tucked under his arm. As most of them were sleeping, he'd loaded a backpack with food and a few bottles of water and headed out. He figured now that he was properly armed and had a few provisions, he'd slip past the sentries and break out on his own. After that, he'd go someplace and figure out what he was going to do next.

He might even do the unexpected and head back into the city.

Standing up, he hoisted his backpack onto his shoulders and hugged the SIG tight to his chest. Above his head, far off in the trees, he heard a red-tailed hawk cry out. Its tone was mournful and lonely. Deep down, Cleese felt he could relate.

With a last look back to Wolf's encampment, he walked off into the silent forest.

Friday Follies

After having searched the compound for what seemed like several hours—checking the Cafeteria, the Video Library, the Cribs, and the Training Hall—Cleese finally got the bright idea to look for Monk over at Weaver's. He recalled how, on any given Friday night, the two men had a standard appointment and could be found at the same place every week (up on the roof) doing the same thing (getting drunk as skunks and howling at the moon). As he walked across the field, the evening dew soaking the bottom of his pant's leg, it would have been damn near impossible not to notice them. Above the sound of the crickets and the soft breeze blowing, two painfully out of tune voices could be heard limping their way through what might have once been a song. It was pretty obvious that whoever it was couldn't have carried a tune in a Beacon's truck and didn't have the rhythm to masturbate.

Cleese immediately recognized the unfortunate thing being slaughtered as an old cowboy song. The voices rose to a crescendo and cracked like ice. One voice abruptly fell silent, audibly cut-off by the flow of liquid across its owner's palate. The other continued, its volume increased; emboldened more by the alcohol than by anything resembling talent.

"Yeeee-haaaaw!"

Monk.

Cleese found a rickety ladder propped up against the far side of the building. Silently, he climbed up and onto the roof. Once he'd negotiated the retaining wall that circled the top of the building and regained a stable footing, he simply followed his nose. The smell of scotch and cigars was unmistakable beneath the night's melancholic sky. From the sound of their drunken revelry, the party had been going on for a while. Monk was going to no doubt look and feel like shit when he woke up in the morning. It was also pretty much a given that he was gonna miss the early morning practice.

"Gentlemen..." Cleese said from the darkness.

"Who dat?" Weaver said and attempted to climb to his feet. He made it halfway there but then teetered and fell back onto his ass. Monk barked out a hearty guffaw, spraying a mouthful of liquor into the air in an alcoholic mist.

Cleese stepped leisurely out into the silvery moonlight; his legs drifting first into view like he'd materialized from behind a drape. The inky black shadows pulled back, casting his features in a soft, bluish tint.

"Ah, the prodigal son..." Monk said raising his bottle, "returned to claim his due."

"You two sound like you're having fun," Cleese said.

"We are. Ain't we, Weaver?"

Weaver lay flat on his back, like a tortoise, his arms and legs splayed akimbo.

"Weaver...?"

Monk looked over at the fallen man. A look of contempt spread over his face like peanut butter across a communion wafer.

Weaver made a deep snoring sound as a snail trail of saliva soaked into his beard.

"I think he's a casualty," said Cleese.

"Worthless bastard," Monk snorted.

"Mind if I sit down?"

"No... Of course..." Monk scooted over a bit to make room, a wholly unnecessary movement since the entire roof of the building spread out around them. He kicked at Weaver's legs, again calling him a worthless bastard under his breath.

Cleese sat and leaned his back against the retaining wall. As he plunked down, Monk handed him the bottle from which they were drinking. Cleese downed a good couple of fingers in one uninterrupted pull.

"Now that's a man drinking right there," shouted Monk, laughing and clapping his hands delightedly.

"I've had a fair amount of experience at this," said Cleese, drawing the back of his hand across his mouth and smiling, his eyes momentarily drifting off to another time and place. "Don't try this at home, kids. I'm something of a professional."

The older man sniffed another laugh and the two of them sat quietly for a moment, each absorbing himself in the night's idyllic calm.

"You guys been here long?" Cleese asked rhetorically.

"Long enough," Monk said sounding almost sad.

"Hmmm," was all Cleese could muster.

"Cleese," Monk asked after a moment, "lemme ask you something..."

"Sure. No sense in me being shy now."

"How the hell did a guy like you end up here? I mean, you *seem* smart..."

"Looks can be deceiving."

"No, really..."

Cleese pondered his answer for a long time before he spoke.

"Shit, Monk... It wasn't like I had much of a fuckin' choice. Back in The World, there were some bad people looking for me and if they found me it was going to get pretty ugly. That and Masterson made it pretty clear that if I didn't get into that chopper, my life was going to get even more... uh... complicated."

"He does have his way."

"Besides," he continued, settling in and making himself comfortable, "I'm a man pretty much all out of options. I've been poor as dirt for most of my life and the only thing I've ever been good at was hurtin' people and crackin' wise. Add to that the fact that I get lippy when I drink and you get something that's pretty limiting in the job market."

"'Wanted: drunken asshole. Must be good at talking shit and fuckin' shit up,'" Monk said chuckling. "Yeah, there's not a lot of call for that."

Cleese nodded and continued, "If the truth were to be told, my life has always been a bit of a steaming pile and it was never going nowhere good. And then," he paused, grinning, "and then, Masterson showed up on my doorstep with a card and some candy and he brought me to this sunny little corner of Adventure Island."

He waved his hand, the motion encompassing the entire compound.

"This... Well, this just seems to satisfy both my unique skill set and my inherent need to be loved."

Both men laughed out loud.

"Here, I do something I'm sorta good at," Cleese continued, "and I potentially stand to make a grip of cash."

Monk nodded slowly in the darkness as if he could somehow relate. Yeah, the money was there, but then again, so was Death. Before Monk could consider the concept further, Cleese let his train of thought go on along its track.

"Now, don't get me wrong. I don't plan on growing old doing this shit... least not as old as you!"

"Heeey, fuck you!"

"I'll make my scratch," he continued, grinning, "and when they try to fuck me—and don't think I don't know that they'll try and fuck me—I vaporize, like Casper the Unfriendly Ghost."

He paused for a second and looked toward the spot in the dark where Monk sat.

"And besides, where else but here could I meet a caliber of people such as yourself? I mean, God knows where I'd have to go to find men of such high moral fiber."

"You could try a prison," said Monk and he laughed.

Cleese smiled silently and for a moment both men sat quietly again, basking in the still of the night. Far off, an owl hooted and a sudden rustling of wings was heard. A second later, a rabbit's cry broke the silence and was abruptly cut off. It sounded a lot like a woman screaming.

"You ever think about buying it, Cleese?" Monk said with a yawn. "You know, about dying?"

"I try not to dwell on it, Pal," Cleese laughed as he spoke. Absentmindedly, he swirled the remaining liquor in the bottle in his hand. A small whirlpool was created in deep brown liquid which dissipated when he stopped. A lone bubble rose to the top and then burst.

"No, really. Quit bullshitting around and answer the fucking question."

"No, I find it hard enough to keep my mind focused on just what's in front of my nose. I leave the afterlife to the greater minds."

"I do. Well, I have been... lately."

Cleese eyed him and raised an eyebrow.

"Oh?"

"Thinking about it, I mean. I sometimes wonder what lies beyond all of this. I used to think it was shit like Heaven or Hell, but now, what with The Dead getting up and walking around and eatin' motherfuckers... It all just kinda puts a weird spin on the ball."

"What d'ya mean?"

"Well, before all of this shit went down, someone just died and, if you were a religious man, you accepted the fact that he went before Saint Peter at his Pearly Gates. You were judged and spent the rest of eternity either palling around with God or having hot pokers shoved up your ass by Old Scratch. It was just what we were told back when we were all in Sunday School and our heads were still soft. Only now... we've found out that dead isn't always dead and sometimes God makes other plans."

"Do you believe in that—God, Heaven, the shit those guys in the polyester suits tell you every Sunday on television?"

"Hell, I don't know... I will say this though... Over the years, there have been times when I did believe, believed with all of my heart. But then... then this shit happened. And there are times now when I look into the eyes of one of these dead fuckers and I wonder..."

"About?"

"About what they are. What they see. What they feel. If they think."

Cleese nodded, but remained silent.

"Sometimes I wonder what it would be like to be one of them, how terrible it must be. To lose everything you are and only be left with that hunger, that fucking need. I wonder how I'd feel. I... I can't imagine it. I won't let myself. All I know is that I wouldn't want to ever become something like... that." He looked at Cleese and then looked away. "And then I think that if there is a God that he must be a real son of a bitch to let this all happen. How much must He hate us? How much must we have let Him down?"

"Well, lookit you... The Deep Thinker."

"Fuck you! I'm being serious."

"Look," Cleese said, "I don't know shit about religion or Saint Peter or any of that stuff. I mean, I've seen a couple of Cecil B. DeMille films, but I ain't no scholar. I just always thought that anytime someone says that he knows what God or who-ever is thinking, then odds are that man is full of shit. Personally, I think it all falls together like this: Truth or God or The Big Stuffed Panda whoever or whatever it is that you think is running this dog and pony show has a lesson that he wants us all to learn before we die. He's taken all that you need to learn that lesson and broken it apart, like a jigsaw puzzle, and spread them out across different schools of thought. Science has a piece. Religion has a few. Fable, literature, philosophy... They all got a bit. Sometimes, a piece can be found in a holy place or even in a dirty joke. We may be stumbling on one of them right now with this conversation."

Monk nodded while Cleese took a second and re-wet his palate.

"Hell, you never know where you're going find one of them puzzle pieces."

"I think I found one up a whore's cooter once," Monk said with a wry grin.

"Yeah, and how is your mom?"

Monk thrust his middle finger into the air.

"Anyway, our job, the way I see it, is to listen carefully to what everyone has to say—The Jews, The Hindis, The Christians, The Muslims, the scientists, the philoso-phers, the writers—and find those pieces that help us define our puzzle. When we think we've found them all, or as many as we can, then it's our job to put them all together and try to figure out what exactly we're supposed to know. I'll tell you one thing... It's not going to church every Sunday and sitting quietly with our mouths open—like baby birds—waiting for someone else to regurgitate up the answer to all of our prayers. In the end, you die and you move on... to whatever. Hell, who knows? Maybe, you get judged as to whether or not you squandered this life, this gift that was given to you."

Monk sat quietly and stared off into space.

"I don't know," Cleese sighed. "This whole zombie thing... I kind of agree with Chikara and her Budo Warriors. It's a test—a challenge, a wrinkle in the fabric, a monkey in the works—that we all gotta rise up to confront and to defeat or be crushed under its wheels. I believe that it's only through challenge and hardship that we can forge our souls into something more than what we are now. Adversity does indeed temper the spirit."

"Wow..." Monk said quietly, "now look who's the Deep Fuckin' Thinker."

"Well, you asked," Cleese said with a resigned shrug.

"No... no. I'm impressed. Who knew that kinda thinkin' was goin' on in that lump of shit housed in your skull?"

"Yeah, well again, fuck you." Cleese paused for a moment and then looked up. He raised the bottle in a silent toast and took another drink. "How about you? How'd you end up in this little corner of Paradise?'

"Me?" Monk smiled in the dark. "Well, I'll tell ya... After being a Merchant Marine for more than my share of years, I ended up working as a longshoreman on some docks in Anacortes, Washington. I was offloading cargo and doing some repair on ships that sailed down the Strait of Juan de Fuca from the Pacific Ocean. It was grunt work mostly, but like you, I'd sorta run out of options and decided to spend some time up in the Pacific Northwest; getting rained on mostly."

Again, he looked off into the distance and breathed in deeply.

"Anyway, I was working on the docks during days and picking up overnight watchman shifts for BP at their Cherry Point Refinery every now and then. So, one night, I'm at the refinery and an alarm goes off. Work shuts down immediately so they can investigate. Long story short, it turns out that all hell's broken loose back in the world and that hell had come calling at the front gate. Soon, it was every man for himself."

"There was a lot of that going on..." Cleese said quietly to the wind.

"Yeah, no shit. Anyway, I say 'Fuck it!' and hop in my ride and hightail it the fuck outta there. I head back to where I was staying and did my best, trying to lock it all up tight. I did ok considering I ain't much of a carpenter. Later that night, I'm laying in the dark and hearing almost continuous gunshots and screaming. Now, I'm no dummy—despite what you've heard to the contrary from the idiots here—and I knew, from what I'd seen for myself firsthand and from what was coming through on the television, that every one of those gunshots and every one of those screams had a story behind them. And none of those stories was having a happy fuckin' ending."

"Yeah, no shit."

"So, I did what a lot of people should have done and that was grab what I could in the way of supplies and head for the goddamn hills. That part of the country, it's pretty easy to do that."

Cleese nodded and rubbed at his eyes. Monk had, up until now, been pretty tight-lipped regarding his past. He was not going to ruin this opportunity to learn a little something about him by interrupting him now that he was on a roll.

"I manage to find this empty cabin up near the Mt. Baker-Snoqualmie National Forest. The place was this nice "A" frame timeshare or some shit; loaded to the gills with food, water, and was as remote as hell. I didn't encounter too much in the way of UDs up there, but believe it or not, I had my share. I ended up staying there until I finally ran out of food."

Monk paused and seemed lost in the memory.

"Y'know... I could have lived like that forever. Isolated. Nobody to give me shit. Hell, man, it was as near to fuckin' bliss as I've ever experienced."

Cleese smiled again, knowing the place where that feeling from came all too well.

"Anyway, I finally come back down to civilization and the worst of it is pretty much over. The Army is mopping shit up and, by this time, they'd already dropped the hammer on places like New York and L.A. But now... But now, both the docks and the refinery are locked up tight and it's not looking like they're opening back up any time soon. So, I'm pretty shit outta luck job-wise and, you know, Daddy's gotta eat. I bounce around for a while doing what I can to make ends meet, but it's all goin' nowhere fast."

"I hear ya, Buddy," Cleese responded knowingly.

"A short time later, I'm in a bar in Southern California near Camp Pendleton and I hear these jarheads—real Marine-type badasses—talking about this League forming. They're saying how it's cake money, but the risks are inordinately high. I eavesdrop a little and, after buying them a few rounds, I find out where this shit's all getting organized. So, I went out there and met up with Weber and his crew and the rest, as they say, is history."

Monk turned, looked at Cleese and said, "I guess you could say that I—much like you—had an aptitude for this shit."

"Which brings us to the now. So, what brought this all on?" Cleese asked as he looked at the bottle of alcohol and raised his eyebrows.

"This?" Monk said while he feigned indignation. "Oh, we're having ourselves a li'l sell-ee-bray-shun."

"And me without my party hat. What is it that we're celebrating, if I might ask?"

"Well, with Lenik and Cartwright now on the D.L.—The Dead List—management has decided to move up our time table."

"Oh?" Cleese leaned forward, his interest now piqued.

"Ay-yup. Looks like you're gonna see rotation sooner than any of us thought."

"When, pray tell?"

"Two weeks."

"Two weeks!?!" Cleese exclaimed, now more than slightly annoyed. "Am I the only one who remembers the Cherry who's trained with unharnessed UDs but once?"

"Oh, they remember all right. In fact, they consider it to be a little bit of a perk. Corporate's been watching your training tapes and they think that you're ready. They're already running ads for the event everywhere: television, radio, even the Internet. Breaking Cherry has always been a fan favorite, you know that."

Cleese leaned back against the short wall. His brain now spun from a combination of the alcohol and the knowledge of what lay ahead.

"What about you?" Cleese asked.

"Me? I'm being cut... Well, 'retired,' actually."

Monk grabbed the bottle from Cleese's hand and drank deeply.

"No fuckin' way." Cleese said astonished. Monk was the best there was. Why would they want to retire him? It just didn't make any sense.

"Ay-yup. First, I'll do a short hitch in the UFL, but you know as well as I do that that league is strictly 'bush.' It's just a convenient way for them to ease me out of the public's eye. It lets me pass from 'Hey, there's Monk!' straight to 'Whatever happened to that one fella... That whaziz name?' in a matter of a few, short months."

Monk snapped his fingers loudly and took another long pull on the bottle.

"It's not like I didn't know though," he continued, almost to himself, "I'd agreed to it before you even got picked up. You were to be my last recruit. My legacy." He raised the bottle as if in toast.

Cleese stared at his mentor for a long time as they sat together in the moonlight. Secretly, he was damn disappointed. He'd always known that Monk would someday move on. He just didn't think it would be this soon.

"Besides, I'm getting too old for this shit. And what with Cartwright buying it today..."

Monk wiped at his nose with the back of his wrist.

"Fuck, man. Cartwright and I signed on at about the same time, Cleese. The man had family."

Cleese stared at the toes of his boots and said nothing.

"You heard about Michaels, yes?"

"No, but I know I haven't seen him around lately."

"Well, after that little dance you two did in the gym, they'd almost let him go, but then thought better of it," Monk said and scratched at his thigh.

"And..."

"As it turned out, your thumpin' must've fucked with his confidence a bit because people say he went at his training even harder than before; taking stupid risks."

Cleese looked Monk in the eye.

"Aaaand..."

"Well, he went and got himself bit during training shortly thereafter."

"No shit," Cleese said as he leaned back to sigh. It sucked that the guy got himself hosed like that, but getting bitten was a risk they'd all assumed from the get-go. The fact that that fat fuck had pushed the wrong set of buttons and gotten himself knocked around a little and then not been able to handle the ass-whuppin' was not something Cleese felt he should take responsibility for. It's just how things went sometimes.

Monk stared off into space for a moment and went back to what he was saying; Michaels' death serving as only an unfortunate blip on his personal radar.

"It's better that I go, anyhow. I need to learn what it means to live again. I need to surround myself with a bit of Life while I still have some of it left in me."

He looked off into the night, not wanting Cleese to see his eyes as they glassed over with moisture.

"I've been around Death for far too long," he continued after a moment, "I'll do my hitch in the UFL and then I'm fuckin' out, Baby. I just want to spend the last years of my life in some place normal, where dead is dead."

He paused, as if deep in thought.

"The dead should stay dead, doncha think?" he whispered to the night.

Cleese nodded silently in the darkness.

Monk lay back, relaxing, and continued to stare up into the stars. After a moment, he looked over at Cleese and smiled. "Did I ever tell you that I got me a little girl?"

"No, you didn't."

"Aileen is her name, only she's not such a little girl anymore."

His eyes took on a far-off, dreamy aspect that could be seen despite the gloom.

"She has this nice, little farm back in Iowa with her husband. At least I think it's Iowa... maybe it's Ohio or Idaho... Damn places all sound the same. Anyway, I've never seen the grandkids and she says that I should come visit... maybe think about coming to live."

"Shit..." Cleese said, took the bottle back, and tipped it up. "You? A goddamn farmer?"

Both men laughed out loud. The sound of their laughter was healing and, given the gravity of the past conversation, much needed by them both.

"Closest you ever gotten to farming, Old Man, is the produce section of the grocery store and you know it."

"Hey, I could learn. Watch this," he said and raised his head slightly. 'E-I-E-I-O, motherfucker.'"

Cleese took back the bottle and chuckled into it. As he did so, he looked up. The stars above twinkled in the night's sky with their eternal indifference. He drank languorously, the liquor burning its way down his throat in a good way. His stomach groaned briefly and then battened down its hatches for what was sure to be stormy weather ahead.

As he set the bottle down, he noticed Monk had drifted off to sleep; a deep rumbling came from his chest as he began to snore. Cleese quietly looked over at two of the few men on the planet that he'd ever considered to be his friends and smiled. Weaver and Monk lay drunk and slumbering on the roof of their place and Cleese decided that, for now, that was just fine. He'd watch over them, finish what was left of this bottle, and keep them both safe from harm up here in this spot that somehow seemed above all the stench, away from all the blood—and all that death seemed like nothing more than a story they'd all heard one time long ago.

He settled in, got himself comfortable, and lifted the bottle for another drink.

"A farmer..." Cleese said, the words sounding hollow within the emptiness of the bottle. "Shee-it."

Consanguinity

The ground burned hot beneath Cleese's boots. The sand had soaked up enough heat from the overhead lights to make the Pit's floor a griddle. Humidity drenched everything in a thin layer of moisture and it pulled what little oxygen there was from the air and made it difficult to breathe. Cleese stood—baking beneath the scorching lights—and watched as the UD before him aimlessly wandered around the vastness of the pit.

The thing hadn't caught his scent as of yet, but it would and when it did, it would come clawing its way after him with teeth grinding and eyes bugging out maniacally. Infectious saliva would be slithering down its chin in long, ropey loops like malignant taffy.

This one had been a woman once; kind of short and matronly. Her back was stooped and her gait was doddering, but her eyes dripped murder and her teeth gnashed together in long, expectant strokes. She walked, swaying, past Cleese and he denied the impulse to reach out and touch her. He wanted to extend this moment, to savor it.

Momentarily, he thought this was what a predator felt like as it eyed unsuspecting prey.

The woman swung around slowly, her arms swaying like a chimp. As she stumbled past, she caught a hint of Cleese's scent on the wind. Her nose managed to snag just a ribbon of his odor and her senses honed in on him like a viper. She turned and stared darkly across the sand. Shadows hung over her sallow face, obscuring any facial features, however, her eyes burned from behind her messy, oily hair.

"HAAA-aaa..." she hissed, her breath poisoning the air as soon as it touched it. She reached out for him, slowly, as if the act caused her great pain. Her hands opened and closed, wanting to touch, wanting to hold, wanting to tear. She'd locked onto his scent now and was coming; coming fast. Her feet were tripped up sporadically by the unleveled surface of the sand, but her speed steadily increased as she lurched wildly across the pit.

Cleese dropped down into a Muay Thai crouch; chin down against his chest, hands open and loose. He rose up onto the balls of his feet and bobbed toward her. His mind instinctively clicked over to pure instinct, and having done so, it never once looked back. A right side kick knocked the dead air from the woman's lifeless lungs. A left upward hook yielded some broken ribs. The spinning right back fist loosened her jaw. An overhand left elbow erased her nose. The woman dropped to her knees and vomited blood and spoiled meat onto the sand.

Sh-tinkt!

The spike was out before he even realized; the metal shimmering in the floodlights. The weapon glowed brightly as if it possessed great power within its metal. Telepathically, the gauntlet sang to him its songs of glory, of fortune, of fame. It was an oracle that radiated Truth and offered up glorious images of his future. It was, it seemed, the very Hand of God. An instrument of great wrath, it was Excalibur in the hands of a vengeful psychopath.

He reached out and twisted his fingers into the woman's graying hair and roughly cranked her head back. She looked up at him, her eyes sinister and brimming with a foul corruption. Her mouth drew open and a blackened tongue emerged over the fencing of her ruined bridgework. Cleese slid the point of the spike into the opening of the woman's ear and steadily pushed.

An inch.

The sound of the crowd above The Pit pounded deep within his chest.

Two.

The woman stiffened against his legs, briefly grabbing a fistful of his pant leg and squeezing. Her back arched and contorted, then went slack. Her features slowly collapsed into an almost peaceful repose.

Three inches.

Four.

The UD's eyes suddenly slid open, like dingy yellow roll-up shades. As her after-life winked out into an unending emptiness, her gaze tore through Cleese's murderous rage. It was like an arrow shot through a rice paper screen. He locked his eyes onto hers and slowly—painfully—he recognized certain contours of her face: her soft eyes, her slightly upturned nose, her kind lips. As she lay there on her knees in the sand, she slowly returned to being just an old woman; hair twisted back, brain now impaled. Recognition took hold and Cleese's mind made its own horrifying connections.

"Ma...?"

"Ma!"

Cleese bolted upright, panting. His heart thumped heavily in his chest and sweat shimmered in the half light across his brow. His head still reeled from the alcohol he'd drunk and his mouth tasted like someone had dumped an ashtray into it. He raised his hands to his face and rubbed them up and down.

A dream...

"Shii..." he hissed into the palms of his hands, "...it."

He parted his fingers and looked around the roof but saw nothing strange; Monk on his back, mouth open and his legs spread out, Weaver, a yard or so away, snoring and scratching at himself. Darkness lay over them all like a cape, but it was otherwise quiet.

He looked out over the compound and it, too, was as quiet as a church. The moon fell down on the grass and the blades reflected the light as silver. He stared out across the fields and saw the Holding Pen brooding in the distance. He couldn't be exactly sure, but he thought he heard a far off moan drift across the compound.

Cleese lay back onto the roof and turned onto his side. Shifting around on the concrete, he tried to find a comfortable spot on the cold, hard surface. Finally, he pushed his back up against the retaining wall and settled in. A shiver abruptly ran down his spine and prompted him to take one more look around. Then, like a child with a favorite blanket, he tugged his jacket tighter around him and hugged it close. As his heart rate slowly returned to normal, Cleese closed his eyes against the encroaching shadows and, in time, fell back asleep.

The Cost of Killing

The repeated crunching of Cleese's feet on the coarse red soil of the compound's track was the only sound that broke the silence of the warm afternoon. His breath came in short rapid huffs which forced his tissues to fight one another for every molecule of oxygen. The metronome-like drumming reverberating up from his legs marked each step of his progress as he made his way around the flat oval track. He'd lost most of the feeling from the waist down four or five miles ago, his mind feeling a distinct separation from the rest of his body. His intellect floated like a balloon somewhere between a blissful, endorphin-infused reality and a torturous hell of physical agony. As he ran along, a song drifted into his consciousness and stuck there like mental gum. He wasn't even sure what the name of it was, but the tune hammered in his brain and kept time with the pounding of his feet.

It was weird how things bubbled up in the consciousness when the body was running on fumes and it wanted to puke its guts up in the azaleas. He was just finishing up what he calculated to be his seventh mile and was feeling like powdered shit; completely drawn and drained. He silently wondered, when the time came, if his legs would obey him or keep on going and not allow him to stop. He would just continue to run around and around until his bones wore themselves down to bloody stubs.

God knew... He felt as if he'd been running in circles—both figuratively and literally—forever. Why should he stop now? As he looked down, he saw multiple sets of his own shoe prints pressed into the soft red clay. In his exhausted delirium, he thought of how he was chasing after himself; following his own tracks in the dirt. He half expected to look up and see his phantom figure running ahead of him at the furthest corner of the track.

Man, I'm getting fuckin' delusional.

Alongside the benches which sat at one side of the track, a thin man with long strands of hair hanging in front of his face stood watching as Cleese sweated his way around the track for the umpteenth time. It was warm out again today, but that in no way deterred the man. He was grateful for a chance to be out in the fresh air, away from the smell of puke and bile and blood and festering gore. If only for an hour or so, he was happy to smell something—anything—other than death.

Adamson had been at the compound for longer than he cared to remember and was beginning to wonder if he'd ever get the stink off him. He'd had a bit of that dead smell back before the world went to shit and life got itself all twisted around, but this was different. This was a stench that had worked itself into the marrow of his bones, infected him to his very soul.

As he watched Cleese running, he remembered a time when he too ran; ran for everything he'd been worth. He'd run from his place of work—a place that was in and of itself a place of death—and, when his car died on him, he'd kept on running until he finally fell exhausted in a warehouse on the outskirts of town. He'd awoken surrounded by men with guns and had, for a moment, forgotten all about Mr. Robinson, Mrs. Jacob, Mrs. Devon, Mr. Lodene and the fat Mrs. Harvey. He'd opened his eyes and saw nothing except the endless abyss one can only see if one is looking deep inside the barrel of a locked and loaded gun.

Once the armed men figured out that he still possessed a heartbeat, they'd brought him to a bivouac and gotten him showered, fed and clothed in something more battle-ready than the soiled business suit in which they'd found him. Then, after a good (and safe) night's rest and quick lesson in firearms later, he'd been out on the front line "droppin' Zs"—the term the militia used for the killing of the reanimated dead.

As the weeks went by, and after a whole lot of practice, he'd gotten pretty good at it. His knowledge of anatomy told him exactly where to aim the rifle for maximum effect. It also helped him to judge at a distance how quickly the undead could move once they'd engaged them—the more progressed their state of decomposition was, the slower they were. As a result, he'd become known as The Dead Guy due to his almost encyclopedic knowledge of Them.

If they only knew...

Then one day, as he finished the clearing of a large office building, a savvy and persuasive man approached him accompanied by a huge bear of a man he'd called Jimbo. The guy had all the subtleness of a used car salesman and, after many drinks and a large steak dinner, talked some shit about these big plans he had. Adamson thought the guy was as crazy as a soup sandwich, but after a few more drinks he felt more than willing to entertain such madness. This guy, Weber, heard about Adamson's unique body of knowledge from some of the men and wanted to brainstorm some ideas with him as to how to keep a large number of the undead. Like everything about him, all of this Weber fella's ideas were big and just this side of crazy. Apparently, Weber had these plans and if Adamson could develop a way to do what he was asking, there could be some big money in it for everybody.

And boy, he wasn't kidding...

Adamson's mistake was that he didn't read Weber's fine print when he signed on. As promised, there was indeed money enough for everybody.

The problem was Adamson was nobody.

Flash forward to today and Weber is a multimillionaire living in a swanky high rise and Adamson a schmuck living in a hangar with a couple of hundred corpses. And when all was said and done, all Adamson had left was what he'd come with: a very specified body of knowledge and his commitment to giving the dead their respectful due. Yes, the idea of making some real money was important, but in the end it was always secondary to his reverence and protection of the dead.

As far as Adamson was concerned, the living were hypocrites and liars and they could go fuck themselves. With a deep, resigned breath he sighed and ran his fingers through his greasy hair. Almost as an afterthought, he wiped his hand off on the seat of his pants and continued watching Cleese as he made his way around the far end of the track.

Cleese powered into the home stretch and decided (based on the sun's position in the sky) that it was getting late and he should probably call it quits. He was supposed to meet Monk to review more fight tapes and wanted to grab a quick shower before he caught up with him. He pushed himself to make his legs pump even harder as he approached the Start marker etched into the track. As he crossed the line and stumbled to a stop, his legs went rubbery and he almost thought that he was going to fall, but managed to maintain his balance.

He walked stiffly until able to catch his breath and then bent at the waist to stretch his already tightening hamstrings. They were still sore from the hack squats Monk insisted on him doing the day before. This running shit on top of that wasn't doing him any favors. His muscles cried out in protest with every movement. Standing upright and walking slowly over to where he'd piled his gym bag and water bottle, his quadriceps and calves now added their voices to the polyphonic pain opera already in progress. He picked up his stuff and slung the bag's strap over his shoulder. Walking off the track, he pulled the top off his water bottle and drank heartily. Once his thirst had been more or less sated, he opened his eyes and noticed someone standing up by the benches at the side of the track. As he came closer, he recognized the guy. He'd seen the dude at the Holding Pen when Monk had taken him there.

Adamson was his name or something like that.

The guy was lanky and had a distinctly unkempt look about him—as if he'd just said, "Fuck it!" and given up on personal hygiene. Cleese was no fashion plate himself—his taste in clothing leaned more toward boots, jeans, black t-shirts and, if the weather was less than perfect, a beat up old leather jacket—but he at least liked a good hosing off now and again. Adamson looked like he'd not seen a shower in quite a while. His clothes looked even worse.

Cleese wasn't sure what the guy wanted, but it looked as if he was about to find out. As Cleese approached, Adamson straightened up and once again ran his fingers through that greasy hair of his. Cleese idly wondered where the guy got his hair care products. Union 76 was his first guess.

"Cleese," Adamson greeted him and reached out to shake hands.

Cleese grinned, bowed slightly and apologized, "Sorry, but I'm all sweaty. I don't want to get you all slimy." Somewhere deep inside his brain, Cleese thought how ironic it was that here was a guy he didn't want to come in physical contact with.

"Nice day," Adamson said, looking around.

"Yeah... Since coming here, I don't get to see as much of the sun as I might once have. It's good to get out into the fresh air once in a while."

Adamson smiled widely and said, "Preaching to the choir, Buddy. You're preaching to the choir." He smiled and then the expression evaporated from his face like an ice cube on hot asphalt. "I wanted to talk to you, if you have a minute."

Cleese nodded and motioned for him to sit down. Cleese took a seat, his legs singing out in appreciation. As his ass hit the metal of the bench, Adamson came around and sat down near him. Immediately, Cleese caught a whiff of the same sour smell coming off of Adamson that he'd encountered when he went into the Holding Pen. It smelled like sour meat and week-old grease. It was the kind of smell that made the stomach churn and the bitter taste of bile come unbidden to the back of the throat. As subtly as he could, Cleese slid slightly further down the bench.

"What did you want to talk about?"

"Well," Adamson said and ran his hand through that hair once again, "I was looking over my log the other day. I keep pretty good notes on how many UDs come in, how many go out, and who it is that makes one change to the other."

Cleese nodded. Other than a few of the fighters he'd met, everyone he'd run into in this place seemed to have a pretty advanced case of OCD. It didn't surprise him that the guy in charge of keeping track of The Dead could tell you the exact number of Them he had in his grisly inventory.

"Yeah, and...?"

Adamson stretched his legs out in front of him and scratched at some bit of slime embedded into the fabric of his pants.

"It got me curious... I noticed you're doing more than your share of incapacitating my Stock."

Cleese nodded and said, "Ummm... sorry."

Adamson laughed and his tone brought a chill to even Cleese's jaded senses.

"No... no. It's not that. It just piqued my interest."

Cleese took another swig from his water hoping the liquid would cut the sour taste that was beginning to develop at the back of in his mouth.

"Anyway," Adamson continued, "like I said, it got me curious, so I dug out one of your training tapes."

Adamson turned and gave Cleese the eyeball.

"Impressive."

"Ah, shucks..." Cleese said with just a hint of irony. "'tweren't nothin'."

Again, Adamson laughed and the sight was like watching a corpse kiss your sister.

"Look, I'm not going to bullshit you..."

"Good. I hate being bullshitted."

"I've seen my fair share of fighters come through this place and not all of them left happy. Shit, most didn't leave with a proper pulse."

Cleese nodded and figured he'd already heard what he was about to hear again. 'This place is dangerous. This place will get you killed. Yadda yadda yadda...' Not wanting to appear too rude, he figured he'd give this guy about five minutes and then use meeting Monk as an excuse to leave.

Adamson surprised him though by saying, "You're a different kind of animal though. I'm guessing that you'll do fine here. You'll undoubtedly to make yourself a shitload of money, but I don't think you will make it outta here without some damage."

Cleese looked at him and grimly shook his head. "Well, that's reassuring."

Adamson leaned forward just a bit, "Even if you are able to survive your time in the pit, the damage you need to worry about..." Adamson raised his right index finger and tapped it lightly against his temple. "...is mental. You need to figure out how to protect yourself against that."

Well, Cleese thought, here's a new twist.

"Have you ever heard of someone named Martin Seligman?"

Cleese shook his head in the negative.

"He was this old school scientist who developed the concept of inoculation from stress by studying the learning in dogs. His experiments put dogs in cages that had an electric shock pass through the floor at random intervals."

"Fun guy..."

"Yeah, well... The dogs would jump, yelp and scratch at first as they tried to escape the shocks, but after a while they'd fall into a depressed, hopeless state of apathy and inactivity that Seligman termed 'learned hopelessness.'"

While Cleese wasn't exactly sure how any of this applied to him, he was now interested enough to keep listening. Besides, he silently hoped that Adamson's story ended with this Seligman clown being ripped to shreds by his own electrified doggies.

He was, after all, a romantic at heart.

"Once that learned hopelessness set in, the dogs wouldn't try to avoid the shocks any longer even when they were provided with an obvious escape route. Some of the dogs were shown a means of escape after receiving some shocks but they were shown the door before they fell into this state of learned hopelessness. These dogs learned that they could and would eventually escape from the shocks. After only one such escape, they would become inoculated against this condition. Even after periods of random, inescapable shocks these inoculated dogs would escape when finally given a means to do so.

"However, and this is the important part, if the dogs were allowed to develop learned hopelessness, they'd sit in their cages and, with a blind sort of resignation, just endure the shocks as if they were an accepted and expected part of their lives."

Cleese looked at Adamson and saw a slowly dawning sense of sadness in his eyes. The guy looked like someone who'd just been given a terminal prognosis.

"As interesting as that is, I don't really see how electrified puppies have any-thing to do with me," Cleese said clandestinely checking his watch.

"This place... these people... are not your friends, Cleese. These people... they are the one's delivering the shocks, Son. And you... you're a dog who's hopefully smart enough to figure it all out. You need to understand that these are the kind of people who would give Anne Frank a fuckin' drum set if it meant they'd make a little more money or gain a little more fame."

Yikes, Cleese thought, *'Bitter Fuck, party of one.'*

Adamson continued talking, but it was pretty clear he was doing so more to purge his soul than to make simple conversation.

"The language and the culture of The League is designed to help you be able to deny what it is we do here and why the system is set up the way it is, but it's only so that the whole thing will seem more palatable. Do you understand what I'm saying, Cleese?"

"Money..." Cleese said and took another drink from his water bottle if only so he'd have something to do with his hands.

"You're going to have your first fight soon and I don't doubt that you'll do fine. You'll see, afterwards, you feel fuckin' invincible and wanted and important. Never doubt for a minute though that the feeling will pass."

Adamson looked up and earnestly stared into Cleese's eyes. His gaze was haunted and had a doomed quality to it.

"I guess all I'm saying is to try to remember who you are and what you really want out of all of this. Then, try to keep in mind what you really mean to these people and decide for yourself if this is someplace you want to spend the rest of your days."

"Well, I appreciate that..." Cleese said quietly.

"There was another guy," Adamson interrupted, "named J. Glenn Gray who once wrote a book called *The Warriors: Reflections on Men in Battle* and in it he said, 'Few of us can hold on to our real selves long enough to discover the real truths about ourselves and this whirling earth to which we cling. This is especially true of men in war. The god Mars tries to blind us when we enter his realm, and when we leave he gives us a generous cup of the waters of Lethe to drink.' Do you understand?"

Adamson abruptly stood up and, without waiting for a response, looked almost embarrassed; as if he'd suddenly come to the realization that it had been a mistake to come here and that he'd maybe said too much. He looked around nervously and then clapped Cleese on the shoulder.

Despite himself, Cleese felt as if he was definitely going to need that shower now.

"Just watch yourself," he said and stepped back. "These people are only here to mine you for what they can. The League does not give up its resources until they are ready. Believe me when I say that they are never ready. Trust me... I should know. I once tried to get out, but... Where was I going to go?"

Adamson turned as if to leave.

"Once The Dead have put their mark on you, Cleese, it's damn near impossible to get it off."

"Well, I appreciate that..." Cleese repeated because it was all he could think of to say. All of this fatalistic talk was starting to creep him out. The whole omnipotent corporation thing, the dog torture, and the "sitting this close to a guy who smelled like a crypt" was starting to put the zap on his head.

"And..." Adamson said and took a couple of steps back in the direction of his Holding Pen, "the rest of the world doesn't know how to deal with you now because of the things they know you've seen. You've taken a peek behind The Veil. They can't—or won't—forgive you for that. It's something they refuse to think about... much less try to understand."

Cleese sat quietly and watched as the sad, broken man walked off across the grass.

"Remember, Cleese," Adamson called back over his shoulder, "we all want Heaven, but few of us are willing to die to get there. A good friend of mine, many years ago, had three things he used to always say, 'Know thyself,' 'To thine own self be true,' and 'Screw the bastards before they get a chance to screw you.' You're gonna need to keep your eyes open for your chance to save yourself and, when it comes, you need to take it...."

Cleese stared as the man walked further and further away.

From the distance, he heard Adamson say, "You need to take it before that window of opportunity closes on you forever."

Cleese sat for a long time as the sun slowly set and the birds chirped far off in the trees. Far off, across the stillness, once again Cleese thought he heard the ever-present moaning of the dead coming from the direction of the Holding Pen.

💀 💀 💀

The Art of War

The air outside of the Training Hall was calm and cool as the sun made its way over the surrounding hills and up into the early morning sky. Large crows spiraled in the air and came in low across the grass, landing periodically to snatch up a tidbit or two wherever they could. The walkway leading away from the building was slick and coated with a thin veneer of moisture. A shimmer of morning dew threw a patina of frost across the heavy, metal doors which led back into the building.

Cleese had risen at first light and left his crib long before any of the others were awake. He'd wanted to get into the gym earlier than usual since the machines and workout spaces always got more and more crowded as the day wore on. There was nothing worse than building up a good head of steam only to be brought up short by someone who was moving along through their workout at a snail's pace. He liked to do what were called "super-sets" which meant jumping from one machine to another quickly in an effort to shock his muscles. Fucking around and wasting time were two things he could never stomach much.

As he stepped into the building, the door closed loudly behind him. The smell of the place, in some weird way, made him immediately feel relaxed and welcomed. It had been a while now since he'd come to the compound and its sights and smells were already making the necessary connections in his brain to equate this place as "home." The whole concept of feeling comfortable, much less "at home" anywhere, was still new to him. Hell, he'd never stayed put in any place long enough for that to happen.

Bit by bit though, this place was becoming something different.

As he entered the open space of the Hall, he was surprised to find a group of people already training out on the mats. From the look of things, they were going over some close quarter combat maneuvers; what Monk called "snatch and strike" drills and established martial arts like Wing Chun called "Pak Sao." He saw, even at a distance, that this wasn't just any group of fighters: they were Chikara's Budo Warriors.

Cleese had wanted to get a closer look at their workout for some time now, but they did most of their training under the cover of secrecy with late night sessions and, from the looks of things, pre-dawn gatherings as well. He had to admit it— Chikara was doing a fine job of honing her fighters into something very special. Their abilities were evident in their matches and their cohesion as a team could be seen in their tightness as a group.

As he got closer, he could see the admiration for their leader in the fighters' eyes as they carefully watched Chikara explain a technique or concept. It was obvious that, to them, she was more than just a leader. Through her philosophies and

No Flesh Shall be Spared

training such as this, she'd managed to keep all of them alive in a sport where death was pretty much a given. For that, they were understandably grateful. Cleese figured all of this samurai "I live to die" shit was just that—shit. No one wanted to die and anyone who said they did was a goddamn liar. Chikara was someone who'd kept them upright and fighting and so anything she had to say was worth giving their utmost attention—and their respect.

As Cleese got even closer, he saw Chikara in the middle of the circle of men doling out her knowledge like it was mother's milk. She looked even better than she had when he'd last seen her meditating on the hill out by the Firing Range. Her hair was just washed, her skin showed the blush of exertion. He saw for the first time a bit of the tattoo he'd heard so much about. The intricate lines were visible around the neckline of her shirt and at the bottom leg of her training pants. The tattoo's colors shone brightly and as a result, Cleese's curiosity sat up and wriggled at the back of his skull.

"Now remember," she said as she paced back and forth within the confines of the circle of men, "the UDs will, based on their instinct, want to swarm you. The idea is to let them. They will want to come in close but will be hindered by their own numbers. Jacobson, what is our credo here?"

She looked over to a fresh-faced kid who appeared to be in his early twenties. From what Cleese could see, it looked as if Opie had done some growing up the hard way before leaving Mayberry.

"'They are many, Sensei,'" the kid recited. "We are one. They are hampered by their numbers and therefore cannot attack effectively. We can strike from any angle, from any position since we stand at the center of the fighting nucleus. We are able to react to the threat around us with im... with im...'"

"With impunity. Correct. Now, the trick is..." she explained as she gently drew one of the other fighter's into the center of the circle. "... to keep your center line constant. You must pull them into your 'sphere'—the circles of influence that whirl around you at all times—in order to control them."

Cleese knew what she was talking about. It was the Aikido concept of "circuits of neutralization." That is to say, every fighter has several spheres which rotate around him at all times: a vertical one, a horizontal one, then two oblique angles. The sphere's energy went in whatever direction the threat was coming. Draw your opponent into one of those spheres and you control his actions. To suddenly reverse that flow could oftentimes be... damaging.

Chikara stepped across from the fighter next to her and dropped into a loose fighting stance.

"Come..." she said to him.

The man took two quick steps forward and made a swift reach out for her throat. In an instant, she grabbed hold of his wrist and spun around in a tight circle, effectively pulling the man's arm around her. She wriggled within his grasp for a moment, did something Cleese couldn't quite see, and then, the other fighter was flipping through the air and landing on the mat with a painful sounding *whump*.

Cleese had to admit, it was pretty damn slick.

"Very nice," he said in a raised voice pitched so that Chikara would be able to hear him across the Hall. Immediately, all of the fighters turned and glared at him. Two of largest started across the mat, looking downright pissed. Cleese laughed and absentmindedly scratched at the back of his head.

"Easy boys...," he said, raising one arm like a traffic cop.

"Teiryuu!" Chikara shouted at the approaching men. They immediately came to a halt, but he noticed they did not retreat. She turned from her group and directed her attention toward Cleese.

"Cleese... You are interrupting an important training session. This time belongs to my fighters. If you would like to talk with me, you will have to wait. I would appreciate it if you would move along."

"Hey, no problem," he said as he continued moving toward her, "I was just admiring your skills."

"Well, thank you," she bowed slightly at the waist as she spoke. "Coming from a man of your reputation, I appreciate the accolades."

"I was only wondering though," he said having now come within normal speaking distance, "if it would work on someone a bit bigger than your man on his back over there."

"Like you, for example?" she said with a wry smile.

The Warriors all smiled and stepped back. They'd been around Chikara long enough to know an accepted challenge when they heard one. They also knew when an ass kicking was about to be doled out. Each of them had been easily beaten by her in one previous training session or another. They were all glad that today's punching dummy was to be Cleese and not one of them. What the outcome would be if these two ever were to brawl had grown to be a hot topic of discussion with many of the men in the compound.

In fact, there was even a clandestine pool being pulled together.

"Well, yeah..." Cleese answered, scratching himself behind the ear. "Simple physics contradicts the theory behind your technique."

"Well, come then," she answered and extended her right arm as if to say, *Right this way.*

Cleese strolled across the mat and stepped into the widening circle around Chikara. Once he got to within an arm's reach of her, he was once again stunned by her sense of power and the way she seemed to occupy one hundred per cent of her body space. With her Warriors gathered around her, she seemed a lot more dangerous than she had previously.

"Ok, Tough Guy, go ahead." She spread her arms out as if she was going to hug him, but her eyes said the polar opposite. "Hit me."

Cleese smiled, shook his head in amusement and then stepped forward. Chikara remained motionless, merely waiting for what she knew was inevitable. Cleese stared deeply into her eyes and saw her eyebrows lower in concentration. Despite all of the bravura, he could tell even she wasn't completely convinced of the outcome of this. Once he caught her attention, he winked at her quickly and then bobbed to the left, caught himself, and then weaved to the right. As his body moved past Chikara, he flicked out a powerless right jab. He didn't want to really hit her, merely to touch her so that she'd know he could have.

Chikara caught the force of the blow with her left hand and, just like before, spun into it. She whirled in a tight circle, and moved along the line of the punch, pushing her back up against Cleese's chest. In an eye blink, her left elbow came back like a jackhammer digging itself into his solar plexus. Cleese felt the air in his lungs rush out of him and then, suddenly, his sense of gravity abandoned him. Remotely, he felt her hip dig into his groin and he pretty much knew what was coming next—she'd draw him into that circle of hers, distract him with a nut shot and then try to hip-toss him.

The Warriors had already begun to relax when the saw Cleese's feet leave the mat. They'd all sparred with Chikara before and they knew that these matches always ended up with her opponent flat on his back, flat on the ground.

It was as immutable as a Law of Nature.

Cleese rolled with the judo throw and then, halfway through, he twisted at the waist. As he came up and over her back, his mind quickly rifled through his options. He needed one that wouldn't get him hurt or injure Chikara. As his mind raced for a solution, he had to admit it, he got lucky. His fingers caught hold of the waist of her pants and, as he continued to fall toward the floor, he dragged her with him. They both hit the mats and he clung tightly to her body, continuing with the roll until he ended up on top of her.

The furious look on Chikara's face was priceless as she lay beneath him. Her eyes blazed with anger and her lips were drawn tight with frustration. It was obvious that ending up this way was not what she'd planned. In fact, it was the furthest thing from it.

Far off, he heard the Warriors collectively gasp. No one in their memory had ever bested Chikara in a sparring match. Not even the most elite of them.

"Hmmm," he said with a smirk to hide even his surprise, "impressive."

Chikara wriggled under him and tried to shake him off.

"Get! Off! Of! Me!"

"No," he said with a mischievous grin.

"With one word, Cleese, I could have these men tear you apart."

"How? With more of your chop-socky stuff?" Cleese laughed and leaned in toward her. "Somehow... I don't think so."

He bent down further until his face came to within a few inches of Chikara's. Her eyes still burned, but in this position there wasn't a lot she could do about it. Her hands lay trapped at her sides, pinned under Cleese's muscular legs.

"Has anyone ever told you," he whispered so only she could hear, "that you're quite pretty?"

Beneath him, her wriggling got more furious.

"No? Not lately?" He winked at her. "Well, you are."

Abruptly, and so none of the other fighters might see, he placed a kiss on the tip of her nose and quickly jumped off. The instant that he moved, Chikara fired off a knee-strike directed squarely at his nuts. Only his quick reflexes saved Big Jim and the Twins.

"Hey," he said with a chuckle and wagged a finger at her. "No fair aiming for The Boys."

By now, she'd gotten back to her feet and was coming on fast. Her jaw was set firmly and her hands were balled up tightly into fists. Cleese had seen the look before. It meant someone was mad.

Once she'd gotten to within arm's reach, she threw three quick punches at him. The left jab whistled past the side of his face. The right hook struck him just under his ear. The spinning, open-handed back fist slapped him across the face. His cheek pinked up immediately.

"How dare you!" she shouted through gritted teeth,

"Wait! Wait!" he said still laughing and rubbing the side of his face. He ran away from her and pulled two of her younger fighter's in front of him.

Chikara stopped her advance and shot a quick glance toward one of her men. As one, the group moved toward him. Cleese had fought groups of men before, but they were usually drunk and sloppy. These guys were well trained and, he knew, each one of them would die for their leader. All she had to do was ask and, he suspected, she just had.

"Matte! Matte! Matte!" Cleese shouted. The group hesitated just slightly, but in that second Cleese started rattling off his explanations.

"Ok... I admit it. I cheated," he said and then turned grinning toward Chikara. "I apologize. I've been...uh... reviewing your fight tapes from St. Louis and saw you did that same thing in your fourth round. I figured what you were doing halfway through it and countered."

The Warriors had come almost to within arm's reach of him and a few circled to his left and right flank. Cleese kept them in his peripheral vision, but his main focus was on Chikara. He knew she could end this before it started with but a word.

Chikara stared at him open-mouthed and eyes wide. Then suddenly, she burst out laughing. The Warriors were confused by this evidently because their forward progress ceased. Cleese watched as they looked at one another and tried to figure it out. When he looked back, Chikara had dropped to a sitting position and tears from laughing had begun to stream down her face.

For a second there was an uncomfortable pause, but little by little the tension eased.

"Let this be a lesson to you, my Warriors," Chikara said, raising her voice. "A little research can go a long way." She rose to her feet in that same weird way that she had when he'd last seen her and moved toward him. "A little subtlety can work miracles as well."

Cleese felt her come up behind him and touch him on the tricep. Gently, she led him away. For a brief moment, he focused on the feeling of her touch. He wanted, for reasons he wasn't quite sure of, to remember what it felt like. With a small chill that ran up his neck, he realized that it had been a long time since a woman—any woman—had touched him in any way other than wanting to see him dead.

He'd forgotten how pleasant that sort of thing could be.

"Continue with your drills, Gentlemen," she said. "I want to have a talk with Mr. Research here."

The group of fighters hesitantly broke off into groups of two and began practicing the throw Chikara had demonstrated. The bravest of them even tried their hands at the counter Cleese managed to pull off.

As he watched them spar, Cleese felt another slight tug at his elbow, then it released. The two of them moved off, away from the mats.

"You really think you are something..." Chikara said.

"Me? No," he said. "I just try to keep myself amused."

"I see..."

"By the way, I meant that 'pretty' remark."

Chikara smiled again and her cheeks reddened. Then, a shadow passed over her face and she got a far-off look in her eye. It was pretty obvious past memories had reared their heads in her mind. It was also clear that not all of them were pleasant.

"Please don't," she whispered and her eyes seemed to glisten with wetness in the light. "I... I can no longer allow myself those kinds of feelings."

"Why?"

"Look, I like you... Please do not think otherwise, but..." for the first time he could remember, she was at a loss for words. As she stumbled for what to say and how to say it, she looked like a little girl trying to talk her way out of trouble. "I have lost too much, Cleese, far too much," she said and looked toward the floor. "I cannot allow myself... I will not allow myself the luxury of starting over."

"Hey, join the club, Sweetheart."

Her look of surprise at his answer was almost comical.

"In case you've been too wrapped up in your own personal tragedy, a lot of people lost every goddamn thing they had when this shit all went down. Don't think that you've got some kind of monopoly on pain and suffering. Sooner or later you have to let go of it. Sooner or later you have to let the pain die, too, because if you don't, it'll eat you up from the inside."

Once again, Cleese saw Chikara's eyes glimmer in the half-light and he reached out and gently touched her forearm. Her arms were a contradiction, cords of hard muscle beneath smooth soft skin.

"Look... I'm not asking you for anything that you aren't prepared to give. I just thought we could talk once in a while; be friends."

She looked up at him and a smile slowly unfurled across her lips. She ran her finger unhurriedly around her ear again, brushing back the errant wisps of her hair like she had the last time they'd talked. That movement had driven Cleese crazy the last time he'd seen her do it.

This time kept the tradition.

"I... I'd like that," she whispered. Almost imperceptibly, she reached out her hand and tugged at the bottom of his shirt, just at the hem.

Now it was Cleese's turn for a broad smile to break out across his lips.

"I'd like that indeed," she said leaning in and grinning mischievously. "Oh, and for the record, pull a trick like that again in front of my men and I won't pull my punches." And then Chikara turned and silently walked back to rejoin her Warriors.

◉ ◉ ◉

The Corral

Before...

An immense flock of birds circled high in the air over the rag-tag compound set up in an open field on the outskirts of town. The spiraling cloud was made up of aggressive crows and seagulls mostly, but smaller robins and sparrows flew along-side the larger birds like Pilot Fish. They shadowed their larger brethren and eagerly picked up any bits of meat left discarded. Having been reduced by their hunger and fear to a ravenous scavenging horde, the avian multitude wheeled about in the early morning's sky like a pulsating Rorschach inkblot. Their mass cavorted in the air like kites set lose from their tethers, whirling reminders of an innocence now lost.

The green pastures spread out below were once fertile farm land, but now the fields lay forsaken and well on their way to seed. The hills rolled like emerald waves; terra firma breakers created by the undulating spasms of the Earth. Abandoned farms punctuated the silent and foreboding landscape like forgotten play sets, their crops left to rot now that no one was there to tend the fields. Half-starved farm animals milled about the hills and glens aimlessly; lost livestock dutifully sought the care of farmers, most of who were either dead or still in hiding. Cows and sheep grazed on low-lying grasses. Milking cows lowed with discomfort as their udders swelled to almost bursting. Columns of acrid smoke billowed dark and pungent from smoldering fires on the ground, their onyx plumes obscuring any view. Deep within the flames, corpses lay smoldering.

The flock lazily spun above the mass of activity which ebbed and flowed within the roadside encampment. The birds' small, obsidian eyes locked in on the commotion as they continually scanned the landscape for any remnants of food left behind by Men—either living or dead. In truth, they weren't in any position to be picky. Food was food and when the world went as crazy as it had, both man and beast were grateful for whatever provisions they could find.

Groups of heavily armed men and women roaming the countryside had become a common sight in the past few weeks; masses of humanity whose sense of dread could only be calmed by the possession of their weapons and by the safety of their vast numbers. In reality, it was their fear that brought them together and—like glue—kept them that way. An uneasy alliance had been forged more out of necessity than any real desire or sense of camaraderie, for when The Dead crawled from their moldy graves, men became afraid and their fear hung in the air like the black smoke from their fires. Every species responded to this fear in its own way: birds took flight and searched from overhead for food, stray livestock searched in vain for their own-ers, and Man had come together into a tribe and did what it had always done best—fight.

The militia was more than a hundred people strong and they wandered the camp in fits of nervous energy. More and more though, it was becoming obvious that the fear they'd felt in the beginning was being replaced by something resembling an unbridled bloodlust. In the last few weeks, these men and women had begun to work more as a fluid army rather than as a frightened mob. They had set about forging themselves, despite their panic and the obvious sense of danger, into a small but entirely self-sufficient military.

Every man, woman and child gathered here had endured the initial terror and confusion and was now bound and determined to be a survivor of this dark page in human history. Some had been lucky and got picked up by the group early in the conflict. Others were not so fortunate and were left to fight The Dead alone for days. Of those assembled, there were few who could not tell, if asked, horrible stories of loved ones and their "Changing."

The compound was not really anything more than a dozen or so Winnebagos pulled off-road and parked in a haphazard circle. Here and there, tents had been thrown up hastily, if for nothing else than to keep the cloud of flies from the group's hastily scavenged food and to offer a safe place to catch an hour or two of much needed shut-eye. It was a slapdash set-up, but it was proving to be an effective one.

Off to one side, near the back, a corral for the captured Dead had been erected using split rails and whatever nails could be found lying around the nearby farmhouses. The fencing wasn't particularly strong, but then again, it didn't need to be. The Dead were fairly weak when alone, banded together it wasn't their strength that was proving dangerous, but rather their numbers. Across the entrance to the pen, someone had spray painted a board to read "Purgatory" and hung it with some old baling wire.

A gathered crowd was a constant around the railings. The Living all stood there, smoking and drinking and gawking at the restless Dead. All of them were sure to keep a safe distance from the railing and out of reach of anything inside, each having seen the cost of getting too close. But gather they did for they all felt a deep compulsion to try and understand—or rather to confront and come to terms with—the very beasts which had thrown their lives into such chaos.

"These dead-assed sumbitches... They ain't shit!" one good ol' boy was saying over the dusty top of his Meisterbrau can. He looked around at his red-eyed audience and gauged their compliance. He then cursed under his breath and wiped his hand absentmindedly at a dollop of bird shit that had splattered down one sleeve of his faded green Army jacket.

"The fuck they ain't, Bubba. I'll tell ya... I saw a group of 'em tear that ol' boy Richard Johnson limb from fuckin' limb over at McGurgie's Feed Store," another man was saying. "You remember Dick Johnson, doncha? He was that big ol' boy what worked over at the aluminum chair factory over in Harbison County. He married that ugly, thick-ankled gal from Eatherton with them big hooters. I tell ya, those dead bastards went after him like he was the main course at a got-dam Chinese boo-fay!"

Bubba shot a look of annoyance and absentmindedly crossed himself. "Don't speak ill of the dead, Cecil."

"Shit... why the hell not? It's not like they's gonna hear us!"

The crowd laughed at Cecil's wit which was usually about as sharp as a bowling pin.

"Anyway," Bubba continued, "seeing 'em thisa way... Hell. I don't think much of 'em, ya know? Buncha slack-jawed, drooling motherfucks is what they is."

Cecil sensed more comic gold here and offered, "Well hell, Bubba... If they ain't nothing and you're so goddamn brave, why don't you just jump inside that pen and give 'em a few licks?"

The crowd nodded its approval and punctuated the air with guffaws, half-formed opinions and snorts of hillbilly derision. As one, they all looked questioningly at Bubba, waiting for either an answer or for him to wisely back down.

"Sheee-it, Ceese, I may have fallen offa the goddamn stupid truck, but it wasn't fuckin' today," Bubba said wiping at the accumulating dust in his eyes.

The crowd collectively nodded their approval at Bubba's newfound wisdom. Most had come to know the man as just a "cunt's hair above a retard," but sometimes, even a retard could have what the alkies called "moments of clarity." The group fell silent and considered the depths of what many called "country wisdom."

A sudden slow ripple started toward the back of the crowd; a slight disturbance in the throng which spread outward. A pair of men pushed their way through the multitude, politely asking to be excused but insistently moving forward, until they arrived at the side of the corral. To the crowd, it was evident that they were not from 'round here. Both their dress and demeanor said as much. The first man, the one who looked to be in charge, was built well, although not particularly tall, with short business-like black hair and a heavy brow which cast his eyes in perpetual shadow. The other guy was a regular Baby Huey: big, broad and muscular with hands like Easter hams.

"Gentlemen..." the in-charge guy said, pitching the volume of his voice at just below a shout. He bowed slightly toward one of the women in the crowd and smiled broadly, "...and ladies... My name is Weber... Joseph F. Weber and this..." He made a grand gesture toward his compatriot, "...is my associate, Jimbo. Say 'Hello,' Jimbo."

"Howdy!"

Jimbo's face broke into a smile that was more painful grimace than overt cordiality and the crowd collectively took a small step backward in response. He stood there, grinning like a corpse and absentmindedly working his huge hands open and closed. The two stood silently, the group having given them respectful breathing room, looking like bizarre versions of Steinbeck's George and Lennie.

Weber leaned congenially against one of the wooden rails and gazed out over the scene before him. Casually, he crossed his legs at the shin and breathed in deeply, allowing the crowd a few minutes to settle down. As silence descended back over them, he took a moment and gazed out over the corral. He'd come here wanting to be heard and, if he was anything, he was a patient man. He would wait until they were ready to listen to all that he had to say. When an expectant quiet was in effect, he cleared his throat and began to speak.

"Did I just hear you one of you boys say something about jumpin' in there and mixing it up with this... thing?"

Bubba looked over at the man and then quickly away. It was one thing to talk this kind of bullshit to idiots like Cecil and the others, but once strangers such as this got involved, he stood to potentially lose some pride.

"Shee-it, Slick," Cecil said. "We was talking about it, but 'round here we also talk a lot about assfuckin' Shania Twain. Both have about the same chance of happening."

Weber smiled and stood there, as if thinking over the likelihood of both ideas. To his mind, he was willing to watch either of these events taking place. But then again, one was going to adhere to his agenda... and one was not. Finally, he decided to get back on point. He looked the crowd over and pitched his voice slightly louder so that those in the back could hear.

"Folks..." he said, his manner now demanding both attention and admiration, "I just happen to have a hundred dollars caysh money in here," and he patted his right breast pocket, "and it's been burning a hole in my pocket for a while now. So... I am willing to wager any of you—or all of you—that my boy, Jimbo, here will not only step into that corral with these Undead bastards, but I'm willing to bet that he'll step out of that very same corral again with neither cut nor scratch. Further... I'll bet that he will, before he leaves the confines of that pen, send each and every one of them back to Hell!" His voice rose to a full shout on the last word.

The crowd laughed as one. They'd seen some crazy shit during the last few weeks and they'd heard tales of some things that bordered on the impossible, but this...

This was just beyond ridiculous.

"I'll go you fellas one better," Weber continued. "Jimbo will not only go in there and kick this thing's zombie ass, but he'll make good and sure that the slobbering sum-bitch is dead—and dead for good this time."

Bubba looked over at Jimbo and tried to size him up, to get a sense of the kind of man who would agree to such nonsense. Upon closer inspection, Bubba decided that the man was big enough, but he sure didn't look crazy. He looked about as stupid as a circus freak, but the behemoth just wasn't selling "crazy" all that well. After a bit of thought, Bubba decided that the giant must just be too goddamn dim-witted to be afraid of dying. Either that or he was just plain suicidal. Hell, being as ugly as he was, who could blame him?

"You're either a fuckin' liar, Mister, or your boy here is stupider than he looks," laughed Cecil, as he looked over toward Jimbo. "No offense, Haystack..."

"None taken," was the grumbled response.

The crowd nodded its agreement with Cecil and was soon muttering a host of varying opinions. They knew Cecil to be about as full of shit as a colostomy bag, but... hell, when a man was right, he was right.

"Well," Weber continued, "shall we put both my comrade's skills and his mental instability to the test then? A hundred bucks, folks... is all it's gonna take."

Weber looked at Cecil and Bubba.

"You want in on any of this, Boys? Hell, if he is indeed crazy and destined to die, it ought to be worth that much just to see these things tear him to shreds, right?"

The crowd muttered quietly, their heads moving back and forth as they discussed the idea. All of them had seen people die at the hands of the dead before, it had become pretty much standard operating procedure these days. But none had ever seen one go to his death willingly. And besides... entertainment was sort of hard to come by, given the current state of things.

Finally, a man named Hansford Tillman who'd once worked alongside the aforementioned (and ultimately doomed) Richard Johnson at McGurgie's Feed Store stepped forward and held out his hand. Benjamin Franklin's crumpled face smiled up from his sweaty palm.

"Ok, I'm in!"

"Hot damn, Son!" Weber shouted, clapping Jimbo on the back. "Now, we got us a right fuckin' sportin' contest here."

And with that, Jimbo silently pulled his shirt off over his head. Once off, he balled it up and handed it to Weber. He arched his back, stretching the muscles in his shoulders and stooped down and under one of the corral's rails.

Weber deftly pulled a small spiral-bound notebook from his pocket and took any and all action, dutifully writing down the amount of each bet by its maker's name. After all of the bets were made, he stuffed the notebook back into his pocket. A hush fell over the group while others, who had also been in the camp, wandered over to see what this new brand of commotion was all about. When they saw Jimbo step into the corral, every eye locked on the center of the pen. Inside the enclosed space, the lone zombie milled about, seemingly unaware of the man who had entered into their midst.

Jimbo strolled lazily out toward the center of the corral, raising and lowering his arms as if he were a great bird trying to fly away. A pink blush of exertion blossomed over his previously pale skin. He took in big lungfuls of air as he worked to infuse his muscles with oxygen.

"What the hell's your boy doin' in there, Mister?" asked Bubba. "That dough-head think he's a chicken now?"

"Pheromones, my good man," Weber explained. "He's sending out his body odor to attract the bastards. Pay attention now. Despite your disparaging opinion of him, Jimbo is a true artist. He won't be doin' this more than once."

Those who were close enough to hear the exchange looked at Weber like he was a couple of wheels short of a skateboard. They'd all been trying their damnedest to not attract these things for weeks now, and here was this big ol' boy trying to do that very thing. The general mumbled consensus was that both of these city boys were about as crazy as shit-house rats.

Cecil snorted, spit, and pronounced, "This is gonna be a goddamn slaughter."

"Indeed it will. Care to get in on the wager there, Buford?" said Weber as he looked the older man clearly in the eyes.

"Ok, goddamnit , you're on, Slick!"

Weber and Cecil shook hands to seal the bet and then they, along with everyone else who had been listening, returned their attention to the corral. Weber smiled slightly to himself and nodded to Jimbo. It was a reaction that went unnoticed by everyone as they were all too interested in what was happening within the confines of the pen, but the giant man caught it and understood it all too well.

Jimbo continued to wave his arms about but he now moved toward where the dead man stood. Before long, the corpse caught hold of his scent. The man had been young, about twenty-three, when he'd met his maker from what looked like a rifle blast to the lower abdomen. His frame was not particularly muscular, but it still looked like he'd had some agility back when he still had a heartbeat. He was overall a little smaller than Jimbo in size, but even to this crowd's uneducated eyes, it almost seemed like a fair fight.

None of them, however, had ever seen the kind of damage someone like Jimbo could dish out when properly motivated. Weber had spent a good deal of time since meeting up with the Big Guy finding and utilizing those motivational tools.

Now Jimbo was pretty much a "point-and-click" kind of guy.

Wherever Weber pointed... Jimbo clicked.

And when Jimbo clicked, things got hurt.

The dead man turned sloppily on his feet and stumbled across the pasture toward this newfound meal. He moved with big, loping strides and gathered momentum quickly. His arms slowly rose, fingers outstretched, and reached hungrily for what lay before him. His mouth chewed the air expectantly, drool dribbling from his lips and wetting his chin. In a flash, the thing's gaze passed from blunted confusion to murderous intensity. At nearly a full run now, it came at Jimbo and the crowd held its breath in anticipation.

Jimbo had always been a big guy and one who never had much call to use what little brains God had given him, but fighting was something he knew down deep in his bones. He'd grown up fighting off his older brothers for lunch money, dinners, extra desserts, even for his first taste of liquor and women. As he grew older, he'd been able to turn his natural ability and hard head into a rather decent income. He was a man who instinctively knew how to hurt people and, if he were to be completely honest, he sorta liked doing it. So, when the undead man lurched his way toward him, Jimbo had already set his mind on the task at hand and developed a plan.

The dead thing took another couple of steps toward Jimbo, coming in wide open and accessible. The thing's hands reached out and clawed feverishly at the air. Its mouth was a pitiless, wet wound which tore savagely across the lower part of its face. Saliva continued to pour from its chops like a rabid dog's. Dirt and dried blood lay caked in clumpy lumps across the vicious wound in its belly.

Seeing as how the dead thing had yet to meet much in the way of resistance in the pursuit of food since returning from the cold embrace of the grave, it now attacked—showing no fear and little hesitation. His deteriorating brain saw no reason to believe that the living man now standing before him would be anything other than his next meal. With an additional step or two, he'd come to within arm's reach of his goal.

Jimbo moved a lot quicker than a man of his bulk should and came in low. He quickly slapped aside the dead man's outstretched arms and stepped into what he called his "pain zone." He drove his arm over the thing's grip and struck him across the side of its head with his forearm, just at the wrist. Its head cracked around like a whip and it stumbled from the concussion of the blow, dropping to one knee. The dead man shook his head to clear his vision and looked up, pupils faded to a milky white. A cold hatred burned in its dead, hungry eyes.

The thing climbed awkwardly to its feet and made another grab for what it still thought to be an easy meal. Jimbo did a little hop in the air and threw a forward "bash in the door" kick, striking the thing square in the middle of its chest. Stale air blew out of its still lungs in a whoosh. In no time, the expelled air reached the crowd, smelling of the grave and rotting meat. Some of the women outside the corral held their hands over their noses in a vain effort to mask the smell.

The dead man's body folded in on itself and fell to the ground by the force of the kick. It landed flat on its back, arms and legs thrashing. For a moment, it wobbled back and forth in the dirt like a turtle trying to right itself. The zombie's limbs flailed about in an uncoordinated spasm, its arms and legs whirling crazily in the air.

As the thing tried to sit up, Jimbo leapt high into the air and came down with both feet—hard—on the thing's chest. His heavy boots were driven with debilitating force onto the dead man's sternum. A loud cracking sound echoed across the pen.

The crowd "oooh-ed" and "awwww-ed" as if they'd experienced the blow first-hand. Blood, black and oil-like, pumped from the thing's mouth in lumpy pulses. A tortured, confused look dissipated like mist from the dead man's features. Its labored attempts at drawing breath broke the stillness in an asthmatic pant.

Jimbo squatted over the crushed thing and, for a second, watched it burble and cough as it struggled for breath. The giant grabbed his opponent and lifted him from the ground and put him in a half-nelson in a quick motion. From a side-sheath, he deftly drew a blade and cut deep into the musculature of the thing's neck. As deep, maroon dribbled out and onto the undead thing's chest, Jimbo cut and twisted the head around on the stalk of its neck, working it back and forth. His actions were accompanied by stomach-turning, wet, crunching sounds. A garbled choking came from deep within the throat of the dead man. Jimbo pulled and wrenched and soon, his efforts were rewarded. The thing's head came away from its body, dragging a portion of its shattered spine along with it.

The crowd became very silent as it watched Jimbo claim his grisly trophy.

By now, Jimbo's bare upper body was drenched in gore. He stood slowly, hefting the severed head by its hair. The dead thing's eyes danced and whirled in their sockets while blood fell dark and cancerous from its mouth, nose and stump of a neck.

Jimbo walked slowly toward the side of the corral, extending his hand and the head it held like an offering to both his partner and to the crowd. The crowd collectively took a step backward. One woman off to the side vomited and turned away.

Weber smiled broadly and turned to the crowd, centering his gaze on both Cecil and the good Hansford Tillman. He dropped his arms around the two men's shoulders and patted them like a brother on their backs.

"Gentlemen... I think our point is made, don't you?"

He turned and extended his hand in anticipation of his payment. The faces of the gathered people were a mixture of disgust and amazement. It was pretty clear that the mountain of a man before them was more than he seemed and could handle the reanimated dead with apparent ease.

"I think it's fair to say that Jimbo and I are both owed our payment."

By this time, Jimbo had arrived at the railing and looked inquisitively at Weber. His boss acknowledged him and continued to keep his hand extended in order to accept the money the locals were digging reluctantly from their pockets.

When Jimbo saw the winnings being handed over, he knew that there would be no trouble. Mr. Weber had taught him to always wait until the money had been exchanged before relaxing. In other camps, at other times, people had periodically been unwilling to pay, figuring some kind of fix was in. Like that was possible.

At those times, Mr. Weber would remind them all of what Jimbo had just done to a thing he cared little to nothing about. He would then suggest to them the kind of damage Jimbo could and would inflict once he had a certain vested interest.

As if by magic, the money would always appear.

"Hell, Mister," Cecil said sounding repulsed. "I don't rightly believe what the fuck I just saw, but yeah... I think you have indeed proved your point."

Jimbo now smiled to this crowd like a child seeking praise and casually tossed the head over his shoulder. The thing hit the ground with a wet "chud" sound and rolled to a stop at Bubba's feet. The dead man's eyes still twirled in their sockets as the severed head rolled to a stop in the dirt. Bubba looked nauseated and pulled away as if his mother's sex-soaked panties had been laid at his feet.

As Jimbo wiped his hands off on the thighs of his pants and stepped out of the corral, Mr. Weber finished gathering up their money. Once clear of the railing, he stood to his full height and once again smiled for all to see. The crowd took a hesitant step back and gave him a wide berth.

Both Weber and Jimbo knew down deep in their bones that they were on to something here. This same scenario had played itself out now for weeks. The two of them would come into a camp like this, wait for an opportunity, and then they'd make their move. The whole deal was starting to look pretty sweet. And if they were careful and played their cards right, this gig could turn into something substantial. Mr. Weber would often talk to Jimbo late into the night about how rich all of this was going to make them both.

For Jimbo's part, he was just happy to have someone he could trust. Life was hard when your thinking was simple and it was important to have someone you could rely on. Mr. Weber could do the thinking and the talking... and Jimbo would do what Jimbo did best.

The arrangement seemed a good one, at least to Jimbo's way of thinking.

As long as Jimbo could keep from making a mistake and keep himself from getting bit, things would be fine. Besides, there was plenty of money and food and women for them both. Mr. Weber was his friend and Jimbo was sure he wouldn't let anything bad happen.

"Well, folks..." Weber said as he rolled his winnings into a tight ball and shoved it into his pocket. "I appreciate your patronage. Now if you'll excuse us, Jimbo and I must be on our way."

Weber had learned that it was important to get while the gettin' was good. Make your score and hit the road was proving to be the best course of action for them. He'd come to know that if you gave the fleeced sheep long enough to think about it, they'd forget about the danger and the implied threat and decide they'd want their money back. Gambling losses had a way of making people braver than they should be. Sooner or later, the image of Jimbo tearing a dead man to pieces would fade and only the hole in their pockets would remain. It would be shortly after that they'd remember the guns in their hands and the vastly superior numbers. It was better that the two of them would be halfway to the next bivouac by then.

Weber patted Jimbo on the back and directed him back the way they'd come through the crowd. As they walked along, the mass of people before them once again parted and made way. Once they'd moved by, the crowd closed again, swallowing them up.

Back by the side of the corral, Cecil looked around at the awed faces of his friends and neighbors. Then, he turned and stared at the severed head laying in the dirt and moving its eyes near Bubba's feet. Still trying to piece it all together, he ran his hand through his hair, scratching his head in thought.

"Well, son of a bitch..." he muttered softly and then wandered off to get himself another beer.

☠ ☠ ☠

Valedictions

The crowd within the Allied Sports Center coiled in upon itself like a viper preparing to strike. Its combined weight squashed down into the seats of the stadium and made the foundation of the building growl like a hungry animal. 19,939 paying customers had packed themselves into the building for tonight's televised broadcast of The World Gladiatorial Federation's *Fight Night*. The event was being broadcast to an estimated 19.4 million Pay Per View subscribers in the US and another 240 million worldwide via the Internet.

Teams of baton-wielding security guards were out in full force patrolling the coliseum both inside and out; making sure that no one in the crowd got carried away by the night's festivities. People could often get unruly at these events, especially when the matches had been exciting and there was plenty of blood on the sand. When there was more than the usual amount of carnage, the people responded to it and could get caught up in the moment. If unchecked, there were usually a lot of fights and more than a fair share of stabbings. The presence of a heavily armed security force ensured that people behaved themselves.

It was shortly before the night's opening match and Cleese found himself sitting out behind the arena, immersing himself in night's cool air. He'd already gotten into most of his gear and wanted just a few minutes to himself before his first match was scheduled to begin. He still needed to hook up with Weaver and get the finished gauntlet, but he thought he deserved some time alone. He glanced at a clock mounted above one of the loading ramps.

It was still early.

He figured that he had a little time to kill before it was time to kill.

He leaned up against one of the League's large Mack trucks parked regimentally in the loading bays behind the stadium. The metal of the truck felt cool against his back as he rested against it. He'd only been sitting there for a few moments when he heard footsteps come up softly behind him.

"This a private moment?" he heard Monk ask, half-kidding, but also not. No one knew better than Monk how nerve-wracking the time just before a match could be. He was sensitive to it and didn't want to cloud his protégé's mind with unnecessary blather.

"No... Of course not, Buddy." Cleese made room on the fender for his mentor and friend.

"Lemme guess..." Monk said paternally, "you're out here keeping yourself busy chewing over the hows, whys, and wherefores..."

"Of what?"

"...of how exactly it is that you ended up in this predicament."

Cleese stared at him silently for a second and then said softly, "Yeah, something like that."

"I wouldn't beat myself up too much over it, Cochise. Look at it this way: you're just a guy to whom God—or The Big Stuffed Panda—has given the wrong set of skills," he said with a grin. "Put that into a blender along with poverty, debauchery, and you being a bit of a sociopath and—voilà!—welcome to The League."

"Well, that certainly is helpful. I don't know what I was thinking."

Monk shrugged and continued, "Fuck it, Slugger. Why ask why? All you gotta do is go out there and play the hand you were dealt." He leaned back and settled in against the truck.

"Life just made you one badass motherfucker and now..." another shrug, "now it's time for you to show Life a little appreciation."

Monk gently nudged Cleese in the ribs with his elbow.

"Shit, I know nothing ever comes at a cheap price, Son. But, listen... This is your time. These people ain't ever seen the likes of you. You were born for this shit. Hell, I've seen lots of guys who thought they were, too," he shook his head, "They weren't shit. I watched as they scraped every one of them dumb motherfuckers out of the sand with a kitty litter scoop."

Cleese looked over at his friend across the darkness. Monk had become, over the last few short months, a closely-held and valued person in his life. There were far too few of those growing up.

After his Dad left, the only men he felt he could trust were the ones he'd found in books. He'd read once—and growing up he was someone who haunted the public library like a ghost—that Nature abhorred a vacuum and, like it or not, something always rushed in to fill a void. Without a male role model in his life, he was drawn to the heroes that lived in fiction. The men he found there were men of strength and courage. They were men of ideals—of honor—who possessed a deep-seated sense of loyalty. They had all of the qualities that the men he'd met in real life lacked. To him, the heroes he'd found in books were like gods and, as a result, he dreamed of one day being like them. And so, names like Conan of Cimmeria, Solomon Kane, Bran Mak Morn, John Carter and Miyamoto Musashi were hallowed and inscribed upon his heart and into his soul. They were the personalities who'd made him into the man he was and remained ideals for the kind of man he wanted to be. *Now*, he thought to himself, *Monk's name would be written there as well.*

Deep down though, he knew that after tonight both of their lives were going to change... and change for good. Monk was off to do his time in the UFL and then to live out his days with his daughter and her family—to tend cattle or sheep or some shit like that.

Cleese... Cleese would continue on to whatever fate The Pit had in store for him.

One man stood at the end of his road and the other stood at the beginning

Cleese knew without a doubt that after tonight nothing would ever be the same.

"You ain't gonna try to kiss me, are ya?" Cleese asked, coming apart with laughter on the last word. He leaned back and chuckled to the emptiness of the night's sky.

"Like fuck..." Monk guffawed, shaking his head. "You're one stupid motherfucker. Do you know that? I ought to just go back in there and get a bird's eye view of you getting your dumb ass torn limb from fucking limb."

"I love it when you talk dirty."

Monk stepped away from the truck and started to walk away. He looked back, almost forlornly, and smiled at Cleese.

"Welp... I guess I'm a ghost. My ride leaves in a few and I'm off to my greater glory. It's time for me to share my immense body of knowledge elsewheres. It's been a real pleasure, Fucknut," Monk said and waved his hand casually into the air. "Try not to get killed out there."

Cleese smiled.

"Well... Considering that I was trained by you... I oughtta be dead in just about a minute or two."

Monk put on a stern face and silently pointed his index finger at his friend. Then he turned and walked away. He was never a man for soppy farewells. Monk figured that in a game as close knit as this, sooner or later, they'd see each other again. If not in the near future, then someday.

"When this is all over for you, come visit me," Monk said over his shoulder. "I'll show you how to milk a sheep."

"You don't milk sheep, you ignorant sop," Cleese said smiling. "You milk cows."

"Sheep... cows... same fuckin' difference."

Cleese watched his friend's back recede until his form disappeared back into the shadows.

"I'll be seeing you, old man," Cleese said under his breath. He looked towards the door of the arena and smirked, "...hopefully in a better place than this. Although, with the kind of luck we both have, it'll probably be in one a whole helluva lot worse."

Cleese walked off grinning toward the back entrance of the arena.

Weaver caught up with Cleese as he waited at the entry to the walkway which led down to the Pit. He walked hurriedly, toting a small canvas bag under his arm. The large man waddled as he walked and when he got up next to Cleese, he was short of breath.

"Cleese," Weaver panted, "Admit it, you didn't think I'd make it."

"I was getting a little nervous there, Buddy. I was beginning to think you were going to stand me up and I'd have to go out there with nothing but my dick in my hand. Is that my shit?"

"I just wanted to put a few finishing touches on it," he said as he handed the parcel over.

Cleese pulled the bag open and reached inside. Weaver had been running prototype after prototype of his gauntlet design by him for weeks. After each time he'd taken the thing back mumbling about some new aspect he wanted to change. Cleese was happy with each revision, but Weaver, it seemed, was a perfectionist.

"I was able to install pressure sensitive pads on the inside of the back panel. With these, you'll be able to flex your wrist and unlock the spike. It shouldn't just pop open like it was doing in practice. You'll still have to slap the release on the back to get it to withdraw though, but I figured that, with this new design, you'll be able to draw it out without having to use two hands."

Cleese pulled the heavy object from the bag. Its metal shimmered brightly in the dim light. The gauntlet was a large sleeve-like thing which covered most of his forearm. At the furthest end, there was a place into which his gloved hand could slide; a small strap fitted snugly between his thumb and index finger. He slid his arm into it, pulling the straps that ran around it tight.

"I've tried to minimize the weight in order for it not to be too heavy. I've tested it out and it seems to work pretty well," Weaver continued.

Cleese raised his arm and felt the thing's mass. He did some shadow boxing and, feeling quite satisfied, he smiled.

"I'll be damned if I can even feel it," Cleese said astonished.

Weaver just stood back and grinned like a parent watching his kid open a Christmas present. Behind the scenes, he'd put a lot of work into the piece, but Cleese was a good guy and a friend of Monk's and that meant a lot.

Cleese threw another couple of quick punch combinations—a right, a left, a couple of quick uppercuts—and barely noticed that he had something strapped to his arm much less this metal monstrosity. He was amazed.

"Squeeze the band between your thumb and index finger and flex your wrist," Weaver advised. "Careful though... the fucker's sharp."

Shinkt!

The spike sprang out with a slight jerk and locked into place.

"Well, fuuuuck me runnin'..." Cleese said, clearly happy. "This is some diabolical shit you got here, Weaver. Who'd you work for back in The World again, S.P.E.C.T.R.E.?"

Weaver bowed and executed an elaborate flourish with his right hand.

"I aim to please. Now, slap the release on the back..."

Cleese did as he was told and the spike slid back into the sheath that was hidden in the gauntlet. The withdraw of the spike was more noticeable than the draw, but given the complexity of the mechanism, no complaints were forthcoming.

"Niiiiice..." Cleese said quietly.

"You like?"

"I do indeed, Pal. I owe you a couple bottles of Scotch for this one."

"You got that right. I've already cleared this little slice of Heaven with the Rules Committee so all's kosher."

"Cool. Thanks!"

"By the way, they thought the same thing I did."

"What was that?"

"That you needed some professional fuckin' help."

"I'll make a note of it and schedule an appointment... if I live through this, that is."

The two men laughed and Weaver clapped Cleese on the back.

"You'll do fine..."

"Thanks, man. I appreciate all of your hard work," Cleese said.

"No problem, Kid," Weaver said. He took the canvas bag back, tucked it under his arm, and turned to leave. "I'll see you after all of this is over with. We'll go get a drink and celebrate."

Cleese nodded and watched as the big man walked away from him.

"Listen... don't get stupid out there," Weaver called back over his shoulder as he left. "I ran into Monk on the way here and he's right, you know. This sport's never seen anything like you or that greeting card you got strapped to your arm. That crowd out there is going to love you... Just keep your head and don't pop off. You'll be fine."

The old man's voice echoed hollowly as he got further away.

"You'll do us proud, Son!"

Cleese turned and looked down the long, dark hallway which stretched out before him like a tomb. Fleetingly, he wondered if he was really ready for this. After a second of consideration, he realized that he probably wasn't, but it was too late to turn back now.

"Fuck it," he said—neither for the first nor the last time.

W aiting in the W ings

"Good evening, Ladies and Gentlemen and welcome back... to WGF Fight Night! Tonight... here at the renowned Microsoft Sports Center, we've assembled another night of combat featuring fighters so talented that you will be glad you stayed up for all of this one. I'm Bob Wester..."

"And I'm John Davis and so far tonight, we've had five fully unharnessed fights and things are looking stellar for our next match. By far, one of the more interesting bouts we have seen scheduled is our next one—a fan favorite—our Cherry Match. The untested fighter is a new-comer hailing from the city of Old San Francisco. He's a big one all right and someone who, if you will recall, first made a name for himself by being one of the few who were able to fight their way out of the city by the bay. Word is that he did it with nothing more than a baseball bat!"

"Yeah, John, The League has put a lot into him, so he's sure to be something else. I've seen some of his training tapes and I can assure you that we are in for a real treat with this one. And then, following that match-up, we'll be bringing you our Main Event, but more on that later..."

"Yes, indeed. Another roster of first class altercations all brought to you by the good folks at Weber Industries. Ok, Bob... I'm being signaled now that it looks as if we're ready to begin our next bout. So, put down the popcorn, Ladies and Gentlemen... and get out the plastic sheets, this one could get wet."

"Why don't we get things rolling and go down to pit-side and Al Sanchez..."

Cleese stood within the confines of the cramped hallway which ran under the stands and led to the underbelly of The Octagon. The place smelled like a bus station and looked a whole lot worse. Encased in cement, it was really nothing more than a long passage which tunneled under the stands above and on into the side of The Pit. From where Cleese was, it was like standing at the throat to Hell.

I feel like I want to puke.

He was a far sight beyond nervous now and he felt adrenaline scream through his bloodstream like a freight train fueled by a bellyful of crystal meth. He paced back and forth, constantly adjusting and readjusting his hardware. He patted the pistol tucked securely under his arm. He pulled on the straps. Absentmindedly, he ran his hands over his exposed stomach and felt the clammy skin under his finger-tips. He reached down further and cupped his testicles, silently hoping they'd still be there when this shit was over and done with.

He flexed his right hand, hit the release, and the spike Weaver made for him sprang out and locked into place. Cleese pushed against a lever on the back of the mechanism and the spike of metal slid back into place with a barely audible "sh-tik." He looked at it and repeatedly flicked it open and then closed. Open. Closed. Open. Closed.

Weaver's a goddamn genius with the way he built this thing.

The old bastard had taken Cleese's idea and run like hell with it. The gauntlet was (as he'd expected) a formidable piece of hardware which danced merrily along the edge of what The Rules would allow. Given its potential for drawing blood and the cool way it looked, Cleese was sure it would make him very popular with the blood-thirsty crowd. It would also no doubt turn him into a bankable commodity within The League.

He thought of Monk then and felt instantly disheartened. Cleese was going to miss his partner. He'd been a good friend to Cleese at a time when he most needed one. Monk could have easily declined the opportunity to train him, but he hadn't and that counted for something.

At least it did where Cleese was concerned.

As he checked his equipment one more time, he wondered whether Monk would really be happy spending the rest of his days kickin' it at his daughter's ranch. Would he really be able to come to terms with Life now that Death had left its unmistakable mark all over him? Cleese wished that they could have talked a little bit longer, but in the end he knew it was better this way. Short and sweet.

Somehow, it all fit Monk's way.

Cleese's stomach twisted in his gut, greasy bubbles percolating through his colon. He touched the exposed skin of his stomach, just below his tunic one more time and waited for the doors to the Pit to open.

Gawd, I want to puke...

"*Thank you, guys. What we have on tap for you tonight is sure to be an amazing fight. A Cherry bout with the combatant having been rushed into service after an unfortunate training accident resulting in the deaths of two fighters: Victor Lenik and Franklin Cartwright, both of who will be sorely missed. The tale of the tape on this new man is pretty impressive. He stands at a whopping six foot two inches and weighs in at a hardened two hundred and fifteen pounds. He's a street fighter... with a record of 0 wins—0 losses. So, this oughtta be good. Ok, the pit door is just now opening and we can see him stepping out onto the sand. Yeah, holy mackerel... he's a big boy, ain't he?*"

"*Al, sorry to interrupt, but this is Bob back in the studio.*"

"*Yeah, Bob?*"

"*Al, I don't see a blade on this fighter.*"

"*You're right about that, Bob. There isn't one in the conventional sense, but take a look at the end of his arm. Cleese has reportedly brought along with him a weapon of his own design. I've not been able to get a look at it, but I'm sure it has something to do with that metallic sleeve he's wearing over his arm. Rest assured though, folks, that the WGF Rules Committee has looked the weapon over and given it their official approval.*"

"*Ok... Good enough. Well, I can hear the start of our new fighter's music, so let's go back down onto the sand for his entrance and the beginning of this match*"

I'm having a weak moment
A moment that may not end
Lonely in my own... skin

The thing Cleese noticed instantly as he stepped out onto the sand was the heat; the heat and the light. Both were a lot more intense than they'd been in the Training Hall. They were absolutely overwhelming. Jeez, it felt like he'd stepped into a sauna standing out here beneath the bright lights; all that heat and air that felt so heavy as to be barely breathable.

Everything is changing
Everything seems changed
As if quietly replaced by something soulless

The music he'd given the sound guy was pulsing through the sound system. Its deep, synthesized beat throbbed seductively throughout the stadium, rattling those in attendance right down to their molars. Its effect was something he'd pondered long and hard over. The pounding rhythm was at once infectious and menacing.

He walked out onto the sand in quick, bold strides, timing his movements so that they would be more or less in synch with the beats of music. He figured the crowd would like it and he wasn't wrong. When he got to the center of the ring, he extended his arms (as Monk had suggested during the last of their training sessions) in a Christ-like pose and held it. Then, slowly, he turned in a tight circle so that the crowd could all get a good look at him.

Burn it down

The crowd out in the darkness erupted with a thundering applause which growled up from the floor and soared over all of their heads like a flock of angry vultures. It was a roar that, momentarily, made his guts pound and his head swirl.

What happened to the spirit with all its endless strength?
Did they swallow him up and put me in his place?
Did I grow within my shadow or simply melt around myself?
The human put back on... the... shelf

Yeah, Baby...
Looking up at the throng overhead and the television cameras pointing at him, Cleese wondered if this was what rock stars felt like as they stepped onstage. It was like a drug and he instantly understood why people worked so hard to be here in the spotlight. It was instantly addicting. Enjoying himself, he decided to play it up a bit to see how far this crowd would follow him. He wanted to see how much adoration they could rain down upon one man.

Burn it down!

Cleese looked the fighting space over as he continued slowly turning and saw that this Pit was very different from the one he was used to. The sides of this arena were not scarred metal but a clear, bullet-proof plastic; like hockey glass only thicker. Manning their cameras like gun turrets, the crew could be seen through the stuff even though the panes of acrylic were tinted slightly to cut the glare. It was a perfect six camera shoot of what could only be described as televised mayhem.

I have seen through the eyes of the opposition
The one who defines my failure
At touching that place in the heart
Where emotions bow their heads in wonder
You have encountered me
Familiar with my immediacy
In a wisp of melody
A neglected phrase unexpectedly heartfelt
In this world I may tap you on the shoulder

Cleese spun lazily to a stop and stood quietly, head hanging down, as if in prayer. His posture was, as previously planned, like that of a Corpus Christi. Hell, if these people were going to treat him like Jesus, he might as well *look* like him. With a grand solemnity, he raised his arms over his chest, crossing one over the other at the wrist. He was careful to make sure that his right hand—the one with the gauntlet—was on top.

Ignite
Burning down your Effigies
Ignite
Burning down your Seems of Change

He stood still a moment longer and waited. The music seemed to hesitate: its beat stalling in the air overhead like an airplane just before it crashed. The crowd hung there right along with it, anticipating his next move. He could almost feel them above him, leaning forward in their seats anxiously awaiting whatever he next had in store for them. With an almost silent snort of contempt, he let them hang there, twisting in the wind. Abruptly, he flexed his right wrist and the spike slid out with a vicious metal on metal sound and locked into place.

Ignite!

As soon as the spike appeared, the crowd went crazy. The weapon materialized on the back of his hand as if by magic. The fact that it did so in perfect time with the ending of the song was icing on the cake. The throng's feet aggressively kicked at the backs of the chairs in front of them and stomped against the concrete floor. Their hands came together in a deafening din of approbation. Their voices made great whooping sounds which pulsed and contorted in the air.

They were, for that one, single moment, a mob united in their furor.

"Whoa-ho, Bob. I didn't see that comin'. The crowd here is on their feet and they already love this guy. Let's see if he can live up to the promise of that entrance once the first buzzer sounds."

● ◗ ●

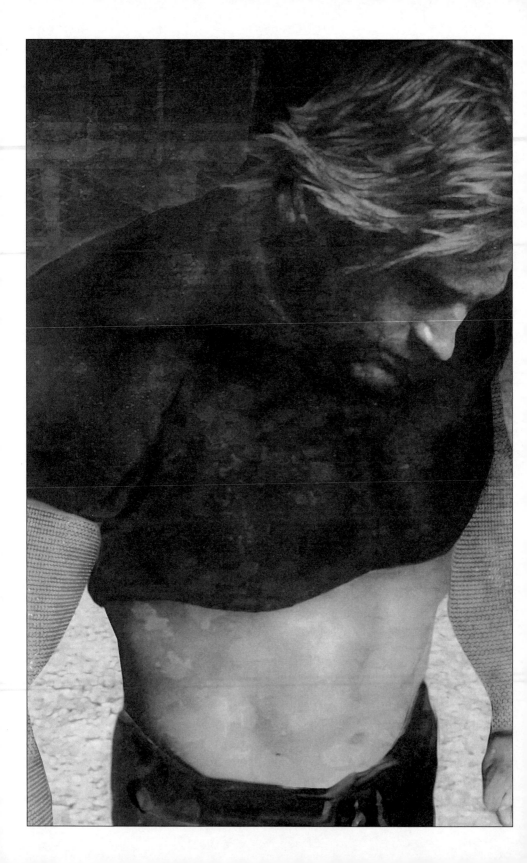

Prima Nocte

The buzzer went off a lot sooner than Cleese expected. His nerves jumped from a stoic calm to full blown panic and back again in less than a heartbeat. His muscles went suddenly slack and he began, as an old friend of his used to say, "shaking like a dog shitting pizza." Then, just as quickly as it had started, the feeling was gone and a sense of absolute tranquility returned to him. The entire episode took only a second and then it was over.

The crowd overhead in the darkness whooped, the lights flashed in his eyes, spindles suddenly turned, and it was Showtime! He had planned and planned for this moment and now that it was here, he felt as calm and focused as a diamond cutter.

Cleese lowered himself into an open-legged stance and quickly surveyed the pit from a crouch; immediately assessing his situation.

Out of the eight spindles that made up the Pit, five had something inside them. At stations One, Four and Seven swayed disoriented UDs. At Eight and Three, there were magazines of bullets, each one of them sitting like twins of salvation.

Thankfully, the other three spindles appeared empty.

The crowd up in the stands hunkered down into their seats as all eyes were directed in anticipation toward the center of the pit. Wives gripped their husband's arms just a bit tighter. Fathers hoisted their sons up onto their shoulders so that the youngsters could see what was about to occur. The children's faces reflected their parents' unashamed blood lust.

The three UDs stumbled out of their spindles and wandered around the sand looking pie-eyed toward the bright lights overhead. They seemed utterly mesmerized by it. Like moths before a flame, they floated drunkenly toward the illumination and reached out their hands plaintively. Their dead mouths clambered and slopped drool as they tried to respond to whatever it was that the light whispered to them.

The Dead had seen a bright light like this once before—in the time of their resurrection, back when they'd first posed their question—*why?* Each one of them dimly remembered the Light and what it once murmured to them, what it had once promised. They'd denied its allure before and there had been, quite literally, hell to pay. Now, as these dead folks stumbled across the sand and reached up for the Light, they once again asked of it their question: *Why? Why have we been denied our eternal rest?*

And, this time... The Light answered them.

Cleese fell out of the overhead glare and landed on the sand between the UDs at positions Seven and Four. He pivoted and moved fast toward Seven who was the largest and most fearsome of the trio. He figured that once he had his hands on him, he could use the thing's stumbling body as a shield to protect himself from the others.

Cleese reached out and slapped the dead man *(late thirties, bigger than the others, squinty—as if he'd lost his glasses and couldn't see, a savage gash had been torn across his lower belly)* across his blood-stained mouth with his gloved hand. It was a risky move, but Cleese felt confident that the Kevlar glove would protect him from the thing's biting force should it come to that. The hide made a seal of the glove and turned the man's infectious mouth into a more or less moot point. In a move he'd liberated from aikido, Cleese twisted the dead man's head around on its axis, directing him toward Four *(teenage male, stoner build, chest showing signs of a shotgun blast)*. The controlled man careened and stumbled, but basically went where he was pointed.

By this time, Four had caught a whiff of Cleese on the breeze and was coming on pretty fast. His eyes bugged out from the depths of their sunken sockets and their violent intent was pretty obvious. As the kid came at him, Cleese pushed Seven in his direction. The stoner swung his arms in a windmill fashion, nails scratching at Seven's face and torso. The boy flailed his arms blindly, gradually becoming more and more agitated as his assault yielded no worthwhile results.

Seven, for his part, had yet to realize where he was, let alone what was going on. His eyes rolled around and were just visible over Cleese's hand. Beneath his glove, Cleese could feel the thing's mouth moving.

Suddenly, Cleese pulled Seven closer and cruelly manipulated his head. A couple of crunching sounds later and the dead man's body twirled to the ground; its neck having been cranked to an impossible angle. With its spinal cord irreparably damaged, the thing's skull sat oddly askew atop the pole of its neck. The UD's body collapsed to the ground and lay motionless, its limbs spread out like a broken star. Only its eyes moved within their sockets as it lay in the soft sand.

The crowd voiced its approval at the spilling of First Blood with another thunderous ovation. Their roar was deafening and the sound had begun to get more than a little bit distracting. Funny how things change.

Four, who continued to reach out across an obstacle that was no longer there, stumbled forward in two great, sloppy steps. Cleese ducked inside, spun under its grasp and hit him twice with powerful rights to the chest. He followed up by coming across with a quick yet powerful left cross.

Four's head snapped around like a sprinkler.

Cleese continued doling out the punishment with an underhand blow directed at just below the kid's sternum. He spun away from the collapsing corpse and stood back to assess his handiwork.

Four wheezed once, twice, and then collapsed to its knees. It tried to draw a coarse, stuttering breath into its lungs, more out of a dimly remembered habit than from any biological need, but that seemed to be something it just couldn't manage. As its milky eyes roamed the ceiling, it blew a crimson bubble out of its left nostril.

Cleese quickly knelt down behind Four, his chest to the UD's back. He hooked his chain-mailed right arm under the wounded thing's armpit, and secured a hand hold on the back of the kid's neck. He tugged the zombie's head downward until its chin rested firmly against its chest. Putting his full weight behind it, Cleese flopped forward onto the sand.

Four's neck snapped like a branch.

Cleese rolled forward and then up and onto his feet. He stood under the light for a second and he tried to catch his breath.

This isn't so bad...

He walked over to the immobilized Seven. The man lay there, prone in the sand, eyes darting about like marbles set loose in his skull. A frustrated expression danced across its features as it tried to move its incapacitated body, but the connection had been severed by the sharp edges of its fragmented vertebrae. Despite the thing's body's damaged condition, the UDs' jaws continued moving wetly, chewing at the sand beneath it as if it were flesh.

Cleese gazed up to where he imagined the heart of the crowd lay and smiled. He raised his right arm slowly and—with a flick of his wrist—the spike flashed into the light. He moved to where the UD lay and impaled the corpse's brain with a single downward stroke. He drove the polished steel into the flesh at the back of its skull where the spine met up with the Occipital Bone. The spike's insertion made a wet, crunching sound. Once the head's eyes went blank and vacant, he slowly pulled the blade back out again. Blood ran in dark rivulets down the chrome spike as it was withdrawn into the gauntlet.

The crowd predictably roared its hearty approval.

Man, I got this shit knocked.

Cleese regained his footing and once again stood fully erect. Menacingly, he scanned the pit. Behind the thick glass walls, he caught sight of the television cameras and smiled for The World. He could just make out the guys who were running the cameras and could tell that they were going crazy: all shouting, waving their arms. Pointing.

Cleese momentarily wondered what all the fuss was about.

His left arm unexpectedly rang out in a painful pinch. He quickly looked down and saw One *(a little girl—maybe eight or nine, her hair mussed, eyes wild, a ragged, open wound that ran across her chest, over her shoulder and down her back)* had her teeth clamped firmly around the meat of his forearm. Drool ran thick and syrupy down to his wrist as her jaws worked against the chain-mail-covered flesh. She looked up at him with a mixture of hatred and hunger in her little eyes.

Shit, this was only a kid. Younger than even the stoner had been and *he'd* been fucking young. Hell, she was nine, if she was a day. Dressed in a torn and soiled pinafore, her head moved back and forth from side to side as she gnawed greedily on his arm. Her cold hands gripped him at the wrist and the elbow and, for a moment, she looked as if she was working on her first Thanksgiving turkey leg.

Cleese's stomach made an oily, gurgling sound.

The crowd sat silently, expectantly, for this was an important moment in all Cherry Matches: the moment when every first-time fighter made his decision to kill. It was a choice made not out of necessity, not out of self preservation, but out of pure, raw vengeance. It was largely held that even if a new fighter did make the kill, he could be so demoralized that he made mistakes later in the match and mistakes *always* proved fatal.

Killing a child—zombie or not—was where a lot of fighters drew their moral line.

Cleese looked down at the kid as she hungrily gnawed on his protected arm. He tried to imagine what she'd been like back when she'd been alive: her first birthday, her first steps, her first bicycle. She'd been called "daddy's girl" by someone, no doubt. It was all too easy to imagine her mother saying that she had the eyes of an angel.

Now, those eyes were cloudy and refused to stay still in their sockets.

The girl's mouth worked against the metal of the chain-mail, grinding and biting, while her eyes danced to their own silent tune. Finally, her attention managed to focus on something cold and oily-smelling that had been pressed into her limited field of vision. It was hard and pointed and pushed forebodingly against her turned-up nose. She tried to make her eyes see the thing, but it was difficult and her vision just wouldn't stay still. Her corrupted brain knew that it was something she'd seen before, but she just couldn't recall when or where or even what the invading thing was.

Then, a sound was heard that helped her to remember.

Cli-Click!

Cleese felt the Beretta jump in his hand before he even realized he'd pulled the trigger. To be honest, it surprised him just as much as it had the crowd in the stands. 19,939 people jumped in their seats as one and then exuberantly let out another explosive cheer. The sound came down like a torrential downpour, drowning out even the sound of Cleese's heart beating in his ears.

The whites of the little girl's eyes were washed away by an internal explosion of blood. Her milky gaze pierced Cleese's own and then she let out a long, gurgling snort. Smoke swirled up from one nostril in a looping curlicue of bewilderment. Those eyes, now set free, rolled up toward Heaven and returned home, back to the angels.

Cleese's bullet sheared its very violent way through the child's nasal cavity, turning bits of bone and meat into secondary projectiles and churning what lay beyond into paste. The slug ricocheted wildly within the confines of her skull and quickly carved her reanimated brains into mush. The back of her head immediately exploded outward, throwing blood and grue into the air and splattering it like a Rorschach drawing across the sand.

Cleese watched with a sudden sense of detachment as her little, fragile body briefly teetered and then dropped to the ground like a felled tree. It was as if, having already pulled the trigger, his compassion for her evaporated in a red mist of apathy. He felt nothing as he watched her body crumple to the sand. His lack of sentiment, much less guilt, toward killing this child troubled him more than anything he'd encountered thus far in The Pit.

The stadium crowd was still on its feet, screaming and applauding, their din rattling the timbers of the building. Instinctively, they sensed that a new champion was in the making; someone who could make good on the promise of communal redemption that the Octagon held. Having eradicated the first round's dead so effectively, they know knew that Cleese was somebody worthy of their love. He was someone that they could revere.

Ok that sucked... that really, really sucked hard.

Cleese dropped to his knees, now somehow out of breath and bowed his head. He blindly reholstered the Beretta, the metal squeaking into the oiled leather. As the crowd above showered their adulation upon him, his attention focused on his fingertips as they swam hurriedly over his forearm as he searched for any signs of injury.

No blood. No wound.

Hot shit, he was ok!

He was all right. He'd made it.

He smiled and felt himself begin to relax.

And then the buzzer sounded for the second round.

The Three Stooges

The foyer of the Joseph F. Weber Industries building stood as both a testament to the man and to the business he'd created. Predictably, it was an amazing thing to behold: ostentatious without being overly flamboyant, classy despite the nature of the firm's stock and trade. The structure was a colossal monument of rigid steel and shimmering glass which towered over the city and cast the buildings and streets around it in perpetual shadow. It stood like a giant middle finger jutting up from the fist of the city.

Inside, a huge atrium—fully four stories high and impeccably decorated—greeted visitors as they entered the building through the massive bronze and glass revolving doors. A multitude of plants had been place about the foyer and were so plentiful that the place had a distinct jungle-like feel. Jutting down like stalactites from the ceiling high overhead, large fans made of bamboo and oak spun lazily above, their motion gently stirring the air-conditioned atmosphere. Their movement created a soft breeze which wafted refreshingly across the expanse of the lobby. The building was a magnificent showplace and one that had won several architectural awards since it had first been erected. The place was almost too nice.

Cleese hated it immediately.

Although he was astounded by the building's stateliness and its inordinate sense of style, there was something about it that just didn't sit right with him. It was all *too* sanitary. The place felt restrictively clean, annoyingly orderly, and utterly, utterly spotless.

Hell, you could probably eat off the floors.

God knew he'd eaten off of dirtier tables in his life.

Shit, he'd eaten off of dirtier *plates*!

Walking briskly, he was able to pass the front desk without the receptionist noticing. He continued toward the bank of elevators tucked away in a small alcove at the far end of the lobby. His appointment was in an office up on the fourth floor and he'd left his hotel early so as not to be late. Punctuality was something that had been drilled into his head since he was a kid. He hated being late. He hated it even more when others were.

It all boiled down to a respect thing, he guessed.

He'd been summoned to Corporate via a note—meticulously typed on League stationary—from some marketing cat named Monroe. It had been sent to his dressing room along with a bottle of scotch immediately after his match. No one would tell him anything about it or what it meant. He'd just been "called." After checking with several of the more seasoned fighters around the compound, he got the impression that it was best not to ask. It was better to just go where you were directed and hope nothing bad came of it. Cleese figured after the night he'd had, it probably wasn't anything too terrible.

A short, heavyset woman with curly grey hair stood waiting patiently for the elevator going up. She wore a boxy overcoat and her shoulders hung at a tired angle. As he approached, the woman looked up and then quickly looked away. Nervously, she glanced askance back at him. Cleese smiled broadly at her in lieu of saying "Hello." She smiled back at him with a worried expression and clutched her purse a little tighter to her chest.

The elevator doors slid open with a hissing sound and Cleese beckoned her to go ahead. Hesitantly, she complied, as if being trapped in a small box with him was the last thing she wanted to do. He stepped in after her and moved to the back of the car. He then turned around, putting his hand into his pocket as he did so. The doors closed with a whisper behind them and, for a second, there was an odd little silence. As they stood there, the woman looked over and managed a feeble smile.

Cleese grinned broadly back at her.

"Gum?"

Her smile fractured like fine crystal.

"Ex-excuse me?" she said, her voice having gained a vibrato from somewhere.

Cleese lifted his hand from the depths of his pocket and opened it so she could see the two pieces of bubble gum held in his grasp.

"Would you like a piece of gum?" he repeated.

She smiled nervously and shook her head.

"No. No, thank you."

Cleese shrugged and nodded his head toward the elevator control panel on the wall near her.

"Fourth floor, please."

A sudden light bulb appeared invisibly over the woman's head and she pushed the appropriate numbers—hers then his—on the keypad. Overhead, somewhere above the acoustic tiling, the sound of gears and pulleys engaging was heard. The car jerked a little as it moved and both of them settled in for the ride, each waiting for their floor. The woman stared intently as the numbers over the door clicked off one by one. It was as if, by the sheer force of her will, she hoped she could make them go by faster.

Cleese looked surreptitiously at the woman out of the corner of his eye. An image of the first UD he'd trained with in the pit—the old woman in the housecoat—flashed before his mind's eye. *Dirty this ol' gal up a little,* he thought, *bloody her nose up a bit, and she was the spitting image of the UD.* He let his gaze wander down to his right arm, the one that had so recently worn the gauntlet, the one that had wielded the spike. He flexed his forearm slightly and watched the cords of muscles dance beneath his skin. His attention drifted and it soon became focused on a spot at the back of her head, where her skull met her neck. All too easily, he saw the chrome shaft sliding in.

Cleese looked back to the piece of gum in his hand.

"You sure?" he asked, offering again, tying to break his morbid train of thought. "I mean, I thought everybody liked gum."

The woman smiled and waved him off sheepishly. "No. No, thank you."

Cleese unwrapped one of the small pink squares and popped it into his mouth. He smiled, balling up the wrapper between his fingers.

"I don't read the comics," he said confidentially. "They're never funny."

The woman smiled awkwardly again and kept her gaze locked onto the numbers above the door. From her expression, the numbers still weren't clicking themselves off fast enough to suit her.

They rode the rest of the way to the fourth floor in silence.

The elevator slowed and finally came to a stop with a nauseating lurch. With a small, metal cry, the doors slid open. Cleese stepped out into the hallway, looking from right to left. The woman stood inside the elevator and nervously looked toward the control panel and again tried to use the force of her will to make the doors close faster. Finally, the elevator began to move and she stole a glance at Cleese.

He looked back over his shoulder at her, grinned, and gave her a little wave.

"B'Bye..."

She offered a half-hearted smile and, as the doors slid shut, he could see a look of relief roll across her features.

Cleese walked down the short corridor that led away from the elevators and paused. He saw a plaque mounted by screws onto the wall. The small square of gold finished metal had numbers and arrows inscribed on it telling which direction in the corridor led to which room. He looked to the right, got his bearings, and resumed walking. Moving along the corridor, Cleese continued to take in his surroundings and tried to envision exactly why he might have been brought all the way up here. He'd had a good night at his fight and everyone seemed pretty pleased. Still, he couldn't help but feel the same way he had when he'd been called to the Principal's office as a kid. To occupy his mind, he went over in his head what he knew about the League.

Joseph F. Weber Industries was an umbrella company which owned the WGF and UFL as well as a number of other, smaller commercial concerns. The corporation liked to call what they did something other than "zombie fightin'." They preferred something euphemistic and a bit more respectable. What was it Masterson had called it? "UD Engagement?" But Cleese's dad had always said to him (when he said anything to him at all), "Son, you can put a pig in a dress and, no matter how nice the dress is, it'll always be just a pig in a dress."

Then again, Cleese's dad also used to tell him, "Here's a dollar, Boy. Go get me a pack of smokes down at the corner market...and be slow... because I'm gonna be fuckin' your momma."

So, there you go...

The more he thought about it, the more Cleese figured this meeting was arranged so that they could discuss a more permanent—and binding—situation between him and the organization. And that only meant one thing... Money. *Real* money—not the chump change for which he'd initially signed on. Real "Fuck you" money! Why else haul some dumbass Cherry all the way out here from the sticks and treat him like he was somebody? He knew he'd had a pretty awesome fight and he'd been told that the audience reaction to his match had been huge. So huge that they were obviously willing to spring for all of this: a four star hotel, a generous per diem, as well as access to the hotel's restaurant and—most importantly—the bar.

First class all the way.

On the plane trip over, he'd come to the conclusion that if he was really going to do this crazy shit, he was damn well going to get paid for it. If only for what he'd been through last night—he needed to live like Elvis... or Howard Hughes... or maybe both.

He continued moving down the hallway and finally arrived at a door with another gold placard in it which read "Suite 411." He retrieved the slip of paper from his pocket and made sure he was at the correct place. Seeing that he was, he stuffed it back into his pocket, knocked once, and then opened the door.

Cleese stepped out of the isolation of the hallway and into a room full of people. He'd walked into what looked like a meeting that was already in progress. Three individuals were gathered around a conference room table; huddled over some reports in manila folders.

"Excuse me..." Cleese apologized as he stuttered to a stop, and began backing out.

"Wa-wait!" one of the men said. He was a tall, rail-thin guy who sported a ponytail and wore a *very* nice suit.

The marketing guy.

"Cleese... Cleese..." Ponytail said as he stood up and lunged toward the door, right hand extended in greeting. "I'm Philip Monroe. I'm the one who wrote you."

Cleese stopped in the doorway and reopened the door.

"I'm sorry," Cleese said, his arms out and palms open ignoring the offered handshake preferring to bow slightly instead. "I thought I was interrupting something."

"No... No... In fact, we were just talking about you." Monroe stopped and made a broad gesture with his arm toward the two other people in the office. "This is Monica Johansson from Sales."

Monica was pretty in a buttoned-down corporate kind of way with blonde hair that cascaded down her shoulders in all the right ways. Her body showed the results of a regular regimen of that useless cardio-kickboxing shit through her trendy business suit. Cleese smiled slightly at the thought of her and forty or so other women all feeling empowered as they threw half-hearted punches at empty air. That all said, she was still pretty hot looking. As Cleese looked her face over one more time, he sadly noticed that her expression said that she knew it because she had a look which spelled "shitty attitude" in any man's language. Her face was perpetually pinched up in a continual sniff as if someone was holding a small turd just under her nose.

Cleese bowed in her direction in lieu of shaking hands. It was generally regarded among the fighters that being in the League had an odd, double-edged sword quality to it. Everyone learned soon enough that one of those edges was that regular people didn't really like to touch you; the *mark of the dead*, and all of that. As it turned out, the other edge of the sword was that there were a *lot* of women who were very turned on by the thought of being touched by you; the *mark of the dead*, and all of that.

Whatever...

Cleese didn't shake hands with people now because he didn't want to embarrass them... one way or the other. It was sort of beside the point that he'd never particularly liked the feeling of people touching him.

"Yes," and the woman actually preened. "Mr. Cleese. Saw your fight... loved it." She smiled and did a quick squint, pinching her eyes and betraying the corners she'd cut on her plastic surgeon. "Loved it and loved *you*! Absolutely fantastic! And, there's been quite a reception forthcoming from our audience, I might add. They absolutely *loved* your arm thingy. Hell, the Internet message boards are positively *sizzling*!"

And she actually winked at him.

"Uhhh... thanks."

Cleese cautiously stepped just a little bit deeper into the room. It was funny... Here he was someone who'd just fought a pit full of the living dead, but *this* was a room he was anxious about entering and closing the door behind him. This whole situation was exactly the kind of interaction that always made him feel all wonky inside. He'd never been the kind of guy who liked the sensation of having smoke blown up his ass. His face said as much now, but from the look of things, these three chuckleheads weren't the type to pick up on such subtleties of body language. Too self-absorbed. He silently hoped that it was not going to get too terribly smoky in here.

He didn't think his ass could take it.

He took another step deeper into the room and quickly cataloged the minutiae of his surroundings as a force of habit. There was a large, mahogany conference table set in the middle of emerald green wall-to-wall carpet. Along the walls, dark wooden bookshelves held row after row of very legal-looking books. The whole decor struck Cleese as being very Christmas-y. Gathered around the table, sat Monroe... Monica... and another guy who was balding and had an expression on his face like someone had just shot his dog. Cleese decided straight away that the guy looked like a mortician.

"And *this* is Richard Murphy from the networks."

Well, I was close.

Cleese smiled and bowed again slightly.

"Cleese..." Murphy said, standing and then adjusting posture just a little bit straighter, pulling his gut in just a little. "May I call you Cleese?"

"Sure..." Cleese said dryly, "after all, it *is* my name."

"Of course... well—um, yes. Cleese, I think I can speak for everyone here at the League when I say that your performance at last night's *Fight Night* was sens-sational. I mean, you really did us proud, Son. Top notch! Weber Industries is *very* pleased."

Sniff! Sniff! Oh, great... Smoke.

"Well, thank you," and Cleese smiled broadly, "Dick."

Murphy's posture sort of deflated and he sat back down.

"Uh-ok...," blushed Monica. "Well, we here at Corporate just wanted to get a chance to meet with you today. You know, get a chance to talk, get an impression of you... and for you to get a feel for us." She directed the emptiest of smiles in his direction. "We wanted to make sure that everyone was happy in their situation and to check and see that we were all on the same page."

She looked briefly to her colleagues as if she were getting a consensus.

"You see, Mr. Cleese, we'd like to offer you a more permanent and substantial spot on the roster."

The men at the table nodded, smiling stupidly with all the sincerity of Cheshire Cats.

"How would you feel about that, Mr. Cleese?" Monica asked. Her drawn-in eyebrows rose expectantly.

There was something in the woman's tone and manner that irked Cleese. Maybe it was the way she was banking on her good looks to seal an already assumptive sale. Like it was *that* easy. It might have been the fact that they'd hauled him all the way here as an obvious show of wealth and power. He couldn't really put his finger on it, but the whole thing was like a burr under his saddle. A voice deep inside of him told Cleese that these were people who were not to be trusted. Monica had a way about her that struck him as oil-slick smooth and about as sincere as a gigolo's promise.

It was the same with the old guy. Dick.

And Monroe—with that dorky ponytail and Euro-trash suit... Shit, that was one pretentious motherfucker if he'd ever seen one. What that guy needed was to do an honest day's work... or maybe spend fifteen good minutes in Cleese's world sometime. The experience might just wipe that smug look off of his Botox-deadened face.

Monica, Dick and Monroe.

Federation Weasels.

Corporate fucks.

Cleese looked around the room as he carefully considered his response. He had always hated this kind of bullshit: Corporate America. It was a culture based on stabbing your friends in the back; a community made up of snakes and sharks. At least on the street, if someone was going to fuck you, they'd at least take the time to look you in the eye as they slid the knife between your ribs. Here, the knife was usually delivered in conjunction with a pat on the back. You know, all friendly like.

Although... Cleese had to admit it, these *were* some very nice digs and what kind of loser was he, living in dorm rooms and sweating bullets, punchin' holes in the heads of reanimated corpses and risking his ass day after day, night after night? Meanwhile, these people sat back in their plush corner offices and made bank on his blood, sweat and fears. The more Cleese thought about it, the more it all seemed unfair to him—promise of an ass-load of money or not.

After all, where was Monk's payday? Hadn't he worked diligently for these imbeciles for too goddamn long and, when all was said and done, all he was getting was that knife-filled pat on the back, a gold watch, and a one-way ticket to Palookaville. Cleese then considered what happened to Lenik. That fuck deserved everything he got, if for nothing else than his own damn hubris. But, where was Cartwright's payday? Cleese saw the way that guy left the compound: in a pine box, wrapped in plastic, bound by twine, with a tag tied to his toe.

Toes up...

Silently, he decided that it was worth the risk and just about time to kick this thing in the ass.

"Well, Monica, both me and my arm thingy would really love to play a bigger part in the League. We really would. You give me a pen and I'll sign on the dotted line right now. It is, I believe, why I was recruited in the first place, correct?"

He looked around the table for a bit of that down home consensus.

"I mean, I imagine you guys didn't bring me on board for my health. It was always the idea that one day I would be signed," he leaned over the table menacingly, "'officially.'

"However, as for my *situation*... My situation is that I kick the shit out of dead guys, old ladies, and children with their throats torn out for America's amusement... and *your* League's profit. Every one of us fighters risks our lives each and every day so you and the rest of these suits can pull down your comfortable paychecks and feel that you're involved in something dangerous. It would probably be a good idea for both of us if we were all, in the future, to bear a little of that in mind, ok?"

Three very unhappy faces met his gaze.

"You know..." he shook his head and let out a hiss of air, "there are days, Mon, when it takes real soap-and-water-scrubbin' to take the stain of the coagulated blood out of my skin. Do *you* ever have days like that?"

He paused for another moment to again gauge their reactions.

"I thought not. So, bearing all that in mind, you tell *me*, Monica... are you all good in *your* situation?"

The three of them continued to sit at the table and silently stare at him for a long time, their expressions still polite, but decidedly unhappy. Cleese saw the quick and furtive look that was exchanged between them. It told him all he needed to know about their opinion of him. He'd seen it too many times before to not know what it meant now.

The look told him two things: "Fuck" and "You."

In a way, that suited Cleese just fine. He'd decided before coming here that he would probably need to develop an exit strategy for this little side-of-the-road freak show and get it in place right quick. Now, after meeting them face-to-face, his gut told him that these people would do exactly as he has suspected: they would fuck him the first chance they got. So, pillaging the situation for every red cent he could get his hands on was now paramount. He'd rat-hole every dime he got his hands on in a place so remote that none of them could ever find it, much less get their hands on. He also knew that he would need to keep his mouth shut about it. He figured he could probably trust Weaver or even Chikara, but if he were to be completely honest about it, even that would only go so far. He'd learned a long time ago that in this life you could only really ever trust yourself.

After that, the Three Corporate Stooges pulled a complete Mount Rushmore. They shut down and didn't say much more unless they absolutely had to. When the subject of money and amenities came up, Cleese threw out numbers and conditions that he knew were exorbitant. Monroe didn't bat an eye. He said that the company's lawyers would draw up the necessary contracts and he'd contact him if there were any questions regarding specific details.

And that was it.

Meeting over.

In and out in under an hour... like this was some kind of Lenscrafters.

Cleese had walked in here just another poor schlub possessing more gnads than I.Q. points and now he was walking out of here a *very* rich man. It was all that simple. It didn't make a lot of sense, but then again, at these prices, it didn't much matter, did it? He had known that he needed to get a look at the lay of this land and, now that he had, he knew he'd need to watch his back and keep his head clear. He couldn't really be sure, but he had a sneaking suspicion that he'd burned a couple of bridges here today.

Did he care?

Fuck no...

He'd been burning bridges for so long that he'd grown rather fond of the smell.

He nodded once more to Moe, Larry and Ponytail and turned to leave.

Hell, if the corporation was going to give him a big, fat pay day, then who was he to argue. He knew that, sooner or later, they'd try to bone him—either financially or the way they'd done with Monk when they didn't let him walk away on his own terms—and that knowledge incited in him a distinctly libertine way of looking at things. Cleese just hoped that he'd live long enough to enjoy the pay-off.

As Cleese was leaving, that smarmy git, Monroe, made it a point to catch Cleese's eye. He smiled a slow, peeling smile at Cleese. It was a smile full of venom and self-satisfaction. It was a grin that would have been utterly at home on the face of Iago as he whispered his conspiracies into Othello's ear.

"Good luck on your next *Fight Night*," and he winked and pointed.

The fuck.

After Cleese left the room, Monroe sat back in his chair, tossed his pen onto the table, and sighed heavily. He looked around the room with eyebrows raised as he blew another breath out of his nose in a whoosh. From the looks on Monica's and Richard's faces, things could have probably gone better.

"Well, *he's* a bit of an asshole," Monroe muttered under his breath but just loud enough for the others to hear.

"About what I thought he'd be really," said Monica unhappily. "What was it that Weber called these guys— 'Jimbos?' That sounds about right."

"I don't know what they expect us to do with the damn thugs they keep sending," Richard sighed. "I can't make League stars out of common criminals."

Monica leaned forward in her chair and gathered together the papers before her. From her the way she stuffed them together, Monroe could tell she was more than a little pissed off.

"Look, I don't much care about these thugs—these Jimbos—in general and that one in particular. We brought Cleese here to see if he was the type to play ball with us long-term. The League wanted to get an assessment of him and how we thought we could utilize him. I have my answer. How about you, Richard?"

Richard rubbed his fingers across his brow as if he was trying to erase a major headache.

"Yeah, I saw what I needed to see," he said. "I had hoped for better."

"Monroe?" Monica asked now standing with her leather folder tucked neatly under her arm.

"Yeah, just another dumb pug who has yet to learn which side his bread is buttered on."

"Then it's settled?" Monica asked. "Monroe, he's your and Masterson's property now. Get him back into the Pit and keep him there for as long as he continues to make us money. He's yours to do with what you will. All The League wants is for him to generate the two Rs—ratings and revenue. We'll need you to accomplish that..."

She paused and looked at him. Her gaze spoke volumes.

"... one way or the other. Everyone agreed?"

Richard nodded his head and stood up.

"I'm good," he said.

Monroe began gathering up his things as well. As he did so, he quickly considered the pros and cons of what had transpired here today. Cleese was a complete and utter asshole—that was now a given—but he was also a talented fighter. Monroe silently thought through how he might turn all of this to his advantage. With the newly given blessing of Monica and Richard, he knew he could do just about anything with the man and not have any real blowback. Since no one cared if Cleese ever made it out of the Pit, Monroe thought that he just might keep continually upping the danger level until Cleese was either turned into a celebrity or a corpse. And, on the off chance that he continued to make it out alive, the only thing that could happen as a result was that ratings would increase. The higher the ratings, the more clout Monroe felt he would have. If Monica and Richard were washing their hands of Cleese on an official level, the only one to benefit from any spike in ratings would be Monroe. And that could only be seen as a good thing. Should Cleese be killed his next time out, then so much the better. They'd just throw what was left of his carcass to Adamson over at the Holding Pen to be used as he saw fit.

Either way, Monroe couldn't see any outcome from this other than his coming out of it smelling like a rose.

Besides, it wasn't like this was the sort of thing that could ever blow up in his lap. He was way too smart—and way too careful—for that to ever happen.

"Sure, I'll regard him as my own little special project. If he makes it through his next match, his ranking will increase and so will our ratings. If he gets tagged by the UDs, then he's out of our hair and the League needn't pay off his contract."

"Ok, it's decided then. I'll let Mr. Weber know the results of this and assure him that there will be no further problems," Monica said, effectively ending the discussion. "He's your Jimbo now, Monroe."

Monroe smiled and walked toward the door.

"Not a problem. I've got this whole thing well in hand. I can personally guarantee that everyone will benefit from how this all plays out."

With that, he pulled the door open and held it as Monica and Richard walked out. He shut the lights off and, closing the door behind him, took one last glance back into the room. He wanted to commit the image to memory as it being the place where his success first manifested itself.

An Ill Wind at The Grab-Ur-Grub

Before...

There was a strong wind which blew through the trees huddled around the outside of the Grab-Ur-Grub convenience store out on the Old Semiyamoo Highway. The gusts shook the boughs and stripped the branches of their dead and dying foliage. An undulating hissing sound, like that of waves cascading onto the shore, punctuated the relative silence. The store's pink-painted, brick structure stood straight and firm indulgently bearing the brunt of the onslaught. The structure withstood the gentle assault as it had for many years. Leaves blew about on the roof, collecting in large, wet piles at the corners and choking the rain gutters.

The front façade of the store was made up of three large floor-to-ceiling panes of glass in stout metal frames with a double door set in the middle. The huge windows were designed so that passersby could see that the store was open all the time and to show a bit of the merchandise sold inside. Across the glass storefront, banners announcing the availability of Lottery tickets, "2 Dogs for a Buck," and ice cold drinks hung from hooks and whipped back and forth in the breeze.

The sale of gasoline was what drew most patrons off the Interstate and it had kept the little store alive when the rest of the town dried up and blew away years ago. It had been rough going there for a while, but between the few remaining locals and the steady stream of travelers seeking road supplies, they were still able to keep the lights on. Unfortunately, every day had become a dance with insolvency.

Out front, three gas pumps squatted like sleeping Indians. Small signs on springs which read "Get Your Gas On" swayed back and forth in the wind. A blue Ford Taurus sat next to the pumps; its driver's side door left hanging open. A lone shoe laid abandoned just under the car's chassis. At the far end of the row of parking stalls, a beat-up red Hyundai Accent was parked; its bright paint obscured by a thin layer of road dust and bird shit. At the other end, a Mercedes E-class coupe sat looking regal and out of place.

Inside the store, a dozen rows of fluorescent lights lit up the place and gave the stock an all-too-white appearance both day and night. Along the wall on the left, an open cold case sat humming, brimming with an array of sodas, juices and energy drinks. At the back were the Beer, Dairy and Bulk Soda refrigerators with several glass doors set in a rubber-gasketed metal framework. A thin layer of frost coated the metal racks inside.

To the right, the L- shaped checkout counter was set up, its surface littered with impulse items like candy, lighters, and snacks. To one side of the cash register was a Quik Pik Lottery machine. Behind the counter, small pints of alcohol lined up like soldiers on long shelving with racks of cigarettes, cigars, pipe tobacco and prophylactics to one side. Below that, a small rack of men's magazines stood, their covers obscured by black cards which read "For Adults Only." At the far end of the counter, the coffee station and fountain drink machines were surrounded by racks of condiments, creamers, cup lids and assorted straws.

The leftover floor space in the center was monopolized by six aisles which offered everything from candy, cookies and chips to bags of charcoal briquettes and loaves of bread. For the most part, if it could conceivably be needed in a car or in the middle of the night, the Grab-Ur-Grub stocked it in abundance.

An air of "inconvenience" hung over the little convenience store now as several people nervously milled about the place. Most were either looking disgruntled or complaining loudly. Up until a short time ago, these people had been simple customers, who—for one reason or another—had stopped in for some necessity or to cure a craving for something sweet. Now, they were besieged—having become little more than hostages. As they paced up and down the aisles, the mood in the place was becoming more and more agitated and, in some cases, downright angry. They'd been stuck behind the store's locked doors for about a half an hour now and, from the looks of things, no one was leaving any time soon.

Every now and then, one of them would cast a wary look outside and shake his head in disbelief. Each in his own way questioned what in hell was going on: some silently, some quite vocally. Oddly enough, "what in hell" was, given the present situation, exactly the correct terminology.

Betty Gillespie stood anxiously behind the counter in her green and red striped uniform and tried her best to settle everyone down. She was the afternoon clerk at the Grab-Ur-Grub and while she had precious little experience telling people what to do, she was working on being able to assert herself. Betty was a plain woman with a heavy smoker's voice and a look about her that showed she'd had her share of hard knocks. Married young, divorced early, and having raised two kids who'd both ended up doing some time, the job at the Grab-Ur-Grub was the best thing ol' Betty could manage this far out from civilization. A good worker, she'd hoped to land a shot at a management position should one ever open up. From the look of things outside, those dreams were rapidly going up in smoke.

"Ok, folks," her voice wavered nervously, "I'm not sure what's going on out there, but I'm sure there's a reasonable explanation for it all. So, if we can all just remain calm, things should be ok."

Across the counter, five people looked at her with unabashed exasperation. A couple of them were regulars, but the others were unknown to her. Just some folks who had simply been in the wrong place at the wrong time and had become stuck here like the rest of them.

Stanley Dillard was one of her regulars and had been coming here for as long as she could remember. His usual order of beer, smokes and an occasional girly book were as constant and dependable as the hands that wiped away the afternoons from the clock's face. Stanley was an older, widowed man with skin like a worn saddle who always came dressed in a pair of bib overalls and a plaid shirt. His bright blue eyes which could be seen beneath his cowboy hat looked—even at this distance—confused.

Another local, Cody Chenault, was a kid whose parents owned the flower ranch out on the frontage road. His was a lonely life out here with few other kids his age to hang out with. Betty did what she could to take the time to talk to him, but the vast age difference between them always made their conversations consist of the smallest of small talk. He was a bright kid with a wide smile and an almost puckish nose who rode that bike of his all over the valley. His favorite topic of conversation was where he was going to go once he was old enough to drive. His plan pretty much started and stopped with him getting the hell out of Dodge.

"Look, Cody," Stanley was saying, "are you sure you saw what you think you saw? You have to admit it all sounds pretty far-fetched."

"Honest to God, Mr. Dillard," the boy said, his arms outstretched and his face pleading to be believed. "I was sittin' over by the newspaper machine eatin' that Abba-Zabba I just bought," he quickly shot Betty a glance for corroboration, "and I saw Boyd Chambers come walkin' down the highway there."

He pointed off down the road and continued talking at a feverish pitch. "At first, I thought he didn't look right, y' know? I mean, he was all pale and his face looked like he was sick, really sick, ya know? Or about to *be* sick. Anyway, he was walkin' down the side of the road like he was drunk, stumbling over his own feet and moving like his balance was all off... like that time he got all plastered at the County Fair and started pissin' near the kiddie rides."

Cody looked around to make sure everyone, even the people who weren't from around there, understood what he was saying. He knew coming in here that his story was going to be pretty hard to believe, so he figured he needed to make sure he got each and every detail exactly right in order to stall any questions before they got asked. Even then... with what he'd seen, he wasn't so sure he believed the facts of the matter himself.

"Anyway, the guy that was drivin' that blue Taurus there was fillin' up on Pump #3 and he had his back to the street. He'd just about finished fillin' up when Boyd came stumblin' up behind him. I swear to God, Boyd looked like he was going to get sick all over the hood of the Taurus when he got close enough for me to get a good look at his face."

Cody looked around again for more of that confirmation he was now so interested in. He took an abrupt pull off of the soda can he held tightly clenched in his fist. The bump in his throat bobbed up and down as he drank. His tongue no longer dry, he went back to the telling of his story.

"So, Boyd comes up behind that fella and for no reason whatsoever he grabs him see. Grabs him from behind and..." He shook his head in disbelief. "I know how crazy it sounds, but... he bit him; bit him hard, he did."

The group all looked at one another and shook their heads as if the boy was just talking crazy. The stranger in the back of the store tisked incredulously.

"I swear!" Cody's face was pulled tight in its anguish. "The guy he bit started screaming and trying to bat him off, but Boyd was like a dog on a bone. He just kept huggin' him and tearin' into the side of his neck with his teeth."

Cody took another swig off his can.

"It was about that time I noticed Jocelyn McNabb coming up from the opposite direction. She was near the pumps and she went over to Boyd and sort of grabbed the man he'd bitten by the arms. Then, she took a bite out of him as well. I mean she bit his arm right through his shirt!"

"Jesus..." Dillard sighed and shook his head. "Are you sure..."

"Look, if you don't believe me, just ask *them!*" Cody said and pointed toward the front glass.

Outside, the aforementioned Boyd Chambers and Jocelyn McNabb stood staring wall-eyed into the store. Both of their faces looked jaundiced and a dark maroon—almost black—substance coated their faces from the cheeks down. Their eyes were empty and their mouths hung open. Drool dribbled from their chins and mixed with whatever it was that soaked the fabric of their clothing. Both kept touching the glass and, as if trying to reach through it, extended their arms toward those inside. Behind them, looking confused, was the guy from the Taurus. More of the dark fluid coated the front of his shirt. The meat of his neck looked like it had been hacked into by a garden cultivator.

"This is bullshit," the voice from the back of the store said. The man, who'd come in with the pretty brunette standing by the magazine racks, was busy microwaving himself something to eat. He looked over the racks of merchandise with a haughty and arrogant look on his face. He'd not asked for permission nor yet paid for whatever it was he was heating up and from his demeanor, he probably wouldn't be doing so, either. He was tall, thin and wore black slacks and a Polo shirt. His hair was pulled back into a tight ponytail which somehow added to his "I think I'm better than you" vibe.

The brunette stood quietly by the magazine racks off to the side and seemed as if she was more fashion accessory than real person. She was pretty, there was no denying that, but there didn't seem to be a lot going on between her ears. Dressed in a denim jacket, a tight tank top and even tighter jeans, her attire was obviously designed to garner attention. However eye-catching her appearance was, she seemed to be the intellectual equivalent of a child. As she occupied herself with fashion magazines and the sunglass rack, it was almost as if she was blissfully unaware of the danger that was quickly unfolding around her.

"No, sir," Cody said. "I saw 'em do just that."

In response, Boyd and Jocelyn pounded feebly against the glass. Their fists left dark smears across the clear panes. The group looked at them and watched as they both pressed their mouths against the window and slobbered all over it.

"Say..." said the middle-aged woman who'd come in to use the public bathroom when all of this first started, "is that glass going to keep them out?" The lady, who'd earlier said her name was Irina Kovalenko, wore her brown hair in what almost looked like a bob. It fell limply down, but not so far as to reach her shoulders. Bangs hid her forehead and the hairstyle served to frame her face. She wore a single strand of pearls, a grey sweater and Capri pants. Her car sat idling next to the Handicapped space outside. She'd left it running since she was only going to be inside the store for a minute.

At least that was what she'd thought, anyway.

Stanley Dillard stepped up to the window and looked the panes of glass over.

"It should. I mean, it's plenty thick," he said patting the surface of the glass. Outside Boyd made a feeble attempt to bite at his hand through the clear window "I doubt even a gang of men could beat their way through."

Betty suddenly spoke up from behind the counter and all eyes turned to her. "Well, if things ever get bad and they somehow get in here, there's a Count Out

Room in the back. We use it to balance the tills. It has a safe in it and it's kinda small, but there are no windows and the door's reinforced metal."

"Well, that's good to know," the man at the microwave said sarcastically. "We can all pile in there like it's a fucking clown car."

"Mister," Stanley said, "I didn't quite get your name."

"Monroe. Phillip Monroe." He nodded his head toward the brunette. "This is my fiancée, Claire."

Claire smiled and waved as if it were a very real pleasure to meet everyone.

"Hiiii-eeee," she cooed.

"Well, Mr. Monroe, I'm not sure how you do things where you're from, but out here in the sticks, we use a tone that's a little more polite when people are talking about things that could save your life. Y'hear?"

"I'll try to bear that in mind, Mr. Ziffel."

Claire giggled and walked back over to where Monroe was standing. He smiled at her and opened the microwave in order to retrieve his now hot food.

They all stood around in silence for a bit, just staring out the window and watching Boyd and Jocelyn French-kiss the glass. After a few minutes of being frustrated that she had been unable to get through to the sheriff, Betty reached under the counter and switched the radio on to see if any of the local stations were broadcasting any clues as to what was going on.

At first, there was just a lot of static coming out of the little speaker, but as Betty spun the dial, snippets of different conversations could be heard. As each one tumbled into the next, a story began to unfold and, from the sounds of it, it wasn't going to have much of a happy ending.

"...any dead person should be isolated..." a man's voice said.

"Human remains are returning to life... and... and... *attacking* the living."

"Stay indoors."

Betty continued working her way through the stations. Only a staccato of hissing white noise and modulated voices came out of the speaker. She kept turning the dial—at first in an attempt to find something that didn't sound crazy. Then, she kept at it in order to try to find something that didn't make her feel more afraid.

"Do not attempt to leave your homes," another man intoned. "These creatures seem to stay alive, as improbable as it sounds, by... by *consuming* human flesh."

"Every person who is killed will become one of them. If you are bitten, you will eventually die and become one of them as well," a woman's voice said, sounding like it came from a place just this side of desperation.

"These are not your family, folks. They are not your neighbors. They are not your friends... not any longer."

The group all looked at one another once again; eyes scanning eyes in a vain attempt to gain understanding. The radio's terrifying voices tumbled into the room like inebriated sailors.

"...the brain...

"These things must be eradicated as quickly as possible. There's no time for sympathy or compassion. There is no time for religious services to honor them, no time for what one might call a dignified internment. There is only time enough for their destruction and their burning."

Finally, Betty had had enough and switched off the radio.

"As long as these things have access to a food source... in other words, us," the commentator said sadly, "they simply will not run out of food."

As the speaker went silent, one last sailor fell.

"If a day were to come that they did run out of things to eat, it would only mean that we were all dead and gone."

Silence enveloped the store and the only sounds audible were the soft tapping and guttural moaning coming from the front window.

"Well, that's just fucking crazy," Monroe sputtered over his mouthful of microwaved burrito.

"It certainly is, Son…" Dillard said in a soft voice. "It certainly is."

The gathered group stood silently, each going over in his head what they'd just heard. The more each of them thought of it, it could only be that everything that was being broadcast on the radio was true. Given that Boyd and Jocelyn still stood leering in at them through the front window and more and more people who looked as bad as they did were now wandering the parking lot, it couldn't be argued that something horrible was indeed happening. There were now at least a dozen of them outside, each with the same drawn appearance and the same sorts of splatters of red and black on their clothing.

As all of their eyes scanned the crowd outside, one by one, the locals were able to identify them. Fred Norwood, the mechanic at the Union 76 down the road was there, his face lacerated savagely. Nick Buford, who delivered the town's newspapers in his little truck, wandered the parking lot aimlessly. From the looks of things, his Datsun had hit something very big and very hard because his arms appeared to be broken and his chest looked caved in. Jorge Velasquez, the short order cook over at the diner, was just standing out by the phone booth; his face and upper body a landscape of hot oil burns and feverish blisters. The list went on and on. One after another they picked out both long-time friend and casual acquaintance; each of them was smashed and injured beyond repair.

As more of the reanimated dead gathered in front of the glass, the group inside became even more concerned. All of this was like nothing they'd ever imagined and so they had no past experience from which to draw. This kind of thing just didn't happen in this small town.

Hell, this kind of thing just didn't happen.

Period.

"Are you sure that glass will hold them?' Cody asked. "There's getting to be quite a few of 'em out there."

Dillard nodded.

"That glass is pretty thick, Code," he reassured. He turned and spoke to Betty behind the counter. "Betty, you remember last summer when those kids shot at the front of the store with that huntin' rifle?"

Betty nodded and assured everyone, "It'll hold.

"Look," interrupted Monroe as he came up from the back, wiping his hands on a napkin. "I'd love to sit around and discuss old pals and how solid the construction is on this dilapidated shithole, but… quite frankly, I'm more concerned with how we're going to get help and get the fuck out of here."

Even though it had been put rather rudely, everyone had to admit the fella had a point.

However, any further discussion of the topic was halted when the sound of whining tires was suddenly heard from the street and all eyes turned toward the front of the store. A large brown delivery truck came careening into the parking lot; its ass end fishtailing and weaving erratically. In the seconds between the time when the truck bounded over the curb on the street and when it hit the pavement and angled toward the gas pumps, it was pretty clear that there were several more of those people—like the ones outside—hanging off the sides of the vehicle. A couple more were holding onto the back gate. A pair of legs stuck out of the passenger window, kicking at the air. On the driver's side, a large man was holding on for all he was worth, his head angled into the window and he seemed to be fighting with the driver.

"Jesus, he's going to hit the pumps!" Cody cried out and took a small step backward.

"Oh, my God..." Irina said dumbstruck, but remained standing near the two front doors.

There was a moment when everyone agreed that impact was imminent, but at the last second the truck veered away and, back end sliding, skated around the small but potentially explosive island. Abruptly, relief turned to panic and, to everyone's horror, the truck high-sided and headed straight at the building. Its speed never let up as it hit the curb stops out front and became airborne.

"Ooooh, shit..." Claire whispered from her position near the magazine racks.

The truck smashed into the door and instantly shattered all three of the large panes of glass. In a shower of glittering hailstones, the windows went from protective barrier to lethal shrapnel. It all happened far too fast for anyone to document, but the end result was the same. One second they were safe and sound behind the supposedly bullet proof windows and the next all hell had broken loose. The truck continued on through the glass and crashed into the first few rows of groceries. Irina Kovalenko, who thought fleetingly of how she'd only stopped in for a moment to use the bathroom, took the brunt of the truck's front fender in the chest. The weight of the vehicle bore down on her and slapped her to the ground. Blood gushed up and out of her mouth and in the milliseconds that it took her to draw in a breath to scream, the bulk of the truck's weight came down on her and crushed her head and chest into paste.

Cody, who had been standing to Irina's right, was knocked back and into the Hostess display. Cellophane-wrapped baked goods exploded around him and he fell hard to the linoleum. Dazed, it took a moment for him to gather his wits and begin to climb to his feet. No sooner did he stand up then two of the people who had been hanging off the sides of the truck sprang up from where they'd landed and swarmed over him. The three of them went down and the boy's blood curdling scream rang out. Blood spurted into the air and painted the image of Twinkie The Kid in a deep crimson.

Once the explosion of glass and metal settled, Betty (who, when she saw the truck jump the curb, ducked behind the counter) came up and into view. She looked at the demolition that was, seconds before, the front of her store and began crying. She was desperately trying to take it all in and therefore never noticed Boyd and Jocelyn climbing through the empty window frames. Before she even knew what was happening, they were on her and the three of them disappeared behind the counter. Her screams and the sound of tearing cloth echoed in the ensuing stillness.

Stanley Dillard saw all of this go down and instinctively knew that they were in a heap of hot shit. With the store front collapsed, their only source of protection was gone. Dillard, who by now had moved away from the demolition and toward the back of the store, turned to Monroe and Claire and pushed them both in the direction of the backroom.

"Run!" he bellowed.

Monroe looked around bewildered.

"Where to?" he shouted while looking around frantically. "There's nothing back there!"

For a split second, Dillard glanced about and realized he was right.

"The room..." Claire said. Her previous humor gone, she now sounded extremely scared. "The one that lady was talking about."

"Right! That a girl!" Dillard nodded and shoved Monroe back again. "Go!"

With that, the three of them were off and running. Claire rounded the corner first and scurried toward the storage area of the store. It was basically a long hallway which ran along the length of the back of the building. Looking quickly to the left, she noticed the back access doors to the Beer and Bulk Soda refrigerators. To the right was a roll-up door which led presumably to the loading dock outside. Next to that, set in a sturdy metal frame, was a small room addition which looked recently built. The structure looked strong and heavily armored. Its walls were made of cement and thick metal rebar could be seen threaded through the concrete. On each side of it, stacks of soda cases and metal CO_2 canisters stood like sentries. Thinking that must certainly be the Count Out Room, she ran off to open the door.

As Dillard and Monroe rounded the corner, they could both hear movement coming from behind them. Small racks of food and large displays were being knocked over and a chorus of low moaning could be heard. From the sounds of it, there were at least five or six of those things running up behind them, coming on fast. Monroe's feet suddenly went out from underneath him, his designer shoes slipping on the slick concrete. He went down with a painful sound.

Dillard heard Monroe fall and slid to a stop. He looked back and saw the people coming up the aisle toward them. They were moving far faster than he'd thought possible, but he felt as if he still had time. It wasn't like he could just leave the guy there to be killed by those things. He raced back and grabbed Monroe by the wrist and hoisted him to his feet.

"Go! I'm going to try to hold them off!" Dillard shouted.

Monroe needed no further urging and was off like a shot. He ran to where the small hall they were in met the long one at the back of the store. He whipped his head around, trying to decide which direction he should head next.

"Phillip!" he heard Claire shout to his right.

Monroe turned and saw her holding open a metal door. Frantically, she pointed inside. He smiled and started running.

"That's my girl!" he said between frantic breaths.

Dillard managed to grab several milk crates as well as some flats of soda which were stacked against the wall and dumped them into the aisle. It wouldn't deter the quickly approaching crowd for long, but it should delay them long enough for him to catch up to Monroe and get inside the protection of the room. He took off running as the sound of people stumbling through the wreckage reached his ears.

He ran off and turned the corner in time to see Monroe and Claire reuniting at what could only be the Count Out Room's door. Monroe was pushing Claire inside and he turned to grab the door's handle.

Dillard sprinted toward them as fast as his legs would carry him. Behind him, he heard the sound of his pursuer's feet begin to slap on the concrete. He knew he'd have to be quick or they'd catch him with the metal door open and they'd all be lost.

He ran as fast as he could, pumping his legs harder, and judged that he'd just make it.

Monroe saw Dillard coming toward him and then his focus shifted to the crowd moving rapidly behind him. There were almost a dozen of them now and they all seemed to be moving impossibly fast.

He's not going to make it!

As Stanley Dillard got to within an arm's length of the door, his eyes met Monroe's. For a split second, he thought he saw Monroe silently urging him on. All of a sudden, Monroe's expression changed and it seemed as if he'd just given up on the old man. It was as though he thought it would be too close and risking his and Claire's lives was too much of a gamble.

As Dillard took his next—and final—step, he saw Monroe tug the door closed behind him. With a heartbreaking finality, the metal door slammed in its frame just as Dillard felt the first pair of hands latch onto his shoulders. Slamming into the door, more hands grabbed onto him and pulled him down toward the unforgiving ground.

Inside the small room, Monroe and Claire panted and held on to one another. Claire started crying and Monroe pulled her tighter. Over the sound of her sobbing, a frantic thumping and hysterical screaming from outside could be heard.

The next morning, Monroe and Claire awoke on the floor of the cramped Count Out Room. Once the noise from outside subsided, they'd cleared some space by pushing the chairs and assorted boxes out of the way and created a makeshift bed for themselves. The floor was freezing, so they'd spent most of the time with their arms wrapped around one another for warmth.

Lying there, Monroe repeatedly ran the scenario of what had happened to Dillard over in his mind and, as was his way, he'd even managed to convince himself that he'd done the only thing he could have by shutting the door on the man.

After all, if he hadn't, they *all* would have died.

The only thing Monroe now found himself regretting was him not having had the foresight to grab some food before locking themselves in here. It had been a while since he'd eaten the microwaved burrito and his hunger was now something he couldn't ignore. Claire was hungry as well. She'd been bitching about not having anything to eat since she'd woken up. Monroe wasn't sure what she expected him to do, for chrissakes. It wasn't like he could just unlock the door and go grab them some snacks.

The only choice they had was to wait.

So, that was what they did.

And as the hours passed, they'd done little else except lie there on the cold floor and bide their time. Hopefully, someone—the cops, the army, *someone*— would come along at some point and find them and rescue them. All they had to do was be patient. However, if too much time passed, there would be no recourse but for one of them to take the risk and go out into the store in search of rations. It'd be dangerous and, if there were still any of those things still around, that person might not make it back.

Somewhere in the back of his mind, Monroe was sure he could talk Claire into it.

And as the hours wore on, Monroe closed his eyes and he began to formulate his side of the argument.

☠ ☠ ☠

The Mouse Print

The fading light of day came spilling in through the polarized windows of the high-rise office; rays of diffused illumination splashing across the lush carpeting in broad strokes. The slate-colored floor covering was deep, soft and very expensive. The fibers soaked up the light's warmth like a sponge. The thick ply was not only a comfort to the feet that trod upon it, but it was also an eye-pleasing accent to the room's deep brown mahogany walls. Near the floor-to-wall panes of glass at the far end sat a large, regal cherrywood desk. Regimented piles of paper were set in very ordered rows near a thin, white computer monitor that jutted up through a hole in the desktop. Behind the desk's leather upholstered chair was a wall covered with framed 8x10" photos. In each, the same man grinned out excitedly from the frame with one arm around someone. Upon closer inspection, those someones were all political dignitaries, film stars, recording artists and fashion models.

Off to one side, the man who appeared in the photos stood looking out of the window at the teeming city far below. The view fell away sickeningly and it was easy to get the impression that to fall from such a vantage point would mean a very long time might be spent hurtling through the emptiness of space. Looking out, vertigo clawed at perception. All that glass and open air was enough to make a person feel dizzy and off-balance when he entered the room.

It was exactly the response Joseph Weber wanted to inspire in his visitors.

Almost sadly, he turned and ambled over to the bar hidden in the bookcase on the other side of the room. Pulling the cabinet open gently, he snatched up a handful of ice and filled a short glass. Scanning the array of bottles set out before him, he selected his poison and poured three fingers of bourbon. The frozen cubes crackled and settled deeper into the squat, pre-chilled tumbler.

With drink now in hand, he returned to his vantage point and sipped the harsh, smoky liquid. The fluid coated his tongue and made his mouth burn in a soothing way. It had been a rough day. This respite was a welcomed diversion from a schedule chock-full of meetings with sponsors, bitch sessions with networks, and the ever-present chore of filling his talent roster. Off in the distance, a lone hawk circled the sky, hunting the concrete and glass landscape for prey.

Weber knew exactly how that sort of thing felt.

He drew another mouthful of liquor and swirled it in his mouth before swallowing. The scotch's intoxicating effect nibbled at the edges of his consciousness and he felt some of the stress he'd accumulated begin to melt away. He knew he'd have to be careful and not let the alcohol carry him too far. He still had one more meeting to get out of the way before calling it a day and heading upstairs to the penthouse he called home.

As he stared out over the spires of the city, he dimly recalled a quieter and far less prosperous time from what seemed like lifetime ago. His reflection told of the years that had passed. His face had a few more lines carved into its flesh. His hair had a bit more gray. His eyes looked more worldly... and also more weary.

"So much..." he whispered to himself. "So much has changed."

Back once upon a time, he'd been a poor day laborer—a grunt—working long hours on construction sites hauling heavy loads of wood and concrete for some very shitty pay. He'd been dead last on a fast track to nowhere. At least that was what everyone—his boss, his friends, his white trash family—kept telling him. All he'd had to look forward to was a lifetime of backbreaking work, maybe a loveless marriage or two with some ungrateful kids who would no doubt grow to resent him, and then a good ol' fashioned chest-crushing heart attack before being dumped into a low cost casket and buried deep in the ground, ultimately to be forgotten. The only thing that would mark his time on earth would be his name and a couple of dates chiseled into a concrete marker somewhere.

Then, that depressing future had all been changed by some multicolored streaks of light tearing across the sky, a sky not unlike the one he now found himself looking out over. With one swipe of Fate's hand, everything that had been in his cards was shuffled away. The whole game got changed when that first dead body opened its eyes and began its search for breakfast. He'd been one of the smart ones and had managed to suss out the whole walking dead situation pretty early on. He figured being forced to cave in the skull of a foreman as he tried to chew his arm off was a pretty big give-a-way.

Weber was not a man who learned fast... but he did learn well.

So, as quickly as he could, he found himself a safe haven and tried to think things through. By luck or by providence, he met up with a guy named Jimbo who, while not a mental giant, was a physical behemoth. An alliance was quickly formed and a plan was just as quickly hatched. By the time the dead gathered enough of their numbers to be a consideration, he and Jimbo had been ready and waiting.

Looking back, those were some fine days and he and Jimbo had definitely had themselves a time. It had been just the two of them, like a modern day Harold Hills, travelling the countryside, sleeping where they could, and methodically bilking the yokels out of their cash and commodities with a grift that was anything but square.

Livin' off the fatta' the lan'.

The way he and Jimbo had it all figured, the dead were dangerous and could be a real handful if you found yourself surrounded by a group of them, but... one on one, they were a manageable threat if you were smart (which Weber was) or built like a Caterpillar track loader (which Jimbo was). Together, they made a formidable pair. As the public's interest in what they were doing grew, Weber was smart enough to see the potential in their little enterprise and had already figured a clear cut way to make some big cash in it. With a business model based more in professional wrestling than in anything out of Forbes, he was patiently waiting when the television boys came snooping around with their Brooks Brothers suits and fancy watches.

Now, years later, he'd parlayed it all into a bonafide empire.

Yeah... Jimbo was gone (he'd gotten himself bitten by one of those things when he'd one day gotten a little too lazy and lot too complacent) as were the four other Jimbos after him.

But, Weber had prevailed, and in the end wasn't that the most important thing?

It was the way *Weber* saw things.

Jimbos came and Jimbos went, but the business...

The business continued.

Forever and ever... Amen.

Weber sipped at his glass and then casually glanced at his Rolex. His Acquisition Team would be here any minute, so he downed the rest of his drink and went and put the glass away. Closing the cabinet, he reached into his pocket and retrieved the small bottle of breath spray he kept there. Two quick spritzes and any trace of the alcohol was gone.

A soft, tinkling chime came from the intercom on the desk and his secretary's throaty—and downright sexy—voice came pouring out of the small speaker.

"Sir, Monica Johansson, Richard Murphy, and Phil Monroe are here to review the contracts on the new fighter."

Weber walked behind the desk and pressed the small red button on the console.

"Ok, Alicia. Give me a moment and then send them in."

He took his seat and got himself settled. He'd worked very hard with the building's designer to make it so that the first image people got when they walked in the door was one that exuded power and influence. He always judged how successful they'd been by the awed look that bloomed in people's expressions when they first walked in. It was a testament to their efforts that it happened no matter how many times the guest had been here. Every time he saw that look, it filled him with a sense of pride.

It was, after all, important to enjoy the little things in life.

As he waited, he took a second and went over what he knew about the Jimbo his team was here to discuss. From the video he'd seen, this one was impressive. Although not exceptionally big, he was strong and seemed to be a dyed-in-the-wool natural when it came to doling out The Pain. The three people waiting outside had come from a meeting with him earlier in the day and would have more information on where this Jimbo's head was.

Not that it much mattered.

The Jimbos all came to The League with stardust in their eyes and dreams of being rich in their hearts. Such simple-mindedness was almost endearing. The truth was, however, that Weber was not about to give any of them a glimpse at the true reality. He was far too smart a man for that. He and his people would promise them that they'd soon have more money than God and see more pussy than a goddamn litter box. It wasn't his fault these dopes never had the sense to read the fine print of their contracts before signing on. The writing there was small and concealed by legalese, but it was there.

In fact, it was Weber's favorite part of the whole friggin' contract.

"In the event of the employee's death or critical injury, all assets of said employee revert back to Weber Industries and its holdings."

In a nutshell, it meant that when—not if, but when—the Jimbo got himself tagged or injured, all of their assets—the money, property, stocks, hell, even the Jimbo's body itself—was to be returned to the League to do with as they saw fit. One small sentence hidden away in the mouse print at the bottom of the contract made sure that what had once been The League's stayed The League's. It was a flimsy codicil which— if the person was smart enough or if he had a lawyer savvy enough—could be broken, but... Jimbos were known for their brawn. Brains were something they didn't exactly have in abundance.

Abruptly, a knock sounded on the heavy wooden door at the far end of the room.

With a grin like that of a cat with an unending supply of canaries, Weber looked up to greet his employees.

Living Forever Learning to Fly

The door to the limousine, which brought Cleese from the hotel to the airport, slowly swung open. With his body still feeling tired, he hauled himself out of the dark, luxurious interior. As his boots hit the sidewalk with a thud, he sighed heavily—feeling the weight of his body more than usual. The air outside the car was hot and humid. The atmosphere felt suffocating and inhospitable. Heat vapor could be seen shimmering off of the pavement a short distance away. He reached back into the limo and hurriedly grabbed his bag so that he could get inside the air-conditioned airport as quickly as possible.

"It's been a pleasure driving you, Sir," his driver, Charles, said as he held the door open and smiled. The man was older, black, and had salt and pepper hair cut close to his head. Cleese felt glad that he'd been hired to drive him. The guy was sharp and had made an already difficult trip a *lot* easier. He'd been all too accommodating and, to Cleese's relief, he didn't talk much. Charles had managed to get him where he'd wanted to go and to get him fed without too much trouble or conversation. Being efficient and quiet were both pluses in Cleese's book.

Since his match, he'd lost the ability to move around in public with any sort of anonymity. In the past, he'd always had a way of making people nervous. It was as if the sheep suddenly sensed a wolf somewhere in their midst, but were unable to identify exactly where. It was something intangible, but it was enough to garner him his share of their attention. But this... this was different. His face was recognizable now by everyone from children to their grandmothers to the family dog. Lately, it seemed as if crowds followed him wherever he went, which was fine except that they'd sometimes swarm him in a way that was a little like how the UDs behaved in The Pit. Things could get tight and, even though they meant well, his defenses would go up. The last thing he needed was to react poorly to an overzealous fan. It wouldn't do for him to deck someone out of instinct and then come to find out all they wanted was for him to sign something.

This driver had seen to it that incidents like that were kept to a minimum.

As he pulled the strap of his Alice bag over his shoulder, Cleese palmed a hundred dollar bill and shook the driver's hand.

"You sure you don't want me to see you to the gate, Sir?" Charles asked.

"No, man... I think I've got this handled."

"Well, you be careful... both in there," and he nodded his head toward the metal and glass of the airport terminal, "and out *there*." It was pretty obvious by the way he'd raised his eyebrows that "out there" meant out on the sand of The Pit.

Cleese chuckled and looked Charles in the eye. "Will do, my friend. Will do."

He let go of Charles' his hand and hitched his bag up over his shoulder. Without any further goodbyes, he headed off toward the terminal door. Already he was catching glimpses out of the corner of his eye of people turning to notice him. It'd all started to follow a familiar pattern. First there was the opening wide of the eyes. Then, there was the dropping of the jaw and the subsequent smile. Finally, the person would turn to whomever they were with and begin whispering excitedly. If he was lucky, it stopped there. If he wasn't, they'd make the walk over and the autograph and photograph requests soon followed. He tried to be understanding and as cooperative as possible, but even after such a short amount of time it had already gotten tiresome and annoying.

He purposefully strode across the sidewalk and the electric doors slid open invitingly, welcoming him into their air-conditioned embrace. Like being wrapped with a cool, wet towel, the air swirled around him and he felt the perspiration that soaked his skin begin to dry. He felt worlds better already; so much so that the awkward meeting with the Three Stooges was becoming a distant, albeit unpleasant, memory.

Well, almost...

At first, he'd been amused by how easy the negotiations had been. Sure, he popped off a little, but for him, that was a given. His mouth had a way of getting him in Dutch, but this time things were different. This time, he had something they wanted. This time, he'd proven himself. This time, he'd made good on the promise of being the commodity they'd thought he was in the beginning.

Then, a thought started itching at the back of his brain. It was slight in the beginning, but as the hours wore on, he realized that they'd been almost *too* compliant, hadn't they? It was almost as if they'd been willing to agree to just about *anything* he wanted. He probably could have asked for the moon as well as a blowjob from ol' Monica Johansson herself and they would have gone for it. She probably would've even worked his balls without complaint.

The question was, *why*?

Maybe they believed in him.

Maybe they saw his potential.

And maybe they *knew* he'd probably not live long enough to collect on any of it.

It was an intriguing thought, but one he decided to put out of his head for now. He made a mental note to spend some time considering everything that had occurred some other time; a time when there were no distractions and he could reflect on things more fully. Right now, all he wanted to do was just get back to the compound and spend a night in a familiar bed.

The airport lobby before him was a wide, open space with a tile floor set in colored squares radiating outward. The ceiling was a cavernous metal framework with banners that welcomed travelers to the airport in several different languages. Hanging like sleeping bats beneath the metal struts, set every fifteen feet or so, were dozens of large televisions. Their placement around the airport was strategic and literally everywhere. High-def images ran the same scenario again and again like plasma-screened déjà vu.

As Cleese walked across the foyer, he glanced up and saw multiple images of One, the little girl from his match, splashed across the screens. In ultra slow motion, the Beretta slid into view like a hungry black mamba and the barrel butted up against her little upturned nose. Her eyes crossed in confusion as they focused on the pistol being shoved in her face. Cleese turned away in shame as an abrupt explosion of dark maroon filled the screen.

It was harder than he thought it would be to see himself shoot a child in the face.

Continuing on his way, he saw the smiling face of a newscaster on the screen out of the corner of his eye. The pretty blonde clapped her hands and laughed in delight. Then, to his disgust, the image cut back to a replay of the bullet slamming its way up the kid's nostril and the whites of her eyes blossoming a sudden red. He lowered his head and made a note to avoid looking up until he was out of the airport.

An information booth sat in the middle of the room like a squatter in a tenement. Behind its counter, a middle aged woman in Fifties cat-eye glasses sat looking tired; the caterpillar from Wonderland come to life. All she needed was a hookah and a mushroom to sit on.

The lobby wasn't too crowded this early in the morning, but as the day wore on, it was sure to become a nightmare. Travelers would come and go, the ebb and flow of their passing as sure as the tides. As he moved through the lobby, more heads turned and gawked at him. Word certainly did get around. He considered himself lucky when he saw the ticket counter he needed and found no line there.

A plain-faced Asian girl was working the desk and she looked up as he stepped up to be helped. Small of frame and wide of smile, her hair was pulled back into a tight bun which left her face looking open and inviting. Her blue uniform looked almost military with the exception of the brightly colored scarf that circled her throat like a floral python. Her nametag read, "Akiko Yamashita."

"Ohayo gozaimasu," he said and smiled. "I have a reservation that I need to pick up a Boarding Pass for."

The now familiar look of recognition lit up her face and she smiled a wide and welcoming smile in return. "Do you have a confirmation number, Mr. Cleese?"

Cleese handed her the slip he'd been given back at the hotel and she began busily typing into her computer.

"Ok, well..." she said and smiled that smile again as she picked up a telephone handset. "It would seem that you are expected. I will page an escort to take you to your gate."

Cleese nodded, bowing slightly. He thanked her and stepped to the side of the counter and waited patiently. This new treatment was definitely something he felt he could get used to. Normally, calls to security would have been made by now and, at the very least, undercover guards—most of who were about as unnoticeable as a cat at a dog show—would be lurking nearby. Instead, he was being called "mister" and "sir" and being thanked for his patronage. Celebrity did have its advantages after all.

All of a sudden, he felt a slight tugging at the hem of his jacket. For some reason, he immediately thought of Chikara. He looked down and saw a small boy of maybe eight or nine years old looking up at him. The kid had a round face with a small button of a nose and wore a knit toque and BMX tee shirt. Puffs of blonde hair poked out at odd intervals around the rim of the cap. He gazed up with the bluest eyes Cleese had ever seen. A mental image of the girl from his match flashed before his eyes and then was gone.

"Ex-excuse me," the boy said.

Hey, at least the kid was polite; many weren't these days.

"Hey there!" Cleese said and smiled. "Can I help you with something?"

"You're Cleese from the WGL, aren't you?" he asked and then looked down toward his shoes. The kid pointed upward toward one of the TVs and quietly said, "You sure look like him."

Cleese set his bag down and squatted in order to be eye to eye with the kid.

"If you promise not to tell anyone, I'll tell you," he said and looked around as if nervous. "You promise?"

The kid nodded his head vigorously, his cap shifting like a bowl on his head as he did.

"Ok, then..." and he leaned in closer. "Yes, I am."

The boy got excited immediately and clapped his hands. Words fell like lemmings from of his mouth.

"Omigod, I saw you on TV at home too and you were *so* great! I totally thought you were going to choke during the first round when that girl snuck up on you, but... Man, it was *so cool*!! I told my best friend, Johnny Mischon from school, that you are my totally favorite fighter now."

The boy's voice had gotten loud and Cleese noticed more and more people were looking his way.

"Listen, Pal, can you keep your voice down, ok?"

"Oh," the kid said and clapped his hand over his mouth and then whispered, "Sorry," through his fingers.

"Thanks, Buddy."

"Cleese," the kid said leaning in, "will you sign something for me? Johnny Mischon ain't never gonna believe I met you."

Cleese looked at him for a moment was struck by how weird his life had become. A short time ago, a kid like this would have avoided him like the plague. He cut an imposing figure and many grownups were oftentimes leery of interacting with him. Kids treated him like Frankenstein. Now... Now, they looked up to him—idolized him.

It was funny how quickly things change.

Cleese fished a League promo card out of the front of his bag and found a Sharpie.

"Ritchie!" a female voice cut in excitedly. "I told you to stay with me. You promised me you wouldn't run off."

Cleese looked up and stared straight into the eyes of a young woman, roughly early thirties, who bore a remarkable resemblance to the kid. She was pretty: blonde hair like his that tumbled across her shoulders, and eyes you could fall into, drown, and feel good about doing so. Her attire was sort of business casual with a large Prada bag slung over one shoulder. The whole look was a carefully constructed façade that was designed to get her noticed.

"Cleese," the boy said, looking down as if he were almost waiting for his mom to steal his little thunder, "this is my mom. Mom, this is Cleese."

For a moment, his previous excitement returned to his face.

"Cleese is a WGL fighter, Mom."

"Yes, Ritchie," she said, running her fingers through her hair in an attempt to straighten it up, "I know. The television has been playing highlights of his match virtually non-stop."

Cleese stood up and bowed at the waist.

"Nice to meet you," he said.

The woman smiled and put one arm around the young boy's shoulder.

"You're quite the media star," she said with a flirtatious pout. It was an obviously calculated move on her part and one that had undoubtedly worked on men before. "I hope Ritchie hasn't been bothering you,"

"No, he's fine."

"Well, we're both big fans of yours. We've enjoyed all of your fights and the last fight was one of the best I've seen."

An internal bullshit detector went off like a fire alarm in his head. He had, after all, only had one fight. The woman was obviously making an attempt to ingratiate herself. It might have helped if she'd done a bit of homework. He was merely a target of convenience. The whole thing made him feel a little played.

Cleese looked down and saw a wave of embarrassment wash over Ritchie's face. He felt sorry for the kid. He knew it was hard to grow up male in the shadow of a single mom. With no dad, he would have little he could call his own—male-wise. In order to survive, he'd have to be tough... and receive a little encouragement.

"Thanks."

Cleese started signing the card and then stopped.

"Ritchie, was it?"

The boy nodded and smiled.

He quickly scribbled, "To Ritchie, I'm glad you're in my corner. Your buddy, Cleese" and handed it to the boy. He was happy when he saw the kid's eyes light up like a neon sign.

The kid's mother plucked the card away from him and looked it over.

"Oh, isn't that great, Ritchie?"

She looked up and smiled again.

"My name's Judith."

"Nice to meet you, Judith," he said and playfully plucked back the card from her and smiled. He handed it back to the kid and ruffled his cap and hair.

"I could sign one of those for you as well, ya know."

She laughed and lightly touched his arm; another calculated move. Cleese liked the kid right off. Mom, however, was quickly becoming a manipulative pain in his ass. He'd seen her type before... in bars. Brassy and sporting a lethal combination of a severely inflated sense of self and an egotistical sense of entitlement, she'd made presenting herself to men into an art form. Richie had undoubtedly come about as a result of some bad planning and a few missed periods.

Now, he was little more than a fashion accessory.

Looking down at the kid, he felt all the more sorry for him.

Then, to Cleese's relief, a man in an official looking white shirt walked up and saved him from further interaction with Judith Painintheass. The dude's hair was cut high and tight and Cleese immediately figured him for ex-military. His posture was a little too straight and his tie was tied a little too perfectly to be anything else. Black epilates and official patches augmented his uniform. A clip-on TSA credential hung like a Christmas tree ornament from his pocket.

"Sir," he said in an authoritative voice, "my name is Paul McDaniel and it'll be my pleasure to escort you to your flight."

Jesus, Cleese thought, *what's with everybody calling me 'Sir?'*

Cleese excused himself, once again smiled at Judith, and then patted Ritchie on the head.

"Be good, Ritchie," he said. "And tell that Johnny Mischon I said you were The Man."

The boy's face almost split in half from the smile that blossomed there.

As Cleese turned and walked away, he could feel Judith's disappointed gaze heat up his back. For some reason, he was sure her ego would live.

Paul the Security Guy led the way past the metal detectors and x-ray machines and on toward the departure gates. About midway down the main corridor, he turned and, pulling at the keychain connected to his belt by a retractable cord, used a key to unlock a side door.

"This hallway will get us to your gate faster and help avoid any unwanted attention, Sir," Paul said. He held the door as Cleese walked through. Cleese got a good vibe off the guy and relaxed a bit. The dude just seemed like someone you'd want to have some beers with; someone who'd done his service when things got tight and was now riding out his time keeping order in the civilian world. Cleese kind of respected that.

"Sir, if I might say something?" Paul asked.

"You can say anything you want there, Paul, as long as you stop calling me 'Sir.'"

"Fair enough," he said and smiled.

"Before doing this security gig, I was in the Marines..."

"I sort of figured that out for myself, Paul. You don't strike me as someone who set out to be Airport Security. No offense."

"None taken. It's a paycheck, ya know?"

Cleese laughed.

"I do indeed, Paul."

"Which brings me to my point."

Paul looked over at Cleese as they walked with a genuinely questioning face.

"I've seen some shit—Iraq, Afghanistan, Iran, Central America, hell, I even got caught in Newark when the shit with The Dead went down—but I gotta tell ya..."

Cleese interrupted him having already heard this rap a time or two before.

"You'd never do what I do, right?"

"Correct, Sir."

"Well, Paul, I'll tell ya... I do what I do, quite frankly, because I was never much good at doing much else. Truth is... you've probably done some things I wouldn't have. So, we're probably even there. I guess what I'm saying is that we all play the cards we're dealt because we don't know no different or we're too stupid to see a way out."

Cleese looked over and shook his head.

"For me, it was a little bit of both, actually."

By now, they'd reached the other end of the hallway. Paul was working at unlocking the door so that they could go out onto the tarmac to where the League's private plane undoubtedly waited.

"Does that make any kinda sense, Paul?" Cleese asked.

"It does indeed." Paul said and grinned. He pressed against the bar that released the lock and then once again held the door open. Sunlight spilled into the hallway, momentarily blinding them both. Cleese walked through the doorway and into the morning's heat.

"On your left," Paul said and pointed toward the Learjet 60 XR waiting on the airstrip. "It's been a pleasure, Sir."

"For both of us, Paul." Then, "I appreciate your help."

Cleese took a few steps and then turned. He quickly snapped off a quick military salute. Reflexively, Paul returned the gesture. Cleese pointed at him with his index finger and the man raised his eyebrows in surprise and smiled.

"Old habits die hard, Paul."

"They do indeed, Sir," and he laughed. "Good luck at your next match, Sir."

"From your mouth to God's ear, Buddy."

"A request, Sir."

"Go ahead."

"Nail one of the bastards for me, ok?"

"For you?" Cleese asked, already knowing the answer.

Paul got a faraway look in his eyes. He seemed lost in thought for a moment and then, just as quickly, he returned.

"For my daughter."

"Consider it done, Paul," and he walked off toward the waiting plane, his thoughts already returning to the place that he was coming to think of as home.

The War of Art

Cleese moved around the mat like a shark circling a sinking ship; a predator looking for any hint of weakness or opportunity. His simple grey sweats and wife-beater were wet with a sopping layer of perspiration; moist patches of sweat darkened the cloth between his legs, under his arms and in vertical splashes across his chest and back. The exposed skin of his arms, face, and neck shimmered in the dull light of the Training Hall. His long dark hair, pulled back into a loose ponytail, left his face exposed. The pinkish blush of exertion colored his skin and made his cheeks red and fiery.

His right foot came up off the rubberized mat and slid cautiously to the side. His bare feet left moist prints on the already glistening padded surface. As it touched down, he remained up on the balls of his feet, all the better to facilitate his next move when the time came. And the time would come. The time *always* came. For time and its subtleties were—as Musashi once said—everything.

His posture was all business: hands raised and loose, back slightly bent. The point of his chin was tucked tight to the top of his chest, making it a harder target should his opponent try to hit him there. The point of the chin was well known by seasoned fighters as being a sure spot for a knockout. It wasn't called The Button for nothing. If a punch could be landed there solidly, the jaw got pushed back and slammed the jawbone against something called the temporal mandibular nerve causing a sensory overload, which effectively shut the brain off. It could also happen if a sharp blow made contact with either side of the jaw at the spot where the posterior condyle of the mandible fit together with the mandibular cavity of the temporal bone just under the zygomatic arch. At least that was what one of the anatomy books said. Both were a means to an end and that end was your lights getting shut off, but quick. Cleese was damned if he was going to serve that shit up on a silver platter.

Anyone worth his salt knew that keeping your chin protected was Job One.

Job Two was to know a thing or two about anatomy—hence the books. Cleese figured that to understand how to take something apart, it was important to know how it went together. In his opinion, the first book someone should get their hands on if they were going to learn how to fight was a book on anatomy and physiology. It just made sense.

Cleese moved around the mat bobbing and weaving, just to keep his opponent guessing, but it was mostly for show. It'd been a while since he faced a living adversary and he found that old habits really did die hard. With UDs, it was all pretty straightforward. "Grab—Kill—Move," as Monk had said. You tended to come at them like a freight train, a murderous force of nature.

Hit 'em hard. Hit 'em fast. Hit 'em with everything in the toolbox.

Living opponents were a different story. They were quick, agile, and some even had half a brain in their head. You just couldn't wade in and start wailing. You had to show your opponent a little respect... especially when you were starting to harbor hopes of getting them into your bed.

Chikara crouched into a deep yet relaxed Horse Stance and followed Cleese with the eyes of a hawk as he danced around the mat, baiting him to rush her. He was skilled and one of most facile fighters she'd ever seen, but it was pretty obvious that he put a lot of faith in his size and physical strength. It was a common mistake a lot of men made. They thought of their fists in the same way they thought of their penises: big, meaty clubs that could beat whatever lay before them into submission. More often than not, they'd end up flat on their backs with an incredulous look on their faces when she showed them what a little leverage and some feminine ingenuity could do.

Since first arriving at the compound, she'd been through this dance time and time again. Sooner or later, every swinging dick that came through here lined up to show The Chick how rough and tumble this sport could be. She'd taken some awfully hard knocks in her time and some serious damage, but she'd decided a long time ago to never let anyone see her break. There were many late nights—far too many for her liking—when she'd hit the showers and cry silently as she cradled herself and quietly nursed her wounds.

As she continued to follow the movements of the man before her, tossing out half-assed jabs and crosses, she kept her eye on his centerline. Long ago, her mentor, Sebastian Creed, told her, "Follow the body's centerline and you will be able to better predict where your opponent will go and what he had planned. Learn to read the centerline and you'll know what they're up to even before they do." Time and time again, he'd been right about that... as well as a number of other things. The lessons she'd learned from that man were still ingrained in her mind and carved into the meat of her flesh.

Cleese reminded her of Sebastian in many ways. Much like him, Cleese was strong, smart, and a very good fighter. He was also honest, compassionate, and trustworthy almost to a fault. And while it was true he was a hulking pile of muscle and had a somewhat coarse way about him, he'd also shown during their numerous talks a depth that all of the others—even Creed—had lacked.

Beneath all that sinew and testosterone, there was a good man buried in there somewhere.

As usual, it would take a good woman to bring it to the surface.

Cleese bounced lightly up onto the balls of his feet and kept moving, pushing Chikara to her right. He'd spent a lot of time reviewing her fight tapes and, by now, they'd been committed to his memory. He pretty much had her and her fighting style figured out; or so he thought. She was a gifted fighter and a helluva smart woman, but she was a slave to her training and relied way too much on the flow of the sticking to her already decided upon game plan. Budo bullshit or not... it was a dangerous thing to do and a habit he felt needed to be broken. That was not to say that she was a pushover, far from it. She was one of the best fighters he'd ever encountered, man or woman.

It just meant she wasn't a perfect one.

As he batted away her half-hearted punches, he kept waiting for her to cut loose and really go for it. He kept waiting for her to hit him—*really* hit him. Maybe she was afraid of hurting him, like *that* was possible. Maybe she was just waiting for him to commit himself so she could level him with something a little more solid. Whatever the reason, this pitter-pat shit was getting old and pretty damn annoying.

He wanted fury and ferocity from her.

He wanted passion.

He wanted *contact*.

"Look, Darlin'..." he said between breaths, "how much of this slap fighting you plan on doing here today? If I'd wanted a massage, I'd go get one."

A smile spread across her face and her eyes seemed to brighten up.

"Oh, you want some of this?"

Cleese was just about to say just how much he wanted all of it, when he saw her back foot dig into the mat. Planting the rear foot like that usually meant your opponent was planning something; usually something big. He lifted his right foot and, just as he was starting to take a step back, two sharp, quick open-handed slaps lashed out and struck his cheek.

He had to admit it, she was fast.

"Tag, *Darlin'*," he heard her say and then cock her head and laugh, "you are It!"

Cleese touched the side of his face and the skin burned hot beneath his fingers. Two quick, shuffling steps forward and he was on her. A left hook, a right, then a quick uppercut later and he'd already let his mind move on to picking up the pieces of what was left of her. The problem was... the punches never landed. When his loosely clenched hands arrived at their intended destination, Chikara simply wasn't there. The bad news was that his momentum and committal to the attack had over-extended him. He felt a gentle—almost loving—push at the small of his back and then he was toppling over. The force of his own weight carried him down and to his knees.

Stupid.

Cleese's body fell past Chikara as soon as she stepped under and to the side of his anticipated combination. The push on the back was done not for any effect other than to let him know that she was there; to know it and to also know that she could have done a lot more damage than just give him a simple push. He may have had strength and size on her, but that didn't always win the ball game. As she saw the all too familiar look of exasperated indignance appear on his face, she almost had to laugh.

Men...

With an annoyed *woof*, Cleese fell onto all fours, his head hanging down.

"What is the matter, Tough Guy?" she said giggling. "You need to take a break already?"

Cleese smiled to himself and looked down at the mat. He felt like an asshole after all that mental pontificating to have made such a rookie move. He slowly climbed back to his feet and turned back toward her, his face now a slightly deeper shade of red than before.

"Careful..." she said and she wagged a castigatory finger at him, "you do not want to let emotion cloud your thinking, now do you... *Darlin'*?"

Cleese grinned and took several abrupt shuffling steps forward. He threw a punch high, aimed just above her head, and then quickly went to grab her arms. His blood was getting hot now and, even though he was beginning to have feelings for this woman, he was not about to let her—or anyone else—get the best of him in a fistfight.

As he bore down on her, she firmly stood her ground. At the last moment, he noticed her stance change ever so slightly as she braced for impact. His thick arms came toward her and a beatific smile lit up her features. It was not unlike the look martyrs got on their faces just before they died. It was a look of utter peace and complete contentment.

Of course, it was all orchestrated bullshit.

As his arms again closed on thin air, he heard her voice speak from over his shoulder, "Our flow cannot become disrupted by our feelings. We must stand to one side of our emotions: anger, fear, hate, wrath... Emotions can only cloud the clarity of our thinking."

Cleese stumbled to a stop and spun around. He shook his head and quietly chuckled.

"You sure do talk a lot. You sure you weren't a teacher in another life?"

A forlorn look momentarily passed like a shadow over her face and then her features reset into a firm resolve.

"We must rely on our training," she continued matter of factly. "We *must* stick to our plan."

Cleese sighed and decided it was about time to cut the chivalry and passive courting. It was time to remind this fighter of the physics of their relationship. He lunged forward and, as expected, she glided to one side. As he reached where she'd been standing, he pivoted on one foot and leaned into her. He felt his back bump against her chest. His heart fluttered just a bit when the soft point of her breasts came in contact with the meat of his back.

"The problem with sticking to any plan is..." he said and quickly threw his right elbow back and then the left. The blows, while light and without much force, rocked her head to and fro and still succeeded in scrambling her attention. He bent at the waist and, reaching between his legs, grabbed both of her ankles. Then, by simply standing up, her feet came up and off the ground. Once her stability was compromised, the rest of her body dropped to the mat with a slap that echoed through the Training Hall. Now that she was on the ground, Cleese simply dropped to his knees, sprawled back, and trapped her torso to the mat with his body weight. With his bulk covering her, she was more or less pinned. Her arms and legs thrashed wildly beneath him, but it was clear to them both that she wasn't going anywhere any time soon. Lying across her, he felt her breath on his neck as she panted near his ear. Her turned his head and looked into her now very pissed off eyes.

"...that sometimes Life doesn't give a shit about your plan."

Beneath him, he felt her wriggle and attempt to throw him off.

"What was it Woody Allen once said, 'If you want to make God laugh, tell him about your plans'?"

"Maybe it's you who should've been a teacher," she groaned, crushed under his mass.

"I actually thought about that..." he said and now it was his turn to sound wistful, "once upon a time."

"Ok... point made," she grunted. "Now, d'ya mind getting the hell off of me?"

Cleese stretched and put his hands behind his head like a man relaxing in a hammock. He then wriggled his body back and forth, settling in and pressing his weight down even further. He heard her moan and then give up a strangled giggle.

"No, seriously..." she said still laughing. "Get off me. You weigh a ton."

Figuring she'd had enough, Cleese rolled over and onto the mat smiling.

Once she'd gotten her breath back, Chikara slowly got to her feet.

"Jesus, I think you broke one of my ribs," she gasped, holding her side.

"Ok, Smartass, I'm not *that* heavy." He gently pushed her and she took two stumbling steps away.

"The hell you're not."

After a brief moment of rest, it was time to get back to business. They both stood to their full height and again squared off with one another. Chikara fell into her relaxed stance, legs slightly bent, arms hanging loosely at her side; an old school Aikido stance. Cleese came up onto his toes, chin tucked, with his hands open and in front of him; in a bastardized street fighter-meets-Muay Thai form.

"Ok," Chikara continued, looking relaxed, "your point aside, I still say that proper training can and will counter any anomaly."

She tossed a sharp left jab followed by a quick cutting oblique kick toward his inner thigh—both he expertly batted aside.

"Look..." he said as he returned to his stance, "any training that is too structured, by definition, doesn't leave room for variation." His hands dropped from his en garde position and his attention became fixed on his explanation. "Bruce Lee said, 'All fixed set patterns are incapable of adaptability or pliability. The truth is outside of all fixed patterns' and he was right. A fighter needs to adapt to the fight and not expect the fight to adapt to him..." He bowed slightly, "...or her."

She dutifully bowed back.

"You can argue the point all you want," he continued, "but nothing's going to change what is."

Seeing Cleese caught up in his thought process, Chikara came on strong. Three quick steps and she was within arm's reach of him. A flurry of left jabs and right crosses followed, some of which landed, but most didn't.

Cleese stumbled back to avoid the onslaught then planted his foot and, redirecting his energy, surged forward. He rolled with her last strike, turned and spun and ended up standing directly behind Chikara. Almost as an afterthought, he wrapped his arms around her at her waist, trapping her limbs against her sides. Bending back, he lifted her off her feet. He thought briefly about slamming her body to the mat, but decided against it as he knew it would undoubtedly hurt her; maybe even break one of her ribs for real.

She wriggled and thrashed in his arms; her legs kicking futilely. Holding her this close, he couldn't help but be aware of the feel of her flesh in his arms. Her skin was smooth and soft, but underneath lay musculature that was firm and supple and very well defined. His face pressed into the base of her neck. His nose was buried in her hair that was damp with the sweat of her exertions. The smell of her was intoxicating; a delicate mix of jasmine and wild honeysuckle.

It had been a long time since Cleese had smelled anything as amazing as that.

"See there...!" he said trying to clear his head and calm the stirrings coursing throughout his body. "Despite all your Zen posturing, you have a habit of being so committed to your plan—of slaughtering what's right in front of you—that you end up leaving your back exposed. You gotta think in *three hundred and sixty degrees!*"

He quickly let her go and she dropped back to her feet.

In a conscious act of pure self-preservation, he took two giant steps back and away from her. As he did so, he could see her deeply thinking about what he'd said. It was pretty obvious it was not the first time she'd heard it. She stood there thinking and for some reason subconsciously rubbed at a spot on her left elbow.

"Monk recently told me something that has stuck in my head...," he added, driving the point home. "He said, 'It's not the one you hear that'll get you... it's the one you don't.' Become a slave to your plan or to your training and you leave yourself open to becoming a victim to it as well."

He let her stew on that for a minute and then said, "Again?"

She nodded and they stood facing one another once more. This time, it was Cleese who threw the first punch. The blow just missed the side of Chikara's jaw line, but at his arm's full extension, he flicked the tips of his fingers, snipping the tip of her ear. The snapping sound caused her to flinch, which surprised him. She seemed unflappable, but he could tell that his zeroing in on what she felt was a perilous weakness deeply troubled her. It was almost as if he knew her inside and out even though they'd only been spending time together for a relatively short time.

Her response to the ear flick was quick, sharp and had none of the self control he'd come to expect. Two quick punches struck him in the chest and hurt. The follow-up uppercut to his solar plexus made those, by comparison, seem like a walk on the beach. The air was kicked from his lungs and he quickly decided that the best move at the moment was to get the hell away from her, for both of their sakes.

It wouldn't do for him to get pissed and let fly with anything near his full strength. She could undoubtedly take the force of the punch, but... Again, it was hard to put your best foot forward with a woman after breaking her jaw or cracking her one on the nose.

As he moved further around her—almost as an afterthought—he abruptly reversed direction. Her confusion by the ploy was obvious. Hastily, she tried to counter with a back fist, but it was sloppy and ineffective. The thing was... that in doing so, she once more left her back open and exposed.

He wrapped his arms about her and pinned her arms to her side for a second time. He pushed down with most of his weight and felt her legs buckle a bit under the burden. She groaned slightly as she attempted to support his weight. Once more, his face was buried into her hair and he could feel the heaviness of her breasts as they rested on his forearms. This closeness was making it really hard to think.

"Girl, you did it again!"

Chikara went tense and he could tell she was pissed; not at him—he was only the catalyst. She was clearly more ticked at herself.

He backed off of the pressure on her and loosened his arms just a bit. She stomped her foot and turned around in his embrace, facing him.

"It just pisses me off. Creed used to tell me the same thing back when he was training me. I've been working on breaking the habit, but... I can't seem to help it!"

"Hey, we all have our shortcomings. I mean, look... I am well aware of the fact that I tend to shirk technique and rely on my power *way* too much. Nobody's perfect," he said, rubbing her back with the flat of his hand. "Just don't go and kill the messenger, ok?"

"No... no." she said looking up at him. "I appreciate your honesty and your willingness to point it out. Others... would not be so forthcoming."

Cleese stared down into her eyes and watched her lips as they continued to move. His attention drifted away from what she was saying and settled on the line of her jaw, the arch of her eyebrow, and the gentle bowing of her lip. After a minute, the fact that she'd stopped talking tapped him on his shoulder.

"What?" she asked, a soft blush reddening her cheeks.

"Huh?" he said, stupidly.

"You're staring."

"Oh, sorry... It's just that... You..." and he looked down toward his feet and then slowly back up into her eyes. "You're... Well... You really are a beautiful woman."

Chikara looked away, but settled into the warmth of his embrace. It had been a long time since someone she thought so highly of had said anything like that to her. Not since Creed... Her heart, while still knowing it should proceed slowly, beat perceptibly faster.

"You aren't so bad yourself," she whispered and slowly put her hands on his waist. "You're... Well, you're different."

Chikara felt a wave of emotion well up inside of her and suddenly there were words pressing against her tongue, fighting to get out. She fought them off for as long as she could, but then she felt his hand slowly slide up the small of her back.

"I... I missed you when you were gone. Missed seeing you."

"Yeah... me, too" was the best he could come up with.

Baka!!!

"Look," she said, "I had a simple life once upon a time, Cleese. I had *a life* years ago and that was taken away from me. I had people I cared for and *they* were taken from me. I had Creed, and he..." She stopped and swallowed hard. "...and he was taken from me. Jesus, I've been doing *this* a long time... too long... and I... I mean, I know the score."

He looked deep into her eyes and saw tears slowly fill them. Wisely, he said nothing.

"But now... now that I've met you... things have become... I don't know... *different.*"

He smiled broadly and winked at her. Deep down, he sensed this train of thought, this view into the things that were important to her, didn't happen often. He knew better than to interrupt its flow.

She shot a quick glance over his shoulder and then slowly turned back to him. The smile remained on his face. She saw it and mistook his pleasure for self satisfaction.

"Well, don't let it go to your head... *Darlin'*," she admonished him and then poked his belly firmly. "It's just that... now..." She looked away as if she were unable to say what she wanted to say and still look him in the eye. "Now that I've found something... *someone*... worthwhile, well... I just think it's time for me to do a little taking of my own. I..."

Cleese reached up with one hand and took her chin in his fingers, tilting her face up to meet his. Her eyelids hung at half-mast and her lips softly parted, wet and inviting. He smiled and she returned it warmly as if she were bestowing a gift. Not wanting the moment to end, he gently inclined his head and lowered his lips to meet hers. As they touched, a spark passed between them. They held each other closer and, like travelers lost in the desert and dying of thirst, they drank deeply from one another's mouths. When they regrettably pulled away from the kiss, they continued to hold onto each other and, for the moment, forgot all about The Dead and The Pit, and how either of them could die at any moment. For now, they were happy to have found one another and both silently made a wish that this embrace would never end.

Across the empty Training Hall, hidden deep within the blackness of the shadows, a lone form, hair tied back in a ponytail, silently watched and considered all the ways that this new development might benefit him.

The QFM

or

"The 'Oh, Fuck' Moment"

"Ladies and gentlemen, you don't need us to tell you that it has been one exciting first half. There's been plenty of blood already spilled and, as we head into the second half of this match, there's bound to be plenty more. As all of you have seen over these past few months, Cleese has proven himself to be nothing short of amazing in his matches. Absolutely hell on wheels and tonight is proving to be no exception. He's really been pulling out all the stops here and this crowd is eating it up."

"That's right, Bob. This fighter has been taking no prisoners and giving no quarter. He's completed each and every round with minimal difficulty and has, as of now, sustained no damage. I mean, he's completely unscathed! However, that may all change now that we're heading into these later rounds and the danger level is even higher. For now, he's looking pretty good out there with no obvious signs of fatigue. The rest of this match oughtta be a good one!"

Once the last of the UDs was down, Cleese felt exhaustion hit him like a hammer to the solar plexus and his knees abruptly gave out. Bent over, down on all fours, he tried to catch his breath; pulling in—as best he could—great heaving gulps of air. His lungs burned like he'd been free-basing napalm and he was trying hard to forget about the knot that was twisting painfully in his side. He made a quick accounting of his arms, stomach and neck and was relieved to find no cuts, no scrapes and no bites.

Well, that accounted for *something*.

He'd dropped the final UD in short order, making sure that it was dead by plunging the spike deep into its left eye. The metal tip came out of the thing's head like an antenna just above its ear. Dark blood oozed out onto the sand and soaked the granules in a blue-maroon.

By his admittedly unreliable count, this was Round Eight and he was looking at four more UDs coming up. Or was it six? He couldn't quite seem to remember which. Shit, for all he knew, it might be eight. Whatever it was, it was going to seem like way too many.

He fought his exhaustion hard for both a rational perspective and any oxygen he could get as he tried to gauge how much time he had until the next buzzer. Thirty seconds, at best. He knew that, for now, he needed to just stay still and breathe; replenish his lungs with oxygen as quickly as possible so that his muscles didn't cramp up on him. Forget about the crowd. Forget about the cameras. Forget about how much he wanted to puke his guts up onto the sand. He had to conserve his energy while he was able since it was still a long way to go until the final round and some of that big-titted dick suckin' Monk had once talked about. Truthfully, he'd skip that last part in exchange for a hot bath, a good stiff drink and maybe some face time with Chikara, but he was willing to take whatever he could get.

"Miles to go before I sleep..."

He figured that whenever the buzzer went off, he would take a few seconds to survey the situation from the ground and, only then, would he decide a definitive course of action. If the UDs happen to catch him as he was halfway to his feet, he'd hit them low and hard from this crouch. Once erect, he could always spin off to a safe zone to gather his wits and plot his next move.

Far above his head, the crowd's incessant roaring throbbed like a bee sting at the back of his skull and made it hard to think. Cleese had once heard that, in the movies, when they needed a crowd to talk, the director would tell the extras to simply repeat the word "rhubarb" over and over. He'd thought that silly at the time, but now, standing on the receiving end of it, that was exactly what it sounded like—"rhubarb."

Cleese had always hated rhubarb.

He hated it even more now.

Ok, John, so we're seconds away from the next buzzer and the start of Round Eight. So far, we've really been getting our money's worth in this fight. Cleese has dominated the action with some vicious hand-to-hand skills and that spike of his is an amazingly effective weapon. He's even managed to get some time to rest between rounds. Now, here it is the beginning of the Eighth Round and he's still looking pretty fit out there although the physical strain of any match can crush a man.

"That's right, Bob... We've seen seasoned athletes get buried in few rounds."

"Boy, I'll say... Ok, we're getting the signal now that the next buzzer is just about to go off, so let's go back down to the pit for more action..."

This time, when the buzzer went off, Cleese was almost ready for it—*almost*. Still out of breath and knowing he was a little past halfway through with this thing, he hoped it would *surely* all be downhill from here. At least, that was what he kept saying to himself. Then, he remembered that the closer he got to the end of the match, the more UDs would be coming out of the turnstiles. The more UDs there were, the greater the danger.

"Danger! Danger! Danger!"

Wasn't that what that crazy Aussie used to say on television back before a fish stuck his dizzy ass and killed him? They'd called that idiot "The Croc Hunter," hadn't they? Cleese had always thought that anyone who would willingly crawl into a cage with a dangerous animal like a crocodile simply had to be a loon. As he glanced around the pit at the corpses and the blood, he wondered just who was the crazy one now.

"Crikey..." Cleese snickered aloud as he huffed in another breath.

The turnstiles spun and locked with their now familiar booming sound and Cleese quickly made note of where everything was. Positions One, Four, Six, and Seven had UDs in them. Position Three had a fresh clip. The other three spindles were empty.

Things could be a helluva lot worse.

Knowing that there was a new full clip waiting, Cleese decided to expend a few bullets to make his life a little easier. He sprang to his feet and briskly strode toward Six *(late teens/early twenties male, punk rocker with a crushed Mohawk, wearing a shirt with the words "Dead Kennedys" printed on it, a series of bruised heroin tracks ran up one arm)* and Seven *(forty-ish white guy—big, looked like a cop, a bullet wound was visible in his upper abdomen)*. The other two UDs seemed to be having a bit of trouble getting out of their turnstiles, so Cleese bet they wouldn't be posing too much of a problem, not for a few seconds at least.

When he had just about reached where Six and Seven were standing, he pulled his pistol out of its shoulder holster, and shot Six three times between the eyes as the boy came teetering toward him. Sure, it was overkill, but he knew deep down that the crowd would react positively to the splash the blood would make on the sand.

This early in the round, those fuckers'll go crazy.

The bullets shattered the bridge of the kid's nose on impact and blew most of his slack expression out the other side of his head. The punk's Mohawk flopped limply to the side as his scalp slid from his skull like a rotting orange peel. Cleese figured it was pretty safe to say, he was now officially down.

The dead cop came up unexpectedly from behind and wrapped his meaty arms around Cleese's chest, trapping both extremities at his side. He felt the thing's rank breath fall cold and clammy against the skin at the back of his neck. A chill ran like a thief down the length of his spine. The cop drove his mouth onto Cleese's trapezius muscle and slobber ran wetly down the meat of his arm.

Fuck!!!

Luckily, the thing had clamped its jaws over the leather of his shoulder holster rather than on anything he needed. However, it did manage to scare Cleese more than a little. He had missed being bitten by a quarter inch of oiled leather. Simply put, he couldn't let something like that happen again. Ever! Next time, he wouldn't be so fortunate. A quick, reverse-headbutt broke the cop's nose and caused the UDs eyes to water enough so that it had no choice but to let him go. It was a risky move, but given the circumstances, it was the only option open to him.

Once free, Cleese drew out the spike, spun around, and, putting his back into it, slashed diagonally across the cop's chest. The metal edge of the blade went in through the bullet wound in his chest, cut through muscle and ribcage and slanted downward. The flesh parted like a sausage and let loose the dead man's intestines in a squiggling heap. The reanimated cop acted as though he'd been slapped with a pillow. His hands flew up and clawed voraciously at Cleese's chest, fingernails scraping against the chain-mail on his arms.

Over the sound of the crowd overhead and the snarling of the cop, Cleese could just make out the sound coming from the other UD's as they stumbled their way out of their turnstiles. He could tell from the hissing sound of their feet lumbering across the sand that they were coming, and coming fast.

He'd have to make this quick.

He whacked the gauntlet's release with the side of the Beretta's barrel and felt a jerk as the blade fell back into place. He raised the pistol and fired the last of his shells with a "double tap" into the centre of the cop's snarling face. The hollow points slapped into his upper lip, splitting it, and then proceeded straight up the cop's nose. The back of its head exploded in a fireworks display of blood and bone. With a look of complete surprise still plastered on his face, the cop teetered briefly on its feet and then crumpled to the ground like an unwanted doll.

Immediately, Cleese turned toward Position Three and made his way straight for the new ammo. As he ran across the sand, he pushed his thumb against the pistol's magazine release and the now empty clip slid out, falling to the ground. He reached the turnstile and, with a practiced move, snatched up the fresh magazine. His bullet needs now cared for, his attention shifted and he spun around and attempted to get a fix on the other UDs. He hastily slapped the magazine into the butt of his gun and, in one smooth movement, thumbed the slide. He felt it "klack" back into place and knew the gun was now ready to be fired once again.

By now, One *(a once-cute woman, about thirty or so, wearing a bloody pullover and light, green pants with no visible signs of trauma)* had managed to come within ten feet or so of him. At first, he thought about taking her out with just his hands, but he'd lost track of Four and didn't want to get caught on a half-blind flank like he had with the cop. So, Cleese raised the pistol, sighted in on the middle of the young girl's face, and pulled the trigger.

The hammer fell and the gun went off in his hand.

The woman continued coming and had, in fact, begun to pick up speed.

He sighted in on her forehead and shot her again.

The gun fired sending up a small cloud of smoke, the air suddenly charged with the smell of cordite. Through the haze, he saw that her progress had not been impeded in the slightest.

What the fuck?!?

He took a couple of shuffling steps back and pointed the barrel at the ground. Pulling the trigger, he was not surprised to see the sand "jump" as the pistol's discharged force tore into the soft ground. However, now that his attention was focused on it, the "jump" was nothing like a live round would have made hitting the ground. It was different—more dispersed and not as powerful.

Looking up, he saw that the woman was even closer now and so, bending slightly and using all of the strength in his legs, he jumped into the air pushing off with his left leg. Putting the musculature of his lower back into the kick, he front mule kicked the woman with his right leg. When he landed, he pivoted on the balls of his feet and threw an almost instantaneous spinning heel kick that hit her like a phone book on the side of her jaw. She flew back from the force of it, arms reeling. The foul air that had been trapped in her lungs was knocked out by the front kick with an audible "oof" and she fell heavily to the ground.

Far too quickly for his liking, she scrambled back to her feet and renewed the attack.

As he watched her coming toward him, Cleese took another quick couple of sliding steps back to buy himself some time. Deftly, he pulled the magazine out of the Beretta and inspected it. Sure enough, the damn thing was loaded with nothing but blank cartridges. He looked back quickly toward the magazine he'd just ejected and saw that it, of course, lay useless in the sand. The warning Monk had given so long ago came whispering out of the back of his brain: "You go in shootin' up the place and you'll find that you're out of rounds when you need them the most."

It figured that old drunk would have been right about some things.

Who knew he'd be right about *everything*.

"Son. Of. A. *Bitch!*" Cleese hissed.

They've given me a clip full of blanks!

Monroe's arrogant little voice rang in Cleese's ears.

"Good luck on your next *Fight Night.*"

That little fuck.

Cleese quickly decided that he would have to consider the many different ways he was going to put the hurt Monroe on later. Right now, he had more pressing concerns in the way of a very undead pissed off Valley Girl now coming toward him like a maniacal freight train; not to mention the still unknown quantity that was Four.

One came straight in his direction, reaching out hungrily for him. Cleese focused in on the ten clawing nails that were coming toward his face like whirling blades. The observation part of his brain noticed that her French manicure had gone to shit. Dried blood and tissue lay caked under the beds of her bent and broken nails. Behind the clawing fingers, slightly out of focus, he could just make out the girl's perfect set of snarling, snapping teeth. She looked as if she had come from a bit of wealth: perfect manicure, perfect teeth. *Someone's parents once had enough money to pay a top-flight orthodontist,* Cleese idly thought. Her tattered shirt, while not exactly haute couture, looked as if it had come from a more than upscale shop.

Like, totally!

He angrily tossed aside the useless magazine and holstered the empty pistol, the black metal seating itself firmly into the oiled leather. Cautiously, he approached the girl. Her hands were his first problem. As they came clawing at him, he slapped the left hand aside, and circled her right wrist in his grasp. Quickly, he spun it, twisted the radial and ulna bones in upon themselves, and shoved the limb back up into its shoulder socket. Her elbow bowed up, drawing the skin taught across the soft underside of the joint. With the heel of his free hand, he struck her in an upward motion just at the point of the elbow, pushing it back and hyper-extending it. The joint snapped with a loud, cracking sound, like wet wood thrown onto a bonfire.

Overhead, the crowd gave up another wave of frenzied shouting.

The girl screeched in what could only have been—undead or not—agonizing pain, but her cry was cut short as Cleese followed up with a savage knife-hand blow to the front of her throat. The scream sounded cut-off as if she'd gulped the remainder of it. His blow snapped the hyoid bone deep in her throat with a muted *scrunch*. She took a small step, then another, and then stumbled to her knees.

As she fell, Cleese turned his head and quickly surveyed the pit. He still couldn't see where Four had gone. He needed to get an idea where it was pretty damn quick, but for now, he had his hands full with the wounded creature before him.

The girl, down on all fours and crawling away, moaned coarsely while she nursed her shattered arm. She may have been no longer alive, but her sense of self-preservation remained firmly intact as she tried to scuttle as far away from him as possible.

Cleese next threw a short, oblique shin kick that struck the girl across her already damaged throat. Her larynx collapsed fully and folded in on itself with a wet, gurgling sound. Cleese knew there was no real point to the blow, the damage had already been done. He just did it because he knew it looked good and it made a *really* cool sound.

The crowd, predictably, loved every second of it. They lapped up every burble and drowning gasp as if it were fine wine.

He stood towering over the girl, her usable hand now cupped over her shattered airway. Their eyes briefly met, but Cleese quickly tore his gaze away. Monk always told him, "Never look into their eyes. The hopes and dreams of what they once were remain there. Look into the eyes and you look into the soul, and that breeds sympathy and sympathy breeds hesitation. You hesitate down here and you're dead before your body hits the fuckin' sand."

Cleese grabbed a healthy handful of the girl's hair and jerked her head back. Her eyes rolled wildly about in her head and her mouth was pulled slack-jawed by the extension of the muscles in her neck. He slapped the release on the spike against his thigh almost as an afterthought. The spike slid out and locked itself securely into place. He raised his right arm and the spike sparkled menacingly in the light.

The crowd overhead continued applauding and stomping their feet in the stands, creating a deafening racket. The pounding made the entire building shake to its foundations. It was Thor's Hammer battering the world into submission. Cleese could feel the thunderous booming down deep in his bones.

After what he determined to be a sufficiently dramatic pause, Cleese brought the spike down and drove it into the top of the woman's skull. Its tip exploded through her head and out the front of her perfectly capped teeth. As the polished porcelain fell like shattered china from her mouth, her voice wailed in a crescendo and then trailed off into silence.

More rhubarb cascaded down from the crowd.

Suddenly, behind him and off to his left, he heard a low moan: a deep and sorrowful sound. It was a voice that mourned for a precious thing long lost; a keening for something it had once cherished, but had now misplaced.

Four.

Cleese pulled on the spike and had already mentally moved on to how he was going to take out his next UD. However, to his surprise and panicked dismay, he found that the weapon was firmly lodged in one of the fissures between the bones of One's skull. He pulled again but the metal still wouldn't budge.

He looked up toward the direction of where he'd heard her moaning and saw Four (*another gramma of all things, about sixty, flowered running suit, the skin on the lower half of her face missing*) shuffling across the sand toward him. Her neck was cocked at an odd angle and she squinted malevolently as she tried to focus her eyes on him.

Cleese hastily glanced down and inspected the mechanism of the gauntlet. It was coated in a sticky veneer of blood, but it all *seemed* to be okay. Nothing looked like it had been damaged. It was just that the metal had somehow gotten itself caught in a crack of bone or something deep within her skull. With the spike stuck where it was and the gauntlet strapped to his hand, his right arm was essentially useless to him. The woman's dead weight not only deprived him of the use of the limb, but it gave him an additional hundred pounds or so to lug around. The trapped arm would continue to be a hindrance to him until he could figure out a way to dislodge it.

Four lurched into him from the side, screaming and clawing, and almost pushed him off his feet. The old woman's arms wind-milled crazily as her hands tried to claw Cleese's face off. It was as if she was trying to make it match her own. He backhanded her firmly with his free hand and sent her reeling.

He quickly bent his knees and dragged One's body over to the side of the pit by the spike. A streak of deep crimson painted the sand in her wake. He hoped that he could somehow pin her body against the wall and, by see-sawing the metal spike back and forth, force the damn thing loose. All he had to do was keep this old bitch away from him long enough and he just might be all right.

Well, it *sounded* easy...

By now, Four had managed to get up onto her hands and knees. She crawled arthritically over to where he stood. She clawed hungrily at his boots and tried to drag herself up his legs with her arms. Cleese irreverently kneed her twice in the face. Her nose made a small "cricking" sound and her jaw shut with a snap. When she opened her mouth again, the tip of her severed tongue fell unnoticed to the sand.

For the life of him, Cleese wasn't exactly sure how what happened next occurred, but somehow, in the midst of the commotion, his legs became entangled amidst Four's frantic arms and One's inert form. Between the wriggling motion of Four and the dead weight of One, he felt his center of balance pitch sickeningly forward and the three of them fell to the ground in a heap.

"He's down! Ladies and gentlemen, Cleese is down!"

The crowd, of course, went hysterical. Their excited cries rose into the air like signal flares. It almost sounded as if they were happy to see him fall.

Ungrateful bastards.

From the ground, he threw a couple of quick Savate kicks at Four's geriatric bridgework, sending pieces of it out of her mouth. Her head whipped around and her body collapsed back onto the sand. The move appeared to have bought him some time in which to deal with One and the still-wedged spike. With no small amount of effort, he pulled himself across the sand on his back, dragging One's inert body along with him.

Abruptly, he felt his shoulder press up against one of the pit's cold, Plexiglas sides. He looked around to get his bearings and found himself right where he wanted to be—next to one of the walls, near a turnstile. The glass felt cool, almost refreshing, against the back of his neck. As he pulled One the rest of the way to the wall, he kept a vigilant eye on Four, who was still drunkenly trying to regain her footing.

Once he'd managed to prop the dead girl's body against the wall, he pressed the arch of his foot unceremoniously against the side of her face. Her features contorted into a Picasso painting against the glass. With a grunt, he used his leg muscles to help push her off of the metal. He felt the spike come loose and slide from her skull with the sound of a creaking door. Her head finally came free and it fell back to the sand with a wet *sh-lup.*

Casting a quick glance backward, he looked through the glass and saw a cameraman on the other side giving him a thumbs-up motion, as if the images he was capturing in his lens were good ones. If the situation had not been so dire, he might have laughed, but all things considered, there was still too much for him to do for any of that.

With his arm now free, he retracted the spike and spun himself up into a fighting crouch. Almost immediately, Four, having now pulled herself more or less upright, pounced on him. She pushed her snarling face toward him. Somehow, he managed to get his hands around the soft tissue of her throat without getting his fingers bitten.

The old woman let loose a strangled scream and pressed her gnashing mouth down in an attempt to get at the pliant skin at Cleese's wrist. Pushing her away with the strength of his upper body, he twisted at the waist, dragging her with him. She pitched over his hip and landed on her ass in the sand. Her momentum carried her backward and, in a vain attempt to save herself, she twisted as if she were trying to roll up onto all fours. Instead, her face slammed against the clear wall leaving an oily Shroud of Turin-like smear across the glass.

Cleese immediately saw this situation for what it was: a major league fuck-up. He was on the ground, his pistol was empty, a snarling UD was all over him, and the beginning of the next round was surely not that far away.

He wasn't exactly sure how he would get out of this, but he knew however he managed it, it was going to require some good, old-fashioned dumb luck.

Using some Greco-Roman wrestling moves he remembered from a lifetime ago in high school, Cleese gradually managed to gain control over the old bitch. He straddled her doggy-style and, chicken-winged both of her arms behind her back. Using his hips, he drove her—hard—face first into the seam where the wall and the turnstile met. He shoved her again and again, slamming her face against the wall, repeatedly ramming her mug into the glass. For a moment, he imagined the television audience being treated to a sight not unlike him bangin' this old broad from behind. This time, he couldn't help himself but to chuckle at the image it must've presented. He even went so far as to make a couple of quick "fuck me" faces before he rammed her face even harder against the glass.

Take this, *Gramma!*

Cleese's run of bad luck abruptly changed for the better with the unlikeliest of sounds.

The buzzer went off, signaling the next round.

The turnstile spun and as the two metal surfaces came together he pushed one more time. The spindle caught the top of Four's head between its metal edge and the wall's framework and pinched it off. A wash of blood and brains splashed Cleese across the chest as her head collapsed like an over-ripe watermelon.

Not a pretty kill, but Four was now officially out of the running.

Now though, with the spinning of the turnstiles, a whole new set of problems hit the table—a new round was beginning. His problems were mounting and they were painting a rather dismal picture. His gun was empty. He was physically tired and mentally exhausted and hadn't had any time to rest.

He was pretty fucked from the looks of things.

Cleese frantically crawled away from the woman's decapitated corpse and scrambled to his feet. He quickly assessed his newly released opposition: Positions Two, Five, Seven and Eight held UDs.

Not exactly what I needed to see...

As his momma used to say though, "every dark cloud has its silver lining" and this one was no exception. For sitting there, in the turnstile of Position Three, not more than a half dozen feet away and purring like a contented kitten, sat an idling McCullough chainsaw.

Groovy!!!

Cleese ran over and scooped up the weapon. He grinned broadly as he hefted the chainsaw's weight and turned back toward the center of the pit. He looked at the oncoming UDs, revved the McCullough's motor, and then revved it again. As he strode toward the group of oncoming UDs, he continued his list of all the things he was going to do the next time he found himself in the same room as Monroe. And as the mental images mounted, he grinned malevolently and raised the McCullough over his head for the first strike.

The Blood of Eden

The light of the moon shone down silvery and bright as it poured like mercury through the blinds covering the window of Cleese's crib. The air outside the window was cool, but not cold, the heat of the day having not yet fully dissipated over the open fields which surrounded the compound. Striated clouds hung like lace across the perpetually surprised lunar face. Only the mournful call of a Red Throated Loon broke the silence of the night.

Cleese sat on the edge of his bed, quietly contemplating the day and its painful lessons. It had been a long, hard day of training and he felt exhausted to his core. He knew he'd pushed it a little too hard today. His muscles still felt raw and sore, but his mood remained light. After all, he'd passed a milestone today—well, tonight, really—and he was still trying to figure out what *that* all meant and, more importantly, what it would mean for his future.

He sighed and looked over his shoulder as the milestone stirred slightly in his bed.

Chikara lay face across the sheets; her ass the only thing covered by the sweat and lust stained sheet. Her hair swirled about her head like an onyx halo. Even though she wore it short, it still managed to hide the majority of her face. From this angle, he could only make out her cheek and a portion of her full lower lip.

Cleese took a long, slow look over her. His eyes wandered over the contours of her form like a canoe lazily drifting upriver, bound for nowhere and going there in no particular hurry. As he gazed at her, he felt his heart pulse deep within in his chest. The longer he stared at her, the more he was aware of it. In the moonlight, she looked beautiful; much more so than he'd ever seen her look. Her skin blushed with the slowly disappearing flush of afterglow.

Tonight, he'd finally gotten a good look at her in all her glory and she was something. Powerfully built and beautiful, every contour of her body was a treasure trove of wonders. And each of those wonders came finely documented by their own map— her tattoo. It was just as much a thing of beauty as was its owner, truly a marvel to behold. The artwork itself was that of a dragon, but it was so much more. The tail began just above her left ankle and it swirled around her calf, continuing on up around her thigh. The main body of the beast wrapped itself like a lover around her waist and up around her lower rib cage, circling up her back and over her left shoulder where the neck and head came over her trapezius muscle and down the front of her chest. The head was a horrible thing to see; its face set in a malicious frown with deeply set, cruel eyes. Its mouth was thrown wide; drawn as if the beast were just about to bite down on the nipple of her breast. Just under the swell of her lower breast, the monster's hand came up from under her arm, gently cupping her. The artistry was amazing.

She'd felt compelled to explain the tattoo early on in the evening, just before she disrobed and climbed into his bed. The image was commonly referred to as a "focus image" and it was mostly for distraction purposes. In the early days of martial conflict, it was noted that an opponent's attention could be drawn away by the sight of an unexpected image in an unexpected place. It was the main reason a lot of fighters got tattoos in the first place. In the first few days of the dead coming back, Chikara had noticed that the reanimated corpses—despite their limited intellect, and sometimes because of it—would respond in the same way, particularly when there were flashes of color. It was a discovery that, up until now, she'd kept to herself, but she'd gotten the tattoo immediately after joining the League. Her thought was that if a little color could distract a UD, then a whole lot just might give her the edge she'd need to stay alive. She'd asked the tattoo artist to simply draw the most fearsome thing he could think of. From its effect on both UD and Man alike, she guessed that it worked.

And then, there were her piercings.

These took a little more explanation. She'd told him how she wore seven closed rings of varying size on her body. She said they were done in atonement for the fabled seven deadly sins. The three large rings in her left ear, she said, symbolized Gluttony, Sloth, and Greed. They were three rings of slightly decreasing size as they arched up her earlobe. The largest if them was about the size of a nickel. Her right ear held two hoops that represented Wrath and Envy. None of the hoops closed all the way and thus the circle was incomplete. Her reasoning was that all of the emotions were empty ones and therefore pointless. The ring in her left nipple was just over the heart for it was in the heart that Pride dwelt. It twinkled softly deep within the dragon's jaws. The last of them signified Lust and that she wore through the hood of her clitoris.

It was, she said, a ring that few men had seen.

Cleese looked her over again, for what must have been the thousandth time that tonight. He used all of the self control he could muster to sip at her image as if it were a fine brandy. Small pools of perspiration beaded up across her back and were set like small oases dribbled sporadically across a desert of bone and muscle. The subtle changes in light and shadow caused by the moonlight played across her musculature and created a landscape of what could only be described as paradise.

She's *so* beautiful.

"You're staring again."

He nearly jumped out of his skin when she spoke, he'd been so lost in the sight of her.

"Sorry. Just thinking," he said.

She stirred and turned languorously onto her back. She smiled and reached out for him to join her on the bed. He laid back and fell into her arms.

It felt like drowning—only more sublime.

"You do that, don't you? What were you thinking about?"

"This place. The League. You. Me. Us. Pick one."

He gently kissed her, tasting himself on her lips.

"Want to talk about it?" she asked as she brushed some of his hair away from his eyes.

He sighed heavily. He wasn't sure what he was feeling could be put into words, the fear, the despair, the unavoidable feeling that he was about to be fucked.

And not in the pleasurable way he'd just been.

Abruptly, and for reasons he wasn't too sure of, he decided to try.

"I don't know much, Chikara," he whispered, "but, I do know that this place... This place isn't good for me... for us... for *anyone*. It's poison. It's like the decay and infection of The Dead has touched everything here and soured it."

He felt her reassuring hand on his arm.

"It's a dead thing—cancerous—and its sole purpose is to leech the Life off of anything and everything it comes in contact with. And once it's taken all it can while its host still lives, it doesn't stop. It changes its agenda and begins to take all it can from its dead."

He smiled at her and almost stopped talking, but what he had to say refused to stay bottled up inside of him.

"The only thing it wants is to sour each and every one of us and it will succeed if we aren't careful. The place is filled with a sickness that we can't survive if we're ever infected and I'm not talking here about being bit by a UD. *If* we play by League's rules, they'll use us up and spit us out. I understand that now. Do you?"

"Yes," she whispered and looked away into the darkness.

He turned in her arms and looked toward the ceiling for a second, trying to decide whether to tell her the rest of it. Slowly, he looked back and stared deeply into her eyes. Then, he decided that she, of all people, deserved to know the truth.

"I didn't tell you before—shit, I haven't told anyone—but... during my last match, when the spindles turned... The clip they gave me was loaded with blanks."

Chikara leaned up on one elbow and look at him.

"What?" Her expression deflated like a soufflé.

He nodded and pulled her back down to him. Right now, as he told her this, he needed to feel her body close to his. For some reason, being near her made it all not seem as bad.

"I can only figure that it was someone with enough juice to pull it off—my guess is either Masterson or Monroe. With the exception of the armorers, who let's face it, don't have the brains let alone the malevolent nature to pull something like that off, they were the only ones who could make the substitution—swap blanks for the live rounds."

"Why? How would they stand to benefit?"

"Who knows what motivates these pricks. Ratings. Animosity. Shits-n-giggles. Hell, I could have pissed the wrong someone off up at Corporate. I have the tendency to do that if you haven't noticed. Who the fuck knows and, quite honestly, who the fuck cares?"

He watched her as she took a minute more to digest everything he'd told her. A cavalcade of emotions fluttered across her face. It had taken him a while to put it all together. He was patient enough of a man to give her the time to do the same. He wasn't surprised when she arrived at the same conclusion a lot quicker than he had.

She was a smart woman.

"So, what are you going to do about it?"

"Honestly?" he said as he pulled her body even closer. "I plan to bounce."

"What, really?" Her eyes again went wide.

He nodded and continued, "I figure I'll gather up as much as I can on the financial end and hit the bricks as soon as possible, some time when no one will notice me gone... until it's too late. I mean, it's not like we're prisoners here, right? They may think they own my soul, but they don't. And as for my body... Hell, that's always been up for grabs."

He gently pinched her bare butt cheek and laughed.

"Not anymore, Baby," she said punching at him, but missing. "You have *my* scent on you. No other woman is gonna dare come near you," she said as she laughed along with him.

She lay there for a long time then as if in great thought. Finally, she pulled back from him slightly and her face took on a look of bound determination.

"I'm going with you."

"What?" Now it was his turn to go wide-eyed. "Are you sure? You don't want to take a minute and think it over? You know, once the post-coital euphoria wears off?"

"I am," she replied as if it were an admission of guilt. "Before this..." she motioned her head toward the bed, "I didn't much care whether I lived or I died here. It was the thing that gave me freedom; gave me my edge. But this... this is somehow different. Now... Now, I want to have a life. Now, I want to find some kind of solace... some kind of happiness and live the rest of my life someplace safe. Someplace..." and she burrowed deeper into his arms, "like here. After everything that's happened, we of all people, deserve at least that, don't we?"

She drifted off and seemed to become lost in her thoughts. He stared at her and, even before he had a chance to think it over, he knew he'd agree to take her along. How could he not? She was beautiful and his equal both intellectually and on the sand.

If anyone deserved to get away from this Hellhole, it was she.

In the silence of the room, he heard her whisper softly into his chest, "God... I'm just so tired. Tired of the death, of the loss, of the... fighting." The sound of slight sniffling came next. "Where's my refuge? Where's *my* happy ending?"

"Chikara..."

"Cleese, I once had people... people I cared about; people who relied on me. I had *a life*." She stared up at him. "Then, the whole world went... crazy... and I lost them. I lost them *all*. After they were gone, I swore I'd never love anything ever again. Yes, I'd taken lovers before... Creed, for one, but that was just scratching an itch, y'know?"

He looked her in the eye and nodded.

Yeah, he knew all about itch scratchin'.

"I knew I'd never have that kind of life again," she continued. "So, I gave myself to the League and killed hundreds—hell, *thousands*—of UDs. It all stopped... mattering to me."

She lowered her gaze and stared back into his chest, slowly running a finger through the hair there.

"Then, you came along," she continued, sounding almost embarrassed, "and now, everything seems to have changed. I don't *want* to die, Cleese. I want to try to live again. I want to spend whatever life I have left away from this place... with you. Now, I only want to get away from all of *this*..." and her voice abruptly cut off.

He hugged her and felt the wetness of her tears on his neck.

"Besides, I've gotten kind of used to having you around," she whispered as if betraying a confidence and pulled him still closer. She wrapped her arms around him and ran the inside of her lower leg up his thigh. As she drew lazy circles across his back with a fingernail, she kissed him again, deep and soul-stirring.

Grinning shyly up at him, almost as if she'd just given away some part of her that she thought long concealed. She wriggled up deeper into his arms and buried her head into the well of his neck, this time making his skin wet with her kisses. She giggled nervously and slowly looked back up into his eyes.

It was in that moment that he caught a glimpse of the bright-eyed girl she'd been once. He saw her as she was, back when her days were long and full of hope and her life seemed to stretch out forever like an unchallenged vista. He saw her as she'd been when she was a child; once upon a time. Back when she could drink up a summer's day like sweet cream, relishing its exhilarating taste of exploration.

For a second, he regretted not ever having had the chance to know her when she was younger. He silently wondered how, if he'd only met her years earlier, how things might have been different.

For him.

For her.

For them.

He leaned in, lowering his lips to hers, and once more felt the heart stopping spark of intimacy. He drank deeply from her mouth and savored the taste of her essence. With a full heart, he drew her body still closer to his own. Primal stirrings took hold and they gave themselves over to their rapture.

Afterward, Cleese lay in the dark as Chikara slept beside him. And in that cold silence, he began planning what he was going to do next.

... and to who.

☠ ☠ ☠

Dead Rising

The UD opened its eyes and stared into the surrounding blackness of the Holding Pen. Its eyelids, still painted with the viscous fluid of corruption, were gooey and stuck together as if covered in paste. A thick, gummy liquid coated the lashes and made them difficult to open. Blinking, it rolled its eyes and looked around. The orbs grated in their sockets, feeling like they were martini olives dropped onto beach sand.

The thing had awoken lying on the ground, coiled in a fetal position. Its clothing, spattered with a kaleidoscopic array of mud, blood, bile and excrement, clung to its flesh like a moist second skin. Body torn and twisted, the thing returned to consciousness with no recollection of who it had been or from where it had come.

It only knew that it lived.

Raising its head from the soft, pliant ground, pain roughly wrapped its unforgiving arms about its torso and swept it into an embrace that was bereft of any solace, devoid of any peace. A raw agony twisted like a blade deep in its guts and blood pulsed like syrup within its necrotic veins. Its limbs felt stiff and its muscles were as taut as harp strings.

Overhead, fixtures suspended by cables from the ceiling cast columns of dull yellow light; pools of illumination splashed across the wet, uneven ground. The soft glow was quickly swallowed up by the icy black. Steam rose from the expansive enclosure and swirled lazily in the air only to evaporate into puffs of nothingness. A low moaning droned in a despondent chorus and imbued the Pen with a palpable sense of foreboding. Dreadful things were afoot in this profanatory place. It was as if even God himself had turned His eye away from it in disgust.

Circling about in the emptiness, other things such as itself walked. The things shambled back and forth, in and out of the sparse light, moving like schizophrenics in ever widening circles. Having lost their chance at salvation, their overriding instinct now was to hunt.

To hunt and to consume.

To find and to eat.

A woman clad in a blood-sodden medical scrub blouse stumbled drunkenly into one of the circles of light. Naked from the waist down, deep gashes had been torn into the meat of her legs. Nodules of bright, yellow fat erupted from deep within the gashes. Spaghetti-like blood vessels bobbed and dribbled globs of coagulated plasma within the folds of the lacerations. Bite marks, red and inflamed, were evident in the meaty folds of her labia.

A man stepped into view—dressed in a flight suit and covered with a black, inky substance—and clumsily bumped into the woman. His lower jaw was missing, the skin beneath his eye torn roughly away. As he turned in the light, a limbless sleeve swayed from the motion.

The two beings moved about one another in a macabre two-step, neither of them seeming to be aware of the other. Each existed in their own world, a solitary realm of famine and horror, of fatality and need. Behind them, a dark mass of putrefied humanity undulated like a heavy velvet curtain.

The newly awakened thing on the ground rolled over and onto its stomach. It felt acidic bile rise in its throat. The taste was sharp and sour on its tongue. Drool slithered from between its lips in glistening strands and pooled in the dirt. The creature pushed against the soil; urine and feces soaked mud pulsed up from between its fingers. Muscles groaned out painfully and fought back as weight was put upon them. Tendons cried out like abandoned children. Cartilage grated as bone slid against bone. Pain unspooled throughout every fiber of the thing's tortured being as if it were a murderous snake.

As the corpse finally got to its feet, it teetered like a toddler taking its first steps. Its center of balance shifted and settled only to shift once more. The ground itself seemed to heave and gimbal just to spite it. The shifting perception did its best to thwart any feeble attempts at locomotion. It lifted a leg arthritically and did its best to walk. Almost as soon as the foot left the ground, gravity pulled mightily against the thing's bulk and nearly toppled its delicate balance. After a bit of trial and error, the thing discovered that short, shuffling steps were all it could manage.

For now.

The dead man raised his head and tried to vocalize its frustration. For reasons it couldn't understand, a distant memory of speech seemed like a natural thing for it to try and do. Only a hoarse, croaking sound tumbled from its lips. The tone was brittle and laced in a vivid torment. Memories flitted across its fractured perception, but the images were hazy and scattered; random sensations culled from a life long gone and now half forgotten. The recollections brought nothing but more confusion and consternation. Nothing, it seemed, could calm the soul-crushing bewilderment of being unexpectedly brought back to consciousness. Any attempt at understanding was met with a slicing blade-on-bone distress.

The thing slowly ran its mud covered hands over its trunk. Its fingers traced their way up its once muscular chest as if in search of something; something of great importance. It was a sensation experienced through a numbed and inadequate anatomy. Deadened fingertips moved in spasmodic motions and stuttered their way up to the cords of the thing's neck. There, bestial bites dug savagely into the flesh of his throat. Long, raking furrows tore deep and were then pulled backward across the shoulder and down the back. As the dead man raised his hand to his face, deep crimson painted his palm and digits.

A deep and unabiding hunger once again twisted tightly in his stomach, calling him to a dark and single-minded purpose. The thing shut its eyes and tried to comprehend what it was that it was feeling. This onslaught of sensation was insistent and refused to be denied, much less ignored. Only one thought stood paramount: hunger. The need spoke to him as a conspirator might and told him how complicity could make all of this pain and confusion go away. It spoke of its plan and a way to get back a share of the peace that had been denied by death. It whispered of a possible respite from this world of torment.

Meat...
Meat held the answer...
The tearing of it...
The biting of it...
The oh so sweet taste of it.

The creature continued to hold its hands in front of its face. Beyond its gnarled fingers, reanimated bodies swayed and stumbled about in a dance of the living dead. The beast looked down in disgust and his dull, listless eyes caught a glimpse of his reflection in a puddle of urine on the ground. It was an utterly altered and decimated countenance that stared back from the depths of the dark pool. The skin of his face draped from his bones like a flag on a windless day. The flesh was drawn and tired looking; its skin leeched of its hue and the complexion as bloodless as a lizard's underbelly.

Realization of what it now was, what it had become, carved its way roughly through the haze, through the hunger, and through the pain. The epiphany pummeled its rudimentary sense of reason with a truth that was undeniable. A minute sense of what it had once been took hold and its impaired brain aggressively chewed over this new reality. A long feared consequence of its Past had become its horrifying Present. The once unthinkable had indeed come to pass.

Feeling an overwhelming sense of shame, the thing that had once been a man ran its hands over his face, coating the sallow flesh with mud and gore. Moaning plaintively, it raked its fingers through its sweat-soaked, salt-and-pepper hair. Slowly, it raised its face toward the light and cried out in an inconsolable wail of mourning.

Connubiality

Cleese stood alone on the roof of The Chest and somberly looked out over the darkness blanketing the compound. The night had grown cold around him but it retained its calm and quiet ambience. The stars spread out across the night sky like a comforting quilt. Sporadic clouds hung like cotton balls against the clear, dark sky. He took in a deep lungful of air and breathed it out in plumes of cottony vapor. With each breath he infused his lungs with frigid air; the brittle oxygen helped clear his head and allowed him to think.

He lifted the fragrant Macanudo, which barely smoldered in his fist, to his lips and rolled the soft tobacco around on the tip of his tongue. He pulled a matchstick from his front left pants pocket and struck it sharply against the stucco of the retaining wall. The match flared with a soft and somehow reassuring hissing sound. He brought the fire to the end of the cigar in order to relight it and its brilliance dimmed as he drew the hearty smoke through its bitten-off end.

"This is for you, Monk," he said under his breath so that only the stars could hear him, "wherever you are, you grumpy old bastard."

He took another long pull on it, rolling the smoke across his palette where it felt silky and warm on his tongue.

"I was hoping I'd find you here," a familiar voice came drifting in from across the vast emptiness of the roof.

Cleese looked across the flatness of the roof, over the ventilation ducts and idle air conditioning unit. At the place where he'd left the ladder propped, he saw a large shadow of a man coming over the retaining wall like a hippo over a yard fence.

Weaver.

"Cleese..." greeted the baritone voice once he'd gotten closer. "Jesus... that ladder gets higher and harder to get up every goddamn day."

"Is it that it gets higher or you're getting older?"

"A little bit of both, Son..." Weaver said chuckling. "A little bit of both."

"I didn't know whether you'd make it tonight. I mean, I figured seeing as it is Friday after all. I was just coming up here to burn a Mac in Monk's honor."

"Hell, Son, I was coming along to do that very same thing." He pulled a cigar his own out of his breast pocket with a sly grin and a flourish.

Cleese handed over another stick match from his pocket and returned the smile. Weaver took it from him with a nod of gratitude and raked it against the stucco. Soon, his cigar was burning as brightly as Cleese's.

"I was beginning to worry that this tradition of ours was going to fall by the wayside now that Monk's moved on," Weaver said as he sat his big ass against the short wall. He adjusted himself and then spit a bit of tobacco over the side of the building. "He and I spent far too many nights up here and I was a little sad when I thought we might not get to do it again."

Cleese nodded and said, "Tell you what, Old Man... I'll take his place up here with you for as long as I'm around if it would make you feel any better."

"It would indeed. It would indeed. And I'd be damn glad to have ya, Son."

Cleese looked over at Weaver and grinned.

"I didn't know if you'd be here or not, but just in case you were, I brought you something," Cleese said as he reached into the shadows at his feet. He pulled a slender bottle into the moonlight, hefted it in his hand once, and then handed it over.

"Saaaay, now we're talking!" Weaver exclaimed, turning the bottle over in the half light so that he could read the label. "Glenmorangie... eighteen year old, single malt Scotch." Weaver laughed and shook his head. "People will say we're in love."

"If they do," Cleese responded with a wry grin, "then you're The Bitch."

The men laughed and eased themselves down into a comfortable sitting position; backs pressed against the stucco. They sat, both looking up into the sky as Weaver pulled the lead foil from around the bottle's neck. With a squeak, he tugged the cork out and set it to his side. He lifted the bottle to his lips and opened his mouth. The rich, brown liquid poured over his tongue with a hearty "glug-glug" sound.

"Aaaaaaah..." he sighed after he'd swallowed. He handed it over to Cleese, his face reddening in the dim light. "That's mother's milk right there, Buddy. Fuckin' A!"

"Glad you like it. I was meaning to give one of these to Monk before he left, but what with Corporate moving ahead everybody's plans and everything getting so crazy, I was never able to get around to it."

"Are you saying you have another one of these bottles lying around?" Weaver said, cocking an eyebrow inquisitively.

"Yeah, I do. I'll bring it next time, you fuckin' lush."

"Ahem..." he said and he gave a little bow, "I prefer the term *connoisseur*,"

"Whatever you want to call it, Pal. Your liver is just as screwed."

"Prolly true..." Weaver took the bottle back and raised it in toast. "To Monk then..." He took a large slug of the stuff and then handed the bottle back to Cleese.

Cleese accepted it and raised the bottle in kind.

"To Monk."

The two men sat, their conversation falling into a comfortable silence, passing the bottle back and forth between them for some time. Neither saying a word nor feeling the need to. It was enough that they were together, hanging out and drinking themselves into a state of forgetfulness. It was a well deserved respite from all that they'd been through in the last few weeks. With Monk gone, Weaver and Cleese had become closer, like acquaintances drawn together by the absence of a mutual friend. Their interaction could still be awkward at times, but Cleese was content in the knowledge that their friendship would find its own path in its own time. Soon enough, things would fall into their own rhythm and things would grow to be more natural between them.

After a few minutes passed and they'd both begun to feel the first wave of their buzz, Weaver looked over slyly and nudged Cleese's elbow with his own. His expression was comically conspiratorial. His thick eyebrows arched and a mischievously insinuating grin spread across his face.

"I notice you and the filly spending more and more time together now that

Monk's gone AWOL." The caterpillars that passed for Weaver's eyebrows danced up and down on his forehead. "What's doin' there?" he asked.

"You know... I'm not sure," Cleese responded honestly. Feeling slightly embarrassed, he scratched himself behind the ear. "She's not like any woman I've ever known before. I mean, she's strong, capable, smart... She doesn't expect anything from me and asks for even less." He trailed off and shrugged. "I'm just enjoying her company is all and I plan on taking it as it comes, to spend time as time is spent, y'know?"

Weaver nodded in the darkness. "I do indeed. She's a nice girl... good in The Pit, too."

Another pause settled in and the two men sat quietly smoking and absorbing the stillness of the night. Cleese was encouraged by Weaver's acceptance of his blossoming relationship with Chikara. It felt a lot like having a dad approve of the girl you were dating.

"So," Weaver said, handing the bottle over, "you hear anything from Monk?"

"Nope. You?"

"Not as of yet. I'm thinking he'll wait until he finishes up his hitch in the UFL. You know, wait 'til he gets to his daughter's place and he has something to report other than how jacked up that dog and pony show is."

Cleese nodded almost imperceptibly in the moonlight.

"He wasn't exactly happy with the way things finally went down, you know," Weaver said, shaking his head in disgust. "He told me that he wanted to make sure you were going to be ok before kicking you out of his nest."

"He was mothering me."

"Well, the hardest thing for a parent to do is to take their hand off the back of the bike. I doubt he had any desire to see you get your ass ripped apart in front of him." Weaver looked Cleese in the eye. "He liked you, cared for you like a son."

"I hate to admit it," Cleese said over the lip of the bottle, "but I'm gonna miss that son-of-a-bitch. He beat my ass—and I cursed him—more times than I'd like to admit, but he was also more help to me than I could've ever told him." He took another long draw of the Scotch. "He kept me alive in this damned place."

Now it was Weaver's turn to nod. Monk had dragged his meat out of the grease more times than he could recall as well. They'd befriended one another in the early days of The League and both considered themselves to have a deep and abiding affection. He felt a pang of remorse when he thought of how he might not ever see his friend again.

Cleese handed the bottle back to Weaver and they were both once again left to drift on the stream of their own thoughts. There was no pressure to fill the void with unnecessary chatter or small talk. It was enough that they could sit and smoke and drink in silence.

And so they did.

Finally, Cleese, coming back to the here-and-now, broke the stillness.

"So, how long are *you* gonna stick around here? I mean, you ain't getting any younger."

"Hey, you can go fuck right the hell off, Pal. I plan on doing this shit for another ten years *at least*," Weaver said laughing. As his chuckling fell under his breath, he said, "Some people's fuckin' children..."

"Hey, no offense meant."

"None taken, ya prick."

Cleese smiled and reached over for the bottle.

"No, seriously, don't you have plans for your Golden Years?"

"Listen, Cool Breeze, I'm not even pushing sixty. I ain't got no retirement plans just yet. My job here is something I do without much thought and I'm really fuckin' good at it."

"Agreed, but don't you have family? I mean, back out in The World?"

Weaver got suddenly quiet, almost sullen, and looked away. A dark cloud passed over his expression and his mood darkened. After a minute, he took the bottle back.

"I did... once," and he lifted the bottle and drank. "Same old story, y'know?"

"Sorry," Cleese said meekly. "I didn't mean to dredge up any bad memories."

"No, it's ok," Weaver said and lightly touched Cleese on the arm with the lip of the bottle. "See, back in the day, I used to work in, of all things, the electronics industry. Did that shit for years. I kept track of thousands of parts at a semiconductor manufacturing plant. I did what they called 'destructive analysis.'"

"Sounds fitting."

"Yeah, well... it was all pretty meaningless, but I had me a wife, a home and a good life goin'. The old American Dream, y'know?"

Weaver's gazed drifted off as he began wandering the meadows of his memory.

"It's funny how things can change, eh?"

Cleese nodded silently and settled back, not wanting to get in the way of whatever it was Weaver had to say.

"Anyway, one day, I'm on my way home, drivin', y'know? And—bam—I hit this massive gridlock on the freeway. Ain't a car moving for shit. People are cussin'. People are honkin'. Then, in the next car over, a radio starts blarin' on about how there are people goin' crazy: mass murder, cannibalism, all kinds of craziness. Shit, you know how it was...

"At the time, the news guys were all talking about everything from Venus probes to some kind of infection, like a virus. Whatever it was and wherever it came from, it was makin' people to go crazy."

Cleese again nodded remembering that day all too well.

"Honestly, I figured it was all one of them *War of the Worlds*-type things. You know, complete and utter bullshit. Anyway, I'm sitting in my car for quite a while, waiting for the gridlock to break. All I wanna do is get home and get back to my life, but as time goes on, I start getting more and more nervous. Not really sure why, but this anxious feeling starts skittering up my spine. So, I pull to the side of the road and drive up onto the shoulder, thinking I can circumvent this shit by doing some off-roading and get my ass home faster. I go four-wheeling through the toolies and get to the next exit. I bounce up and over the curb and come screaming down the embankment."

Weaver had a faraway look in his eyes as he continued. From the look on his face, it was like he was back there, seeing it all play like a movie across his mind's eye.

"Anyway, long story short, I finally get to my street and as I pull up to my house I see the place surrounded by a dozen or so of those motherfuckers. They're all milling about, but gathered around something on the lawn. At first, I was like, 'what the fuck?' and start fearing the worst. Little did I know that not in my wildest dreams could I have imagined 'the worst.' I start turning toward the house and, as I come up the driveway, I see that the thing on the ground is Fran Johnson from next door. She's lying on the ground and her clothes are all pulled open and there's blood and guts and who knows what else spread all over my lawn. Now, I'm still thinking that this is some kind of joke, like a Halloween prank, but the look on her face told me that it was all real as shit. These animals had torn Frannie to pieces and, from the blood on most of their faces, they looked like they had, as weird as it sounded, been eating her. I mean, fuck me..."

He chuckled in disbelief.

"Anyway, as soon as these fuckers see me coming, a whole slew of them, all pasty-faced and bleeding gashes, come lurching across the lawn, toward the driveway. Unable to stop, and not really wanting to for that fuckin' matter, I hit the sidewalk and plow straight through them sons-a-whores. I mean, I *slammed* into 'em. A handful goes under the front wheels and their bodies make loud thumping sounds under my wheels as I run right over them. The others bounce offa my fender like bowling pins."

Weaver lifted up the bottle and drank again to both wet his whistle and to calm his nerves. In a moment, he cleared his throat, swallowed, and continued talking.

"I slide to a stop near the front door and I'm about as scared and pissed off as a cat in a washin' machine. Not really thinking about whether it could or would be dangerous, I jump out and get a clear look at the situation—Frannie torn open on the lawn, the blood, the people I'd run over starting to get back to their feet, the whole mess—and I know *somethin'* ain't right, y'know? I mean, I'm just fuckin' smart like that.

"Then, I see *Frannie* move..."

Weaver paused long enough to take another pull on the bottle.

"So, I dive back into the car and pull an old tire iron out from under the seat. I get back out and just start swinging. I mean, I'm cavin' in heads and breaking off fuckin' limbs."

Weaver looked over at Cleese in the waning light and smiled.

"You'da been fuckin' proud of me, man."

Cleese grinned and nodded.

"Anyway... It was about then that I hear my Dora screaming from inside the house and I *panic!* I start beating my way through the crowd of these sons-a-bitches. I must have flattened a football team's worth or so, I swear to fuckin' God! So, with my adrenaline now pumping, I make it to the front door and kick the motherfucker down. Inside, there are one or two more wandering in the front room and entryway. I lay them out and go running through the house and up the stairs toward our bedroom. I get to the doorway and I see Dora..."

Weaver's voice cracked suddenly, tied tight with emotion. His eyes welled up with tears that he quickly swallowed down. Bolstering his resolve, he looked out across the compound and continued.

"I see her... and she's surrounded by like four of those things. The only thing I can figure is that they must have gotten in through the back patio door, coming over the fence from the neighbor's house. They were all gathered around her, trying to negotiate the furniture, knocking it over and scattered shit off of the dresser as they did whatever they could to get at her."

Tears were streaming freely down the big man's cheeks now and Cleese didn't blame him one bit. Weaver was a tough guy, but... every man had chinks in his armor and they usually were gathered somewhere around his heart.

"I'll never fucking forget the look on her face as I came into the bedroom, Cleese," he said wiping away at the tears which had gathered in his beard. "Her eyes were wide—scared, scared as I'd ever seen her—and her face was covered in these scratches. It's kinda funny... Through all the commotion of those things in the room and the ones that were trying to break in outside, through all of that shit, I heard her softly say my name when she saw m..."

Weaver's eyes brimmed over with a new wellspring of moisture and his voice cut off, suddenly sounding constricted. He coughed softly and cleared his throat and did his best to continue.

"And that was when they got a hold of her. I remember her screaming as they dragged her down to the floor. I mean, she sounded so fucking scared. By the time I was able to beat 'em off of her, she was gone; torn apart. There was blood *every-where*." His voice trailed off into nothing. "There was just *so much* blood..."

Cleese looked deep into his friend's face, but quickly realized that he was no longer telling the story for his benefit. He watched as tears freely spilled out of Weaver's eyes, rolled down his face, under his glasses, and soaked into his already wet beard.

"Later, Emergency Rescue crews showed up in the neighborhood and started rounding up The Dead. I never saw if Dora came back or not. I assume she did, but I wasn't there to see her... or take care of her. I was taken out to the EMT vans and checked out for any bites or signs of infection."

Weaver wiped at his running nose and took another drink from the rapidly emptying bottle.

"Anyway, once things were relatively safe, they took survivors off to some of the Shelters. There, they had some real doctors check me out and, once they saw I hadn't been bitten, they let me go. The only problem was... I had no place *to* go. With Dora gone, my life meant shit. It was fucking rubble, man. So, at first, I joined the cleanup crews and helped trying to get things back under control. For the longest time, I went out on the 'house to houses' and I'll tell ya... I took great delight in watching each and every one of those bastards I came up against being put down. Hell, I still feel that way some times. With every one of them being killed, it's like a little bit of my pain, a tiny bit of my grief, gets washed away. My heartache seems a little more tolerable anytime I feel as though I had even a small hand in putting those fuckers back in their goddamn holes."

He paused again, obviously trying to get control of his emotions. He took an-other shot and wiped his mouth with the back of his hand. Cleese idly thought that, before this night was out, he was going to need to go get that other bottle from his Crib.

"It wasn't too long after that that things settled down and we got back to what we all remembered as 'normal.'"

Weaver turned and looked Cleese in the eye.

"But... who gave a flyin' fuck? A lot of us had no place to go. Most of us couldn't—and wouldn't—go back to our homes. Hell, everything at my house only reminded me of what had been stolen from me, of what I'd lost. I'd heard from some guys on one of the cleanup crews about this guy Weber and his plans for this League thing. When it looked like it was a go, I signed up right away.

It seems that I still needed to see some blood spilled before I was ready to call things square," he chuckled and shook his head. "Once I signed on, it was pretty apparent that I was no fighter. Fuck, I usually come out on the losing end of a pillow fight. So, since I'd always had a head for organizational shit, I volunteered to head up their armory. And with that, The Chest was born."

Weaver lifted the bottle in a half-hearted toast and drank deeply.

"I've been here ever since."

"Jesus..." was all Cleese could muster. He went over Weaver's story and had to admit, it was something. One thing wasn't clear though and that was closure. "So, are things about even between you and The Dead, Weaver? Are things any closer to being settled?"

Weaver looked at Cleese, his normally jovial face now grim and set in stone.

"Well, I've considered that a time or two, to be honest. And after a lot of thought, I've decided that things will never be even or settled between me and those fuckers, Cleese. Not ever. Never. Ever... Ever..."

Cleese nodded and looked away, somehow understanding. Some men, when everything important in their lives is stripped away, have only the pain and the anger left. Their anguish becomes the one thing they can count on and they cling to it like a life preserver because, in a lot of ways, that was exactly what it was. Cleese didn't fault them for feeling that way. Everyone walked their path in life and they held the things that worked for them close, the things that nurtured and protected them. Anger and hatred could oftentimes be as reassuring as a warm blanket on a rainy day. However, sometimes that comforting blanket wrapped around them, weighed them down, and dragged them to the depths of despair. Cleese silently hoped Weaver was the type of man who could one day learn to let go.

"It's one of the main reasons why I appreciate the work you do," Weaver continued. "I mean, you cut a swath through those fuckers and nothing seems to affect you," Weaver laughed and slapped Cleese on the thigh. "You're a baddass, Son, and you're able to do the very thing I wish I could have..."

"And that is?"

Weaver looked away, up toward the piece of sky where he liked to think the love of his life waited for him to one day return to her.

"Save my Dora, I guess."

☠ ☠ ☠

Ridgeway Elementary

Before...

The afternoon bell rang out across the crowded playground, signaling the end of the lunch recess period. The sharp, shrill sound made many of the children playing there jump in their shoes. Some of the more excitable girls squealed in surprise and then immediately cupped their hands over their mouths as if trying to catch their voices before they could be heard. Balls bounced and swings swung, but all that soon came to a stuttering stop once the Yard Duty Teachers blew their whistles and gently herded the kids toward the main building. There were a few stragglers—that was to be expected with children of this age—but the women soon had the mass of waving arms and runny noses all heading in the right direction.

Chikara Pressfield walked toward the red brick façade of Ridgeway Elementary School, stopping every now and then to gather up an abandoned jump rope or orphaned Four Square Ball. She tried to soak up as much of the midday sun as she could since it would be her last chance of the day to feel the warming rays of the sun on her skin. The rest of the afternoon would be spent in her classroom, her time monopolized by what she'd come to think of as "her kids."

She'd been teaching at Ridgeway for most of the school term, having received her teacher's certificate the prior year, and she'd come to really enjoy her new vocation. In college, she'd ridden an athletic scholarship for all it was worth and at one time even thought herself destined for the pro tennis circuit. She had a backhand that was—or rather, had been—pretty devastating, if she did say so herself. But after a car wreck had more or less shattered the elbow of her left arm, those dreams had been set aside. After months of rehab and a heart full of tears, she'd found that she'd been unable—and unwilling it would seem—to invest the kind of energy it took to make a full recovery. Now, incapable of competing on a professional stage, teaching became the best of a set of limited options.

At the large double front doors of the school, she dropped off the playthings in the bins kept by the entrance to the playground and—as she was the last one in—turned to shut the doors behind her. The midday sun had just reached its epoch and was beginning its long slow slide toward the horizon. Birds could be heard chirping in the trees that lined the soccer field, their song joyful and carefree. Momentarily, she envied them.

As she pulled the door closed, through the glass she noticed a man standing far across the playground outside of the fence which encircled the perimeter of the school. She continued to watch him for a minute or so as she absentmindedly straightened her long black hair with her fingers. The door's lock clicked into place and a chill abruptly rippled down her back. Shaking it off, she turned and headed down the hallway to the stairs and up to the second floor where her small class waited at the end of the hall.

As usual, her classroom was in a total uproar. The children, still bristling with excitement from the play yard, were jostling one another and bouncing around the room like pinballs. She opened the door, which was flanked on either side by large bulletin boards, and stepped into the room. The class was in the midst of learning the countries of the world and each continent was represented on the corkboard by assorted maps and pages carefully cut from *National Geographic* magazines.

Along the far left side of the room, a whiteboard stretched from floor to ceiling, wall to wall. Across the top was taped a banner which read "Word Wall." Underneath it were all of the letters of the alphabet arranged in orderly rows. Slips of paper with handwritten words on them were taped beneath each corresponding letter.

At the head of the class to her immediate right, a large chalkboard was mounted, the day's lesson plan written in Chikara's swirling scrawl. She approached her desk as the door closed with a hiss behind her, and the class immediately began to settle down.

"Hello, Miss Pressfield," the children called to her in a sing-song tone as she took her position before them. Quietly, but firmly, she redirected the children's energies back to their studies.

"Ok, settle down now, boys and girls," she said, smiling warmly. This being the first real class of her teaching career, she couldn't help but love them all dearly. Despite her best efforts to conceal how she felt, her affection for them was readily apparent. "Can anyone remember what we were talking about before recess?"

A pond of blank faces met her gaze.

"Oh, come on, you guys... we were *just* talking about it."

Sheepishly, a hand rose at the back of the room. The boy had a crew cut and a soft, round face. He was new to the class, having just arrived from St. Louis a month or so ago. From what she'd seen, the kid was pretty smart.

"Yes, Jeffrey."

"We were talking about the... Messopotavia and Youfrageous Rivers."

"Well, sort of."

The class giggled and hid their faces behind their hands.

"We were talking about the Tigress and Euphrates Rivers in Mesopotamia. What many call the Cradle of Civilization. Good job though..." She cast a playful frown toward the rest of the class. "No one else remembered even that much."

The kid's laughter stuttered to an embarrassed stop. Behind a tapestry of faces, Jeffrey blushed and looked down toward his desk. It seemed that Jeffery, like many of the boys in her class, had a bit of a crush on his teacher.

Chikara considered the whole idea quite cute.

"Does anyone remember anything else from our discussion?"

Before any of the children could answer, the Public Address System crackled overhead. A few thumps later, and Principal Borden's voice was heard, peppered with static.

"Excuse the interruption, Ladies and Gentlemen, but we have an announcement."

Chikara held a single finger to her lips as a sign to the children that they should be quiet. As the children had been taught, they dutifully repeated the gesture.

"We have been notified," he continued, "that due to some road closures, we'll be staying after school today until everything is cleared up. Thank you."

The class collectively groaned and shuffled in their seats.

"Ssshh," Chikara said and tapped her finger against her lips. The children again mimicked her. As the Principal began talking again—something about parents having been called and "how everything was ok" and for them "not to worry"—she walked over to the window and looked out at the schoolyard from over the fire escape that ran up the side of the building. The area was empty. A sudden gentle wind swirled and gently pushed the swings to and fro as if invisible children who occupied them were enjoying a ride.

As her eyes drifted across the slides, carousels and Jungle Gyms, she noticed a small group of people congregating outside of the school fence. Just a few of them stood there, but the sight seemed incongruous with the hour of the day. Parents never started gathering until near the time school let out. The sight of folks waiting out by the fence now just seemed odd. At first, they appeared to be talking to one another, but as she watched them more closely, it looked more like they were simply standing and staring at the school from behind the cyclone fence.

At the far end on the right, she noticed the man she'd seen earlier. He wore a black tie and looked as if he'd spilled something (coffee, maybe?) on his white shirt. The dark stain splashed across his chest and down the front of his pants. His manner seemed agitated as he ran his hands obsessively over the wire, but his eyes remained fixed on the school. Seemingly by accident, he found the break in the fence which allowed entrance to the school's grounds from the street and he hesitantly took a step through.

A light tugging at her shirt sleeve brought her back to the classroom. She looked down and saw a young girl with long black hair parted in the middle looking up at her with a questioning gaze.

"Yes, Carolyn?"

"Is everything ok? Are we in trouble? The Principal said we have to stay after school."

Chikara looked up at the class and saw an assortment of small worried faces looking expectantly at her.

"No," she said softly. "No, everything is fine. He just said there was some problem with the road; perhaps a traffic accident of some sort."

"Miss Pressfield?" said a small Japanese boy named Yoshi who was proving himself day by day to be the clown of the class.

"Yes, Yoshi?"

"Uh... I'm scared."

Chikara looked around the room and a good portion of her kids were nodding their heads up and down aggressively in agreement.

"Oh, Yoshi," she said and walked over to pat him on the head. "There is absolutely no need for that..."

As she spoke, she turned her head for one last look outside. Across the soccer field, she saw that the rest of the group of people were now following the man with the stain on his shirt through the fence and slowly making their way toward the school. She mused that maybe they were some of the children's parents who'd heard about whatever was happening on the roads and had come to fetch them. Even as the words were formed in her mind, somehow she knew that wasn't the case. Feeling her stomach becoming uneasy and electric, she stepped away from the window.

Abruptly, the classroom door opened and Mrs. Walters from the fourth grade class next door poked her head in. The woman was older than Chikara and stockier. She had obviously dyed blonde hair set in a style that made her look a bit like a "biker mama." Her clothes more or less confirmed the assumption. She smoked like a train and the throaty, coarseness of her voice and heavily lined face were evidence of that. Since arriving at Ridgeway, she'd come to be the closest thing Chikara had to a friend amongst the staff.

"Chikara," she said, her voice trembling just a bit, "may I speak to you a moment?" She roughly jerked her head back the way she'd come. "Out here... in the hall."

"Ladies and Gentlemen, please open your free-reading books and sit quietly for a bit while I go speak with Mrs. Walters." She turned toward a boy with a bowl haircut at the front of the class. "Luke, you are in charge while I am gone. Please see to it that everyone is *reading*."

She walked toward the door and said, "And please... don't worry. I'm sure this is all nothing to be concerned about."

As Chikara came through, Mrs. Walters stepped back. She nervously looked up and down the hallway while waiting for the door to close behind her.

"What's going on, Helen?" Chikara asked, trying to follow the other woman's gaze.

"Something is *up*, girl," was the only answer given.

"What? Wait. What are you talking about?"

"Did you hear that letch Borden?" she asked. She'd long been complaining about the Principal and his "hands on" approach with some of the female staff. "Well, he was lying..."

Chikara looked at her confusedly.

"About ten minutes ago, I was talking to Phyllis in the office," Helen continued. "She said that Fred got some kind of frantic call from the police just prior to him making that announcement over the PA."

"The police?" Chikara asked, unbelieving. She took a quick glance behind her and peered through the small window set in the door. Predictably, the children were not reading but rather, talking amongst themselves excitedly.

"Yeah!" Helen shook her head up and down excitedly; eyes opening wide enough to show the whites around the irises. "Phyllis said that right after the call, Frank got on the radio and called Jessie, the new janitor, and told him to start locking the doors that lead into the building. After a few minutes, she said that Jessie stopped answering his radio. Weird, huh? She didn't hear much else, but after that, Frank's tone changed... He just sounded *really* freaked out."

"Wait... That makes no kind of sense. We're supposed to..."

"I know! We're supposed to always keep those doors open during regular school hours."

"Surely, Phyllis misunderstood."

"That's what I asked her. But she said she heard him talking to the janitor plain as day. I'm heading down to the office now to see what I can find out. I just wanted to tell you what was going on before I went."

Chikara rubbed a hand over her face in an effort to make sense of it all. For some reason, the image of the people gathered outside flitted across her mind's eye. When her attention came back to the moment, she saw Helen looking around nervously and wringing her hands.

"God, I need a smoke."

"Well, if you learn anything," Chikara said, looking back over her shoulder at the door to her classroom, "come back and tell me, ok?"

The older woman nodded briskly and gently touched her friend's arm reassuringly. With that, she hurried away, her heels clicking against the hard tile floor.

Chikara took another look up and down the hallway and then pulled open the classroom door. As she stepped inside, twenty-three pairs of terrified eyes snapped up to look at her. The kids were obviously frightened, their initial anxiety having escalated to an almost full-blown panic. Kids have always instinctively known when adults were lying and, as a result, grown-ups were not to be trusted. They'd all heard the worry in Mrs. Walter's voice and in Chikara's absence it had fanned the flames of their unease.

Chikara tried her best to smile as she walked toward her desk at the front of the room, but then she caught sight of Roger at the far end of the room. The little boy (with his Dumbo ears and large round glasses) was a human polygraph. The kid could smell bullshit a mile away. He'd caught on to her early in the school year when she'd tried to tell the children about Santa Claus. She decided, given everything she'd been told, that honesty would be the best policy.

"Children, I'm not going to lie to you..." she began.

Roger narrowed his gaze and leaned forward.

"Something is indeed going on and we're all going to need to stay calm."

A few of the girls and even a boy or two stared at her wide-eyed and blinked away some tears. For the most part, the children were putting on their bravest faces.

Lydia, a fragile-looking blonde with small wire-frame glasses, hesitantly raised her hand.

"Yes, Lydia."

"Who are those people?"

"What people, Dear?"

"The ones outside," she said and slowly raised her hand and pointed toward the window.

The collective group nodded like bobblehead dolls. Chikara stepped over to the window and was amazed to see that the entire group of people who were by the fence had now made their way onto the lawn just outside the building. Worse, they were being followed by another large group who were still making their way through the fence and across the lawn. All told, there were forty or so people milling around outside.

Straining to get a good look, she saw that something didn't seem right. There was definitely something wrong with all of them. Blank faces and gaping mouths were unanimous expressions they wore. Their gait was more like a stagger than real walking; as if they were drunk or severely impaired. Their forward motion was a result of their rocking back and forth of their body on stiff legs.

Suddenly, a small itching began at the back of her brain and she got the distinct feeling she was being watched. Turning her head slightly to the right, she caught sight of the man in the white shirt and black tie: the one with the coffee stain down his front. While the others were milling about, he was standing still and looking up at the building, straight up at the window. His gaze bore through her and he seemed to be assessing the structure as if looking for a way in. Having weighed through all of the available options, he seemed to have settled on the window of her classroom.

As their eyes met, the man suddenly looked at the ground and then back up, tracking the structure of the fire escape.

"Miss Pressfield?"

Another small voice interrupted her thinking.

"Yes, Lisa," she said and turned to look at the other girl now standing next to her. The child had shoulder-length brown hair held back by a floral headband. Her front two teeth were missing and her eyes were wide and looked wet with tears barely held in check.

"I... I want to go home," she said, her bottom lip standing out like a fleshy bookshelf. Chikara looked up and the class as a whole was again nodding in agreement.

"As soon as I know what's going on, you can, Dear," Chikara said and she patted the child on the back of her head. "Now, please take your seat, ok?"

Again the classroom door swung open and Helen Walker stepped into the room. The smile she'd pasted to her face was more grimace than grin, but God love her, she was trying to put on a good show.

"Miss Pressfield, can I talk to you for another moment? *Please...*"

"Oh, here we go..." Roger sighed under his breath.

"Surely," Chikara said and nodded to Luke. "You're back in charge, Buddy."

The boy sat up a little straighter and nodded, trying his best to put a "game face" on. Despite his best efforts though, he still looked as if he were about to cry.

Chikara followed Helen back out into the hallway and closed the door behind her.

"Ok, what's up?"

"We need you to come downstairs. We're talking about barricading all of the doors."

"You're *what?!?*"

"Sam Lorning, the shop teacher, pulled a television set into the Teacher's Lounge and you're not going to believe what the news is saying.

"What are they saying?"

Helen took hold of Chikara's hand and pulled.

"You'd better come with me."

"Hold on a second..." said, pulling back her hand.

Chikara opened the door behind her and stuck her head inside. As she leaned in, she reached out and rested her hand on the fire extinguisher hanging from a hook at the side of the door. The children sitting in their desks looked so small and scared. She smiled and waited for them to quiet down.

"Children, I'm going to be right back. Everything's fine. I just need to go check on when your parents can come take you home."

Inside, she felt like shit for lying, but it was the best excuse for leaving them she could think of off the top of her head. At the back of the room, she caught a glimpse of Roger The Human Lie Detector frowning.

"Luke, you're The Man."

Just to be safe, she locked the door as she left so that the kids wouldn't be tempted to start roaming the hallways. She twisted her key in the lock, removed it from the door, and returned it to her pocket.

And with that, she was gone.

When Helen and Chikara got to the Teacher's Lounge, there was already a crowd of people inside huddled around the television. They stood in a semi-circle around the tall metal cart where the TV sat. Most of them were nervously holding Styrofoam cups with rapidly cooling coffee in them. A few held cigarettes between their fingers, but they were mostly just burning away unnoticed. Oddly, they all had the same look on their faces as the children in the classroom.

"If there's no activity where you live," the warm voice of the anchorman was saying, "stay indoors and barricade all means of entrance. This is the Emergency Broadcast System for the greater Columbus, Ohio area. We repeat, lock all doors and windows and remain inside. Bicentennial Park is no longer considered a secure area. Please avoid all areas which would normally attract large numbers of people such as sports stadiums, shopping malls, and all downtown locations. You should proceed as quickly as possible to the areas which are being repeated in our bulletins. Further, please follow all directions given you by any and all military personnel. There have been reports of looting in most downtown areas. Please... do not attempt to travel. Even though you may believe that your loved ones require your assistance, you must remain where you are, or—if you are not safe—in one of the rescue stations. By all means, be wary of any and all people who appear disoriented or confused."

"These people are assholes," Jim Rhodes, the fifth grade science teacher said. He was a short, balding man with a small patch of hair encircling his head. The light overhead shimmered off of the barren landscape of his skull.

Chikara thought to herself that if anyone could know an asshole on sight, it was Jim. Those types could smell their own.

"Ssshh..." Sandy Kirklash, the second grade teacher from the first floor hissed. "We can't hear what they're saying with you talking."

"All right. All right." Irritated, Jim looked away.

"Ssssssssshhhhh!" the group hissed as one.

The scene on the screen changed to some recorded tape from an earlier news conference. The camera shook as it was being adjusted, but the image soon settled down. A stoic black man in a business suit stood before a podium and was talking to a room full of reporters. "I'll take your questions one at a time, please," he said, his eyes looking sad and bloodshot.

A male reporter's voice was heard. "Are we dealing with some kind of contagion? Is this something man-made?"

The man looked down and in a weary tone, said, "It's too early to tell. From all accounts, it is not something of a natural origin."

A woman's voice came next, "How does it spread? Is it airborne?"

"Airborne is likely, but we simply do not have any way of knowing at this time."

"Could it have anything to do with the recent reentry of the orbiting space station?"

"We don't know. At this time, we are open to any and all possibilities."

The first male reporter broke in and asked, "Is this an act of terrorism? Is it a military concern?"

"While we do not think it is an act of terrorism, as the phenomenon is occurring across the globe, it has been made the highest of priorities for the military."

"Sir, are these people alive?" asked the woman.

The man sighed and, as if he were wearing the weight of the world on his shoulders, whispered, "It would appear not."

"What do you think we should do?" Sandy asked, her voice shattering the silence of the room. The teachers looked at one another and silently shook their heads.

"This is just crazy," Josh Giorda, another teacher said. He'd come onboard about the same time as Chikara had. He was young and, if you asked most of the female members of the staff, pretty darned cute. "I mean, really... 'Dead bodies walking around'? It's like a bad horror movie."

"I'm telling you... It's probably all bullshit," Jim said over the rim of his cup.

Abruptly, the Lounge door swung open and Principal Borden entered, looking frazzled. His shirt collar and tie had been pulled open and his face was awash with stress. He cleared his throat before speaking.

"Ladies and Gentlemen, I'm going to need your attention, please."

Someone lowered the television volume a bit with the remote and they all turned to face him. Fred the Letch looked like shit. His eyes were red and his skin had grown as pasty and white as a fish's belly. He was obviously out of breath and you could tell by looking at him that he was barely holding it all together.

"We're going to need to barricade the entrances and exits to the building. The police have contacted me and said that the threat being reported on the news—as ludicrous as it may sound—is very real."

He looked around the room and, just for a moment, they all saw the first glimmers of panic set in deep within his mind. He quickly spoke again to hide it.

"We'll split into four groups, each going to one of the four entrances into the building. Josh, since Jessie has stopped answering his radio..." A sudden distant look passed over his face like a cloud. "I don't know, maybe he decided to leave once he saw those things outside," he said distractedly, almost as if he was talking to himself. Just as quickly, he came back to the now and continued his thought. "I'll need you to head over to the access doors in the basement and make sure those are locked and secure."

The group looked to one another and began exchanging nervous chatter.

"People... People... We need to stay focused on this. This is no joke," he said, his voice cracking minutely. "We have more than just ourselves to worry about here. We have the children."

The soft sound of the television filled the ensuing silence.

"I understand you're having a difficult time killing these things, Chief," a reporter asked.

"Just shoot them. Shoot them in the head," the voice of an exhausted man in a police uniform responded. "They seem to go down permanently when you shoot them in the head."

Chikara felt an errant and indistinct sense of déjà vu.

"Then, you gotta burn them. Beat 'em or burn 'em. They go up pretty easy."

And with that, they set to it. There was some disagreement early on as they broke into groups, but for the most part, they accepted this new reality without complaint. Chikara went with Helen, Jim Rhodes and Ross DeChamp, the fourth grade P.E. teacher, and headed off toward the East Entrance. Not a lot of conversation took place en route. They were all lost in their own uncertainties. Whether it was worry over their own families, loved ones, or pets, no one said much of anything. They just walked down the corridors in hurried silence, passing several closed classroom doors. From inside, several sets of small, scared sets of eyes looked out, their lashes wet with tears.

When they arrived at the doors, Chikara took a second and looked outside through one of the wire mesh-laced windows. There were several more of those people milling about now. At one point, she thought she recognized Sam Theroux, the owner of the nearby bodega. His glasses were gone and his features were contorted into a perpetual sneer, but sonofabitch it sure looked like him. It wasn't until he turned to face her full on that she noticed one of his eyes had been torn out.

"Oh. My," she whispered. "God."

"What?" Helen asked as she quietly turned the key in the locks and carefully wound the length of chain DeChamp had brought along through the door's push-bars. For some unspoken reason, they'd decided to go about their business as silently as possible. It was as if they all instinctively knew that too much noise would undoubtedly mean getting the attention of the people outside. She slipped a padlock through two of the links and snapped it shut. For good measure, she pulled gently on the door to make sure it was tightly closed.

Off to one side, Jim Rhodes stood with his arms crossed indignantly.

"Nothing," Chikara answered. "Never mind."

"Let's get back," Jim said, looking up and down the hallway with a hint of nervousness. He'd been looking through the window on the other door and had not liked what he'd seen. Not one bit. He'd also seen Sam, thus his face had abruptly turned white and a good portion of his bluster evaporated.

As they turned away from the door, Jim and Chikara exchanged looks that spoke volumes and those volumes said the same thing: 'We're in a bubbling vat of shit here.'

Hurrying back down the hallway, they'd not gone more than a dozen steps when they were brought up short by a loud banging sound from the direction they'd just come. Through the window, they all saw Sam's distorted face pressed against the slim pane of glass. His lone eye glared at them and his mouth dripped long strands of saliva. Apparently, he'd seen them as much as they'd seen him. Immediately, Sam banged his fists against the door again and again. His hands rained down against the metal in an insane drumming rhythm which echoed down the empty corridor. As one, the group took another step backward. From where they stood, they could see the double doors shaking in their frame. Sam had obviously been joined by more of those people outside and they were all now pounding with him in earnest.

"We should get back to the Lounge," Ross DeChamp said, his voice sounding small and scared in the large hallway.

"Yeah, no shit," Helen murmured and her words echoed hollowly in the emptiness of the corridor.

When they got back to the Lounge, they met up with two of the other groups, who each had variations of the same incredible story. As the group talked, Chikara couldn't help but feel her gaze being pulled toward the ceiling. It had seemed like a long time since she'd left her classroom and she felt compelled to get back there. The kids were probably scared shitless by now after they'd no doubt looked out the windows and seen god-only-knew what.

As the teachers continued talking amongst themselves, she quietly slipped off and headed back down the hallway to the stairs.

Midway up the stairway to the second floor, Chikara stopped.

She was sure she'd heard something coming from the hallway at the top. At first it sounded like the screech of a rusty door being opened against its will. Slowly, she took another step. Then another. As she reached the last step, she stopped yet again.

Abruptly, an unmistakable shriek echoed down the hallway just outside the stairwell.

Without another thought, Chikara ran up the rest of the stairs and down the hall and as she got closer to her classroom, she heard the scream again. This time she was able to pinpoint its origin and to her dismay it was, without a doubt, coming from inside *her room.*

Those last few steps seemed as if they were being taken in slow motion; like in a dream when, no matter how fast you tried to move, it was never fast enough.

She reached out and quickly unlocked the door. Grabbing the doorknob and twisting it, she pushed the door open with all of her might and rushed inside.

"Say," Helen interrupted the other teacher's conversations, holding up her hand. "Hey, shut up, willya?

Having now gained all of their attention, Helen looked around the room and then back to the Lounge's closed door.

"Did anyone see where Chikara went?"

The group shook their heads and looked stupidly up and down at one another.

"Maybe she went to the bathroom," Jim Rhodes said.

"Jim..." Helen rolled her eyes and walked off to go look for her. "You really are an idiot."

Chikara pushed on the door and it abruptly bumped into something soft yet unyielding. She pushed again and heard a soft thump like the sound that comes from stubbing your toe on a table in the middle of the night. She pushed harder against the bulk of the door, her face slamming painfully against the wood. Stepping back, she looked down and was horrified to see Luke's wide eyes staring up at her. The boy's mouth hung open, his tongue protruding slightly from between his teeth. There was a smear of something dark across the side of his face.

Another scream broke the silence and, putting her shoulder to the wood and planting her feet solidly against the flooring, she pushed the door open. Luke's inert body slid with it, his way greased by more of what looked like the pool of oil he seemed to be lying in.

As she stepped into the room, utter chaos met her gaze. The children's desks were overturned; paper and books littered the floor. Glass glittered like diamonds amidst the clutter and there was more of that dark material spread everywhere. As her eyes adjusted to the light, she saw more figures lying like abandoned dolls about the room. Her vision slowly cleared and her mind put names to those dolls: Sean in his JVC baseball shirt, Angela, Juan, Claudia, Stephanie, the boy they all called Gordo, Tina and Julia.

Her kids.

They lay motionless on the floor, pools of what she now recognized as blood quickly congealed around them. Near her desk, she saw Jeffrey's thin legs sticking out from underneath. It was like he'd gotten caught trying to climb under it. He must have thought it was the one place he'd be safe.

Chikara stepped deeper into the room and her foot bumped into another doll. She looked down and Lisa's cold eyes stared back at her, her headband pulled down and twisted around her neck. Her face was now a mask of tears and circular wounds.

Far off across the room, she saw what look like a fort, but was actually a haphazard barricade made up of desks piled one on top of the other. Behind it, a fistful of kids stared back at her. Their faces were wet with tears and the look in their eyes was pure horror. In front of the desks, several more children lay. They were alive and moving, but all were nursing wounds. Georgette was cradling her arm. So were Meryl and Frank. The shoulder of Ming's shirt was torn and blood was dribbling down her arm. Off to one side, Tia was wailing, a large chunk torn from her cheek. Blood painted the side of her face.

In the seconds it took for Chikara to catalog the devastation, three dark figures pulled themselves from within the cloak of the room's growing shadows. The figures all had the same blank stare as the people milling about the playground. Chikara looked up and saw that the windows had been smashed in.

"My god," she whispered to herself, "they must have come in through the fire escape."

The last of the looming figures stepped forward into the waning sunlight which was cascading in through the empty window frames. Chikara's mouth fell open when she saw that it was the same man she'd seen earlier; the one in the stained shirt and tie who'd been staring up into the window.

"You..." she hissed.

The other three figures—a teenager in a football jersey, a fat, balding man, and a woman who would have looked pretty had half of her face not been ripped away—followed suit and took staggering steps forward. Blood covered each of their faces and coated their hands and forearms. The fat one was frantically chewing something.

Chikara stepped back in disgust and bumped into the wall near the door.

Her mind reeled in abject horror at the scene which lay spread out before her. And then, suddenly, painfully, the guilt kicked in. In a series of mental flashes she conjured up what must have transpired here: the people coming up the fire escape, the children's panic, and the invaders hammering on the windows in the same way they'd hammered against the door she and the others had locked.

She drew in a deep, anguished breath imagining what happened next all too easily.

The figures gathered outside, their numbers growing, the malevolent stares, the moans and the pounding.

My God!

Then, the windows giving way and the glass raining in.

Dear sweet Jesus!

The panic. The terror.

No!!

And then, the violence.

My fault!!

Her kids.

This is all my fault!!!

These were her kids... and she'd left them alone. Even though she thought she'd been protecting them by locking the door, she had in reality left them trapped and on their own. With nowhere to run, many of them had been cornered and had no choice but to die an unimaginable death.

This was a guilt that she knew she would carry with her for the rest of her life.

A low moan brought her focus back to the present. The four strangers took another faltering step toward her and she pressed her back firmly against the wall. Her heart beat painfully in her chest. Her gaze lifted to stare upward toward the ceiling. She felt her tongue go dry as her terror grabbed her roughly and tightened the muscles of her limbs.

And as the first of her tears cascaded down her cheeks, she knew... beyond any shadow of any doubt that this was *her* fault. Hers and hers alone. It had been her duty to care for these children, to keep them safe and sound. And she'd failed.

God... she'd even locked the goddamned door!

It was by her hand the kids couldn't escape this fate.

Almost immediately, her growing fear was replaced by deep and vengeful anger. As the heat of that anger gripped her and took hold, she felt the tips of her fingers wrap around a piece of metal protruding from the wall. She pulled against it and a heavy weight abruptly tugged at her arm. Confused for a moment, she looked down and saw that she'd pulled the fire extinguisher off its hook.

It was at the precise moment that she heard a low moan come from a few feet in front of her. She looked up wildly and saw the man in the shirt and tie come another step closer. A hungry grin strained his features and he slowly licked his lips in anticipation of what would come. He opened his mouth and uttered another low, soulless moan. Breath that smelled of the grave assaulted her senses and she saw bits of meat wedged between his blood-soaked teeth.

Teeth, she thought, stained with the blood of her children.

As a kind of madness sidled up to her intellect, she felt its warmth; embraced its momentary comfort. Like a fever dream, the delirium whispered to her and told her what had to be done, what *must* be done. What followed next was pure instinct and unfiltered insanity.

Spinning at the waist, pulling at the weight of the fire extinguisher as if she were delivering one of her devastating backhands, she brought the canister up and smashed it against the side of the man's head. With a satisfying crunch, his skull collapsed in on itself and he was slammed to the floor, his body landing like a sack of meat. She delivered two more crushing overhand blows to his skull before leaving him for dead.

Continuing the onslaught, she swung the metal can around and struck the kid in the jersey across the knee. The sound of the joint breaking was both gratifying and, in a way, cleansing. Another overhand swing brought the cylinder down on the fat guy's bald skull and he went down without too much of a fight. As he hit the ground, the small finger he'd been chewing fell from his lips and landed, rocking slightly, on the floor.

Abruptly, a slender hand with polished nails grabbed at the back of her collar. Chikara bent at the waist, ducking underneath it, and brought the extinguisher upward in a demolishing uppercut. The once pretty woman's jaw shattered and, with an ear splitting snap, her neck broke. Her body crumpled to the floor in a heap.

Now out of breath, she stood panting over her handiwork.

The kid in the jersey had begun pulling himself toward her again, dragging his shattered leg behind him.

"Behind you," she heard Carolyn scream excitedly from behind the barricade.

Adrenaline now leaving her system, Chikara strained to lift the blood splattered weapon over her head, but with what felt like a Herculean effort, she got it there. Now standing with the dripping fire extinguisher held high above her, she screamed incoherently. As she felt the dead thing at her feet touch her leg with cold hands, she drove the weapon downward with all of her might. The metal rim struck the kid just at the bridge of the nose and smashed whatever was above it to mush.

An unnatural quiet fell over the classroom. The stillness punctuated only by soft sobs and sniffles of the frightened children and the heavy panting of their now exhausted teacher.

"Jeez, Lady," Yoshi said, staring wide-eyed from behind the piled desks and wiping back his tears, "what took you so long?"

Helen Walker came out of the stairwell and as she rounded the corner onto the second floor, heard what sounded like a bar fight coming from Miss Pressfield's classroom. She broke into a run and made her way down the long hallway. She arrived at the room, breathing heavily, and pushed the already ajar door open and stepped out of the hallway and into a war zone.

The classroom looked as if a bomb had gone off in it. Papers, desks, and glass were everywhere and some of the windows had even been shattered. Unbelievably, amidst the rubble, were several bodies laying strewn about. And there—and this was the most unbelievable of all—standing over what looked like a corpse and driving a fire extinguisher repeatedly into its skull was Chikara.

"What the hell?" Helen asked to no one in particular.

Chikara, her face, chest and arms now spattered with blood, looked at the extinguisher in her hands with disgust and dropped it. The metal clanked against the floor with a hollow sound. Immediately, she rushed over to the pile of desks in the corner and pulling them away, made a throughway to where her kids cowered. Once a way was cleared, she frantically saw to some children who were obviously injured.

"Chikara..." Helen asked hesitantly. "What's going on here?"

"Helen," Chikara shouted, "get me the fucking First Aid kit in the desk."

The children all got that all too familiar "Ommmm, you're in *trouble*" look on their faces and it wasn't until the two ladies realized it was because Chikara had said the "F word" that they understood. If it hadn't been for all the blood and carnage around them, the two women might have laughed. Instead, they each set their faces and went to work.

Once it was apparent that whatever danger there had been had passed, the children encircled them both and began wildly gesturing and talking, all trying at once to relate the horror of what had happened. A few of the others grabbed onto each of their legs crying, holding on for dear life.

"Hold on... Hold on. We need to see to those who were injured and then we can all talk," Helen said. She'd retrieved the First Aid kit and pulled gauze and antiseptic out of the case.

"No," Chikara said, still trying to catch her breath. She gently started freeing her legs and directing the traumatized children toward the door. "We need to get out of this room and lock the door behind us. There could be more of them coming up the fire escape."

"Right. Come on, children. We need to exit this room," Helen responded as she ushered the unhurt children through the debris and toward the door. "Just like we do when we have a fire drill, ok?"

"Go downstairs to the Teacher's Lounge and tell whoever's there what happened." Chikara called to her. "Roger, honey... I know you're scared, but I *really* need you to run ahead. I need you to go tell the other teachers what's happened here."

Roger, jug-eared and bespectacled, stared at his teacher and fear once again gripped his expression. He looked around nervously at his classmates for support, but his gaze was met by wide-eyed stares which mirrored his own.

"It's ok, Roger," Chikara said trying to soothe his worries. "There's none of those people anywhere else in the building. It's safe. I promise."

To his credit, the boy nodded and stood up, but not before helping a few of the others to their feet. Once he was sure those around him were ok, he looked back at Chikara. She smiled at him and winked as if to reassure him. With a quick nod, the boy turned and took off at a run out the door. The sound of his footfalls slowly receded as he sprinted away from the classroom.

One by one, the children were attended to and carried out of the room. Helen brought the uninjured kids to the Teacher's Lounge where they were given drinks of water and allowed to recuperate from their trauma. Even Jim Rhodes helped out by gently taking the hands of some of them and holding them close as they cried and sobbed out their stories. In the end, he wasn't such an asshole after all. The injured were tended to one at a time and then taken to an impromptu infirmary in the main lavatory on the first floor.

And the dead...

Even though it broke her heart to do so, the dead were left where they lay. There was little choice other than to leave them in the classroom. It would simply be too traumatic if any of the other children were to come across the dead bodies in any way, shape or form. And so, after taking one final, soul-crushing look at their bleeding and broken little bodies, Chikara turned her back on her room and locked the door behind her.

As night fell, all of the children from the other classes were brought to the gymnasium and the rest of the classroom doors had been secured one by one. The injured from Chikara's class were cared for on makeshift litters and left in the infirmary that was set up in the first floor lavatory. Around midnight, the first of them began dying. Poor Tia—who had been bitten so badly on her cheek—was the first to go. Chikara had cradled her little body in her arms and felt her slip away.

In the end, every one of those who'd been slightly injured died; delirious and hot with fever.

Near midnight, on a patrol of the hallways, Jim Rhodes heard the sound of something scratching against the door from inside Miss Pressfield's classroom. When he looked through the small piece of glass set in the wood, little Lisa Jackson, with her floral headband still twisted around her neck and her face hot with festering bite marks, stared back at him from the darkness with cold, dead eyes. He'd stumbled away from the door, his hand covering his mouth in horror, and vowed never to go back.

As the news on the television in the teacher's lounge continued to play on through the night, the newscasters did their best to explain the gravity and extent of the situation. All too soon, it became apparent just how widespread it was.

And what needed to be done.

It was just after the news had switched over to the Emergency Broadcasting System that Chikara quietly searched the school for the kind of weapon she figured she'd need for the gruesome job which surely lay ahead of her. She found a never used fire axe in an enclosed case near one of the toy bins by the front door and decided that it was the best thing she'd be able to find at the school. It was either that or an old aluminum bat. She couldn't ever imagine bringing herself to doing what she knew had to be done with that. As odd as it sounded, she thought the axe would somehow be kinder. It would at the very least be quicker.

However, knowing that didn't stop her from shuddering at the thought of it.

So now, more or less armed, she sneaked off by herself and sat quietly on a folding chair in the lavatory and waited, waited for them each to come awake.

Just her and her kids.

And the heavy, metal axe.

And as each of her small and hopelessly fragile students slowly opened their eyes, their pupils now clouded and opaque, their mouths open and hungry for all things wet and red, she tightly gripped the firm wood of the axe's handle and raised it over her head.

Then, as compassionately as she could, she put each one of them back to sleep.

It was, after all, the least she could do... for her kids.

Poisoned Apples

Cleese stood brooding behind the thick Plexiglas wall of the pit. His right arm raised and pressed against the clear laminate, he glowered and gave off a distinct "don't fuck with me" vibe. Behind him several teams of workers busied themselves with the multitude of tasks necessary in order to put a television show of this scale on the air. Cameramen moved large cameras about like they were gun turrets, each angling for the best shot at incoming enemy zeroes. Others sat behind giant consoles, busily turning knobs and sliding levers. Scores of fresh-faced Production Assistants rushed back and forth like baby chicks as they herded paper from one disorganized desk to another. It was all business as usual for them, but for Cleese it looked like a chaotic mess.

His mood was a foul and malignant thing and it showed. His was a demeanor that very nearly shouted for people to leave him be and, for the most part, they were all smart enough to comply. He'd always been a man who wore his emotions on his sleeve; the good, the bad, and—like this one—the ugly. It was an integral part of his charm. He was not someone who kept things bottled up and now was no exception. His intent gaze burned its way through the glass and a troubled sneer lay fixed upon his face. A few yards in front of him on the sand under the blinding lights stood the catalyst of this grim temper.

Inside the Pit, Chikara had just regained her footing after eviscerating the UD *(an impossibly skinny old man wearing boxer shorts and not much else. His scalp had been ripped away and the shiny whiteness of his skull lay horrifically exposed)* that had stood in front of her. It was technically still a "live" combatant, but with the old guy's guts rapidly cooling in a pile at his feet, he wasn't going anywhere fast. Gutting him bought her some time and had given her, at the very least, some breathing room. Around her, the bodies of the fallen lay heaped like cordwood, their vacant eyes staring blankly upward toward the blackness of the ceiling.

Cleese leaned closer, nearly pressing his face against the glass, and carefully watched Chikara at work. The vapor of his breath made small clouds of moisture on the acrylic. She really was something to behold. Standing there beneath the hot lights, her body glistened with the perspiration created by her prolonged movement. Her short, spiky hair threw droplets of water off and into the air like a sprinkler head. Her face was covered in thick, Kabuki-style makeup: curving, purple splashes of color covered her eyes with deep, lavender shadows. The harsh coloring gave her face a constant aspect of extreme rage. With her chest and shoulders heaving from her exertions, her muscles danced beneath her grue-coated skin.

Standing there covered in blood and sweat she looked—in a word—magnificent.

Cleese had given up trying to decide if throwing in with her was a good idea. When she lay beneath him, it seemed like the best idea he'd ever heard. When she wasn't, he still thought it might be good to have someone there watching his back, especially someone who just might be his physical equal. It'd been a long time since he'd trusted someone enough to do that.

So, without much thought, he decided to give it a go.

In for a penny... in for a pound.

Having made the decision to leave together only made the tableau being played out before him that much harder to sit through. Watching her, surrounded by these lethal creatures, he only wanted to protect her, to keep her safe, to get her the hell out of that Pit. But he knew, like it or not, his only choice was to let this play out. If one of The League's premier fighters suddenly cancelled a match—a *televised* match—it might make the powers-that-be suspicious. And, if they were to get away without complication, their disappearance had to be kept quiet. Otherwise, who knew the lengths these fucks would go to in order to keep them here. They'd already done some pretty fucked up things to drive their ratings up. He could only imagine the kind of shit they'd pull to keep them both in the Pit, earning revenue. So, with a kiss and a whispered prayer, he'd watched her walk down the gangway and out onto the sand.

He didn't like it, not one bit.

But she'd made it clear it was her intent to go through with the match and there wasn't much he could say or do to stop her. Besides... They both knew she was a skilled fighter and had done this shit a thousand times before. She wasn't stupid. She'd do the right thing, make it through the match, and they'd be scott-free.

Still... the compulsion to step in and take the risk for her was maddening.

He looked up from his reverie as motion from inside the Pit caught his eye and returned his attention to the match. From over her shoulder, Chikara drew the katana which rested in the ornate scabbard—which she called a "saya"—she kept lashed across her back. With a flash of gleaming sliver, she drew the blade and slashed it across the space in front of her. The old man's head separated from his shoulders and bounced like a ball across the sand. With a flick of her wrist, she expertly whipped the sword around in a tight circle and dislodged any blood and tissue from its metal with centrifugal force. She turned and expertly slid the sword back into place.

Across the pit, the final UD of the round (*a comic book geek-looking Asian kid with a Moe Howard haircut and a massive gunshot wound to the throat*) was weakly pawing at the sides of the Pit, oblivious to the imminent danger that was now stalking across the sand toward him. Chikara came up behind him, delivered a lightning fast, straight blast of punches to the dead kid's kidneys, and then leveled him with a reverse wheel kick. The kid was unceremoniously slapped to the ground. She stood over him and grabbed a handful of hair, pulling the kid's head back. A flurry of hacking knife hands to his already damaged the throat and he was soon drowning in a cascade of his own blood.

Once more, Chikara reached back for the katana. She was going to make more of a show of things, but she knew that she'd need to make this quick since the round was undoubtedly almost over and another would soon begin; one that would bring a fresh crop of UDs. As her fingers touched the handle of the weapon, she heard the buzzer go off.

Cleese winced when he heard that. He knew better than anyone that having any number of UDs hold over from one round to the other wasn't good. It did nothing but add to the already daunting numbers the fighter faced; especially this late in the match. It meant that she'd be beginning the new round at a disadvantage.

As the spindles turned, he felt their vibrations through his hands which were pressed firmly against the glass.

"Whoa, John, this could be a real problem for Chikara. She has a holdover and she's going up against four fresh UDs."
"Indeed... she certainly going to have her work cut out for her."

Almost immediately, Cleese sensed that something wasn't right. In fact, from the looks of things, something was very wrong. From his vantage point, it was difficult to take in the whole of the Pit, but he instinctively knew that it simply looked too crowded out there. He could see Chikara and the leftover UD. He could see the new UDs staggering out of the spindles. Still, it just looked too damn populated out there.

"Hey, hold on a second there, John..."
"I see it too, Bob. I count the leftover UD, the... one, two, three, four new UDs, but... there are three additional..."
"John, I've just heard from our handlers who, as many of our fans know, are the people whose job it is to load the combatants into the spindles for every round. They tell me that there seems to have been an equipment malfunction that's re-leased a few extra UDs onto the sand."
"Well, someone's job is going to be on the line, eh Bob?"
"I'm not sure about that, John. When you're dealing with things as dangerous as the Undead, sometimes mistakes happen. Now, normally, something like this would mean The League putting a stop to the match, but with Chikara out there on the sand, a few extra opponents should only mean a few more kills."

Chikara heard the UDs before she saw them only because the commotion they made coming out of the spindles was louder than she'd expected. She drew her katana and quickly removed the Asian kid's head just below the jaw line. She turned and crouched in order to get a better idea of where everybody was, drawing her blade before her. Once she got a look, she felt her heart sink.
There were too many of them!
Far too many...
"Fu-" she whispered softly under her breath.

"-uck!' Cleese shouted as he turned and looked toward one of the cameramen. "Get her the fuck out of there!"
The man poked his head out from behind the camera meekly and stared. He nervously looked from right to left as if confused and then went back to looking through his viewfinder. It was pretty obvious he wasn't going to be any help. Cleese maneuvered around the guy and the camera and took off toward the Pit at a dead sprint.

Chikara brought her sword in front of her, using its sharp edge as a shield. The first of the dead *(a middle-aged nun wearing a blood-spattered habit that was torn, half-exposing one of her breasts)* had reached her, its fingers lightly pulling at the tip of the blade. With two clean strikes, the nun's arms fell to the sand, lopped off at the elbows. Another lateral slash and, from either the fighter's momentum or her upper body strength or both, the dead thing before her was cut cleanly in half.

Stepping back, she took stock on the rest of her opposition. It was bad, but not that bad. She'd trained for worse. Bolstering her confidence, she dug her feet into the sand and waded into the fray.

Cleese could barely see Chikara's body through the press of UDs gathered around her as he ran toward the Pit's hatch. He was able to just make out the silvery flashes of her sword through the glass, but the bulk of her body remained obscured from view. Abruptly, she broke free and stumbled into view.

He skidded to a stop and pressed against the transparent wall. Through the glass, he could tell something had gone wrong; very, very wrong. Cleese could see numerous scratches across her midriff, her hair was mussed and she'd taken some blows to the shoulders that were already starting to bruise. It also appeared as if she was favoring her left arm. With the way she was protecting the limb, she may have sustained either a pulled bicep or, worst case scenario, a sprained or fractured forearm. From the looks of things, the UDs had pawed her up pretty good, but she still seemed capable of defending herself.

One of the things *(a girl in her late teens, wearing a dirty prom dress with what looked like a knife wound in the middle of her chest)* came up on her nine. As she turned to address her, Cleese could see that she had a wild-eyed look on her face and the scabbard of her sword had been ripped from her back. All things considered, she looked pretty beat up, but thankfully, she didn't seem to have been bitten.

Then, just for a second, she looked up. Her eyes bore straight through the glass and into Cleese's. For the first time since he'd met her, she looked scared; *really* scared. Gone was the brave fighter who'd led more than her share of men into battle and kept them alive, sometimes despite themselves. Gone was the confident woman who alternately could be tough as nails and then soft and pliable as velvet. Gone was the brave soul who he'd just held in his arms and sent down the gangway. For that second, their eyes met and she made a silent plea for his help.

Her mouth moved slightly as she silently whispered his name.

Cleese had an unnerving sense of déjà vu.

Then, a shadow moved behind her and the world seem to fracture and slow down.

An unseen UD *(a rapper-looking black guy in his mid-twenties with multiple gunshot wounds to his chest and upper abdomen),* who'd been quietly hanging back and observing things while the others attacked, stepped up silently behind her. Despite its brain being addled and driven by a single-minded purpose, it had learned a thing or two from its time being used as a training aid. It knew that although the fighters were fast and strong, they could also be over confident. And it was that arrogance that often led to them leaving their backs exposed.

This one had proven herself no different.

Cleese saw the thing's shadow fall across Chikara's shoulder as it came up behind her. With alarming speed, it quickly wrapped its arms around her, effectively trapping both of her hands at her side. Through the glass, he heard her cry out in pain as her injured arm was pressed tightly against her chest. Her blood-covered katana fell useless to the sand at her feet. The thing bent its face into the nape of her neck and slid its wet mouth to the right.

As Cleese tore himself away from where he stood and raced toward the gangway which led out onto the sand, out of the corner of his eye he saw the thing's mouth slowly open. Its teeth were yellow and rotten within its twisted maw. Its black tongue was raked across its dry, cracked lips. And the last image he saw through the glass before racing out into the Pit was a flash of the thing's teeth sinking into the meat of her neck.

Cleese came through the Pit's hatch moving as fast as he legs could carry him. By his last estimation, there were four or five UDs still left roaming the sand. He quickly scanned the area and found all of them on their knees and huddled in a small group. Two more lay in pieces on the sand, their necks broken, but their heads were still technically connected.

Cleese was moving at a full run now and, as he got closer to the huddled group of UDs, he snatched up Chikara's abandoned sword. Once he'd gotten to within a few yards of them, he saw one *(a middle-aged Filipino woman in a nurse's outfit with the left side of her body badly mangled)* pull a chunk of something wet and quivering away from the crowd. As Cleese lifted the katana to strike, the thing brought the mass of meat up to its mouth.

Cleese stumbled to a stop, the sword raised over his head like an executioner's axe. The nurse looked up at him with an almost sated look in her eyes. Below those empty pools, on the meat it was gnawing, he saw the familiar face of a dragon. A small silver ring glistened in its jaws.

Cleese bowed his back and struck, crying out in pain and frustration, with all of the strength he possessed. The blade hit the nurse with such force that he barely felt it cut through the bitch's neck. Her head fell like an oversized melon to the ground. The satisfied look on her face dissipated like vapor.

By now, he was in a position where he could see more clearly what had happened to Chikara. After having put up what could have only been a valiant fight, the things had, quite literally, torn her to shreds. One of her arms—her right from the look of it—was being fought over by two of them. The two others were busy ripping into her chest as if today was Christmas and she a present to be fought over.

In a flash, he noticed the spot just below her rib cage where he'd once discovered she was the most ticklish. His heart twisted savagely in his chest as he recalled having kissed that spot time and time again. The sensation of it, the warmth, the softness, brushed over his lips like a ghost's touch. Now, the spot—her spot—was a torn and blood-covered mess.

Tearing his eyes away, the image before him being too much to bear, Cleese raised his gaze. He caught a quick glance of Chikara's face as they tugged and tore at her. Her body rocked back and forth from the force of their efforts. One eye was closed. The other was wide opened; her eyelid having been torn cruelly from her face. Cleese saw a small drop of clear moisture pool and then slide away from the corner of her closed eye.

After that, things sort of blurred for Cleese. He dimly remembered wading into the center of the UDs without a care for his own safety. He chopped and slashed with the katana until the muscles in his back screamed in protest. Like a whirling dervish of death, he tore at them. Hunks of meat flew from their bodies and tumbled across the sand. Like a Pollack painting, blood splashed across the glass, creating an impressionist's vision of Hell itself.

When the last one of The Dead had fallen, Cleese turned in the light and saw a cadre of the Budo Warriors now coming through the doorway. They rushed toward him, but quickly slowed when they saw that all of the UDs had been dispatched. Cleese glanced back and took another look at Chikara's ravaged face. He felt his throat tighten painfully.

Even in death, she was still one of the most beautiful things he'd ever seen.

He tore his gaze away and, as he looked up, saw the horrified faces of the camera crews staring at him through the glass. The broadcast must have cut to commercial because the cameras were all pointed away. Now that there was not a need to document what was happening, they were able to react honestly to the horrible tableau before them. Their expressions and demeanor were ones of heartache and alarm. Most of them had known Chikara and, like many, thought her invincible. To see her die like this, rocked them to their core.

For his part, Cleese couldn't stand to look at them; their anguish was a debilitating reflection of his own. He turned away and desperately sought something—anything—on which to focus in order to help hold back the wave of grief and nausea he felt building like a tsunami within him.

Just then, something moved behind one of the cameras across from him and caught his eye. Something—no, someone—pulled from the shadows and stepped into the light being cast inside the Pit. Cleese was able to make out the shape of a thin man, in a business suit, talking to one of the cameramen. Cleese saw the man lift his head and laugh at something said. That was when whoever it was turned his head and Cleese saw that the guy wore his hair long... and pulled back into a tight ponytail.

Just then, Cleese saw the smarmy fuck notice him staring. Through the glass, Monroe never acknowledged him, but instead just stared as if the entire situation was a goddamn science experiment. The self-satisfied expression Monroe wore spoke volumes. It was all Cleese needed to see in order to know that he was involved.

Somehow... in some way... that motherfucker had had a hand in this.

With great difficulty, Cleese tore himself away from Monroe's gaze. He knew that if he looked too deeply and thought about it for too long, he'd kill that son of a bitch right here and now; in front of God and twenty million witnesses.

No. This was something he'd force himself to wait on. He'd collect Chikara's body and see to her burial. Then, when the time was right, he'd slaughter that prissy fuck with his bare fuckin' hands.

Slowly, he turned and walked back across the Pit toward the door. His foot kicked against something and he looked down. There, half buried in the sand, was the scabbard to the sword that he still held half forgotten in his hand. He dropped to one knee and picked up Chikara's saya, dusting it off. Carefully, he slid the blade into the slot in the wood. The metal made a hissing sound as it disappeared into the sheath. With a click, the sword slid into place.

The sound made his heart twist unbearably within his chest.

As deep and painful emotions swirled within him, he fought back the rising tide of his anguish. A knot the size of a man's fist flexed in his stomach and, for a moment, a wave of tears splashed against the inside of his eyelids.

Silently, he cursed himself.

Goddammit, he should have seen this coming!!

He should have... He should have *known*.

All of the signs were there... but he'd gotten too complacent, too full of his own bullshit.

Jesus... the hubris! The fucking *ego!!*

Things had been going too well for him, for them. After all this time, all of the pain and loss they'd both endured, they'd both manage to find someone that could be let inside. Someone who could be trusted. Someone to care about.

If it wasn't exactly Love, he felt it was pretty damn close to it.

So very fucking close!!

And now, thanks to this place and these people... she was gone.

It... was gone.

Moving slowly, he got back to his feet and stiffly continued toward the door. As he moved forward, he was left little choice but to walk past the group of Warriors still congregated on the sand. Most of them stood with their heads down, their world now shattered by the death of their leader. Chikara was someone they'd all thought was as close to invincible as humanly possible. Each of them bore their thoughts—like the Kabuki makeup they wore—on their faces and those thoughts could be traced in the wake of their tears. If Death could come calling for the best of them, what did the future hold for the least of them?

Cleese walked on and the men parted without a word to let him through. He moved past, but never looked one of them in the eye. That would have been too much to bear. They'd all lost someone dear to them today, and that loss was going to take a long time to heal. Cleese strode past them silently with his eyes cast downward and continued on up and out of the Pit.

They'd have to take care of themselves now, he thought. Chikara was gone and Cleese had no intentions of taking on her students in her memory. He had more than his share of memories of her to contend with all on his own. These men may have known her longer, but she and Cleese had shared an intimacy they would never understand. It had been a connection much deeper than simple sex. This was like a twin finding their counterpart and then having them ripped away. He knew getting over this was going to take time, time and some solitary reflection. He decided he would mourn Chikara in his own time, in a proper place.

First, he had to think some shit through.

First, he had to get those ducks of his in a row and line up that exit strategy.

However, before any of that could happen, he had a little something he needed to take care of.

Extreme Prejudice

The Training Hall echoed with an ominous sense of finality as its heavy doors slammed shut behind Cleese. The sound echoed through the place like the news of a loved one's sudden suicide—quick, abrupt and undeniably pitiless. Inside the expanse of the large auditorium, the air was so hot that it suppressed the urge to breathe in those gathered there. The heat sweltered and twisted in the air like the body of a man long dead. Even though the Hall was proving itself to be a hellish sauna, a few fighters still stood idly around. They gathered near the free weight area, but their work-outs were halfhearted, at best. A couple of men lazily practiced grabbing and throwing combinations on the large mat but their movements looked as if it was a great discomfort to move about in the heat. For the most part, those who were in the great hall today just hung out and offered up silent prayers for a cooling breeze.

In such heat, it was difficult to do much else.

Cleese ignored all of it—the heat, the humidity, and the men—as he entered the Hall proper and walked briskly across the mats and on toward The Octagon. As he moved through the open area of the building, his eyes roamed the corners as if he were looking for something specific. His stride was direct and his gait was purposeful. A few of the fighters milling about the mats offered up whispers to one another. A few even crossed themselves as he passed, but none were confused as to the cause of this ill temper. The news of Chikara's death had affected each of them, but they all knew by now of the special connection between Cleese and Chikara and they paid its due respect.

As he made his way across the floor, they made sure to give him a wide and silent berth. It was as if, on some subconscious level, they could sense that whatever his purpose was for being here today, the aftermath of this foul mood would surely put a stain on the walls.

Odds were that it would do the same to a few pairs of underwear.

Down deep inside the pit, a newly recruited fighter and his trainer could be heard as they went through a set of basic drills. This early in the game, the reasoning was to get the new fighter used to being around The Dead without feeling the need to piss himself. Exposure bred familiarity and familiarity bred composure. At least that was how it was in theory. Some fighters never got used to it and they'd all paid the price. The UD they had on the lead was moving about and attacking the Cherry with a murderous intent. The thing's face was a contorted mess and its hands were a blur as they clawed at him. The fighter batted the advances away with a cautious and unsure hand.

Cleese, for a second, had another one of those uncomfortable flashes of déjà vu.

By now, he'd gotten closer to the pit and had moved up toward the bleachers.

In the distance, he was able to make out the suited form of Masterson standing at the foot of the stairs over by the far end of the stands. The big man was gesturing and talking to someone seated in front of him. From this angle, Cleese couldn't really see who it was. He could tell from Masterson's body language that whatever they were talking about wasn't going well. Masterson's demeanor and the forceful way he waved his arms and pointed emphatically betrayed the topic of discussion as being both important and personal. One thing for sure, he wasn't happy.

As Cleese got closer, he heard Masterson's voice hiss a name: "Monroe."

Sometimes... sometimes... life could just be too sweet.

Midsentence, Masterson caught sight of Cleese coming up the stairs and waved a dismissive hand to silence the discussion. As Cleese got closer, he could see from his posture and his expression that he was pretty tense. In fact, the word infuriated might have been a better term.

And rightly so...

The League had thrown out some wild pitches as of late. Chikara's death was a serious and unsuspected blow to Cleese and The Warriors.

Hell, the whole damn League was reeling from the shock of her loss.

But if one took some time and thought about it, a fighter death—even a popular one—wasn't *that* big of a surprise given how dangerous this game was. Sometimes they forgot the truth of what it was they were doing out there on the sand. The Dead had—once not so long ago—nearly eradicated the whole of Humanity. The fact that Mankind had been able to pull itself back from the brink was a minor miracle in and of itself. Time had a way of blunting the memory of how serious it had all been... and still had the potential to be. These were high stakes they dealt with on a daily basis. Death was always just a dumb mistake away, and what happened to the best of them could easily happen to the least of them.

The important thing was that, according to all reports, things seemed to be going well for The League... and what was good for The League was good for the fighters.

Masterson had seen tapes of Cleese's matches, and even he, a non-fan, had been impressed. Revenues were up. Internet buzz was like nothing anyone had ever seen. Corporate was as happy as newlyweds, already gearing up a line of merchandise with Cleese's face on it: shirts, hats, hell, even foam spikes—for the kids. Recent tragedies aside, business was good.

As he watched Cleese continue to approach, Masterson silently considered how God gave every man in this life one gift: some could sing, some could erect buildings, some could paint portraits, but every man had one thing that he was able to do better than anyone else. Masterson felt his gift was his ability to lead and to make the hard decisions that often meant whether men lived or died. For Cleese, his one gift was his ability to put the hurt on other living things. It was this gift that made him a perfect match for the world Weber had made for them. The man was born and bred to be in this sport, and it was that very reason which was, undoubtedly, why his life back in the real world had amounted to such a steaming shit pile.

On more than one occasion, Masterson had tried to imagine the kind of sewer that could have bred a man like Cleese. Poverty, abuse, neglect... they were all just ingredients in a lethal recipe. Spices in a naturally toxic stew.

But then again, Masterson really didn't really give that much of a fuck about the bastard or his childhood, if he were to be completely honest. No one was more aware than he of the fact that Cleese was simply this week's fêted warrior. He was fuckin' Pokemon and not a damn thing more. His time would come and go with a minimum of fanfare. Masterson knew from his tenure with The League that the UDs—given enough time and opportunity—claimed every fighter. No one was exempt. Not even the pretty ladies. Fighter's faces came and fighter's faces went— sometimes literally. Cleese had been a doomed man since he first stepped off of the Black Hawk.

He just didn't know it yet.

"Cleese!" Masterson called and waved. He smiled that oily smile of his and extended his hand toward the approaching fighter.

"Masterson," said Cleese in a monotone and nodded in lieu of shaking hands. His pace, however, never slowed.

"You remember Philip Monroe, don't you, Clee...?"

"Of course, he does," interrupted Monroe as he got to his feet and brushed at the seam of his pants. Casually, he stepped forward. "I got a message you wanted to talk to me, Buddy?"

Cleese had gotten close to the two men and, as he stepped to within arm's reach of them, he brushed past Masterson with the same ease that he'd exhibited time after time in the pit. As he did so, he took an additional step forward, raising his right hand up toward his chest as if scratching an itch; a classic misdirection. Without warning, he suddenly snapped his hand out in an open-handed back slap, its speed more like that of a viper than any human appendage. The hall reverberated with a sharp, clapping sound as he cracked Monroe soundly across the jaw.

Far off across the Training Hall, the other fighters all stopped what they were doing and turned and stared.

Monroe stumbled backward, almost skidding like a cartoon character on the back of his heels. His knees went soft and he fell, flat back onto the bleacher's seat. A dark red imprint resembling the back of Cleese's hand burned hotly across his cheek.

At first, Cleese was kind of amazed. The blow was meant only to get the fuck's attention. He hadn't even hit him that hard, but Monroe went down with surprising ease.

Whatta bitch!

Monroe scrambled across the bench, trying his damnedest to get himself as far away from Cleese as possible.

"How *dare* you!" he shouted through rapidly puffing lips. An incoherent stream of threats of suspensions and legal action followed as he nursed his rapidly swelling face. His ponytail had come undone, leaving oiled hair hanging loosely across his eyes.

Cleese wasn't sure, but it looked as if he was crying just a little.

Cleese crossed the distance between them with frightening speed. He deftly reached out, grabbed up a handful of Monroe's tie and shirt collar and dragged him toward the side of the pit. It was a move he'd performed a thousand times as a bouncer in bars. It surprised the drunk by throwing his balance off and it hinted at the raw power that was at his assaulter's disposal. It also got him up on his feet, out of the bar and into an alley where the real punishment could take place. It was—as they say—a "win-win."

Monroe began, this time as expected, to scream and screech like a little girl.

"You fucking *cunt!*" Cleese spit out, his voice dripping with hatred. "Did you really think I wouldn't figure out your fuckin' hare-brained shit, huh?!?" Cleese shook Monroe like a rag doll and pulled his face within inches of his own. "Who do you think you fuckin' are with this Blofeld bullshit?"

Monroe screamed out, his voice cracking like ice. "Wha...? Let me go! What are... What are you fucking *talking* about?"

"You know damn well what I'm talking about, Knucklefuck! You set it all up, you limp dick *motherfucker! Everything!* You fucking did it all!! And..." he hesitated for a heartbeat, then, "I *know* you had a hand in what happened to Chik..."

An unexpected knot as big as a fist clogged his throat and choked off his voice.

Masterson rushed up behind Cleese and wrapped his arms around him. He did his best to pull him backward, but to his complete surprise, Cleese's position never wavered. The man barely moved. In fact, he was so intent on getting his hands on Monroe and doing what he wanted to do with him that he didn't notice Masterson was even there, much less any of his fervent attempts at containment.

"'Good luck on *Fight Night* next week,'" Cleese said, his voice mimicking Monroe's arrogant demeanor. *"Fuck you!!"*

Monroe finally managed to wriggle his way free and stumbled over toward the railing on the side of the pit where Masterson had been standing.

"You keep away from me," shrieked Monroe. And then to Masterson, "Keep him the fuck away from me!"

Cleese moved again and his speed was something Masterson simply couldn't believe. Masterson was a big man—a life-long soldier—and Cleese brushed him off like an old coat. One second he was standing three feet in front of him, the next he'd moved past him and had his hands once again on Monroe.

To Monroe's credit, he finally screwed his testicles to their sticking point and threw a weak and undisciplined punch at Cleese. Cleese snatched the weaker man's fist out of the air as it flew by. He circled it in his grasp and twisted the wrist. With the bones of his arm torqued in such a manner, Monroe had little choice but to go where he was being pointed. Cleese tugged on his arm, pulled it upward then quickly downward, and Monroe dropped to his knees.

Cleese pushed his knee into the center of Monroe's chest and leaned him against the railing, backward over the Pit's edge. Then, he shook him violently.

"I ought to feed *you* to one of these fucking things!"

In the pit, the fight above had not gone unnoticed and the training UD had begun to get agitated by the raised voices and the palpable sense of aggression. The thing immediately went into a frenzy the moment it saw Monroe's hair dangling a foot or so above it, just out of its reach. Having had little success with the live fighter standing in front of it, the thing immediately made frantic leaps and grabs for Monroe. Its frustration level rose markedly as it felt the tips of its fingers brush through Monroe's dangling lock of hair. The trainer who held the reins pulled the UD backward and it came away with only a few strands of hair caught under its cyanotic fingernails.

Cleese wasn't entirely sure, but he could have sworn he smelled Monroe shit his tailored silk pants.

The fighter and his training partner quickly pulled the agitated UD away from the side of the pit nearest to where Monroe hung. Off in the distance, a raucous chorus of cheers, shouts and applause were heard coming from the other fighters in the Hall. It seemed that there were more than a few people who didn't like Monroe or his methods and watching him get bitch-slapped was riotous sport.

It sure as hell beat standing around and sweating like a pig.

Finally, Masterson was able to pull Cleese from on top of Monroe, but not without a good deal of exertion. Cleese let go reluctantly and brushed Masterson off.

"Cleese, what the hell do you think you're doing?" Masterson asked excitedly, pushing him back. "You can't strike a League official. Do you want to get released from your goddamn contract?"

Now secure that Masterson had Cleese under control, Monroe renewed his shouting and impotent threats as he rose to his feet.

"How dare you! How fucking *dare* you!!" Monroe shouted as he stood up and brushed at his shirt in an vain effort to wipe away the wrinkles. "Don't you get it, you stupid mother fucker? We *own* you, you stupid fuck!"

"What did you just say?" Cleese growled.

"I said, we own you. Lock, stock, and white trash barrel."

Monroe, feeling a bit of his old self now that Cleese was away from him, threw his hands up into the air.

"Let me break this down for you," Monroe pointed an accusing finger at the man who just seconds ago was trying to throttle him. "You fighters..." and he raised his voice loud enough for everyone in the hall to hear, "You are nothing more than commodities. Property. *We* call the shots here."

"Shut up, Monroe," Masterson warned.

"No... No, Masterson... he needs to hear this."

"Shut. Up. Monroe."

"You really don't get it, do you? We... Us... The League... We make the decisions here. *We* decide who gets signed. *We* decide who gets fighting slots. *We* decide who gets play. You've never been anything other than a circus act, you fuck."

"Shut. Up. Monroe. Walk away..."

Monroe stared at Masterson then shot a menacing glare at Cleese.

"You know what... Fuck you! *We* decide who lives, Cleese. *We* decide who lives and who fucking *dies!*"

Cleese grinned malevolently and tried to decide which body part he was going to shove up Monroe's ass.

"Walk. Away!" Masterson warned. "NOW!"

Cleese looked around and decided he couldn't just kill this asshole in front of God and all these witnesses. Better to step back, get some perspective, and decide what to do. He figured it'd be best to decide just how cold his dish of revenge should be before serving it. Slowly turning away, he took a step back the way he'd come.

Then, Monroe went and ruined it all by opening his mouth and letting the other inconceivable shoe drop. Monroe glared at Cleese and smiled.

"After all... if you hadn't noticed, you fucking chimp, shit has a way of happening around here."

Cleese stopped in his tracks. He slowly turned at the hip and stared menacingly at Monroe.

Surely he wouldn't be so stupid as to...

"Shut up, Monroe," interrupted Masterson angrily. "Shut the fuck up!"

Cleese glared in Masterson's direction and then back at Monroe.

"Just ask your girlfriend," Monroe said smugly and looked away.

Almost immediately, he regretted making the statement and glanced over at Masterson. From the look that passed over his face, it was plain to see he knew that he'd fucked up. Silently, he wished he could take that last bit back the instant after he'd said it, but Cleese had laid his meaty hands on him, struck him and made him look like a fool. If anyone needed to be taken down a rung or two, it was Cleese.

Far off, he heard the sound of Masterson sighing in frustration.

As he gazed sidelong at Cleese, his mind almost didn't register the fighter's movement.

Cleese spun at the waist and threw a reverse side kick which hit Monroe square in the center of his chest. The air was kicked out of the man's lungs and Cleese took no small amount of satisfaction out of the sound it made. The only thing better than hearing it was watching Monroe go sailing back into the railing, pitching over the edge and falling headfirst into the Pit. His shocked face disappeared over the edge milliseconds before his shoes did. He went over with the most sublime expression.

"Fuck you," said Cleese as regained his footing. His hands went up into the air in frustration. "Fuck you and fuck your little fuckin' game! Fuck your League! Fuck this..." and he waved a hand in the direction of the Hall.

He brushed past Masterson and, as he walked away, he shouted, "And fuck you too!"

Another shout of rousing consensus from the fighters across the Hall rose and fell in the room like a wave. Cleese sensed a few rounds of free beer in the offing.

Masterson reached out to Cleese, as if to try and stop him, but Cleese was beyond hearing any more of his or anyone else's bullshit. As he walked away, he looked back at him with a look of complete contempt.

"You fuckin' Assclowns," he spat as he continued on back across the Training Hall and toward the door. "You fuckin' deserve each other."

Cleese made his way toward the main door and his form disappeared into the blackness of The Hall's shadowy corners. The applause from the assembled fighters continued unabated until he'd kicked the door open and walked out. Once again, the heavy sound of the door closing echoed through the hall.

Masterson walked to the edge of the Pit and looked over at Monroe who'd by now managed to pull himself up into a panting, seated position down on the sand. His fall had been far, but the sand softened his landing considerably and the only thing injured was his ego.

The two training fighters were not amused as they made their way quietly out of the Pit. When Monroe fell over the railing, they'd had to yank their UD around *hard* to keep it clear of him as he hit the sand. From the look of things, they'd broken the damn thing's neck doing so.

"Ass-*hole!*" Monroe shouted as he stood and set to brushing the sand from his pants. He stood silently fuming for a moment and then glanced up to Masterson with the look of an errant child.

It was immediately obvious to the fighters still in the Pit that they'd been pulled into something of which neither of them wanted any part. Leaving the corpse with the broken neck lying in the sand, they both headed out the hatch.

Sometimes discretion really *was* the better part of valor.

Masterson peered over the top of the railing, his expression not a happy one. Once he was sure Monroe was for the most part unhurt, he stood fully erect and slowly crossed his arms across his chest.

"Nice job... You just *had* to say something, didn't you? Had to open your god-damn mouth, eh Monroe?"

Masterson looked around to see if anyone was within earshot. He had no doubt that the fighters out on the mats heard what Monroe had said. It's not like he didn't fucking shout that shit at the top of his lungs. As he looked out over the Hall, he saw most of the fighters looking away. If they'd heard anything, they were not showing it. Satisfied that things were more or less ok, he stared down at Monroe balefully.

"You might as well have just signed your name to a goddamn confession, you stupid fuck! There will be no controlling him now. Not now... not ever!"

"Oh, bullshit...!" Monroe said with disdain, still trying to pull himself together. "Oh, and thanks a lot for helping me out there. You know you could have done *something* to stop him! He could've gotten me killed!"

"No, can it, Phillip. You've habitually pushed this whole thing in a direction it never needed to go. Things were progressing as they should have: revenue was up, attrition was manageable and everything was fine. We really didn't need you lending a helping hand..." Masterson uncrossed his arms and grabbed the rail before him forcefully. "God knows, there is enough drama and trauma in these damned spectacles to keep people tuning in. You didn't have to fuck with things."

Masterson ran a hand across the back of his neck.

"Now... Cleese has gotten wise to your bullshit and he knows... he *knows*... you're the fucking man behind the curtain. Jesus... Weber is going to be furious over this." Masterson looked down and concentrated his gaze toward the tips of his highly polished shoes before whispering more to himself than anyone else, "We're going to need to be extra careful... now more than ever."

"What?" Monroe said emphatically from the pit.

Monroe paused and looked back in the direction Cleese had left.

"Perhaps there is more to our friend than we'd first believed."

Monroe stared up at Masterson and looked deep into the old soldier's eye as he went back to pulling himself together and rubbing his cherry-red cheek.

"Whatever... That fucking idiot's becoming a liability and a menace despite the money he's pulling in," he whined as he continued brushing sand from his pant's seat. "And don't tell me you haven't thought the same."

The two men each stared into space for a long time, thinking. After a moment, Monroe looked around at the pit in which he stood.

"Jesus... look at this place. It's disgusting!"

Then, he looked up and caught Masterson's eye.

"Do you think..." he asked and looked around for any unwanted ears, "Do you really think he'll be a problem now?"

Monroe suddenly looked more than a bit worried. The League had a lot invested in Cleese and they would remain happy just as long as things continued along the rosy path they'd all been traveling. If he'd somehow managed to push things a little too far and jeopardized all of that, it might cause an inconsolable rift to appear.

"I mean," Monroe continued, "Weber will be really fucking pissed if Cleese got clear. I mean, before the League was done with him and his contract. I mean, if he were to be killed, that'd be one thing, but..."

Masterson pondered the situation silently for a moment. It was good that

Monroe had gotten his head back in the game and was thinking clearly again. The man was an impetuous and manipulative jerk, but he was also pretty adept at climbing the corporate ladder and sensing the ebb and flow of the tides. Masterson wasn't much interested in the upward mobility of his career.

He just wanted to keep his job.

Thinking it through though, Masterson decided that yes... Cleese was indeed pretty hurt and angry—and with good reason—but when push finally came to shove, he was alone in this. Chikara was gone. The League owned Weaver pretty much lock, stock and barrel. He wasn't close with anyone else and had no one he could trust outside of this place.

"Ok," sighed Masterson, "so looking at it objectively, I don't think Cleese can do shit. He's pissed now, you've pretty much seen to that, but give him time. He'll calm down and remember who pays the bills and when he does, he'll either get back on the program or he won't."

Monroe thought it over and decided Masterson was right. He nodded his agreement and then moved to tie his hair back into its ponytail.

Masterson smiled and then added, "Besides, where else does he have to go?"

"You really think so?"

"I do. And besides... something's just been brought to my attention that, I think, should help settle the matter, one way or the other. Once and for all."

Monroe turned and limped painfully across the sand toward the Pit's entryway.

"After that," Masterson said from overhead, again looking over his shoulder toward the Hall's door, "he'll either be on the team or he won't be. Whichever... It's all the same to us, right? And you know as well as I do... It's not like there's a shortage of fighters out there. They may not be as talented as he is, but they're still more than willing to step out there onto that sand. It's like you said, whether they end up living or dying... we win either way."

Monroe nodded and continued hobbling toward the door.

Masterson turned and leaned against the railing, saying, "And if Cleese thinks he can do anything like bailing on his contract, well we have a battery of lawyers just waiting to sue him for more money than he's ever imagined."

Monroe had by now reached the hatch to the stairway. He stopped and waited for Masterson to finish his thought.

"If that doesn't work..."

"There's always the mercs..."

"Right. If he does as he's told, we'll utilize his talents until he's no longer any good to us. After that..."

"I'll just continue to stack the decks against him during his matches until he has a change of heart... or gets himself injured."

Reluctantly, Masterson agreed.

"But just so we're clear... and let's be agreed on this... The man is, as of now, utterly expendable."

Masterson nodded and looked away. For a moment, he thought he had an idea of how Judas Iscariot felt.

"One thing I doubt he ever read was the small print of his own contract," Masterson continued, "and you are quite right... We do own him—alive or dead—and we continue to own him until which time we decide that we're through. Not the other way around. Even if a fighter ends up dying in the pit, The League still has a legal right to whatever is left of his body. Dead... or *Undead*."

Monroe stood at the open Pit door and looked toward the gangway which led up to the grandstands. He'd always figured he could trust Masterson. Now, he was sure of it. He'd only had to take an ass-whipping to find it out for sure. He was convinced now the man would watch his back and, as a result of that, they would both come out of all of this being solid gold.

Masterson watched Monroe as he limped his way around the corner and up the ramp from where the gangway was. He watched him approach in the dim light of the hall and silently wondered how wise it was to be allied with a duplicitous man such as Monroe. He was proving himself to be a bit of a pain in the ass and Masterson was beginning to think it might be wise if he put as much distance as he could between himself and the man's impulsive schemes as possible.

Because, if he wasn't careful, Monroe was going to put both of their asses in a sling.

☠ ☠ ☠

I Shall Be Released

"Well, Bob, we are nearing the end of yet another exciting match for our Fan Favorite Fighter, Cleese. This is the last round—last call—for him and, to be honest, that's probably a good thing. He's looking a little worse for wear out there and that's never good. He'll need to find some energy from someplace though. I mean, he's not quite out of the woods yet."

"You're right, John, we still have this final round to go and, as any regular WGF Fight Night viewer can tell ya, one round can make all the difference in the world."

"Ok, Bob, according to the clock, we're just about ready for that buzzer and hopefully Cleese can bring this already exhilarating bout to an even more exciting conclusion!"

"So, let's go back onto the floor and see how this all turns out!"

Cleese groaned aloud and drew a deep breath in to help clear his mind.

His arms and legs hung at his sides, exhausted. They ached now more than they'd ever had in his life. His tendons had been stretched beyond their endurance; muscle fibers having sprung with the sound of banjo strings. He felt like some hammered shit out here and by his count he still had one more round to go. His back, bent and twisted from his toil down on the floor of The Pit, felt like it was made of shattered glass and bound together by razor wire. He stood stooped and panting as he hovered over the pile of dead bodies at his feet. The omnipresent stench of spent blood, urine and chyme on the sand left a sour tang that clung to the back of his throat like oily smoke.

His eyes drifted over the faces of the corpses at his feet. Some of the UDs bore the countenance of people who had died in great pain. Given their present surroundings, that was about what he expected. Oddly, others bore expressions of a deep peace, as if finally dying—and dying in a way that guaranteed them to be dead for good—gave them an escape from the torment of being what they were. These looks crawled deep into Cleese's psyche and touched a part of him that he was very uncomfortable with. He slowly raised his eyes toward the lights as a shiver tickled its way up his spine.

The crowd overhead continued to drone on into the night. They existed out there within the black folds of darkness, moaning like specters lost in a dwindling twilight. Their voices crescendoed and then crashed like the echo of violent waves breaking on a rocky shore. The sound had become a primal thing, something exultant and yet somehow darkly terrible. There was blood in the air now and that always drove the crowd into a malignant fervor. It was the emotional equivalent of throwing gasoline on a grease fire.

Cleese tried to not listen to them, tried to blot out what they were saying, but doing so was impossible. Their voices were a deluge of sound which rained down from above, a din falling on him from somewhere out there in the darkness; a murderous, blood-parched thing. It took everything he had in him not to scream back at them. To shout and to tell them that their bloodlust, so complete, so all encompassing, had burned inside of them for too long, that it had robbed them of whatever humanity they'd once had. Cleese knew though that it would do no good. He'd once thought he understood their hatred for the dead, but since Chikara's death, he knew he didn't understand shit. Like the Romans before them, these people only craved their spectacle. Deep down, he had come to realize that this was just another coliseum and he was just this day's Champion.

And The Dead... they were just more lions waiting to be fed.

Cleese stood fully erect and pulled the spike from the back of the last UD's head. Grey matter clung to the blade in sticky, wet clumps. He whipped his arm about and dislodged the material by centrifugal force. Then, with a snap, he retracted the blade and stepped out from beneath the pile of the last round's dead.

Once again, he almost didn't hear the buzzer go off; he'd grown so distracted by the chorus of complaints emanating from his weary body. He felt tired and drained mentally. His arms and torso were coated with a thin, slimy veneer of brains, sweat and blood. His skin felt completely drenched in the stuff. He couldn't imagine what he looked like.

Raising his head, he saw his image on the television monitors mounted on the Pit's high walls. What stared down on him looked more like a hellish demon—all red and black with a maniacal, blood-thirsty gleam in his eyes—than a man. He smiled for the cameras, hoping it might soften the image.

It didn't.

God... I'm ready to for this shit to be over—like now.

As he stumbled to the center of the ring, the echo of the buzzer vibrated through the stadium's metallic skeleton. He didn't so much hear it this time as he felt it reverberate down deep to his core. The vibration rattled him down to the soles of his feet. Wearily, he crouched into his loose fighting stance and took a quick look around. The Pit stretched out before him, blanketed in a cold, unforgiving stillness.

Remarkably, the spindles remained still.

A ripple of expectation shimmered through the crowd and, just for a moment, every person in the stadium held their breaths as one. The feeling of anticipation was palpable: heavy and electric.

Cleese walked inquisitively to the center of the ring and looked up toward the control booth. He raised his hand to shield his eyes from the strong, overhead lights, but saw nothing.

The quiet within the stadium soon became a deafening weight that pushed down on the interior of the giant space, pressing each member of the audience into their seats. It was a silence made all the more oppressive by the vastness of the structure in which it was contained.

A heartbeat passed.

Then, another.

Then, with an abrupt teeth-rattling boom, the spindles spun and locked themselves into place. The ear-splitting, metallic sound cleaved the air like a blade. It was a noise that lacerated molecules and carved a savage gash into the meat of the still atmosphere.

Cleese relaxed his muscles and fell back into a half-crouch instinctively. He swept his eyes around the diameter of the pit; scanning the immediate area, looking for any threat. His gaze flickered from one spindle to the other, his brain locked and loaded to catalog any impending threat or hazard.

They're empty!

All of the spindles spread out before him were empty.

No weapons, no UDs, no... nothing.

What the fuck?

Cleese rose up onto the balls of his feet and gingerly walked toward the nearest position to him: Position Five. Quickly and carefully, he checked the interior of the spindle for some hidden menace, but there was nothing.

He did the same with Position Four and got a similar result.

Then, out of the corner of his eye, he caught a hint of motion—from Three—and he whirled to face it. Across the sand, he could just make out a dark silhouette as it rippled deep within the blackness of the turnstile. The form stood back in the shadows, clutching at the back wall of the spindle. Its figure was squat, but thicker than most—at least its shadow was. Its manner was pure fear and volatile confusion.

"Uuuuuuuuuh...???" the thing moaned; sounding confused and almost scared. The voice sounded muffled inside the enclosed space of the spindle.

The crowd erupted in applause the instant they saw that there was a UD in play. When they saw the first hint of movement, their ovation rained down over Cleese in a thunderous waterfall that was overwhelming and suffocating. Collectively, they understood that if there was to be only one UD released, it must be a formidable opponent; perhaps one of the survivors from a previous match. Whatever it was, it meant that the match was on once again and the wave of their blood lust had yet to crest.

Cleese strode across the sand, his gait fatigued, but intent and still very, very lethal. He hadn't been sure exactly what was going on before, but now... Now, there was a target in his sights and that meant there was something toward which he could direct his fury. As he approached the spindle, he slapped the spike back out and into place and aimed the point towards center mass, directly at the thing's un-beating heart.

"What say we get this shit over with, huh...?" Cleese said aloud.

He stepped into the shadows of the spindle, firmly grabbed something inside with his left hand, and then threw a solid blow into the blackness with his right. His fist struck the thing within squarely in the back. The spike slid smoothly between its ribs like a baker's knife into icing. In a live man, the spike would have pierced his heart and death would have been instantaneous. For an undead one, spearing it was merely an efficient way of getting the damned thing's attention.

The dead man in the turnstile arched back with a deep, wet, coughing sound. Blood and phlegm splattered against the walls of the turnstile in thick, coagulated globs. Cleese felt the UD pull backward a little bit against the spike, but it was difficult for it to gain any leverage. There simply wasn't enough room in the tight confines of the spindle to move. It was a lot like wrestling in a phone booth in there. Still, he felt the tug of the thing pull on his arm and strain his shoulder.

"Ok, Bub," Cleese said as he firmly set his feet in the sand. "Time to dance."

Cleese forcibly dragged the figure out and into the light with a vicious tug. The crowd caught sight of the impaled zombie and erupted into more mindless cheers and applause. Cleese got cocky and let the thing go with his one free hand while keeping the other, the one with the spike, firmly lodged in place. Hell, why not? If they were going to give him only one UD this round, he'd make the most of it.

The crowd responded predictably—with more rhubarb.

He stood before both the cameras and the crowd with his arms outstretched. He raised his face, his expression one of raw power, toward the ceiling. An errant cool breeze blew across his cheek and, thankful for the respite, he breathed in deeply and then sighed. Cleese returned his grip to the back of the thing's neck and jerked him fully into the glare of the lights, exposing its face for all to see.

The UD was an older man who stood about five foot eight or so, middle aged, and black hair with liberal dashes of grey in it. His body was a solid frame...

...like... a boxer.

Suddenly, the truth hit Cleese in the chest like a two-by-four.

Oooooh, shit...

Monk stood dumbly in a blinding light and reached back with both hands for the spike which punctured his rib cage. His face had become a bloodless fish of a face as a result of his dying and rebirth. His mouth drooped to one side and his hair lay wetly across his skull. The smell coming off of him was like rancid milk. Deep, savage bites were torn from the meat of his neck from behind. The familiar yellow and red of infection ran hot and fierce around the bite marks.

Cleese felt his heart twist painfully in his chest as he stared at the wounds and thought of how they were in the just about the same place as Chikara's first bites had been. Monk had undoubtedly gone down just as she had. A UD must have come up on his blindside, been just out of his line of sight. In his mind's eye, he could see it all happening all too easily. After all, he'd already seen it in real time once before. This end result was different though.

They'd left Monk in one piece.

Cleese pulled away, withdrawing the spike from Monk's back and stumbling backward. As his mind reeled, he absentmindedly slapped the release and the blade slid back into its sheath.

Monk stood motionless, staring blankly into the air. His numb mind wasn't sure why the pain in his back had stopped, but he was glad for it. It was enough that there was an almost constant whirlwind cycloning in his head, more physical pain only made it harder for him to focus. Above him, impossibly bright lights blinded his vision and there was a roaring sound pounding in his ears. His feeble intellect reasoned that by standing without movement, he might be able to gather what was left of his wits and get a handle on what was happening around him.

It was all just so confusing. The motions, the sounds, the pain...

And the now constant twisting of hunger in his belly.

Cleese stood equally still, desperately trying to put all of the pieces before him together for himself. He stared at his friend, allowing his eyes to carefully catalog the extent of what had happened to him. It broke his heart to see Monk like this.

None of it... None of it made sense.

How in the hell? Monk was supposed to be out of here. He was supposed to be on a farm someplace, living the good life, tending goats and watching his grand-kids grow up.

Cleese looked over toward the cameras and knew that his horrified expression was being seen across a few billion television screens, but he just couldn't help it. Seeing Monk coming out of one of the turnstiles was literally the *last* thing he thought possible. Then again, with what had happened to Chikara... He figured he wasn't scoring too high on the whole "estimating probability" thing.

He narrowed his eyes and tried to focus beyond the glare that spread like mercury across the glass. What he saw was mostly shapes and shadows moving like ethereal ghosts, but after slightly moving his head from side to side, he was better able to make out more distinct shapes. He could see the cameramen hard at work, busily recording the event. They operated their cameras like pros and dutifully racked focus on his personal nightmare.

Then, off to the side of one of the cameras, his eye registered another bit of slight movement. He took another step to the side and focused his full attention on it, being careful to keep a watchful eye on Monk. He gazed deep into the blackness beyond the glass and made out two figures standing in the shadows. He raised his hand and shielded his eyes from the ever present glare. Squinting further, he was just able to get a better look. As his eyes strained to their limits, he saw Masterson standing with the same look of evaluation that he'd had when he first busted into Cleese's apartment back so long ago. And there, stand just behind him and grinning like a retard was Monroe.

Moooother... fuck. Tweedle Fuckin' Dumb and Tweedle Fuckin' Dumber...

A small voice deep in his head told Cleese that getting mad now was not any kind of answer. There was plenty of time for that.... later. Now, there were too many people, too many witnesses, and besides, he wouldn't be able to get to them anyway. The glass and the metal of The Pit saw to that.

No... There was time enough for what he had in mind in the future.

Now... He would wait... and he would plan... and the people responsible for this would come to know the full measure of his wrath. Necessity now dictated that he return his focus to the still-dangerous thing which stood in front of him.

He turned and redirected his attention back toward Monk.

He turned... and looked at his friend.

Monk stood on his feet a dozen or so feet away, rocking from side to side. He was still reaching toward the wound in his back confusedly as if he couldn't quite figure out what had happened. There had been great pain moments ago, and now, there was none. His face contorted as he tried to think it all through. And his jaw... His jaw chewed continually in that way The Dead all had, as if he were literally chewing over the problem that had been set before him. Despite all of his best efforts, his mind just couldn't make the necessary connections.

He looked drunk, swaying on his feet, his head lolling back and forth like a pendulum. It was almost as bad as it had been that night on the roof of Weaver's place except that his clothes were disheveled now. His face and hands were smeared with dirt and caked with dried blood. He'd undoubtedly fought hard when he first awoke from the sleep of death. Cleese could tell his friend had pitched quite a bitch from the deep abrasions on his wrists and throat. It was clear that the collars and restraints the handler's had used on him had not been kind.

Monk stared straight ahead blankly. His gaze remained unfocused and imbecilic. Then, he raised his head and sniffed at the air. Once he caught a whiff of Cleese's scent on the stagnant air, instinct abruptly took over and focused his thinking. The realization that food lay somewhere nearby struck his diminished intellect like an arrow hitting its target. He turned and it was almost as if Monk was seeing him for the first time; like he had no recollection of their painful reunion just moments before. He lunged forward, coming on fast, his hands a clawing dervish aimed at Cleese's exposed throat.

Cleese took a couple of shuffling steps backward in order to give himself some room and to buy himself a little more time. Monk, however, was undeterred and continued coming on at break-neck speed. Cleese slapped Monk's hands aside and grabbed at the front of Monk's bloody shirt, quickly twisting at the waist. His old friend went sailing over his hip and on toward the sandy ground. Monk struck the sand flat on his back, dead air knocked from his now-still lungs with an audible *woof.*

The crowd overhead reacted with an exultant cheer.

Cleese stumbled away in the hope that some more space might also spur a bit of insight. He knew he needed to figure this shit out and he needed to do so pretty damn quick.

As he circled Monk from a safer distance, he quickly ran through the things he knew for sure. This was no chance meeting—not with Masterson grinning like a gargoyle from behind the safety of the glass. Not with the way that cocksucker Monroe looked with that smug expression and self-satisfied grin on his prissy face. No, this was something that was all going according to their fucked up little plan.

Maybe it was payback for that stunt he'd pulled back at the Training Hall. Maybe this was their way of making things more exciting for the home audience. Maybe... it was just a display of power, of what they could do if they wanted to. It was hard to say... One thing was for certain, whatever had happened to Monk, it hadn't been accidental. Sure, he could've gotten tagged while burning up his time in the UFL. His attention could have strayed, been in the wrong place at the wrong time.

Shit, it had happened to Cartwright easily enough.

On the other hand, it was totally within Masterson's and Monroe's playbook to have arranged for Monk to be in that wrong place at that wrong time for no other reason than to pull off this little set-up here. There'd been far too many things like this happening of late to still be throwing the word "accident" around. Not when these little fuckups were happening to specific people in specific situations. It all seemed a little too perfect, a little too pat.

Who the fuck knows...

The important thing was... Monk didn't just wander in off the street. This had most definitely been arranged and someone—or maybe a pair of someones—needed to sack up and swallow a heapin' helpin' of responsibility. Even if that taking of responsibility meant being killed where they stood by Cleese's bare fucking hands.

Cleese stood fully upright and drew in a deep cleansing breath to focus his thinking. He needed some emotional distance away from all of this. He needed some time to sort it all out. He needed to be able to mourn his friend, to come to terms with his dying first. He could come to terms with his rebirth after that.

But... since all of that was evidently impossible, he'd just have to deal with it and sort out his grief and sense of vengeance later.

He watched Monk slowly, awkwardly, climb back to his feet. He stared sadly as his friend teetered and regained his balance like a toddler. What had once been fluidic motion was now replaced by spasmodic convulsions masquerading as motor skills. He felt a deep sense of melancholy wash over him. No one should have to end up this way, especially not Monk. No one should ever be denied their eternal rest. Cleese suddenly felt like an asshole for his part in all of this: the matches, the money, the notoriety, The League.

He closed his eyes and sighed forlornly.

"It's time... Time for us to go home, Pal."

As he opened his eyes, he saw that Monk had gotten back to his feet and was staring at him. Now that he'd decided his course of action and that both Masterson and Monroe were pieces of business that he would deal with later—especially Monroe—his mind was clear to deal with what now stood before him.

Right now, he had bigger problems.

Right now... he had Monk.

His friend had risen to his full stature and begun to lope across the pit toward Cleese. Unlike other UDs who came on like pissed-off drunks, Monk crouched down low, in that all-too familiar boxer's stance. It was clumsy and old school, but it had obviously been hard-wired into the machine.

Cleese had seen that stance before—long ago—in Training.

So, they do remember parts of their lives after all.

If Cleese remembered his friend's modus operandi correctly, Monk would go for his legs first in a bastardized Greco-Roman wrestling move. He would more than likely swoop in and try to pick him up and off his feet and then attempt to slam him onto his back. It was something that was designed to kick the air clean out of your opponent and—if it was successful—make any further breathing painful and laborious. It'd always been one of Monk's go-to opening moves.

As if on cue, Monk ducked in low and made a lunging grab for Cleese's thighs.

Having already expected the gambit, Cleese leapt back and, as Monk came in, he threw a downward slicing haymaker. The blow shattered Monk's jaw and made his open-mouthed gape even more pronounced. Monk's body corkscrewed from the strength of the impact and his body spun to the ground.

The crowd erupted into furious applause. While they may not have fully realized the importance of what was happening down on the sand, the bastards could sense that the fight was back on.

Cleese danced backward in a move he'd copped from Muhammad Ali. As he backpedaled, he looked at Monk's face and was shocked at how much different it was. Sure, it was basically the same face he'd come to know and love, but... it was also noticeably altered. Its fundamental structure hadn't changed, but now every piece of musculature just kind of sagged. It was almost as if someone had pulled downward at Monk's chin and the rest of his face had fallen in line and stuck there.

Cleese's gaze fell, at last, on Monk's eyes and his resolve shifted just a little, just enough. Despite it all—the blood, the death, the danger—staring out at him from behind those clouded eyes was his friend.

Not a UD. Not a zombie.

Just Monk, plain ol' Monk.

And, from the look in his eyes, somewhere deep beneath the anger and the violence, his friend was terrified, hopelessly confused and blindingly hungry. It was as if he'd gone to sleep and had what surely must have been the greatest dream imaginable and then, without provocation or preview, he'd been dragged back into a world he no longer understood.

Similar, in dimly remembered ways, but still changed; still *different*.

Now, there was only the pain... and the disorientation... and the hunger that never seemed to fully go away.

By now, Monk had scrambled sloppily back to his feet and renewed his attack. He came in with his hands up, elbows drawn to his sides; old habits refusing to die. Despite all of the interference his brain was getting in the way of varied signals, Monk still managed to fall back onto instinct and his manner became a little more assured.

He came in fast and hit Cleese at the waist. Monk lifted him off his feet and, not fully being able to compensate for the weight, they both fell to the sand. While Monk had the seemingly superior position, Cleese retained the Closed Mount position and, being the stronger of the two of them, was still able to more or less control his opponent. Cleese could feel his friend's hands crawling and scratching over his chest. With all of his upper body's strength, Cleese lifted Monk up and away from his body. Monk's mouth moved back and forth as it nervously chewed the air. Saliva dripped dark brown and thick from Monk's chin and pooled on Cleese's exposed stomach.

The crowd ooohed and aaahhed above their heads.

"Monk, no!" Cleese shouted, shoving his hands up and away.

Immediately, Monk stopped struggling and, for a moment, simply stared at Cleese. His expression was a whirlwind of emotions scrawled across a slack and deadened slate. He was confused, but still hungry; his rudimentary brain conflicted over which was the more pressing need. The important thing, to Cleese's mind, was that he'd stopped trying to take a bite out of him.

Cleese quickly cleared his head and decided right then and there that if he wanted to get through this shit alive, he had better start acting like a fighter or he else he'd end up just like Monk. And as a great man once said, "Fuck that!"

From his position on the ground, Cleese let go of his hold and threw four fast punches. Two rights landed at a point just to the left of Monk's right temple, effectively stunning him. The next left hit Monk just under the nose, shattering the cartilage there and opening a spigot of thick, black blood. The last punch came in hot on the heels of the last one. It hit Monk right under the chin, shutting his jaw with a click. The accumulated force of all four punches landing within a span of a second or two sent Monk up and off of Cleese. As Monk collapsed to the side, an arc of blood flew back and painted a thick stripe of red onto the sand.

Cleese jumped to his feet and, for good measure, threw his back into a front "field goal"-type kick which sent Monk's head snapping upward. His body went slack and he collapsed onto the sand.

Overhead, the crowd once again did their thing.

Cleese watched as Monk slowly crawled away and then painfully pulled himself up onto all fours. His friend moved with what looked to be excruciating pain. His face twisted up into an agonized grimace with his every motion.

The whole damn thing broke Cleese's already broken heart.

This is what they have done to my friend.

Standing there staring sadly at the milieu round him, an idea suddenly occurred to him. Maybe it was possible to tap into the man Monk once was. After all, he'd obviously retained his fighting style from before. He'd reacted to the sound of

Cleese's voice just a second ago. Maybe there was a way to reignite the man's now dead brain by memory recall.

Fuck... at this point, it was worth a shot.

"Monk!" Cleese shouted. "MONK!"

The old man slowly crawled up and sat back on his haunches. His hands fluttered lazily over his shattered nose, vainly trying to stop the flow of blood. He stared up into the glaring lights from his kneeling position on the sand, his mouth falling open and slack like a carp's.

"Monk!" Cleese repeated.

Monk stared blankly into space.

Cleese tried again, "MONK!"

Monk slowly turned his head and looked at Cleese. His stare remained empty and soulless, but a small spark of recognition could be seen smoldering deep within.

"MONK!"

It was obvious from his reaction that Monk was at least slightly able to recognize his name when he heard it called to him. Surely, if that spark was there, there must be a way to fan it into a roaring fire.

"Monk!" he shouted. *"MONK!!"*

The dead man looked away sadly and stared into space for the longest time. His eyes roamed the pit as if his mind had just tuned into a radio station no one but he could hear. He turned his head and his eyes fell back on Cleese with a heartrending finality. Monk's clouded gaze seemed to bore through to Cleese's very soul. It left him feeling a terrible coldness inside. Then, as if a sun slowly dawned across his slackened features, Monk painfully blinked and then he drew a stuttering breath.

"Cleeeeeeesssss..."

Fuck me...

Cleese stepped back and dropped his hands to his sides. Staring up into the lights, he blinked away more of his tears. He narrowed his eyes against their harsh brilliance and squeezed away his pain. Around him, the stadium's air had gone— whether in reality or merely in perception—utterly silent. Cleese looked back and felt his heart twist once more as he gazed into his friend's sad, doomed eyes.

"Monk? You with me, Buddy?"

Monk sagged in his own skin as if, deep down, he was ashamed of what he was, of what he had become. He turned his face away and sheepishly fumbled at his clothing. With noncompliant hands, he tried his best to straighten away the wrinkles and stains from his shirt's fabric.

"Cleeeeeessss..." he groaned sadly.

"Monk..." Cleese sighed, letting the situation sink all the way in. "No. Not you..."

Bit by bit, Monk's gaze slowly rose and finally settled once again on Cleese's now tear-stained face. The dead man stared for a long time as if he was off, lost in thought. His expression looked almost like he was listening to a voice from far away. His internal radio quietly whispered its message from across the veil of Death. For a second, he made no further movements. He simply stared at Cleese, moving his mouth in that constant chewing motion.

And then...

"Cleee... sssssss," Monk moaned. "Kiiii. Meh..."

"Fuck..." and tears came anew. "Monk..."

"Kiiii... Meh... Cleeesss!!"

Monk crawled arthritically across the sand, painfully prostrating himself before Cleese like an over-whipped dog. He continued to keep his head down, but reached up and grasped at Cleese's hand. At first, Cleese was reluctant to let him take it, but he figured that he'd be able to yank it back if Monk fell back on instinct and tried to bite. At least that was his hope.

"I can't, Monk." Cleese hissed, and the dam that held back his reservoir of tears finally broke completely free. "Not you, man... Not you."

Monk slowly raised his gaze and looked Cleese dead in the eye. For a moment, Cleese was dumbfounded by how ravaged his friend's face was. His gaze was rheumatic and the enamel of his teeth looked stained and pitted. It broke his heart to see Monk like this; beaten, dragged back to life and now abandoned to be ingested by the Pit.

Hadn't he worked hard enough or long enough for them here?

Couldn't he, of all people, be spared this indignity?

Monk slowly reached up, his fingers fumbling at the gauntlet on Cleese's arm. He stared and never broke his gaze from Cleese's, but his hands moved with a clandestine secondary agenda. His fingers ran over the metal like a bland man reading Braille.

At first, Cleese thought he'd been wrong and his friend's need to feed was going to win the battle for his soul. For a second, he was sure Monk was going to try to take a bite out of him, but finally, he felt his friend's fingers touch the release mechanism and pause.

Monk stared intently at Cleese and repeated, "Kiiii... Meh... Cleeessssss!!"

Then, Monk pressed down on the metal latch.

The metal spike sang out of its sheath.

Monk slowly looked up at him with dead, pleading eyes and released his grip on the gauntlet. They were the same eyes Monk always had, only now, the pupils were milky and clouded over.

"Cleee... ssssss. Kiiii... Meh... "

Monk reverently bowed his head and offered up the nape of his neck. Cleese looked up and away, into the light, and lovingly slid his fingers into Monk's hair.

Now, he too asked of the Light that same question, the one that The Dead seem to always be asking, but never had answered.

Why?

The moment hung in the air like the body of a suicide; soulless and as heavy as the sin itself. The Light... as always, kept its thoughts to itself.

Cleese slowly raised his right hand as if it weighed a thousand pounds. He gently placed the tip of the spike against the small indentation at the base of his friend's occipital bone. Oddly, Cleese flashed on the mental image of an old woman wearing a boxy coat standing in an elevator long, long ago. The memory of the taste of bubble gum flitted across his tongue. The image of two young boys—one wearing an eye patch and another with a turtleneck raised impossibly high—flashed across his mind's eye. A small, well of dark blood pooled where the tip of the spike cut into Monk's greasy skin.

"Ye.. ssssss," Monk whispered. "T'aaang... yooooo..."

Cleese stood silent for a moment and looked around the pit. His mind reeled back over all that he'd seen and done since stepping off that fucking helicopter so many, many months ago. He thought of how his life had changed—both for the better and for the worse. From where he stood now, it had once looked a hell of a lot better.

The league had fucked him and fucked him hard, that much was sure. They'd treated him like shit since the beginning and, despite the money and the supposed affluence, that had never changed. He saw that all too clearly. The sickening part was that they'd expected him to just bend over and take it all... and he had. God help him, he had. Willingly. He'd always thought that his soul could never be bought, but he now knew he'd been wrong.

He knew it could...

He could even tell you the exact amount on his fuckin' price tag.

And to think... They'd fuckin' set him up—*twice*—and they'd played him for a chump more times than that. And those fuckers hadn't shown one ounce of remorse over it. Not over Chikara. And now, not over Monk. Who knows what kind of shit they'd done to Monk over the years or what strings they'd pulled in order to get him here in this place tonight.

But in the end, here they all were. Together.

Monk, treated like dirt for years and then retired before he was ready, he'd been thrown away unceremoniously with little to no fanfare much less respect. He'd been discarded without so much as a thought or kind word. But even that was not enough for these motherfuckers. No, they'd knowingly sent him off to be killed in some rat-fuck farm league where, as everyone knew, safety was never a high priority.

And what did he get as thanks for years of loyal service?

His reanimated corpse was sent back into the pit to fight some more.

And then there was Chikara... Yeah, that particular wound was still far too tender to poke at. Her memory was one that would haunt him, he knew, for the rest of his life.

Well, fuck this...

One look into Monk's eyes told him everything he needed to know.

He was outta here. Gone like the fuckin' wind.

The League could, if they were very quick, kiss his lily-white ass.

They'd taken far too much from him to sit still on this one. There was just way too much pain and far too much loss for him to just kick back and forget everything that had happened.

Both to him and to the ones he loved.

And besides, now he had a bankroll—and a sizeable one, at that. He'd been very cautious and had surreptitiously stashed away as much of the money as he could get his grubby little hands on. He'd been careful to continually move it around, never letting his wealth rest in any one place for too long. It had all been stashed in enough different places and in enough different countries that no one—not even those knuckle-fucks Masterson or Monroe—could find it.

And speaking of Masterson and Monroe...

There were two scabs Cleese didn't mind poking at now that this was all said and done. Those two fucktards needed to know a bit of the pain he now felt. They needed to feel a bit of the same loss. Cleese was sure that he'd only need to think on it a bit and some version of a fair and sensible adjudication would occur to him. Soon, it would be payback time for them... and payback was a righteous and vengeful bitch.

But first...

Cleese returned his gaze to the back of his friend's head and closed his eyes.

"You know what, Monk?" he said in a hushed tone.

He slowly opened his eyes and took a long, slow look around the pit for what he was sure was to be the last time. He saw the bodies piled about him, the blood spattered sand, and the cameras behind the glass. He smelled the copper-tainted scent of spilled blood and ichor. And as the sound of rhubarb rained down on him from overhead, he smiled.

"Let's go home, Pal," he said with a sigh. "Let's you and I go home."

Cleese closed his eyes and ran his hand through his friend's salt-and-pepper hair. He gripped it and gently pushed his head just a little further forward. For a moment, the world seemed to go silent, and in the soundless void, the memory of his dead friend's voice echoed:

E-I-E-I-O.

"Abso-fuckin'-lutely..."

And Cleese drove the spike home.

· · ·

Hegira

Weaver stood alone outside of the stadium, alternately breathing in the cool night air and sucking hot smoke from a Macanudo. Both helped, in some small way, to suppress his sense of grief and indignation. The air helped clear his head. The cigar was symbolically being offered up to the memory of his friend; in memory of Monk. *How many of these damn, cancerous things did the two of them smoke together?* he thought. He ran his tongue across his lips, tasting the fine tobacco, coughed softly, and came to the decision that it had been too many.

He glanced around the loading docks, watching the flurry of activity as the groups of thick-necked Teamsters worked at breaking down the pit and all that came along with it. Large, muscular men heaved beams of metal as if they were balsa wood while others—the ones with clipboards and small, bookish demeanors—ran after them like kittens craving affection. They scurried around busily jotting down identification numbers on invoices like accountants with an obsessive-compulsive disorder.

Weaver pulled another mouthful of smoke from the cigar and rolled the heavy tobacco taste over his tongue. His exhalation was like plumes of cotton set adrift on the night's still air.

They've killed my friend.

Tears welled up in his eyes and he forced himself to choke down the lump that grew like a goiter in his throat. Monk had been his buddy longer than he could even remember, longer than he wanted to remember anyway. Since his Dora had died, he'd been the only real friend Weaver had. The person who'd cared about him and vice versa.

And now...

Now, he was dead... and, thanks to Cleese, dead again. Weaver had felt a little bit of himself die tonight when he saw that spindle turn to reveal what had once been his friend. Over the years, Weaver had come to love this sport, but at that moment, that love withered within him and died.

Still, though...

He was thankful that Cleese had been there to do the right thing. Weaver didn't lay blame for any of this at Cleese's feet. He'd sent Monk back into the Land of The Dead with some small sense of honor. He'd also denied those bastards in the expensive box seats their Big Finish. He'd taken from them the one thing they'd more than anything, the thing that would sell more of their precious tickets, get them their fucking ratings. Instead, Cleese had provided something that meant more—more to Weaver at least.

Weaver drew in another mouthful of silky smoke.

The sound of a side door suddenly opening startled him and the big man looked around the front of the truck against which he was leaning. Deep in the shadows, a figure carrying something big and heavy over his shoulder moved like a wraith in the darkness. Whoever it was, he was a large guy and he moved with dexterity of a thief on the prowl. From the way he continued to scan the area with his eyes, it was obvious he didn't want to be seen. For a second, Weaver caught his silhouette against the reflected light from the trucks and suddenly recognized the form as one he'd seen before.

"Cleese?" Weaver questioned of the inky blackness.

For a second, nothing; then, a barely audible voice hissed at him from the shadows. "Weaver?"

Weaver cast a suspicious glance around to see whether or not they could be noticed by any of the Teamsters or pencil-pushers and then walked quietly—almost nonchalantly—over to where Cleese stood lurking in the darkness.

"You...uh... going somewhere?" Weaver asked the inky darkness.

"Ay-yup," came his answer from the gloom.

"Care to share?"

"Not really. I don't want anyone asking you if you know where I'd gone. If you don't know, then you can't tell anybody."

"Fair enough," he said and drew another puff from the Macanudo. The expelled smoke drifted off and dissipated in the cool air. "Can I ask why?"

Cleese set the heavy duffel bag he carried over his shoulder down and stepped deeper into the blackness. If he was going to take a minute to say goodbye to Weaver, he was damn sure going to keep himself hidden from inquisitive eyes.

"Do you really need to?"

"No. I guess not."

"You know as well as I do the kind of shit that's been going down."

Weaver nodded and drew another lungful of smoke.

"You saw what they did to Monk."

Cleese looked down at his hands as if there was a stain there that no amount of washing could remove. Lady Macbeth had nothing on him.

"I did, indeed."

"And you approve?"

Weaver glared at Cleese for a moment before realizing that the question came more out of grief than anger.

"With all due respect, Son... Fuck you."

"You're right. I'm sorry... That was out of line."

"I approve not one fucking bit," Weaver bumped his cigar's ash against the bumper of the truck. The smoldering, grey cylinder fell to the ground and shattered into a fine dust. "He was my friend too, remember?"

"Then, you shouldn't have to ask why I'm leaving this fuckin' place," the words caught like a fishhook in Cleese's throat.

"Look, Son. I hate these fuckers as much as you do for what they did to Monk. They used him and they spit him out," he said. His voice fragmented with emotion. "And I don't think for a second that they wouldn't do the same to you. Or to me, for that matter."

Cleese looked his friend over, knowing down deep in his soul that he was right. Nothing he was being told was anything he hadn't already considered. It was just disheartening to hear his thoughts coming from someone else's mouth. Since this was undoubtedly the last time he'd see Weaver, he let the man talk. As he listened, he made sure to keep his eyes reflexively scanning the area for anyone who might see them talking and report them.

"That all said though," Weaver continued, "no one knew the risks better than Monk. He'd been at this a long fuckin' time. As I know you are well aware. Monk knew the kind of people running this place. He knew the cut of their jib, what was important to them. It's all a part of what we signed on for."

"Maybe it's what *you* signed on for."

"Don't fool yourself, kid. The signs were there all along. Don't go and get indignant now just because you chose to ignore them."

Cleese stared at his friend, but remained silent. He was right, of course. He hadn't exactly been on vacation when Lenik and Cartwright died. They'd been carted off like spent resources and forgotten. Michaels had received even less. While there was a part of him that knew he was expendable, his ego wouldn't allow him to *truly* believe it. It had taken the deaths of two of the most important people in his life to drive the point home.

"And that's why, in the end, he gave himself up. It was his way of cheating the bastards out of their precious ratings points. It was his way of saying one last 'Fuck You' sent special delivery from one James Thelonius Montgomery."

"Well, fuck it. I'm not playin' no more." Cleese ran a hand through his hair and looked away. "I'm out."

Weaver shot a quick glance at Cleese's bag out of the corner of his eye. The handle of a Japanese katana stuck out of it like a bamboo shoot.

"I see you have Chikara's sword," Weaver said sadly.

Cleese looked down at the gold and sharkskin tsuka sticking out of his duffel.

"I do. I wasn't about to let those fuckers get their filthy hands on it," responded Cleese. His gaze took on a lonely, far-off aspect. "It was special to her."

"As were you."

Cleese looked up at his friend for a long time, but said nothing. The expression on his face just about broke Weaver's heart.

"I know," Cleese whispered.

"Where will you go?" asked Weaver finally.

Cleese stared at him blankly. He cocked an eyebrow and softly said, "Somewhere... Somewhere over the rainbow, I guess."

"Ok...ok." Weaver said chuckling, "Don't need to tell me. I understand, but I'll have to say something about all of this, you know. You may have your exit strategy all mapped out, but I still have a job to do. However, before I go running off, I plan to finish this fine cigar here and enjoy the night air. If you really plan on heading out of here, as much as I'll hate to see you go, you should be gone before I'm done."

"You plan on staying on after all of this?"

"Let's be honest, kid..." Weaver drew another puff off his cigar. "What else is an old man like me going to do?"

"What if they have the same plan for you as they did for Monk?"

"Shit... Dying's easy... it's living that's hard."

Cleese smiled and scratched at the back of his neck.

"I thought it was comedy that was hard."

"Son... Life is comedy. I thought you knew that."

Cleese stared into the eyes of his friend for some time. While he didn't condone him sticking around, he sort of understood it. Weaver wasn't exactly a young man and The League was all he'd known since losing his wife. And despite even the noblest of intentions, it was as they say, "Better the Devil you know than the Devil you don't." He extended his hand and clasped his friend's. Cleese broadly smiled at the big man and held tight.

"You're a good man, my friend. I'll miss Friday Follies."

"As will I, Son. As will I."

Cleese turned and slid his hand into the duffle bag which lay like a dog at his feet.

Weaver looked at him and cocked a furry eyebrow over the rim of his big glasses.

From within the folds of the duffel bag, Cleese brought out the gauntlet Weaver constructed for him wrapped in a soft cloth.

The spike.

Cleese handed the bundle to Weaver with a sort of reverence.

"This little contraption of yours saved my ass more times than I could ever count, Man. I want you to have it back."

For the countless time that night, a lump quivered deep within Weaver's throat. It was with this act of returning the gauntlet that he knew it all to be real; an end of an era, a chapter closed, another road mark passed on the way toward the end of his life.

He grinned broadly at Cleese, heartily shook his hand again, and slid the gauntlet into the folds of his jacket. Its weight was heavy and full of bitter-sweet memories as he held it, much the same way he did his grief, tightly against his chest.

"Any loose ends?" Weaver asked.

"A few... Nothing for you to worry about though," Cleese said with a chilling finality, "Now, turn around and go back to suckin' on that stogie. I want to keep you out of the shit storm I know will be coming. You've been a good friend to me, Weaver. I'd like to keep it that way."

The two men looked at one another for a moment and then Cleese set to closing the duffel bag. When he was done, Weaver was waiting with a second Macanudo in his hand. With a smile, he handed it to Cleese.

"For the road..."

Cleese smile and raised the cigar as if in toast.

"To Monk."

"*Requiescat in pace,*" Weaver said and turned his back. He drew in another mouthful of acrid smoke and reminded himself to always remember this moment. He blew the soft plumes into the air with a sigh and silently watched the smoke drift off and into the blackness of the night.

"By the way," Weaver said to the silence, "Monk was damn proud of you, Son. He told me so many times."

The silence didn't respond, but instead spread itself across the loading dock; cold and lonely and all too final.

"Cleese?"

Weaver turned around again, but Cleese was gone.

💀 💀 💀

Requital

Philip Monroe walked into the parking garage and the sound of the elevator doors hissing shut behind him went unnoticed. The low ceilings and close walls of the place gave it a tight claustrophobic feel, like a large concrete mortuary vault. Pillars of rough grey stone were set in organized rows, their upright beams solidly supporting the floors above. The flat of the cement flooring laid cold and gaudily painted with lines and arrows; its slick surface adding to the echo-inducing vastness.

He made his way across the large expanse of pavement with a noticeable sense of determination, the silk of his Dolce & Gabbana suit swishing softly within the thrumming silence of the concrete structure. As he walked down the center aisle, he switched his briefcase from one hand to the other. As he did so, he caught a glimpse of his reflection in a nearby BMW's tinted window. He was pleased with what saw. Despite the shitty day he'd just experienced, he was still managing to look pretty good.

And why shouldn't he?

It was his business to look good. His image was an integral part of what he considered to be his unique skill set; a distinctive collection of talents which helped him time and time again to sway a client over to his way of thinking. He was a man who made it his business to use everything at his disposal to convince other people to see things his way. If he couldn't convince someone by logic and reason, a flash of some gold cufflinks or the glimmer of the pearly whites could usually save the day.

As he made his way through the lot, weaving his way between cars and over curb-stops, he felt a sudden, slightly nauseating wave of fatigue cascade over his body. All he could think about was how much he wanted to get home, and the faster he got there, the better. All day, he'd been dealing with the fall-out from Cleese's rather unsatisfying end to his last match and then his abrupt disappearance afterward. The whole thing left him feeling exhausted and a little sick to his stomach.

Cleese.

That son of a bitch.

Monroe had been hesitant to sign him to The League in the beginning, but he went ahead and did it anyway. Fighters were always a troublesome lot and Cleese had proven no different. They were base, unruly and always dumber than a bag of hammers. Still... he'd sure as hell made them a fuckload of money. The still-accumulating revenue was the only silver lining in an otherwise shit-laden cloud.

For quite some time now, Monroe had thought of Cleese as a revenue stream to be plundered, a work horse. Nothing more than chattel. As everyone knows, before you can put a horse to work, you have to break his spirit. Cleese's spirit had been more resilient than he'd thought it would be. The incident in the Training Hall was nothing more than a sign that he wasn't getting the "who's really in charge here" message.

And there was no way—no *fucking* way—Monroe was going to let that incident slide. The thought of that day and the way things went down still filled him with rage. How dare that crass bastard put his meaty hands on him! How dare he expose him to that kind of danger... in that place. Monroe still bristled when he thought of how close Cleese had put him to one of those... those *things*.

Ok, sure... Cleese had been pissed as hell over how things had turned out. The magazine of blanks ploy had been risky, but well worth it. Monroe suspected that an audience seeing a fighter empty a clip and do no damage would bring in big ratings. And he was right. The numbers on the broadcast had been astronomical. In fact, the surge carried over to the next week's show as well. Who cared if shit like that put one of those reprobate fighters in danger?

After all, it was what those idiots were being paid for.

Then there was the Chikara incident. Yeah, that didn't exactly go as planned, now did it? He'd thought that adding a few more of those things to the mix would make the round more exciting and he was right again. How was he to know she'd get herself distracted and be taken down? But it was a risk all of the fighters took when they signed on their contract's bottom line.

No one was ever guaranteed a Get Out Of Jail Free Card...

No matter how popular they were.

Of course, how Cleese managed to deduce that Monroe had anything to do with any of it was still a question that was up for discussion. It could have been the equipment manager or a production assistant who'd said something to someone who said something to someone else, but there was no way of being sure.

Who knew? People talked.

But then again, who really gave a shit? There was no tangible proof.

And that lack of proof was Monroe's ace up his sleeve.

Plausible deniability, baby.

If it was good enough for Richard Nixon, it was good enough for him.

And, looking back, that was where he probably should have left well enough alone.

But then, Masterson told him how Monk had gotten tagged while pulling some new recruit's meat out of the grease. Monroe took the news as what it was: pure providence. They'd brought Monk back as what he was—a resource. The decision for him to fight was a given. What else were they going to have him do now that he was dead, their taxes?

No, he was a fighter when he was alive and he would be a fighter now that he was one of the reanimated dead. Who he'd be fighting was never really in question. It had pretty much decided itself. Cleese was getting uppity and he needed to be reminded of who held the reigns. He would either have to fall into line—get with the League's program—or he could just as well fuck right off. All of it—the blanks, Chikara's regrettable death and finally the addition of Monk as an active UD— should have been enough for him to see exactly which side his bread was buttered on. That was just the way things sometimes worked.

It wasn't about what was good for the fighter.

In the end, it was only about what was good for the League.

Monroe smiled to himself, recalling the open-mouthed look of astonishment that'd dawned on Cleese's face when he got his first glimpse of Monk.

God, it had been sooo sweet.

"Feed me to those things, huh?" he sniffed under his breath as he turned and made his way to the aisle where his parking spot was. "Yeah, well... how'd that work out for ya?"

He was now within fifty feet of his car, a classic steely black Jaguar XJ220 Pininfarina. He'd paid a pretty penny for the car and it had been worth every cent. During the mid-nineties, the Sultan of Brunei and his brother, Prince Jefri, secretly bought hundreds of supercars and had them customized by some of the best in the business. There were only a few in existence, but sometimes having enough money and the right connections made even the impossible possible. Weber himself introduced Monroe to the Southeast Asian seller and had even helped to have the car shipped. It was a beautiful machine and Monroe doted over it like he would a beloved child.

As he approached the automobile, his mind had already begun to move on to the rest of his evening. He was scheduled to have dinner with Claire and then the two of them would rush off for a "meet and greet" that Weber Industries scheduled in order to celebrate the recent jump in *Fight Night* ratings. Word of Cleese's disappearance had not yet filtered down to any of the affiliates, but Monroe was already putting his spin on that particular ball, for when it did. The official company line was going to be that the man was certifiable—a thug—and, despite the WGF's stringent filtering processes, he'd gotten through.

Yeah, sorry about that...

And even though Cleese had proven himself to be a good earner, his induction into the League had been a mistake, but one that was being dealt with accordingly. The League had too much invested to risk a dime of it on someone with as much instability as Cleese exhibited. The cold facts were that he'd been behaving erratically lately, even going so far as to attack another fighter in the gym as well as a League official. If any of the affiliates doubted it, Monroe still had bruising he could show them to verify the point.

Monroe arrived at the Jag and looked the car over with loving approval. He'd worked long and hard to procure the trappings of wealth and all his plotting and scheming had finally started to pay off. He'd come up from the poor section of Chicago and had lied, cheated and yes, even stolen to make it this far. In that way, truth be told, he and Cleese were somewhat alike. Growing up poor either made a man ambitious or a hoodlum. Monroe had chosen ambition and affluence for his life's course. Cleese chose booze, broads and brawling. Monroe lived in a penthouse with a beautiful woman. Cleese was a criminal who did unimaginable things to pocket change. In the end, Monroe was the one who could look himself in the eye in the mirror and still feel a sense of pride and accomplishment. While Cleese on the other hand... what could he see in his reflection other than the face of an outlaw and a gorilla?

Monroe had done what he'd done for very specific reasons and now he was finally living a bit of the good life. This car was just one example of that. Important people in the WGF had already told him that he was destined for great things and he liked the way that sounded.

Damn straight he did.

Reaching into the pocket of his slacks, he found his key ring and hit the button on it to unlock his door. The chirp of the Jag's alarm disarming echoed through the building. He slid his fingers under the door's handle like he would into a lover's blouse and gently pulled it open. With a sigh, he dropped himself into the leather of the car's driver seat and wriggled into a comfortable position. Once set, he reached over, set his briefcase on the floor in front of the passenger's seat, and then pulled the door shut behind him. Sliding his key into the ignition, Monroe breathed deep of the air inside the car. God, he loved the smell of this car. It had the rich odor of leather and wood that he'd always equated with money.

And if there was one thing that he liked the smell of, it was money.

Monroe lovingly slid his fingers around the key and gently turned the ignition. The starter caught at once and the engine jumped to life. The car purred softly as he revved the engine. Then, slipping the transmission into gear, he backed carefully out of its space. With a gentle hand, he guided the Jag forward. The car slid across the ground like a python. It moved with barely a sound, only the quiet hissing of its tires on the cement to mark its passing. Its engine's power growled under his foot, and, God knew, it felt good.

Monroe carefully angled the Jag down the aisle and toward the exit ramp as he had many times before. Just for a second, he worried whether the car would make it through the tight corridor. He jogged the car around and drove up the ramp and into the blackness beyond.

Weber Industries had designed this building to be cutting edge, like a lot of Weber Industries' holdings. But for the life of him, Monroe couldn't figure out what kind of incompetent would have designed ramps as tight as these. Who were they for, *Mini Me?*

The Jag circled around the ramp and whipped around the last corner before the street. Suddenly, Monroe saw something ahead of him and had to almost stand on the brakes to get the car to stop.

"Ah, hell..." he said, slapping at the leather bound steering wheel.

Parked directly in front of him, blocking any exit, was a beat-up flatbed truck. Its driver had obviously misjudged his departure and gotten the damn thing stuck. Or he'd just stopped, not caring who might be coming up behind him. He leaned his head out his side window and noticed, almost subconsciously, that the flat of the truck's bed seemed slightly too wide for it to have ever made it into the lot.

"This idiot must have been backing up and hit the building," he said to no one but the empty car seat next to him.

He looked in his rear view mirror to see if he would be able to back up and use another exit, when an old Dodge Dart pulled up just behind him. Frustrated by it all, Monroe honked his horn twice, its tone echoing back through the cavernous structure.

After a moment, the Dart's driver slowly got out and he walked past the passenger's side of Monroe's car. Monroe couldn't make out the man's face due to the baseball hat he wore low over his brow, but then again, he didn't much care. If the guy was able to get the moron in the truck moving, who was he to complain?

Monroe sat for a minute or so and watched as the Dart's driver crawled over the back of the truck and on toward the left side. The guy peeked into the driver's side door and then reached into the open window. He took a leisurely glance up and down the street and then crawled back the way he'd come. Once back on solid ground, he came back toward Monroe's side of the car. He kept his head down as he walked, his face remaining cloaked in the shadow beneath the brim of the hat. As he got closer, Monroe noticed the guy slide his hand into his coat pocket.

Monroe looked into his rear view mirror again and checked behind him. There he saw the Dart still idling, the car door still slightly ajar. Monroe lowered his gaze and prepared to talk to whoever the Dart's driver was. He briefly took another annoyed look at the truck in front of him. He assumed that whoever this fucker in the truck was, he must have left his vehicle and just run off someplace.

Some people were just so damned inconsiderate.

Monroe glanced at the clock on the dashboard and momentarily thought of calling Claire. If this shit didn't straighten itself out in short order, he was going to be late for their dinner reservation.

The guy driving the Dart had by now come up to the Jag's window and knocked once and then once again with the meat of his knuckle. Monroe rolled his window about halfway down, enough so that he could communicate with whoever the guy was, but not so wide as to leave himself vulnerable should this guy decide to start some shit. He may live uptown now, but Monroe had once lived downtown and he still retained *some* of his street smarts.

"So, did this idiot leave his truck or what?" Monroe asked and leaned out a bit to look toward the truck.

"Not quite..." was the grumbled answer.

Monroe was startled a bit when he heard the voice. For some reason, the tone and timbre of it sounded vaguely familiar. Monroe wasn't sure exactly where he'd heard it before, but he knew the tone from somewhere. Maybe the guy was a maintenance guy in the building or something. Suddenly, he thought he caught the scent of bubble gum on the air.

"Well, what the fuck then...?" he said, pointing toward the flatbed. "How do people just *do* this kind of shit?"

The man outside bent down and stared Monroe full in the face. His eyes flared beneath the shadow of his cap and he smiled. The smile was malicious and shark-like with lips that slid back and exposed teeth that seemed impossibly white.

Monroe's brain sort of stalled and he felt more than a little bit confused as he abruptly found himself face-to-face with the one thing he thought he would never see again: Cleese.

And yet, here he was... looking smug and lethal and all too real.

"I think that, right now, you have problems far greater than that fuckin' truck, *Phil*."

Monroe sat, mentally vapor locked as he tried to sort it all out in his head. A lot of information flitted before his brain in a cascade of images that didn't seem to make much sense. Despite his best efforts, he just couldn't make the connections fit.

He'd been on his way home.

He was going to meet Claire.

They were supposed to go have dinner.

There was a truck.

A Dodge Dart.

Some people were inconsiderate.

And now... Cleese?

It took Monroe a second to put it all together, but when he did, the conclusion he reached made his bowels suddenly loosen.

Cleese pulled his hand out of his pocket and drove it straight across the lower part of Monroe's face. His head was pushed painfully back through the window. The blow rattled Monroe's jaw pretty severely and he felt his mouth suddenly fill with blood.

"That was for what you did to Monk, you son of a bitch."

Monroe's head spun from the concussion of the punch and the world sort of tilted on its axis as a result. As he tried to clear his head, he reached over feebly and pushed the button to roll the window up. It was the only thing he could think of to put a barrier between himself and Cleese.

It was all for naught.

Cleese grabbed the window by its uppermost edge and, in a series of quick, back and forth yanks, he pulled at the pane of glass. The first tug rattled the glass in its frame. The second sprouted a spider web pattern that radiated out from the top down. The third shattered the window, sending nuggets of glazed glass cascading into Monroe's rapidly dampening lap.

Suddenly, there were thick hands at Monroe's throat and he was unceremoniously hauled from beneath the steering column and out through the broken window. Chunks of the still remaining window scratched his back and legs deeply, allowing blood to flow and soak the material of his pants. Once clear of the window frame, Cleese hoisted Monroe into the air and then slammed him heavily into the cement wall. The force of the impact rattled Monroe's teeth in his jaw and shook his eyeballs in his head.

Again and again, Monroe felt his back and skull crash into the cement. His already dizzy world was further clouded and the black fog of unconsciousness slowly crept in. As his mind fought for some avenue of escape, two uppercuts ploughed into his lower abdomen, kicking the wind from his lungs. Then, he felt his body arc through the air and pound onto the hood of the Jag.

Yeah... that's definitely gonna scratch the paint.

Out of the corner of his eye, Monroe saw Cleese pull something dark and hard and round from his pocket. He clenched the ball tightly in his fist, his knuckles white from the exertion of holding it so tightly.

Then, the hailstorm of punches commenced.

Monroe only felt the first few as Cleese repeatedly pounded the heavy ball into his face and chest. Far off, Monroe heard the sound of his nose crack. Then, his cheekbones splinter. Small, hard chunks of enamel were torn from his gums and fell like pebbles to the back of his throat. The snapping of his collarbone took the breath from his lungs. His sternum ached from the repeated bludgeoning.

Out at the far borders of his perception, Cleese's voice echoed in a stream of profanities.

And then, just as suddenly as it began, the beating stopped.

Monroe made a thick gurgling sound as he fought to catch a breath through the decimated anatomy of his face. So much for that "unique skill set."

As he lay there, Monroe wasn't sure how severely Cleese had hurt him, but he knew it was bad. Blood flowed freely down his throat and he did all he could to either spit it out or swallow it. He tried as best he could to turn his head to keep himself from drowning. The thing was... he was only barely able to keep up with the flow.

Abruptly, Monroe once again felt himself being hoisted slightly off the car hood. Cleese had him by the lapels of his jacket with one hand and by the belt with the other. For some unfathomable reason, he felt his attacker pulling on the front of his pants. An unexpected and extremely localized pain suddenly erupted at his crotch.

Fighting for breath, he realized that Cleese had let him go. He fell back, splayed across the hood of the Jag. He lay there and groaned, alone with the pain in his face and a sudden weight in his groin. At first, Monroe thought Cleese might have stabbed him or cut him in some way.

Jesus... no!

Still trying to catch air, Monroe reached down into the front of his pants and felt around. Shoving his hand under his beltline, he discovered the small, round object Cleese had been hitting him with stuffed down deep into his shorts. The thing now snuggled against his balls like a purring cat. He reached down and got a hold of it by pressing the object deeper between his legs. Whatever the thing was, it felt like a metal apple with what appeared to be a fat stem sticking out of the top of it.

He turned his head and looked back down the ramp through the growing haze. Cleese stood a ways away, back beyond the Dart and just around the corner. His middle finger was raised defiantly.

"And *that*... is for Chikara!" he shouted, his voice echoing dully as he disappeared around the bend. The sound of his receding footsteps echoed in the darkness.

Monroe barely felt a thing as the fragmentation grenade exploded in his lap.

Solemnities

The sun burned overhead like an indifferent parent on the day Masterson visited Philip Monroe's grave. It had been a little over three weeks since the funeral and this was the first time he'd been able to come and pay his respects.

For obvious reasons, he didn't go to the service. He'd been advised by the police as well as League Security that it wouldn't be safe; wouldn't be "prudent." There were still no official suspects in what was being called a deliberate incident. However, if the person who bombed Monroe's car was who Masterson thought it was, he prayed for Monroe's soul and for his own.

He slowly looked around him, glancing over the headstones and foliage of the cemetery. God, this was a depressing place; a dark and lonely dumping ground for people who felt the need to warehouse their past. The idea of squandering good land and good resources just to remember people seemed downright stupid to him. Let the dead be dead and let them fade in the memory of the living in their own good time.

He laughed, deep and with resonance. These were macabre observations coming from a man who made his living dealing with the living dead. He'd seen too much life and too much death to think of it any other way.

The cemetery where he now stood was obviously old, most of its headstones dated back to the early Forties. Once manicured lawns now stood abandoned, its landscaping left to be choked by weeds and kudzu. A lot of the marble structures were blackened at their seams, mildew and rot patiently eating away at the expensive, polished stone. Monroe, who'd had no real family to speak of other than a girlfriend, did, as it turned out, have an aunt who had left him a deed to this burial property in her will. Its placement—in this cemetery, in this plot, in this manner of procurement—implied a grave that was soon to be forgotten. At any rate, it was a joke burying what was left of Monroe in a casket. With what remained, a Tupperware container would have sufficed.

If he allowed himself to think about it, Masterson was almost impressed by how Cleese had moved in such an unexpected direction. A direct frontal attack was not something Masterson thought he'd been capable of. It was a smart move. He supposed that Cleese would be heading his way next. It's what Masterson would have done: minimize the liabilities, take out any competition. And that didn't even take into account the whole revenge angle.

But then again, Masterson thought that Cleese just might give him a pass on this one, preferring to observe him from afar. He could all too easily imagine Cleese watching him spend the rest of his life in paranoid anticipation of the death he'd be dealt rather than simply just killing him and having done with it.

He'd want to fuck with him.

It's exactly what he'd done that first day in the Orientation Room back at the Compound.

Which brought him back to Monroe. That stupid shit had pushed things way too far. He'd compromised them both by not being able to keep his fucking mouth shut. Wishing Cleese good luck... for chrissakes! He'd pushed Cleese and poked him and prodded him until the man had no choice but to react. And then there was that outburst at the Training Hall. He might as well have admitted to complicity in the whole mess. What an arrogant prick. He pretty much slapped a target on Cleese's back and signed his goddamn name to it.

It was right after the initial meeting at Corporate, Monroe told him about deciding to give Cleese a clip of blanks during a match. He wanted to "step it up a notch. Masterson thought it was too risky and had too much potential for blowback, but Monroe was intent on showing Cleese who was in charge.

But it had been Weber who gave the go-ahead. He said it was a solid show of force and would "set the tone" of their relationship.

They all knew it would make great television.

After that, Cleese had been a wild man; totally unchained. He'd fought harder than ever and his ratings soared. Everyone should have been happy. They were all making a ton of money. Upper management and Mr. Weber had decided—with Monroe's cheerleading—to throw yet another challenge at Cleese. For no other reason than to show him who was in the driver's seat here.

Once and for all.

The results had been mind blowing. Ratings for that night's match and the subsequent replays were astronomical. Merchandise revenue went through the roof. Hell, even some station affiliates that were starting to whine about the level of violence on the shows had fallen into line. Cleese had overnight become the most popular fighter The League had ever known.

It was all too perfect.

And then, in the same evening, Cleese up and disappeared.

The selfish bastard.

Masterson had by now arrived at his car, a sleek black Lexus LFA. The car had been a gift from Mr. Weber as a sort of reward for Cleese completing his training in record time. The car was low to the ground with a 4.8 liter, 552 horsepower V10 engine that would purr like a kitten or growl like a beast depending on the person behind the wheel. The car was magnificent.

Masterson hated the damn thing.

Every time he looked at it, all he could think of was Cleese.

And doing so always made his sphincter tighten.

He took a deep breath and looked at the cemetery around him as he dug in his pockets for his keys.

God... what a shithole.

Suddenly, his cell phone chirped in the left, breast pocket of his suit coat. Transferring his keys to his other hand, he reached into the folds of his jacket and retrieved the small black gadget. His finger slid across the front screen and the phone did the rest. He held the phone to his ear and stared across the bonnet of the Lexus.

"Masterson," he said.

Inside the earpiece, a familiar voice spoke, its tone sounding tinny through the small speaker.

"Masterson...? Weber."

Masterson stood a little taller, a result of years of standing at attention when a superior officer spoke. When he realized no one was around, he relaxed just a bit.

"Yes, Sir."

"I asked these fucking morons for an update on this Cleese thing and, well... these fuckers couldn't find their asses in the dark with a flashlight and a map."

"Yes, Sir."

"So... what do you have for me?"

Masterson paused and thought. He hated having nothing to report, but... well, he had nothing to report. Cleese had, by all accounts, vanished off the face of the earth. His crib was empty. The dump he lived in back in San Francisco was a meth lab now. Hell, even Weaver claimed to not know where he'd disappeared to. And that wasn't even the worst of it.

The money.

No one in the organization could explain how Cleese had managed to vaporize with the amount of money he did. There were supposed to be fail-safes to prevent that sort of thing. Once again, Cleese proved himself to be a lot smarter than anyone gave him credit for.

"Masterson?" the voice in his ear asked.

"Yes, Sir."

"The Cleese thing..."

"Well, Sir, we're still looking into it. So far, there's not much to go on."

The voice on the other end was silent for a long time. With each passing second, Masterson felt another bead of nervous sweat crawl down his back. To his surprise, Weber's response was not the one he anticipated.

"Well, no matter... Given enough time and resources, we'll find him."

"I apologize, Sir. I take full responsibility. This whole thing has been a bit of a bust, Sir."

"Nonsense! Have you *seen* the latest financials? Revenue is still climbing. Merch is as well. The Internet is buzzing and people are talking, man. I think Weber Industries can survive some errant bone-breaker walking off with some pocket change, don't you?"

Pocket change? Masterson heard the sum Cleese had disappeared with was a lot more substantial than "pocket change." Rumor was... he could have bought himself a small country with what he'd taken.

"Yes, Sir, but... we did have losses."

"Well, sure... But anything worthwhile comes at a cost, now doesn't it? And if that cost is an employee or two, well..." and he laughed under his breath, "those are acceptable losses. Look, if we gain this kind of revenue and are able to clean our yard of some troublesome debris, well..." another laugh. "Hell, that's a win-win by my count."

"Yes, Sir."

"We'll weather this, Masterson. We'll live... and we'll thrive. And soon enough, we'll find that rat bastard and get my money back."

"Yes, Sir."

"Besides... I have a few new ideas I'm working on that'll make this shit look like a Three Card Monte game. Some new shit, Son! A few new games to play..."

"Yes, Sir."

"Speaking of..."

"Sir?"

"I want you to hit the nearest airport... what is that," the sound of papers rustling could be heard over the speaker, "Chicago Rockford International?"

"Yes, Sir."

"Ok, we'll set up travel. Just get there as quick as you can."

"My car, Sir..."

We'll send someone for it... or fuck it! We'll buy you another one. I just need you on a plane to Tampa ASAP. The choppers are all committed to something else."

"May I ask, Sir..."

Weber sounded as if he'd already moved on to the next item on his To Do List."

"There's a new fighter I want you to retrieve. Ball of fucking fury, from what I hear. Then again, I also hear he's as smart as a fuckin' stump, so... he's perfect!"

"Yes, Sir."

"Ok... we're done. Call me when you have this guy. Geddit?"

"Yes, Sir."

"Got it?"

"Yes, Sir."

"Good!" and the phone went silent in his hand.

Masterson shut the phone off and slid it back into his pocket.

Damn... here we go again.

He turned back toward the Lexus and ran his hand over its painted surface. Once again, the vehicle brought up memories he'd have rather left alone. And even though Mr. Weber didn't seem overly concerned, Masterson knew he'd not feel totally relaxed until he knew beyond a shadow of a doubt that Cleese had been contained.

He just hated loose ends like that.

A cold chill abruptly slithered down his spine and gooseflesh migrated across his forearms. Despite himself, he took one more cautious glance around, first to the left and then to the right. All the while, his eyes kept scanning the area just in case. It would be just his luck that Cleese wasn't gone for good and had instead decided that some Amateur Hour assassin-esque shenanigans were in order. He slowly scanned the grounds and surrounding foliage of the cemetery, its headstones jutting up from the ground like severed thumbs.

It *seemed* all clear. But in the end, who could tell?

Masterson laughed under his breath.

Motherfucker.

It suddenly dawned on him just how vulnerable he was standing out here, not to mention in his everyday life. He knew how easily any person— shit, even a President or his brother—could be gotten to. Cleese had proven that once already.

Having watched Cleese in the pit for some time now, he had a pretty good idea of what was in the man's repertoire; bold and unexpected surprises notwithstanding. As he thought about it, he was pretty certain that, if Cleese really wanted him dead, he would die regardless of any precautions he might take. Masterson had seen that fact clearly in the other man's eyes that day when he tossed Monroe into the pit. Cleese was like a shark in that respect. Once he'd locked in on his target, nothing and no one could get in the way of his objective.

It was the very reason that he'd been chosen for the League to begin with: the ability to kill, without remorse and without hesitation, and to not stop until the target was terminated.

So, what the fuck? Why worry, right?

Right?

Masterson reached down and dug his keys out of his pocket.

He silently wondered whether or not he'd see it coming when the time came. Monroe hadn't.

As he slid his key into the car door's handle, he tried to imagine how it would go down.

A rigged door lock?

He cautiously turned the key in the lock.

Trigger switch on a door hinge?

With a pull, he opened the car door.

Pressure trigger-switch that would go off when weight was applied to the seat?

He slid into the car's seat and put both hands on the wheel.

Poisoned food?

He glanced over at a crumpled fast-food bag containing a half-eaten burger and a rapidly chilling order of fries sitting on the floorboard.

A cut brake line?

He pushed once, then twice, on the brake pedal.

A bomb wired to the starter?

He slid his key into the car's ignition.

So many ways to die.

Masterson hesitated a moment and looked around. Still all clear. Not a soul to be seen. The place was silent except for the far off singing of birds and the gentle swishing of the trees in the breeze. He was alone in this City of The Dead. He smiled slightly as he felt icy fingers of dread run up and down the back of his neck, dancing there like cold regret.

He shivered, despite himself, and abruptly chuckled under his breath.

He looked back in the direction of Monroe's grave and slowly turned the key.

Far off across the cemetery's fields, under an old bent walnut tree, a silhouette sat as if meditating atop a black Suzuki GSX1300R motorcycle. The man and his machine were hidden from view within the shadows and the both of them watched the man in the tailored suit as he talked on his cell phone before climbing hesitantly into his automobile.

The figure in the shadows absentmindedly scratched at the curve of his jaw line and then leaned upright. With a flick of a switch, the bike's ignition caught and the engine roared to life. The rider zipped up his jacket and pulled a small, silver MP3 player from his pocket. He slid the headphone buds into his ears and pulled a full face helmet over his head. Looking down, he scrolled through the tracks on the player until he saw what he was looking for; a little something for the road. He hit "Play" and tucked the small square of metal back into his pocket.

In the small earpieces, a dulcimer played soft and rhythmically within the confines of his head. A woman's plaintive voice cried out and a synthesizer wailed mournfully. Electronic drums thrummed a low rhythm which seemed to perfectly match the vibration of The Busa beneath him.

I walk with phantoms and leaves are burning at my feet.
I walk with phantoms.
Sometimes they rage
Sometimes they fade.
Some must watch while some are
Singing the hum of the walking dead.

The man smiled and pulled on a pair of leather riding gloves. He took a quick glance down and patted the sword which was secured to the side of the motorcycle within easy reach. Always now within easy reach. He looked back and watched Masterson's car begin to roll forward, slowly heading for the stone arch of the cemetery's gates.

I walk with phantoms and leaves are ice at my feet.
I walk with phantoms.
Here is the truth:
Seven wonders and the will to live.
Singing the hum of the walking dead.
Thinking of every word that you said.
Singing as garden walls ripple with the blur of bees,
Sweetly singing as sunlight streams through the aching trees,
Voices trampling the exhausted wilderness,
Singing the hum of the walking dead.

A small, satisfied grin danced across his lips.

Burning like the gaze upon a faithless friend
Burning down the lonely trees always in the end
Voices trampling the exhausted wilderness,
Dragging the heels of the walking dead.
Dragging out every word that you said.

Reaching out, he pulled in the clutch and kicked the bike into gear. With a twist of his wrist, the motor growled and the bike shook reassuringly beneath him. The guitar in his ear cried another plaintive note and the voice continued to whisper its intoxicating tale of sorrow and, for a second, things seemed like they might be ok— the sense of loss he felt might someday subside.

Singing the hum of the walking dead.
Thinking of every word that you said.

He settled a little deeper into the seat and an exhilarating sense of expectation rose up from the depths of his soul. Slowly, he let the clutch out and felt the motorcycle's back tire bite into the dirt. And as dark clouds reached down from the heavens to embrace him, the figure rode off into the distance.

Epilogue

"Well, Johnny, that about wraps up another exciting WGF Fight Night. Next week, we have even more excitement for you all including a No Weapons Match and an always exciting Team Match."

"That's right, Bob. We'll also have a profile on newcomer Alfredo Villanueva, the Spaniard who's scheduled for his very first match that night. Yes, my friends, it's another Cherry match and we'll have it all—right here—on Fight Night."

"So, I'm Bob Wester..."

"I'm Johnny Davis and for Al Sanchez down on the floor and for everybody here at Weber Industries and the World Gladiatorial Federation, we'll see you next time—at The Fights!"

● ● ●

Thank You

First and foremost, I wish to thank my beautiful wife, Catia, for her constant support and love above and beyond the call of reason, for putting up with me, my weird hours, my weirder questions, and for enduring the constant stream of horror and kung fu movies. You've been my partner, my lover, my confidant and my friend. Thanks for believing in me and for never giving up! As Shakespeare once wrote, 'Doubt thou the stars are fire; Doubt that the sun doth move; Doubt truth to be a liar; But never doubt that I love.'

I also want to thank my kids, Jhustin and Connor, for putting up with me and my moods (both good and bad), for listening when I was prattling on about everything from the code of the samurai to the subtleties of blood splatter and for at least looking like you were paying attention, for acting as stand-ins for all of the fight sequences, and for allowing yourselves to be used as a captive audience. You two make me very proud and I love you more than you will ever know.

Furthermore, I want to thank my mother, Ruth, for raisin' me up right despite considerable odds and for being, above all else, my friend; Annie and Chuck, for being indulgent and understanding and for giving me the two gifts that have truly taken my breath away. Without you guys, this book would have never been completed—literally; Joseph Weber for sound legal advice and for being wise beyond his years. 'Nicolo would be proud of you, my man, but then again, so would the Marquis'; Kyle Cornelius for keeping me grounded; Robert Blue Yount for teaching me that it was possible to aspire to greatness even while 'stitching up a post'; Brian Ellison, Kelly Kuehl, and Johnny Keith for being there even when I wasn't; Charlene, Kaiya, and Julian for bringing joy... and Popeye's; Charles Murray for all those nights 'outside' and for making me laugh time and time again; Tony Cress for sitting up with me night after night, indulging this fable, and making sense; Susan Prunty for taking the time to pick things apart and for being kind enough to not spare my feelings; Rob Weber, Monica Enderle Pierce, Christopher Burch, Stephen Santogrossi and Zarina Hawkins for the critical eye and the insight; William Faith and Monica Richards for the kind permission for Cleese's music and for being my friends; Aaron Acevedo for the artwork and for being so accommodating; Scott Pierce and Richard Valentine for taking me seriously; Jessica Von for the photos and the tacos; and to Paul Wein for one day saying, "You really oughtta write this shit down."

And much love to the others who, in one way or another, have allowed me to share their Path with them: Tony Timpone, Michael Gingold, and Chris

Alexander at *Fangoria* & Steve "Uncle Creepy" Barton, KW Low, and Jon Condit at *Dread Central* for giving me a chance and for continuing to believe in me; Clive Barker, Craig Spector, and Terry Castle for the quotes and for being so kind, Brian Hodge and Travis Milloy for once saying, "That's a nice little story you have there" and for setting the bar so high; Philip Nutman for the taking the time to look things over; Neil Gaiman, Joe R. Lansdale, Chuck Palahniuk, Eiji Yoshikawa, Robert E. Howard, Hunter S. Thompson, Philip K. Dick, Stewart O'Nan, and Stephen King for sharing and inspiring; Val Lewton, Jacques Tourneur, George Romero, Jorge Grau, Lucio Fulci, Tom Savini, Greg Nicotero, and Zack Snyder for doing it so well, Goblin & Lustmord for providing the music, John Scoleri for sound advice; Sean Smithson for being rad and for the insight; Jon Edwards for literally being the first person to buy this book; all of the coffee shops this was written and edited in for not kicking me out, and to Howard Stern, Joe Rogan & Redban, Bill Burr, Doug Benson, Kevin Smith, Scott Mosier and Ralph Garman for providing the laughs through the workouts.

I also wish to thank Lee Jun Fan for providing such an amazing example and for the philosophy.

The humblest of praise goes out to Crom.

And to anyone who ever picked up a copy of *Carpe Noctem*: I made a vow to one day make it all up to you. Please accept this book as a token of my most sincere thanks and apologies.

And finally, to Randy Brown, Sydney McFarlan, and Alex Aguilar....
"I lift my glass to honor you, my dear departed friends."

☠ ☠ ☠